YANTO'S SUMMER

YANTO'S SUMMER

Ray Pickernell

This edition published by Accent Press Ltd 2015

ISBN 9781783759002

Copyright © **Ray Pickernell** 2015

First edition 1988 by Morgans Technical Books Ltd

In memory of Ivan Harris, a true friend.

FOREWORD

How well I remember writing that first sentence – 'A cold full moon bathes the wide reaches,' etc. etc. etc. That was over seven years ago now, and any thoughts of it becoming a novel, let alone being published, had not occurred to me, even in my wildest dreams.

It was a very stop-go affair, with a growing bundle of handwritten pages receiving my attention on just the odd Thursday afternoon; this being my half day off from selling cars. After a couple of years I did begin to wonder what on earth I was doing. Was it any good? Would it have any appeal?

It appealed to me, certainly, because it represented a nostalgic romp back to that place which holds the warm and happy memories of my formative years. But was that enough? If I was to continue, it was imperative that I find out.

It was around that time that Severn Sound, Gloucester's local radio station, announced its intention to hold a short story competition. This seemed an ideal opportunity to have my writing vetted by someone other than myself.

By changing character's names and engineering a premature ending, I managed to adapt the first chapter of my manuscript into a short story and duly entered the competition. To my total surprise, my entry won and was eventually broadcast on local radio. My output then increased dramatically for a while, and then, inevitably, the euphoria wore off and once again it was back to Thursday afternoons.

After a couple of more lethargic years, Christopher Musk, a presenter on Severn Sound, informed me that the county had a new writer in residence, and that maybe I should ask him to review my efforts to date. This seemed a good idea, so I telephoned Bryan Walters who graciously agreed to read my manuscript and give his professional opinion.

One night, approximately two weeks later at about five minutes to midnight, the phone rang. Fearing bad news, I answered the phone only to hear a very enthusiastic Bryan Walters extolling the virtues and potentials of my manuscript. It was like listening to a fairy story. It lifted me to such a degree that the book was finished within six months. I feel very indebted to Bryan Walters.

I also owe a debt of gratitude to Chris Musk. It was he who initially put me in touch with Bryan Walters, and it was he who introduced me to Jane Sullivan. Jane is also a member of staff at Severn Sound. I just happened to mention to Chris that I was seeking someone to type up my longhand. When I returned from lunch the following Saturday, there was Jane sitting at my desk in the showroom. Since then she has converted three hundred pages of longhand foolscap into her immaculate type, and steadfastly refused to take a penny piece for her trouble. In this new dark age that we sometimes appear to be entering, it is strangely reassuring to know that such people are still around. Bless your heart, Jane.

Another person to whom I owe much, is that grand retired gentleman of the river, Mr Fred Rowbotham. He probably knows more about the Severn and its estuary than any man living, and is never too busy to share that knowledge. Whether I was sitting in his lounge drinking his coffee, or hanging on the phone, he would answer my questions in a gracious and patient manner. Thank you again, sir.

Gloucester has always had its share of characters and funny men, and Gerry Thomas is certainly one of them. Gerry has been a comedian all his life but is now moving into the big time. He is a regular on *The Comedians* and I am sure he will go all the way to the top. What many people do not realise is that Gerry is also a very accomplished poet. The two poems in this book were custom written by him. Good on yer, Ger.

With the Irish sequence help again materialised in the form of Neil and Dennis Prenter. The brothers lived on the shores of Strangford Lough after the war, and were able to help me considerably. 'Thanks again, boys'.

As I said before, I have spent seven years, on and off,

writing this book. Had it not been for one man, it could have taken even longer. My boss, Brian Powell, turned many a blind eye as I scribbled away at my desk during those rare quiet periods. But for his tolerance it could have taken me ten years.

Then finally I must thank my wife. During that last six months especially, she would sit on her own for hours at evenings and weekends as I worked. Many times, some instinct or intuition, call it what you will, must have told her that I was beginning to flag. She would appear in the nick of time with a large scotch in her hand. Thus fortified, I was able to continue. And so it is finished. The impossible has happened. My grateful thanks to all concerned. I hope you enjoy it.

R.C.P.
1988

Purton East, Gloucestershire

Late April 1947

One

THE CATCH

A cold full moon bathed the wide reaches of the Severn Estuary in a brilliant, ghostly glow.

Several old barges, beached deliberately years before in an attempt to slow down the erosion of the river bank, stood out against the moonlit water like defiant skeletons. Vast stretches of mud, still wet from the last tide, glittered like a carpet of diamonds in the eerie light. A light wind stirred the coarse grass, which grew thick and rough on the eroded banks but thinned to the odd clump as it reached the river's thick, iodine-coated mud.

The tide had ebbed now, leaving a strange quietness along the shoreline. The contrast was startling. Only a few short hours before the world's second highest rise of tide had arrived with that familiar roar, and in a little over three hours had filled the mile-wide estuary with twenty-five feet of salt water. This was the famous Severn Bore tide.

Yanto Gates broke through the blackthorn hedge, which separated the Severn bank from the adjacent Berkeley to Gloucester canal towpath, and surveyed the scene before him. He loved this river, but tonight, bathed in this unusually bright moonlight, it moved him to the point of goose pimples. He gazed up and downstream. The only sign of human life was the beacon light at the end of the pier, which skirted the entrance to Sharpness docks, a mile or so downstream. He needed the loneliness this night. Yanto Gates was a salmon poacher.

He had left the warmth of the Blue Boar after the usual extended throwing-out time, and now felt elated as the four pints of rough local cider began to work on him. Having spent a couple of hours checking his rabbit snares around the low

Severn grounds, the two fat rabbits now secure in his waist bag indicated that this could be his lucky night. It was now 1.30 a.m. Time for the real business of the night. If his luck held, maybe a fine succulent Severn salmon.

Satisfying himself that he was absolutely alone, Yanto sat down on a handy clump of grass and removed his boots, which, together with the two rabbits, he placed under a nearby blackthorn bush. After struggling into his hip-length waders and taking a final look around, he moved towards the mud line.

Immediately in front of him, stretching out into the mud and sand of the now almost empty estuary, was a barrier of salmon traps. They were placed in a gentle curve, about twenty traps in all, facing the outgoing tide.

Made of strong willow cane, the cone-shaped traps were about five feet in diameter at the mouth, tapering to a point. Once the unfortunate salmon had entered the trap, it was doomed. Yanto hoped the recent tide had yielded a fish which he would grab before the traps were checked the following morning.

At low tide the bed of the estuary was mainly hard-packed sand, which stretched for miles up and down stream, and for most of its mile width. Before reaching the high sand, one had to cross a fifty-yard trough of mud and water, the depth of which varied from six inches to six feet. The trough was probably the only reason the area had not become a popular tourist resort years before. It was down this trough that the Severn tide roared twice daily, before relentlessly covering the high sand in the middle estuary at a rate the eye could see.

The locals knew that the trough was traversed at regular intervals by natural rock bridges showing just above the mud. Over the centuries, millions of rip tides had worn away the softer sandstone, leaving the harder rock strata a convenient, if slippery, way for the knowing locals to gain access to the sands.

Every summer, visiting daytrippers could be seen enviously watching the local people enjoying themselves out on the sands and wondering how the devil they got out there.

Yanto recalled talk at the Blue Boar about recent good runs

2

of fish and was full of anticipation as he carefully picked his way across one of the rock bridges. He cursed loudly as his rubber-clad right foot struck off a slimy rock and plunged knee-deep into the mud and water. Using his hands to steady himself, he managed to free his leg from the sucking morass. As he straightened up and regained his balance a spasm of pain shot through his left thigh. The pain was the result of the German mortar fragment which had smashed his thigh at the Battle of Arnhem, three years before.

Yanto had loved the army, and although he felt ashamed to say so, he had enjoyed the war. He loved the tough life of thrill and fear and his excellent war record had made it easy for him when, in 1941, he had decided to apply to join the newly formed Parachute Regiment. The mortar fragment had ended his war however, and by the time he got out of military hospital it was more or less over anyway. He had then returned to the dull monotony of rural country life in his native Gloucestershire. He worked hard as a stevedore on Sharpness docks, but it was still the thrills of life that kept him really alive. Poaching, strong cider, and women.

Yanto reached the end of the rock bridge where it disappeared into the hard sand. The walking was now relatively easy as he made his way towards the first of the salmon traps, or 'kipes' as they were called locally.

Looking into the yawning mouth of the trap, with the moonlight flickering on the wet slimy seaweed within, was not unlike looking down the throat of some attacking monster. Yanto hesitated for a moment then plunged his hands into the evil-smelling mess. Taking care not to scratch his hands on the holding spikes, he rummaged through the weed, feeling for that spasm of movement which would indicate a dying fish. With his head and shoulders inside the trap, he reached to the base. No movement, no luck. With a silent curse he extricated himself from the first trap and moved on to the next.

A full hour had elapsed and Yanto's enthusiasm was beginning to wane. So far his nocturnal activities had produced only scratched hands, a smell on his clothes that would ensure tongue pie from his mother next morning, and a great pile of seaweed.

With his hands deep inside the penultimate trap, his body stiffened. He felt a surge of excitement as something moved between his hands. His hands were cold. He couldn't tell fish from weed. Spurred on by excitement, he snatched out another double handful of weed and there, moonlight flickering on it with every feeble movement, was a small Severn salmon.

Taking care not to damage the fish, Yanto withdrew it from the trap. He was disappointed. 'Just a babee,' he muttered to himself; still, it would keep him in cigarettes and cider for a week.

The last trap yielded nothing. Yanto hit the fish on the back of the head, pushed it into his waist bag, and stretched his aching back. He lit a Woodbine, took a deep drag, and stared about him. Away on the far side of the estuary he could still see the odd lights shining from the cottages in the Forest of Dean.

'Better get moving,' he thought. He stopped as he turned. Had he imagined it, no, he was sure something had flashed in the moonlight. It must have been a good quarter of a mile away, towards the middle of the estuary. Could it have been a stranded salmon? The tide went out as fast as it came in, and it was not unusual for large fish to be stranded in one of the various sized lakes left behind in the sand hollows.

The wind was getting up and Yanto realised he had a problem. The flash could easily have been the moonlight catching a wave top on one of the larger pools. There was also the time element. The next tide could not be far away, and if he was caught by the tide he would be in real trouble. He pondered the problem. It would take him at least half an hour to get to the point of the flash and back to his own bank, even if it turned out to be a wild goose chase and he was able to return immediately. 'I wish I hadn't seen the bloody fish,' he muttered under his breath. To go, or not to go?

The possibility of a big fish was too much for him. Yanto started out across the sand at a brisk pace. Having made the decision he now felt elated again. As always, the element of risk was the icing on the cake as far as he was concerned. He breathed in the fine night air and hummed the tune of 'Colonel Bogey' in time with his silent footsteps. He could have been walking on another planet. The flat, moonlight-illuminated landscape, interrupted by large and small pools of bright water, seemed unreal.

He became aware of the wind getting up a little more, sending the small clouds scudding across the face of the moon. It seemed ridiculous, but a frown crossed his face when he remembered that in a very short time the hard flat sand that he was walking on would be thirty feet under the water of one of the most unpredictable estuaries in the world. He also knew that the tide was usually preceded by a rising wind.

He increased his pace and almost immediately saw another flash, very close now.

He skirted a small lake and walked straight into a patch of quicksand. He was up to his shins before he realised what had happened. Yanto had been in Severn quicksand many times before. As a child between the wars this had been his playground. He and his friends would deliberately allow the quicksand to take them up to their knees before being extricated by the other members of the gang. These things were done without the knowledge of parents, needless to say.

Holding his body rigid, Yanto used the weight of it to fall forward. He fell very slowly until his hands came into contact with the sand, by which time the suction on his feet had been broken. It was now easy to wriggle his feet free of the clinging mess.

He hurried on his way. He was now approaching quite a large area of trapped water, roughly fifty yards square. After studying the small lake he knew instinctively that if there was a fish it was in this pool.

He stood dead still, watching the wind ruffled surface of the water. It could not have been more than three feet deep at the deepest point and as little as six inches in others. Any decent-sized salmon would be bound to show itself as it moved around waiting for the next tide to free it.

Yanto waited another five minutes and became aware of the ever increasing wind as it began to flap his collar. 'Come on, you bugger, show yourself,' he muttered. He decided to wade into the pool. That should stir him up if he's in there, he thought.

Before he could take his first step into the water he saw the fish. It surfaced about twenty feet from the edge of the pool, slid its full length over a shallow sandbar, and disappeared again. For a second Yanto remained rooted to the spot. 'Jesus Christ,' he gasped. From that first moonlight glimpse he knew he had a specimen here.

With a whoop of exhilaration, he charged into the shallow water. His quarry surfaced immediately. As it tried to thrash away from its attacker the fish stranded itself in a shallow section. In his excitement Yanto soaked himself in his effort to grab the fish before it found a deeper refuge. His hand found the monster's tail. 'Got you, my beauty,' he gasped. His triumph was short-lived. With a massive burst of energy the fish broke free of his grasp and leapt six feet in the air. 'Blast it,' he yelled in frustration. 'Calm down, you prat,' he told himself. He knew the fish was doomed. Methodically, he began to splash up and down the large pool, almost falling several times as he traversed the uneven sandy bottom.

To any casual observer it would have been a very comical sight. A full-grown man, cavorting about in a moonlit pool at three o'clock in the morning.

Again, the fish stranded itself. Again Yanto managed to grab the tail, and yet again the fish broke free and leapt in the air. Yanto's already wet head and shoulders received another soaking as it hit the water. That did it. With his well-known temper getting the better of him, he jumped on the fish with both feet. The fish was almost spent. With both hands locked around the monster's tail, the gleeful Yanto dragged it through the shallow water on to the hard sand.

He sat down heavily and while holding on firmly to the still struggling fish, put his head between his knees, panting loudly for a full minute.

Only then did he realise the extent of his prize. 'Bloody hell,' he breathed in admiration, 'you must be fifty pounds if you are an ounce.'

The moonlight appeared from behind a skulking cloud and lit the king of fish in all its glory. Almost reluctantly, Yanto took out the small cudgel designed for the task and struck the fish sharply on the back of its shining head.

With a final spasm, the fish lay still.

Now the problem was getting the fish home. A salmon is slippery enough to handle at the best of times, but one of this size...

He took a hook from his waist bag. The big hook which had once been part of a hanging scales was in the shape of the letter S, and sharpened to a point at both ends. He jammed the point firmly under the great fish's jawbone and used the other curve of S as a carrying handle. Now he was ready for the return journey.

Two

THE TIDE

With the big fish draped over his shoulder and the small one secure in his waist bag, Yanto happily began to make his way back towards the home bank. He laughed quietly to himself as he followed his original footprints, still visible in the hard sand. 'I wonder what Herbie would say if he could see us now, my beauty,' he said, and patted the huge fish's head.

Herbie Connors was the local water bailiff who had been involved in a personal battle of wits with Yanto for as long as he could remember. Herbie had been overheard to say he would happily give up his army pension to catch Yanto red-handed.

The fish began to weigh heavily, but he accepted it happily. He began to work out the probable returns from his nights work. 'Let's see,' he mused 'at ten bob a pound, this fish must be worth twenty-five quid I reckon. If I throw in the little 'un, Sid Watkins will be happy to give me twenty quid. Yes, I reckon Sid will be glad to see our Ma in the morning'. Sid Watkins was the slick manager of the Berkeley Chase Hotel in the nearby town of Berkeley, who never missed a chance of a bit of extra profit.

He became aware of a new sound in the night. It was a rushing, roaring sound. 'Sounds like the Cornishman coming,' he thought dreamily to himself, remembering the time he had watched the express thunder through Berkeley Road station. Then he froze with alarm as the full implication of the sound hit him. 'Christ, the tide,' he gasped, as he broke into a staggering run. 'Of all the stupid bastards.'

With the excitement of the fish he, of all people, had forgotten the tide. The mistake was made even more stupid by the fact that he had known for some time that the big tides were

9

due. The very high Bore tides rarely occurred during the hours of darkness, but he knew this one was predicted to be a twenty-seven-footer, and that meant danger. The thought of it brought him out in a cold sweat as he ran desperately on. Held back as he was by the fish and his clumsy waders, he finally reached his original crossing point. One glance confirmed what the noise had already told him.

The trough was now a fifty yard wide torrent of deafening crazy water, made even more awesome by the brilliantly revealing moonlight.

For a split second he experienced that same numbing fear he had felt the first time he had come under enemy fire. 'Calm down and think, you stupid prat,' he told himself fiercely. Crossing here would be impossible.

After a moment's thought, he decided he would have to try and race the tide. He remembered the last time he had been in this situation. On that occasion he had been ten years old. As children between the wars, Yanto and his friends spent most of their summers out in the estuary between tides.

They could all swim like fish and occasionally, just for the hell of it, he and one or two of his braver friends would deliberately allow themselves to be cut off from their home bank by one of the smaller, less fearsome tides. Once the trough had flooded to a manageable width, the boys would swim for it, usually finishing about one hundred yards upstream by the time they had struggled through the rough water and reached the home bank.

The one occasion flashing through Yanto's mind at this moment involved just three of the local water babies: Yanto, his best friend Simon Midgeley, and that danger-loving, beautiful tomboy, Julie Murchison. Julie was a rich kid who loved to associate with the tougher, more daring local boys. She couldn't resist the challenge of swimming back over the tide when the boys suggested it. What they had not realised however was that the tide they chose for Julie's initiation was a late spring Bore. The noise of the incoming tide had interrupted their games on the sand further out in the estuary. All three ran back to the trough prepared to swim for it as the boys had done several times before. One look was sufficient to make them realise they had made a dreadful mistake. They realised they would have to race the tide. About half a mile upstream the trough was traversed by the Purton breakwater. The breakwater was a finger of massive boulders sticking straight out into the estuary for a couple of hundred yards. Yet another effort to save the banks from the destructive effects of this river.

The breakwater was very effective. It stopped the initial rush of water for a while, but once the large depression around the barrier had filled, like a bowl filling before your eyes, the tide would roar on down the trough on the other side of the barrier.

The breakwater had given the kids the precious time they needed. By sprinting like Olympic champions on the hard sand they had managed to cross the almost empty trough on the far side of the breakwater before the flood arrived. But it had been close and the children had never taken liberties with the river again. On that occasion their predicament had been spotted and a boat had been sent out from Sharpness on a wild goose chase. Yanto's father had got hell from the harbourmaster and Yanto had got hell from his old man.

But there would be no boat tonight. Having decided he must race the tide, he began a desperate cumbersome run along the edge of the trough towards the breakwater. He quickly realised a ten-year-old in swimming trunks can run a good deal faster than a twenty-eight-year-old clad in hip-high waders with a bloody great salmon on his back. As he staggered on he could visualise the young Julie running alongside him, red-faced and tight-lipped. He had loved that girl from afar after that first incident, but she had been too full of fun and the love of life to worry about boyfriends. As the war approached, her father, Colonel Joshua Murchison, had sent her to live with his sister in California. It had almost broken Yanto's heart at the time.

A patch of soft sand almost sent him sprawling. God, he was tired. Should he ditch the salmon? No, he wasn't that tired. He considered tearing off his waders but there might still be time to cross the far side of the breakwater without having to swim for it.

The huge boulders of the breakwater loomed ahead of him, the grey stone showing white in the moonlight. His heart sank. The depression around the breakwater already resembled a great lake, full of swirling whirlpools. He knew the grey tide must already be at full flood on the other side. He pressed on doggedly.

His position was now becoming desperate and he cursed himself again for his stupidity. He was forced to run wider now because of the ever expanding lake. His chest was heaving. He was a big, fit man but he realised he could not go on much longer, and his iron resolve began to melt in the face of the powers of nature surrounding him. As he stumbled around the far side of the breakwater, the hard sand was replaced by thick mud. Getting through it took the last of his energy. He was forced to stop. His war wound which had pained him earlier was now turning to agony. The incessant roar of the tide forced him on again. When he finally reached the trough, it was by willpower alone.

The torrent here was almost as fearsome as it had been at the original crossing point, but not so deep. 'About waist deep in the middle, I reckon,' he told himself. But it was filling before his eyes. He desperately wanted to rest, but it was now or never.

Taking a firm grip on the hook, still jammed securely in place, he lunged determinedly into the rushing water. Before the water reached his knees he knew without a shadow of doubt that he would never be able to stand at waist depth. As the water ripped at his thighs he turned and staggered backwards, using his stronger right leg as a brace against the frightening force of the water. As he reached the middle of the trough, the water was forcing itself over his shoulders. The cold water shocked him as it tore at his bare neck. His fear turned to blind rage. 'You won't get me, you bastard,' he yelled in defiance. At that moment a rock moved under his right foot and he went under.

The cold salt water on his face caused him to come up

gasping. He held on desperately to the dead weight of the fish, but try as he might, he was unable to regain his feet. Relentlessly, the amazing force of the tide rolled and twisted his body along like a dead sheep's. He tried to dig his heels into the bed of the trough in an attempt to slow down his headlong rush, but each time the soft bottom gave way and on he went. He gasped in agony as his knees smashed into a rock. Yanto Gates was afraid of no man, but now he was terrified.

Suddenly his body hit a shallow rocky section of the trough bed. By digging his heels into the rocks he was able to lunge a good six feet nearer the home back. 'A couple more of those and I shall be out of the main current,' he told himself wildly. Mercifully the shallow section continued. Again, hidden reserves came to his aid. Another series of lunges took him out of the central current and somehow he managed to regain his feet.

Yanto staggered and fell the last few feet and finally collapsed on the mud and grass of the bank. Cursing and gasping, he lay there for a full five minutes, the surprisingly intact fish by his side.

The cold eventually forced him to his feet. He looked at the river, which was now in full flood. The roaring bedlam of the tide's initial onslaught was being replaced by a menacing quiet as the deep black water sucked and heaved around the boulders. The moon lit a silvery path across the estuary, interrupted only by the high sand still visible way out in its centre. Even that was rapidly being engulfed by the hungry tide as he watched. Then there was a mile of deep treacherous water separating him from the Forest of Dean.

Three

MOLLY

It felt as though he had been fed through a mincing machine.

After gingerly feeling himself all over, Yanto decided there were no bones broken. Having looked around, he also realised just how far his reluctant running and swimming had taken him upstream. His boots and rabbits would have to wait until tomorrow; that was certain.

He looked across the field-cum-riverbank in the general direction of civilisation, and with the aid of the moonlight was able to make out the familiar gables of the Blue Boar, a hundred yards away. He decided the quickest way home was through the Blue Boar's yard. Once again he threw the cumbersome fish over his shoulder and began squelching his way across the boggy field. After climbing the ancient fence which bordered the pub's premises, he leaned back against the fence for another breather.

The old pub looked cold and lifeless in the moonlight, a total contrast to the turmoil which normally prevailed during licensing hours. The building had originally been a manor house and must have looked beautiful in its heyday.

With its Georgian frontage and those imposing pillars holding up the front porch, it still looked impressive. Ivy draped the whole frontage of the building and mingled with the moss of the large dilapidated lawn. Yanto could imagine crinolined children playing with their nanny on that lawn in more sane and settled times, when Britannia ruled the world.

He shivered. Having rested he now felt the chill from his soaked and muddy clothes. He walked through the Blue Boar's yard and on up the narrow lane which ran directly to the village of Purton, a distance of a quarter of a mile. It was now 3.30 a.m.

and he stopped on the swing bridge over the Berkeley to Gloucester canal and tried to hide the fish as much as possible. It was not unknown for Herbie Connors to be about at this time, and Yanto had done enough running for one night.

He suddenly decided not to go home to the cottage he shared with his widowed mother. Even with his poacher's stealth, his mother always heard him enter the house and he didn't feel like explanations tonight. A sly grin crossed his face as he thought of an alternative billet in which to spend what remained of the night. He felt a stirring in his loins at the thought of it. I'll bloody have her tonight, he decided.

Instead of turning left over the canal bridge which would have taken him into the village, he turned right and began walking out of the village on the Brookend Road. The air was warm for April and he felt comfortable again. The night was dead still now, not a breath of wind. 'What a bloody contrast to an hour ago,' he thought to himself. Even the smell of the spring flowers became apparent, something he had never even noticed before in daylight.

After walking for approximately a quarter of a mile he stopped outside a small detached cottage on his left. The moonlight illuminated a hand carved wooden name plaque on the freshly painted gate: Honey Cottage. Hanging around the gate were various other crudely written notices advertising fresh garden produce for sale.

Yanto carefully opened the gate. There was the inevitable screech which, in the dead of night, sounded like a cock fight. He carefully placed the fish on the wooden water butt at the side of the house then looked around the ash path for a couple of handy sized stones. He tossed the first stone at the small wooden framed bedroom window on the left-hand side of the cottage, keeping a wary eye on the right-hand window at the same time. The stone struck the wooden window surround and fell back, hitting the metal cover of the rainwater butt with a loud clang. He froze for a full minute, but all was silent.

Taking more care with the second shot, he was rewarded by the cracking sound of stone hitting glass.

After what seemed like an age, he heard the metal window catch being released. This was followed by a heavy thump on the warped wooden frame and the window flew open. A tousled head appeared at the window.

'Who is it, what's going on down there?' the head demanded.

'It's me, Moll, Yanto,' he answered with an urgent whisper, still keeping his eye on the other bedroom window.

'What the hell have you been up to?' she demanded, glancing down the road as if she expected Herbie Connors to appear on his bike.

'Let me in for Christ's sake and I'll tell you.'

The head disappeared. Half a minute later the front door was tugged gently open, and there stood the slim nightgowned figure of Molly Hopkins, curlers and all.

'Hello, sweetheart,' he smiled, and walked past her, up the narrow passage, and into the back kitchen. He stood with his back to the fireplace, still glowing with the remains of last night's fire. Molly followed him into the room, struck a match, and lit the oil lamp.

'Good God,' she breathed as she saw the state of him, 'You look like the combination of tramp and fairy.'

'Whaddya mean, a fairy,' snapped Yanto.

'Well, look at all that shiny stuff all over you,' Molly continued, 'you look like a Christmas tree.' Yanto laughed as he realised his shoulders were covered with fish scales which were flashing in the dim light of the oil lamp.

'I've got something to show you' he said, and disappeared back down the passage. When he reappeared carrying the fish, Molly gasped with admiration. She had never seen such a fish.

'You never caught that in the Severn, did you?' she whispered.

'Where do you think I got it, the bloody fishmongers?' he replied, with mock exasperation.

'How much is it worth?' Molly asked, unable to take her eyes off the beautiful specimen.

'I shall want twenty quid off Sid Watkins for her.'

Molly started to rebuild the fire. 'Get those wet clothes off,' she demanded. 'I'll make a pot of tea then you can tell me all about it.'

Yanto sat in front of the now blazing fire, naked except for an ex-army blanket draped around him. He sipped the hot mug of tea and watched Molly remove her curlers with one hand while laying out his clothes by the fire with the other. The clothes began to steam immediately.

'Moll, you're a good 'un.,' he said, as he watched her well-rounded posterior moving under the thin nightgown. He also began to experience that old feeling.

He had been seeing Molly on and off for about six months. She was different from most of the considerable number of women he had known. Sensible, efficient, and a heart as big as a football. When her mother had died early in the war, Molly had smoothly taken over the running of the house and also the more difficult job of looking after Selwyn, the father she adored. All this in addition to her full-time job in the Sharpness dock office. Yanto grudgingly admitted to himself that she was also different by the fact that she was still a virgin.

Molly finished laying out his clothes and put the refilled teapot on the hob to brew. Yanto watched her with affection. She was tall, only five inches less than his own six foot one.

'Right,' she said, as she dropped into the old chintz covered settee beside him, 'what are you going to do with all that lovely money?'

'Well, I've been thinking,' he said, as he slid his arm around her waist and pulled her close.

'Yes,' she said expectantly. Her pretty elfin face, accentuated by her short bobbed hair, looked up smiling.

'Well, you know you are always moaning about me not taking you out enough,'

'I do not –' she started to interrupt.

'Anyway, I managed to save a few bob and Billy Tolboys, my mate on the docks, was telling me there's a motorbike and sidecar in Bert Midgeley's garage in Sharpness and he reckons Bert could be persuaded to sell it.

Molly's smile faded slightly. She had hoped his ideas lay in another direction, like an engagement ring. But then again, she knew him too well. She had never told him she loved him, but she guessed he knew, with the confidence that comes easy to good-looking men. Yanto was one of those men who stood out in a crowd. Tall, and as strong as a lion. With his blue-black curly hair and ice-blue eyes, he could melt most women with a glance. He also had brains. Being one of the few local boys who had gone to grammar school had given him that extra confidence early in life. He was a born fighter. Making a name for himself as a boxer in the army had come easy to him, and had it been peacetime he could probably have gone a long way in the sport.

All that, and a war hero to boot. Molly remembered the day he came home from the war. All the local folk were out in the street to welcome him home in his uniform and red beret of the Parachute Regiment. With just the aid of a walking stick he made his way to the Blue Boar followed by most of the kids in the village, who must have thought he was some sort of God. No, Molly had long since decided to play this one cool.

'Yanto Gates,' she squeaked, 'if you think I am going to hare around the country in all winds and weathers in a contraption like that, you've got another think coming. Anyway, I've heard that the sidecar can come off. I can imagine you turning right in one of the lanes around here, and me going straight on into some duck pond or other.'

Yanto almost laughed out loud, but remembered Selwyn asleep upstairs. 'Don't be daft,' he chuckled, 'just think, I'll be able to take you to dances at Listers Hall in Dursley, even Gloucester if you like.'

'By the time I get there in that thing I shall look like something the cat dragged in,' she chortled. Yanto could see she was sold on the idea. Then he pulled her close and kissed her on the lips. As she melted against him, he caressed her right breast. He kissed her again and her breathing rate increased. Yanto resisted the urge to rush things. He was not in a French whorehouse now with his paratrooper mates. This was Molly.

That was all very well, but the feel of Molly's firm large breast in his hand was having a strong effect on his animal instincts. He took hold of her hand and gently directed it under the blanket which shrouded him. Molly showed a momentary resistance once she realised where her hand was going, but with a soft moan she gave in and her fingers closed around his erect manhood.

'Jesus, I'm there at last,' he thought deliriously. Then allowing his hand to drop, he began a gentle circular massage of Molly's flat soft belly. All the weeks of reluctantly keeping Yanto at bay, plus having her hand on a male sexual organ for the first time in her twenty-five years of life, was too much for Molly.

'Don't let Dad hear, for God's sake,' she moaned quietly, as all her inhibitions went out of the window. That was enough for Yanto. He threw off the blanket, picked up the limp girl, and gently placed her on the mat in front of the blazing fire. From a kneeling position, he turned and doused the oil lamp, hoping to reduce the chance of any embarrassment changing Molly's mind at the last minute. As he turned and looked into her eyes he knew instinctively there was no need to worry on that score. This had a marvellous calming effect on him and made him determined to do the job right, especially as it was Molly's first time. He undid her nightgown and admired her body for the first time. The light from the fire bathed her in a warm flickering glow as he lay down beside her. First he kissed her forehead, then her eyes, her mouth, her throat. Then he gently stroked her stomach in a circular motion, luxuriating in the feel of her pubic hair brushing the edge of his hand. Finally, he could stand it no longer. He gently forced his hand between her tightly closed thighs. With a small guttural sigh she relaxed and allowed him to part her thighs. He lay there rigid with excitement as his hand probed her moist femininity.

'Please, Yanto, please,' she gasped, 'now.' In one movement he lay across her. Remembering to take his weight on his elbows as a gentleman should, and desperately trying to restrain his passion, he entered her gently, but firmly. At first he thought

20

she was going to scream. But no sound came. Instead, she grasped him as he had never been grasped before.

For the next three minutes they experienced sensations that only requited lust can bring. Suddenly, Molly's back arched and lifted his entire weight off the floor as she reached her climax. The noises she made finally triggered Yanto who, with a great effort, managed to withdraw at the last second. They lay there together for several minutes, gasping and perspiring.

Finally the heat from the fire began to burn Yanto's left side and forced him to roll off the still-inert Molly. He sat up and their eyes met.

'That was wonderful,' she breathed. 'I would never have believed it could be like that.'

'You've got to have the right bloke, mind,' Yanto smiled at her, as she stood up and shrouded herself in his blanket.

'You might as well have a couple of hours on the settee,' Molly suggested, then turned away in her embarrassment. 'I'll go and get a quilt.'

Yanto stretched himself full-length on the settee and felt that lovely feeling of total contentment creep over him.

Molly re-emerged and threw the quilt over him. She looked at him quizzically. 'You won't tell anybody, will you?' she said pleadingly.

'Don't be so bloody daft,' Yanto replied, 'What do you take me for, a peasant?' Molly disappeared up the stairs and Yanto heard her bedroom door open and close quietly at the end of the landing. 'Jesus, what a bloody day,' he said to himself as his eyes closed.

Four

DOCKLAND

Yanto awoke with a start. 'What the hell, where am I!' He could feel a moving weight on his legs. He raised himself on one elbow and gingerly felt around his feet. He jumped as his hand came into contact with something warm and furry.

It was Rats, Molly's huge tortoiseshell cat. He fell back on the settee with a thump as the memories of the previous night's activities came flooding back. Rats walked up his chest and began to lick his stubbly chin, obviously enjoying the salt from Yanto's late night swim. The cat jumped to the ground and disappeared into the kitchen as Yanto swung his legs off the settee and sat up.

It was almost light outside. He pulled back one curtain and looked at his watch. Shit! The watch had stopped at three o'clock. About the time he had taken his reluctant swim.

Making a mental note to drop the watch into Merryfield's watch repairs on his next visit to Berkeley, Yanto hitched the blanket around him and walked through the silent house into the kitchen.

Rats looked up from a saucer of milk as the monklike figure entered the room. A horrible thought struck Yanto as he saw the cat eating. Where was the bloody fish? The cat could have eaten half of it while he had been asleep. A sigh of relief whistled through his teeth as he stuck his head into the pantry. Molly had put the fish in the meat safe. The safe being a large cabinet with a fine wire-mesh door to keep flies off fresh food. He opened the safe door and took out the fish as though it were stuffed with rubies.

He dressed quickly. His clothes, although dry, felt stiff and unpleasant. 'Damned Severn water,' he muttered. The kitchen clock read 6.30, plenty of time to walk home to his mother's cottage for a wash and a bit of breakfast. Then on his bike to report for work at Sharpness Docks for eight o'clock.

It was five minutes to eight when Yanto cycled over the low swing bridge onto the wharves of Sharpness Docks. The sun appeared and sparkled on the railway lines, wet after the recent April shower. The rails were set flush with the concrete and he negotiated them carefully. A bicycle wheel fitted into the rail slots perfectly, with disastrous results as Yanto had often discovered after the odd liquid lunch at the Sharpness Hotel.

The great boom of the war years had passed and the docks were settling down to the post-war doldrums. A docker was never sure what to expect when he reported for work in the morning. Sometimes there was work, sometimes not. If he went a week without work there was just seven pounds a week pool money to take home. Not much if you were married with a family.

On the other hand, he could find he had been selected to unload a valuable cargo such as palm kernels. On such a cargo he could easily make himself twenty pounds a week, plus. These cargoes were few and far between, however. Much more likely to be a timber boat. Hard work for about fourteen pounds a week.

Yanto cycled down the wharf, dodging the mooring ropes until he arrived at the berth of a small Norwegian timber boat called *Marit*, registered in Oslo. Yanto and his gang had started work on her the day before.

As he threw his bike into the timber shed Yanto spotted his friend and workmate, Billy Tolboys, leaning over the ship's rail.

'Welcome aboard, Cap'n,' grinned Billy as Yanto reached the top of the gangway. Billy had been a close friend for over a year now and they had had some good times together.

Tuberculosis as a child had kept Billy out of the war, but he was now a fit twenty-six-year old, as tall as Yanto but as thin as a rake. His mop of red hair and boyish good looks made him a favourite with the ladies. 'I don't like the look of yours much,

24

Yant,' was his favourite expression as the two of them prepared to chat up a couple of strange girls. But it was usually Billy who finished up with the lesser of the two.

'What the hell were you doing last night?' Yanto asked as they climbed down into the half-empty hold of the *Marit*.

'Why?' Billy looked at him a bit old fashioned.

'Look at your eyes, they're like pissholes in the snow,' laughed Yanto. Billy laughed in return.

'Well, you know my old man keeps a fifteen gallon cask of scrumpy in the shed?' Yanto nodded. 'Well, he needed a refill so I gave him a hand to push his hand cart into Berkeley last night. He gets his cider from Tom James's cider press.'

'Christ,' interrupted Yanto, 'Old Tom's cider's as rough as a badger's ass.'

'You're telling me,' Billy continued. 'Anyway, Tom wouldn't let us go, kept fillin' them old cracked china mugs of his. We both finished up pissed. Can you imagine what it was like getting that bloody cart home?'

They were still laughing as they stepped down into the hold. The sun was now shining out of a cloudless sky as they removed their shirts and allowed the sunlight to bathe their pale bodies. In the confined space of the ship's hold the air was already thick with the powerful, but pleasant aroma of unseasoned timber. A couple more members of the gang came scrambling down the companionway ladder. After exchanging greetings, Billy turned to his mate. 'Anyway,' he said 'you don't look as though you'd give Joe Louis much trouble this morning. What were you up to last night?' Yanto went through the events of the previous night, carefully leaving out his conquest of Molly. 'Christ,' breathed Billy, 'you were lucky there mate, that was a pretty big 'un for a night tide, I heard it was a twenty-seven footer.'

'You don't have to tell me, you prat, I had to swim the bastard, didn't I?' Yanto grunted.

The rest of the gang arrived swearing and moaning, ex-army haversacks hanging over their shoulders containing their precious bait.

'By the way, Bill,' Yanto turned enquiringly, 'has Bert Midgeley still got that motorbike combination you were telling me about?'

'Far as I know, why?'

'Cause I'm gonna buy it, that's why.'

Billy looked aghast. 'You got that sort of money?' he said. 'Even if Bert lets it go, he will want a pretty penny for it. You can't get 'em for love nor money.'

'We'll see,' said Yanto. 'I get on well with old Bert.'

A huge steel crane hook suddenly descended quietly between their faces and made them both leap back in alarm. Yanto shook his fist at the face of the crane driver grinning down at them through his cab window. 'You shitbag, Tiny, you could have given us a bloody heart attack.' Tiny Bennion grinned again and pointed up the wharf towards the dock office. Obviously Cliff Barrett, the dock foreman, was on his way.

'Did you pick up my tompaw from the stores, Bill?' Yanto shouted, as the gang began to slap the heavy deal planks into slings. Billy pulled a short wooden-handled instrument from his belt and tossed it to Yanto. 'Cheers, pal.' With a quick reflex action he caught the tompaw, a short stout wooden handle with a steel claw set in the end, and thumped it into the first deal of the day.

Yanto worked with a will, making up the slings of timber ready for Tiny Bennion's crane to pick up and dump on the wharf. The other half of the gang, working on the wharf, then took the individual timbers on their leather-padded shoulders, and with that strange loping run, their steps synchronised to the bending motion of the plant, would deposit them into the timber sheds.

The docks were alive now. Alive with the sound of honest toil. The roar of the grain elevators and the slap of timbers rent the sunlit air. It was going to be a good day.

Five

THE SALE

Mary Gates cycled through the village of Wanswell towards the town of Berkeley. Her back was as straight as a ramrod, which made her feel a little more dignified while engaging in what she considered the unladylike art of cycling. The black vintage Humber bicycle was a little unsteady today. This was probably caused by the roll of linoleum, one end of which was tied to the carrier behind her saddle, the other to the handlebar. It looked awkward, but not heavy, unless you took into account the fact that this linoleum was rolled around a fifty-pound salmon.

'The things I do for that boy,' mused Mary, as she jumped off the bike and began to push it up Station Hill. The lino had been Mary's idea. Just as well. Because as she cycled out of Purton, she had passed Herbie Connors cycling in. Herbie had passed her with a respectful 'Good morning.' His back was also as straight as a ramrod and his highly polished black gaiters had flashed in the sun. 'Sly old devil,' Mary had sighed with relief. Herbie's face had also lit in a sly smile as Mary had passed. She had reminded him he would have to speak to a certain young man in the Blue Boar this evening. It concerned a pair of boots and a brace of rabbits.

Mary cycled into Berkeley's ancient square and acknowledged a cheery greeting from 'Old Jesus,' the bearded local tramp, who was resting on the Town Hall seat.

She turned right into the High Street then jumped from the cycle and began pushing it up an alleyway on her left which led to the stables-cum-car park at the rear of the Berkeley Chase Hotel.

As she entered the alleyway she heard someone call. She turned and saw Tommy Hook standing outside his butchers shop in the High Street.

'Mornin' Mary. I see 'e's bin at it again,' he said with a knowing wink. 'Can't you get him to rustle me a couple of bullocks?' He doubled up laughing at his own joke. Mary fixed a frosty gaze on him 'It's nothing like that, Tom Hook,' she countered, going red in the face. Sticking her nose in the air she hurried into the car park and banged the bike against the wall of the hotel kitchen.

The heavy ornate kitchen door swung silently open on well-oiled hinges Mary found herself looking down at the small dapper figure of Sidney Watkins, manager of the Berkeley Chase for the last ten years.

Sid's face lit up at the sight of her. Mary was still a good-looking woman and Sid had admired her from afar for a long time. He had never found the nerve to ask her out. 'Come on down, my love. Lovely to see you,' he said, with an accent that betrayed his Cockney past. Mary smiled as she negotiated the three awkward steps down to a sunken floor of the huge kitchen. 'How's that scallywag of a son of yours?' Sid asked.

'Actually, I have come to see you on his behalf,' said Mary pompously. She always found herself adopting this haughty attitude when entering big houses or hotels of above average splendour. It was her natural defence after her early years of domestic service. From leaving school at twelve years of age until her marriage to Hywell Gates at the age of twenty-five, she had slaved in other people's houses for a pittance. 'That's how I spent the best years of my life,' she often said to her son. She had also instilled into Yanto at an early age, that he was better than most and as good as anybody. Another reason for Yanto's fantastic confidence. When she married she swore an oath that she would never work for anyone outside her own family again. Each time she helped her son dispose of a poached salmon she felt good. It was another smack in the eye for the establishment.

She looked at Sid, a good clean-looking man in his late fifties. With dark hair and moustache, he was always well-dressed, regardless of the time of day. He was in shirt sleeves, but still looked dressed in his dark tie, trousers, and waistcoat.

'What can I do for you then, Mary?' Sid's soft, wide-spaced brown eyes looked at her betraying his obvious affection. Mary knew she could twist him around her little finger. So did Yanto, which was the main reason Mary did the selling.

'Yanto has sent something over for you,' Mary said softly. 'It's hanging on my bike in the yard, inside a roll of lino.'

'I see,' said Sid knowingly, 'Help yourself to a cup of tea my love, while I fetch it in.' Mary poured herself a cup of tea and savoured the aromatic smells of good food for which this house was known for miles around. To be frequented by the blue-blooded followers of the nearby Berkeley Hunt was the ultimate praise.

Mary heard the expected whistle of surprise from the car park. A minute later Sid staggered down the steps with the fish still in the roll of lino. Red in the face, he dumped the burden onto the massive wooden kitchen table, which gleamed white after countless years of daily scrubbing. With Mary holding the roll firmly, Sid took hold of the salmon's tail, and with one hard steady pull freed the fish from its linoleum case.

Sid's eyes opened wide with wonder. 'Jesus   Christ,'   he breathed, momentarily forgetting Mary's presence. 'Sorry, Mary,' he apologised, 'but that's the biggest salmon I have ever seen.' He went to the far kitchen wall and took down a large hanging scales.

'You will find it's just over fifty pounds,' chirped Mary, as he hung the scales on a large nail hammered into one of the exposed beams. Using both hands, Sid hoisted the fish up towards the scales. 'Stick the hook in his gill slit, Mary,' he gasped again going red in the face. Steadying the hook, Mary negotiated it into the fish's gill slit. 'OK,' she said, Sid slowly allowed the scales to take the full weight of the fish. It read fifty-one and a quarter pounds. Sid could hardly believe his eyes.

'Told you,' said Mary triumphantly.

'Well, that's some sort of fish all right,' Sid muttered thoughtfully. 'Mind you, Mary, they don't command as high a price as the small ones. We have to expect more wastage, can't keep putting it in and out of the fridge, could poison somebody. I could go to seven and six a pound.' Mary's eyes hardened.

'Don't give me that rubbish, Sid Watkins,' she began, 'with the average party in this place, that fish would go in one sitting and you know it. Yanto wants twenty pounds for that fish, in which case ...' She hesitated as she went to her large shopping bag. Yanto had told her to give the small salmon to Sid providing he coughed up the twenty quid, but Mary decided she could get something out of it for herself, especially after that uncomfortable bicycle ride. Mary took the five-pound salmon from her bag, wrapped in newspaper. 'In which case, Yanto said you could have this one for a pound, and it's worth at least two pounds ten, as you know. Of course, if that's too much for you, there's always the Princes over at Newport, but they will get all the future fish as well.'

Her bluff worked well. 'All right, Mary. I know when I'm licked.' Sid held up his hands in surrender. He left the kitchen and picked up the hotel cashbox from his office in the foyer.

With Mary leaning over his shoulder, he took out four large white five-pound notes and a single pound note, folded them carefully, and handed the money over to her. 'Tell him not to spend it all at once,' he said with a grin.

'I will, Sid, and thank you.' She put the money in her purse with a reverence shown only by people who had rarely, if ever, had handled notes worth over one pound.

'That's some sort of woman,' thought Sid, as he watched her skip up the kitchen steps and disappear into the bright sunlight of the car park. 'One of these days,' he mused.

Leaving her bike in the Berkeley Chase car park, Mary hurried down the High Street. A wave of cheerful elation swept over her as she separated her pound note from Yanto's fivers. 'Oh, Mary Gates,' she said to herself 'you should go into business for yourself.'

Her smile grew even wider as she walked into Shoreland's dress shop.

Six

THE BIKE

After enduring the terrible winter of 1946-47, this, the first really warm day of spring, was having a remarkable effect on the dockers unloading the *Marit*. They worked with a will, luxuriating in the feel of the sun on their bare backs. They also worked with the knowledge that there was a big Russian timber boat due in on the midday tide. If they could finish the *Marit* today, there was a good chance they would be working on the Russian boat tomorrow. That would guarantee a full week's work.

Yanto attached the crane hook to his latest sling of timber, steadied it as Tiny Bennion took the strain, and watched it disappear through the hatch.

As he stretched his back and wiped the sweat from his eyes, somebody yelled 'Bait time!' It was 10.30. Bait time in dockland meant fifteen glorious minutes of rest. Time to eat their sandwiches and drink their bottles of cold tea or cider.

Yanto picked up his ex-army haversack and sat down beside Billy on a handy sling of timber. Billy mopped his face with a large red handkerchief as they examined the bait of the day.

Whaddya got?' grunted Billy.

'Faggot sandwiches,' came the reply. 'Swap one for a cheese and pickle?'

'OK. Variety is the spice of life,' grinned Yanto.

'Can't you ever stop talking about women?' Billy grunted back. They ate in silence, listening to the murmured conversation and occasional laughs of their comrades.

A noisily closed door made them glance up at the ship's sunlit bridge. A seaman was leaning on the bridge rail, his bland Slavic face scrutinising the resting dockers. Yanto caught his eye with a nod. The seaman returned the nod and jerked his head towards the rear of the bridge.

Picking up his now empty haversack, Yanto climbed up the ladder on to the deck. A quick glance up and down the wharf showed no sign of Cliff Barrett. He went up the companionway ladder to the bridge two rungs at a time.

'Don't forget you know who,' Billy shouted from the top of the hatch ladder as Yanto and the seaman disappeared through a door at the rear of the bridge.

Yanto stood alone in the oily smelling cabin, allowing his eyes to grow accustomed to the gloom after the bright sunshine outside. He listened to the throb of the ship's generators, a noise he associated with every ship he had travelled on. The Campbells steamer his mother had once taken him on for a day trip to Ilfracombe. The troopship which had taken him to war. They were all the same. He hated their claustrophobic atmosphere. He would rather have parachuted out of an aircraft a dozen times with full equipment in the dead of night than spend one night on a ship.

The seaman reappeared from behind the curtained-off bunk section of the cabin. He handed Yanto two bottles of Martell three star brandy and two cartons of American Chesterfield cigarettes. Yanto quickly stuffed the goods into his haversack. The seaman's face split into a grin for the first time when Yanto handed him four pound notes. This was the standard dockland charge. One pound for a bottle of spirits, one pound for a carton of cigarettes. This was always provided the customs boys didn't catch you.

The two shook hands and after another quick look over the deck, Yanto sprinted around the wheelhouse and down the ladders into the hold to join Billy.

'That's two quid you owe me, Bill,' he grunted.

'Pay you Thursday, OK?'

Later that morning, Yanto stopped and stretched to ease his aching back. 'You fancy coming down to Bert Midgeley's with me, dinner time?' he asked Billy.

'Nuthin I'd like more, mate, but it's high tide at twelve

o'clock, and they're opening the gates to let the Russian timber ship in. Josh Cornock was telling me the big tides of the last few days have brought the elvers down. He reckons when they open the gates, the basin will be full of 'em.'

'So what?' said Yanto.

'Well, I promised my old man I would take home a feed for him tonight. I brought my net with me to have a go at 'em dinner-time.'

'Please yourself,' Yanto grunted, and thumped his tompaw into the next section of deal.

It was ten minutes past twelve when Yanto propped his bike against the wall of Bert Midgeley's garage.

Nailed over the doorway of the ramshackle clapboard frontage of the building was a large rectangular sign. He could just make out the name in spite of the peeling paint.

ALBERT MIDGELEY & SON.
MOTOR ENGINEERS.

Yanto felt a tinge of sadness as he looked at the sign. He remembered the morning he had watched Bert proudly hang up the brand new sign. It was the morning that Simon, Bert's son and Yanto's best friend, had joined his father's business after leaving school. That was thirteen years ago, but to Yanto it seemed an eternity.

He walked into the cool, gloomy interior. The signs of neglect were everywhere. The garage had a dirt floor, but decades of oil and grease, plus vehicles and feet, had made it harder than concrete. Several bicycles, left days before for repair, would probably have to wait days more to be completed. Car springs and axles littered the floor; A punctured car wheel that someone was repairing lay in the centre of the floor with half its inner tube hanging out like a paunched rabbit. What a bloody mess, thought Yanto.

'Anybody at home?' he bawled.

The back of the garage was boarded off. With the screech of

rusty hinges, one section of the boarding which served as a door was partly pushed and partly kicked open.

The tall hunchbacked figure of Bert Midgeley came shuffling out. Bert was in his sixties, with a balding head, thin weasel face, and a nose that never stopped running, winter or summer. Yanto could not recollect ever having seen him out of a boiler suit.

'Hello, son,' said Bert fondly, as he took out the inevitable packet of Woodbines and offered one to Yanto. 'To what do I owe this pleasure?'

Bert had always held Yanto in high regard. Being so close to Simon, Yanto had spent a great deal of his childhood at the garage. 'Almost a second son,' Bert had always said. They had joined up together in '39, but when Simon had been killed at Alamein Bert had died with him in spirit.

'Hello, Mr Midgeley. Nice to see you again,' said Yanto respectfully. 'I was told that you had a motorbike and sidecar. Just popped in to have a look. Is it for sale?'

'Not to anybody, lad,' said Bert, 'but for you I might make an exception.'

'Can I have a look?' Yanto tried not to look too eager.

'It's through here.' Bert shuffled back through the door into the boarded off section of the garage, followed by Yanto, who was frustrated by the old man's slowness.

This part of the garage was a little more presentable. It was Bert's private workshop, complete with a lathe and other skilled men's paraphernalia. Bert started to move a huge pile of cardboard boxes which had once housed a variety of motor spares. Yanto could see something behind the boxes, covered by a tarpaulin. The end wall of this part of the garage was almost all window, but it was so filthy and flyblown that it was even darker in here than the front of the building.

'Give me a hand, son,' Bert grunted, 'I'm not as young as I used to be.' Yanto needed no second bidding. He moved the rest of the boxes in less than a minute.

Bert took a long sniff and looked at Yanto. 'I bought it off George Holder's widow,' he said. 'You remember old George.

34

Got killed when that horse kicked him in the head.' He paused as he tugged off the filthy tarpaulin. 'Happened about six months ago, up at Wilf Tillet's farm at Halmore, surely you remember?'

Yanto didn't answer. He was gawking at the beautiful red and silver machine which was revealed as the tarpaulin fell away. 'Christ, Bert, it looks brand new,' he gasped.

'Yeah, she's a beauty all right. She was old George's pride and joy.'

Yanto noted the B.S.A. motif on the petrol tank. 'What model is it, Bert?'

'She's a '37 500cc Sloper, a fine machine, not many around these parts.'

'Will she start?'

'Course she will.' Bert answered Yanto's question with another sniff. 'I'll get her out in the middle of the workshop, then you can have a good look around her.' The bike started with Bert's second kick. The noise was deafening in the small confines of the workshop. After a couple of noisy tweaks on the throttle he allowed the engine to idle. They both listened to the gentle burble of the exhaust for another minute, then Bert cut the engine. 'What do you think then?' he asked, and sniffed again.

'Well I want her, of course, who wouldn't?', Yanto began, 'but what sort of money do you want for her?'

'Well, with the sidecar, plus the condition of the bike, she is worth every penny of two hundred pounds,' Bert said cautiously, 'but from you I would take a hundred and seventy-five.'

Yanto looked a little crestfallen, and he wondered how his mother had fared with Sid Watkins. 'I have been saving for a while now,' Yanto began, 'and by tonight I shall have a hundred and fifty. Not enough, eh?'

Bert looked at him for a full half minute. He could see Simon standing there. He remembered that Sunday morning in '39, when Wilf Bullingham, the local amateur photographer, had come around at Bert's request. Wilf had photographed the

35

two boys in their brand new uniforms outside the garage. He still had the photo upstairs. That was the last photograph ever taken of Simon and it was Bert's most precious possession.

Yanto began to fidget under Bert's gaze. 'I hear on the grapevine you can get your hands on the occasional salmon,' Bert said suddenly, with a wink.

Yanto smiled. 'Occasionally,' he replied.

'Well I am partial to a bit of Severn salmon,' Bert said. 'If you promise me that next half-tidy salmon that comes your way, you can have the bike for a hundred and fifty. How's that?'

Yanto could have hugged the old man. 'Mr Midgeley, you are a gentleman,' he said, and grabbed Bert's bony hand.

'There's nobody I would rather see have it, son,' Bert said sadly.

They walked back out into the sunlit street together. 'Have you got a licence?' Bert asked.

'Yes,' Yanto replied. 'I was in the R.A.S.C. before I transferred to the Parachute Regiment. Did some despatch work.'

'Good,' said Bert. 'I'll service her up for you. Let's see. Today's Wednesday, you can pick her up after work Friday.'

'Bloody marvellous,' came the excited reply. 'I'll pick her up Friday, and pay you in full then.'

Bert watched Yanto jump on his bike without touching the pedals. He looked back over his shoulder. 'Thanks again, Bert,' he bawled.

'You're welcome, son,' replied Bert in his sad monotone voice. He tried unsuccessfully to sniff back the tears as he watched Yanto race back towards the docks.

Billy Tolboys gave a whoop of excitement. Old Josh had been right, as always. The old river man had said this big tide would bring the elvers down and, sure enough, the muddy water of the dock basin was full of them. A half-hour before, the massive lock gates which separated the dock basin from the estuary had been opened to allow the ancient Russian ship to enter.

She was the largest ship to enter Sharpness Docks since the war, and many local people had turned up to watch her berth. After entering the basin she had to negotiate the lock, a narrow channel which connected the basin to the dock proper. As she passed through the channel there had been less than a foot clearance between the ship's sides and the concrete wharf. It had been a slow job, but as all this had been going on the elvers had been flooding into the basin.

What miracle of navigation brought these baby eels from their birthplace in the Sargasso Sea to their ancestral waters in the River Severn, nobody knew. The fact that they did arrive however, was much appreciated by people in this part of Gloucestershire. The eel fry, awaited impatiently each year, provided sport and income. Nobody in the area was happy unless they had at least one feed. When the elvers were running, each tide saw an army of hopefuls with their elver nets, scooping the waters from Sharpness to Gloucester and beyond.

Billy walked slowly along the lip of the dock basin sieving the water, still brown and muddy from the passing of the Russian ship. As he reached the spot where Josh Cornock was likewise occupied, he heaved the elver scoop from the water and was delighted to find it a quarter full of the writhing silver baby eels. Billy whooped again. 'Look at this bloody lot, Josh,' he jabbered excitedly, 'I've never sin the water so thick with 'em before.'

'Well, make the bloody most of it,' grunted Josh, as he stood up and mopped his bearded face with a large brown handkerchief. The hankie had once been white, but Josh liked his snuff. 'You got to keep going when you find 'em, the little buggers disappear as fast as they come.' Billy squatted down on his haunches and took a single elver from his scoop. He was surprised at its strength as it curled its three-inch long body around his index finger, and squeezed. The tiny eel was almost transparent, except for the jet black, pinprick eyes.

'You would never think he'll be a bloody great eel one day, would you?' Billy said thoughtfully.

''E won't, will 'e?' Josh said, with a twinkle in his watery blue eyes, 'cos you're gonna eat the bugger, ent ya?'

Billy ignored the remark as he tipped the elvers into his bucket. He banged the upturned scoop on the lip of the bucket to dislodge several writhing bodies which seemed reluctant to leave the fine mesh cloth of the scoop. The bucket was half full of Severn water. It was important to keep the elvers alive. The traditional way to cook them was fry them alive in hot bacon fat, then add an egg, which had the effect of binding them together. The result was a delicious nourishing meal, and, many swore, an aphrodisiac to boot.

Josh shuffled off down the lip of the basin still sieving the water. He had brought a zinc bath with him which he hoped to fill that afternoon.

Billy watched him as he concentrated on his task. The elvers were important to Josh. When he sold them around the pubs and to neighbours that evening, the money would subsidise his meagre pension. 'It's a crying shame,' thought Billy, 'here's a man who knows more about this river than any man alive. He was a river pilot in the sailing ship days and look at him now, having to catch elvers to supplement his income. I wonder if that's how I shall finish up?'

Billy's thoughts were interrupted by a yell from further down the dock. His boyish face split into a grin as he saw Yanto cycling down the edge of the wharf like a lunatic. As he stood up, Yanto arrived and threw his bike into a beautifully controlled side skid, jumping off just as the bike crashed to the ground.

'Smart prat,' snorted Billy, 'you are going to catch your balls on the handlebars doing that one day.'

Yanto ignored the remark. 'I got the bike, Bill,' he shouted, almost knocking him to his knees.

'You're joking,' Billy gasped.

'No I bloody ent,' Yanto laughed, 'it cost me a hundred and fifty, and my next salmon. Old Bert is one of the best.'

Billy's eyes shone as Yanto told him about the bike. He was already imagining a widening of their nocturnal activities.

'When're we goin' out then,' Billy demanded.

'Well I thought we might give her a spin on Friday night,' Yanto answered with a grin.

'Do a tour of the river pubs, OK?' Billy whooped again. 'I think I will ride pillion on the way out, but I reckon it'll be the sidecar for me on the way back.'

Yanto grabbed the bean pole handle of Billy's elver net. 'I might as well get a few elvers for our mother while we're here. She likes 'em. I can't stand the bloody things myself.'

'Rubbish,' laughed Billy, 'they put lead in your pencil.'

After another ten minutes they had half a bucketful of the squirming delicacy. 'Better get back, I reckon,' Yanto grunted, looking at Billy's watch.

Giving the still busy Josh a parting wave, the two of them started back. After crossing the dock channel by way of the lock gates catwalk, they paused for a while watching and listening to the bedlam of noise from the riveting guns as the shipyard men worked on a small coastal tanker in the dry dock. 'Amazin' how much bigger they look out of the water,' commented Billy. They walked on down the wharf until they reached the *Marit*, still talking about the coming Friday night.

Seven

THE BLUE BOAR

There were three public houses in the village of Purton. The Blue Boar was, however, the undisputed centre of village life. The place where rivermen, dockers and farmworkers could relax after a hard day's work. It was a wonderful gas-lit haven with all the right smells and atmosphere, where a man could laugh, share his worries, and escape from his wife's tongue.

On the odd occasion the jollities would get out of hand and the fists would fly. Maybe a visiting foreign seaman, whose uninitiated brain having been blitzed by the local rough cider failed to appreciate a gem of cutting local humour. Such pugilistic interludes were usually short-lived however, for it meant incurring the wrath of the landlord, one Nathaniel Nelmes, better known as 'Knocker'.

Knocker had descended on the village just after the Great War at the tender age of twenty-five. He had been a successful prize fighter at the time and had the good sense to buy the Blue Boar from the proceeds of the noble art. Knocker was now, in 1947, as much a part of Purton as the breakwater. His feats of strength were legendary throughout the area. He was five feet five inches tall but just as wide, with a face that resembled the rough end of an oak beam. Knocker was also much loved in the area for his kindness and generosity. Many locals had had good reason to be grateful to him when times had been hard. Even now, a hard-up local could be sure of a free pint just by telling Knocker he had watched him fight at Gloucester's annual Barton Fair, back in the old days.

Yes, Knocker was now a much respected and financially secure backbone of society. But he would be the first to admit he owed most of his success to his wife Renee. She was in total contrast to her husband. Four feet eleven inches of skin and bone, but a terrible sight to behold when roused. Born in nearby Berkeley, Renee had been brought up the hard way. Being the second born in a poor family with thirteen brothers and sisters, you had to be tough to survive. The number of times she had had to go to school with no knickers on was nobody's business, she often told her husband.

And tough she was. The most popular story told by the regulars to casual strangers concerned a very large Swedish seaman who had visited the Blue Boar with a couple of shipmates one evening before the war. Knocker had been out that particular night, which had been very fortunate for the seaman. Even so, after several pints of the local brew, the big Swede had leaned over the bar, grabbed Renee's skinny little shoulders, and planted a big cidery kiss smack on her lips. Renee had replied with the most perfect right cross ever seen in the pub, or outside it for that matter, to the seaman's jaw. The seaman had been knocked out cold, helped considerably by the cider, no doubt. Renee's fame throughout the locality had been assured that night.

She had also been the saviour of many local drinkers who were about to get the bum's rush from an irate Knocker, always a painful experience because Knocker rarely bothered to open the door first. Brought running from the living room by the yells of the unfortunate wretch, she would subdue her husband with dockers' language and a series of smacks across his massive crew-cut head. Then, after watching Knocker slink back behind the bar, she would throw the drunk out herself. Between them, the Nelmeses were a formidable pair.

Pay day in this area was generally Thursday, so on Wednesday nights the Boar was usually quiet. If a man was lucky it was a case of pop in for a quick half, then home to a meal of bubble and squeak with the missus.

It was nine o'clock on Wednesday night when Yanto walked into the Blue Boar's yard. He stopped and surveyed the river bank. It was high water time and, in spite of the fading light, the flat mile of water stood out bright and menacing. Some stretches of the river seemed to be racing downstream while the adjoining stretch, maybe fifty yards wide, raced in the opposite direction causing silent eddies and whirlpools. It created a picture of calm silent menace.

Yanto shivered slightly as he turned towards the Blue Boar's front porch. As he reached the porch the door opened and the tall skinny frame of Sammy Pockets came walking out. Had it been any night other than Wednesday, he would have staggered out. Sammy was a retired bargee and local character.

The inevitable long loose mackintosh and knitted scarf were in evidence, which along with his totally bald head had long made Sammy the victim of local humour. 'Hello, my babe,' he chirped, as he almost walked into Yanto. 'Quiet in there tonight,' and jerked his bald head in the direction of the bar.

'That's what I need tonight Sam,' Yanto replied, 'and mind how you go on that bike. We don't want to get the grappling irons out tonight.' He smiled as he watched Sammy cycle a little unsteadily out of the yard. Sammy lived in a small cottage on the bank of the Berkeley to Gloucester canal. It was only necessary for him to cycle three hundred yards down the canal towpath to get home, but three times to Yanto's knowledge he had ridden his bike into the canal. Some said his wife didn't turn a hair any more when Sammy was carried in like a drowned rat.

Yanto walked through the front porch of the pub and on into the flagstoned lobby. Up two steps on the right of the lobby was the lounge, with its ancient piano. This room was rarely used except by posher locals, who were very thin on the ground, or on really big occasions when people overflowed from the public bar and snug. The last such occasion had been V.E. night, two years before.

Knocker's bored-looking battered features brightened as Yanto walked in and leaned on the well-used but polished bar. 'Ow bist goin on then?' he beamed.

'I'm OK. How's yourself?'

'Well it's Wednesday, en it?' Knocker shrugged his massive shoulders with a look of resignation on his face. 'Still, never mind, pay day tomorrow, then look out.' He picked up a pint mug and leaned towards the cider barrel.

'No. I think I'll have a beer tonight, Knock, give the jake a rest,' said Yanto.

'Suit yourself,' Knocker replied, and drew off a pint of bitter which he held up to the light. 'Not bad for a cider house, eh?' he said proudly.

Yanto took a deep swig. 'Beautiful mate, just beautiful,' he confirmed, and lit a Woodbine.

A cackling laugh from the snug doorway made Yanto turn. The laugh came from Sooty Hill, the Blue Boar's famous wit and practical joker. 'I hear you tried to swim the Severn last night,' he chortled.

'Christ,' grumbled Yanto, 'that didn't take long to get around. Who did you hear that off? I haven't even told Knocker yet.'

I've been in the snug,' said Sooty, 'your mate's in there with his new girlfriend. He told me all about it. Another pint of God's liquor please, mine host,' said Sooty, mockingly, holding his empty mug to Knocker.

Knocker re-filled Sooty's mug with rough cider and gave him a disapproving look at the same time. He didn't approve of people abusing their bodies the way in which Sooty did. 'This scrumpy will be the death of you, Sooty,' he said seriously, 'they'll find you in a ditch one night, all blue in the face.'

'Look mate,' replied Sooty, 'when you sweep chimneys for a living, you need plenty of liquor to swill out your guts.'

'What guts?' countered Knocker. 'This stuff must have burned out your guts years ago.'

'Bollocks,' Sooty replied, and walked unsteadily to the far corner of the bar to talk to Maisy Miller. Maisy was a spinster, and appreciated cider almost as much as Sooty.

'Silly old bugger,' muttered Knocker, 'but he never makes any trouble, so what can I do?'

'I shouldn't worry about it,' Yanto replied, 'there's nothing wrong with his head. Remember a couple of weeks ago when you were taking the piss out of him for being scruffy, you told

44

him not to come in again unless he was wearing a tie. What did he do? Came in the following Sunday morning with a tie on, no shirt or coat, just a tie. No. There's nothing wrong with him, mate.' They were both still laughing at the memory when the off sales bell rang. As Knocker went to the slide window to serve, Yanto picked up his pint and walked through into the snug. A large framed photograph of Joe Louis in fighting stance looked menacingly down at him from a supporting beam as he walked through the saloon bar doorway.

The snug looked very snug tonight. A small open fire burned in the grate even with the April weather getting warmer daily. In here the wooden benches had padding on them, and the firelight flickered on the horse brasses and old muskets that festooned the walls.

The gas lights were kept dim in the snug to compliment the cosy room. The tall lanky figure of Billy Tolboys was slouched in the corner seat by the fire. Sat primly by his side was a slim little blonde that Yanto remembered from somewhere.

'Where ya bin?' demanded Billy, 'I thought you was never comin'. You met Mary?'

'I've seen you somewhere, haven't I?' Yanto replied, his wide-set eyes scrutinising the girl.

'I work in Sharpness Co-op,' the girl replied, and looked away shyly. 'I've seen you come in for cigarettes.'

'That's it,' said Yanto, 'I was watching you cut up that damn great lump of cheese with that wire contraption.' The girl laughed behind her hand.

'Anyway, where have you bin?' Billy repeated his original question.

'I went for a stroll down the river bank,' replied Yanto, with a wink. 'I had to pick up my boots and rabbits, but I found somebody had nicked the bloody things.'

'They weren't nicked mate,' Billy said earnestly, 'Herbie Connors found 'em so look out.'

'Oh Christ,' groaned Yanto, 'those boots were nearly bloody new. Who told you it was Herbie?'

'Sammy Pockets,' replied Billy, 'he said he saw Herbie

walking along the bank behind his cottage. He saw him pull a couple of rabbits out from under a bush so he must have had the boots too.'

'The old basket,' growled Yanto. 'Still, he can't prove they're my boots. He must have eyes like a bloody owl.'

'Anyway, what you drinking?' he said, dismissing the subject by the tone of his voice.

'I'll have a pineapple juice, please,' said Mary in a weak voice. Billy wanted cider. Yanto took the empty glasses back through to the main bar. The bar was empty now except for a couple of old boys playing dominoes. A bored-looking Knocker was leaning face in hands, looking into space. 'Roll on to-bloody-morra night,' he moaned, as Yanto banged the empties on the counter. As he re-filled the glasses, Knocker leaned over to Yanto. 'Hey,' he said, in a low voice, 'who's the little wench with Billy? E's getting as bad as thee.'

'Oh just a little piece from Sharpness. Seems a nice kid.' As Yanto spoke the bar door was thrust purposefully open and there, framed in the doorway, was the tall moustached figure of Herbie Connors. Straight as a ramrod, Herbie marched to the bar. Herbie had been in Kitchener's Army. With his highly polished boots and gaiters, corduroy trousers and tweed jacket, he looked the epitome of authority. Every inch a bailiff of the old school. He dumped a bag of empty bottles on the bar. 'Evening, landlord, Master Gates,' he said in a loud voice, and exercised his usual habit of momentarily standing on tiptoes as he addressed them.

'Evening, Mr Connors,' replied Knocker respectfully. Yanto nodded in return.

'Three bottles of cider to take away, if you please,' he boomed. Herbie never drank at the pub. He regarded the locals as a bunch of peasants generally. He did have a sneaking respect for Yanto however. His war record and the fact that he had never been able to catch him poaching red-handed appealed to his old world code of honour. He often wondered what he would do if he did manage to catch him. He had heard many stories about Yanto, and knew he was a rough handful.

46

As Knocker busied himself filling the bottles, Herbie turned to his main adversary. 'Master Gates,' he said, again in a loud voice, 'were you by any chance on the river bank last night?' The two old boys looked up from their dominoes. Herbie diverted his gaze to them whereby they both took a sudden renewed interest in their game.

'Not me,' Yanto replied, looking hurt, 'I spent the evening at Selwyn Hopkins' place, with his daughter Molly.'

'I see,' Herbie said. 'Only I found a couple of freshly killed rabbits and a nice pair of boots under a bush on the bank early this morning. I dropped them into Sharpness police station, if you know anyone who might have lost them. Of course, they might ask a few questions.' He paid Knocker and picked up his bag of bottles. As he turned to leave he smiled evilly at Yanto. 'I can see I shall have to pay more attention to the river now the fish are running,' he said. 'Goodnight all.' He marched stiffly to the door and was gone.

'He'll bloody have you one of these days,' said Knocker, looking into Yanto's grim face.

'Ahh, he couldn't catch a bloody cold,' snapped Yanto and carried the drinks back into the snug. Billy was still slouched in the corner with his left leg stretched across the seat and his right arm around Mary's neck. As he had walked through the doorway, he just caught a glimpse of Mary snatching Billy's hand off her right breast.

'Better leave the salmon alone for a couple of weeks, I reckon,' said Billy, who had heard every word through the connecting hatch.

'Forget it,' said Yanto and they changed the subject.

They talked for ten minutes about their pending motorised pub crawl planned for Friday evening. 'We must test the bike before we give the girls a ride, mustn't we,' chirped Billy. He looked at Yanto and laughed.

'When will we get the chance of a trip on the bike?' Mary interrupted.

'Suit yourself,' Yanto replied.

'What about Sunday, we could have a picnic,' Mary said

47

with a slight plea in her voice.

Yanto looked at them both. 'OK by me,' he said, 'Ain't doing anything on Sunday. Where'd you like to go?'

'Oh lovely,' Mary giggled with delight, 'it's getting so hot already! What about Ham Park?'

'Good idea,' said Billy. 'There used to be a load of deer up there, but I expect they ate the buggers during the war. Still, it's nice and quiet, with plenty of woods and mossy banks to lie on.' He grinned evilly at Mary, who coloured up instantly.

Yanto arranged to pick them up outside Sharpness Co-op on Sunday morning, after which Mary said it was time for her to go home. They walked back into the main bar and found Knocker mopping up. After Billy and Mary had departed, Yanto walked over to the counter. 'Quick half before I go, please, Knock.' Knocker grinned as he handed Yanto his pint mug, two-thirds full. He jerked his head towards the bar door. 'He'll be in her pants before the night's out, I'll be bound.'

'More than likely,' grinned Yanto and took a long swig.

Knocker suddenly stopped mopping down the bar and looked at Yanto. 'I knew there was something I wanted to tell you. I was talking to Joe Asnett in Berkeley yesterday. Nat's coming home.' The news caught Yanto unawares and caused a jolt in his stomach, but he showed no sign of concern as the dark-skinned handsome spectre of Nat Asnett, his arch rival, appeared in his mind's eye. 'Yeah,' Knocker said, 'it seems he's done his time, and he's coming home. Bad news that one, but you used to be pretty friendly, didn't you.'

'Yeah, we knocked about a bit,' Yanto replied and looked thoughtfully into his beer. As children he and Nat had ruled the roost. They were both big, tough, good-looking boys. Yanto and his gang of faithful followers regarded Sharpness and the dockland as their stamping ground, while Nat and his crowd of reprobates guarded the juvenile world of Berkeley. The gangs had clashed many times. But the leaders, probably through mutual respect and fear, had never fought. It had been the same after their school days. Rivalry over girls had brought them almost to blows many times; but not quite. It was then that Nat

48

started going bad. Several assault and battery charges had brought him trouble with the police. The last couple of times Yanto had seen him before joining the army, it had been touch and go. Nat's taunts and sarcasm, usually in front of girls, had pushed Yanto's self-control to the limit.

The last time they had met was on V.E. night in Berkeley. Nat was on leave from the navy and had been impressed as he watched Yanto hit a drunken sailor who had tried to grope a young girl.

The sailor had gone straight through the casement window of the Red Hart, into the street. The window had cost Yanto a lot of money, until the girl's father heard about it and reimbursed him. Nat had returned to his ship after that leave and almost killed a petty officer in a drunken rage. The last they heard was that he had gone over the wall for two years.

'Let's hope the military nick knocked some sense into his head,' grunted Knocker as he wrung out his bar cloth.

'I doubt it,' replied Yanto. 'I can see me and him having it to go one of these days.'

'Well make sure it don't 'appen in my pub,' said a concerned Knocker. 'This place wouldn't be worth a twopenny fart after that little incident.'

Yanto smiled, bid Knocker good night, and walked out into the cool night air. As he walked through the yard he heard Renee's shrill voice.

'Them buggers all gone yet?'

Eight

JULIE

Julie Murchison stood on the platform of Berkeley railway station and gazed around. Absolutely nothing had changed. The nine years that had elapsed since she last stood on this spot could have been a dream. The little Victorian station house stood there mellow in the sun, with tubs of flowers adding to the colourful scene. The neat pile of coal used to fuel the open fireplace in the waiting room lay to one side, just as she remembered it. Tom Cotter, the little fat station master who had gawked unashamedly at the beautiful girl on his platform, could still have had the same shirt on.

But it was the tranquillity she remembered most. The only sound was the birdsong and the breeze rustling the honeysuckle-laden hedgerows. It was all a total and welcome contrast to San Francisco, her home for the past nine years. It was good to be home. She had been the only passenger to alight from the two carriage train which she could still hear dimly in the distance, chuffing its way over the Severn Bridge on its way to Lydney.

She picked up her two large suitcases and walked through the small cool ticket office on to the station forecourt. As she put down her cases a large shiny 1935 Armstrong Siddeley came around a bend in the station drive and braked to a halt a short distance from her. She smiled as she recognised her father's car, and smiled even wider when she saw who was driving it.

Barney Summerville slid nervously from the driving seat of the Armstrong and stared with unbelieving eyes at the girl with the cool smile who stood before him. Could this possibly be the same human being he had transported here in the pony and trap before the war? The same little girl who he had loved like his own, who had waved wildly at him until the train had disappeared around the bend.

It must be so. She came towards him, threw her arms around his neck and kissed him on his ruddy moustached face. 'Barney, darling,' she whispered in a soft mid-Atlantic accent, 'how lovely to see you again. How are you?' She stood back, still holding his hands and saw tears appear in the eyes of the old man who had been more of a father to her than her own father.

'I'm well, Miss Julie, all the better for having seen you. I would never have recognised you,' he spluttered, 'America must have agreed with you.'

'Oh, it was wonderful, Barney. It would take a million years to tell you all the things I've done, and some of the things I wouldn't tell even you,' she said mischievously, 'but it's great to be home. How's Father and Mother? I must admit I am surprised Mother didn't come to meet me.'

'She can hardly wait for you to get home,' Barney assured her hurriedly, 'but she is in bed with flu, nothing serious.'

'And Father,' Julie enquired, 'is he OK?'

'He's well, Miss Julie. He would have come himself, but he is so busy at the estate office.' Barney sounded almost apologetic. Julie needed no explanations. She knew her father too well. Joshua Murchison had always been a tough unyielding man who had made it quite clear to Julie that he would rather she had been a boy. It was probably the reason that the young Julie had been such a complete tomboy.

As Barney began stowing her luggage in the boot, Julie slid behind the wheel of the Armstrong. 'Do you mind if I drive, Barney?' she giggled.

'Can you drive, Miss Julie?' Barney showed surprise. Most local girls were lucky to have ridden in a motor car, let alone learned to drive one.

'Yes,' Julie said, 'I've been driving Aunt Polly's Chevy for absolutely ages in the States.'

Barney slammed the boot shut and slid nervously into the front passenger seat. 'I don't know what your father will say,' he began. Julie terminated his hesitancy with a curt 'Don't worry!' She turned the key on the shining walnut dashboard and pressed the starter button. The big in-line six cylinder engine boomed into life, then settled into a barely audible whisper.

Barney explained the intricacies of the pre-selector gearbox, after which Julie engaged first gear and, with a slight jolt, moved the big car slowly down the station drive. Turning left into Station Road, Julie gunned the Armstrong towards Berkeley. As the car moved into top gear, Julie turned to the still tense Barney. 'Tell me, Barney,' she said quietly, 'are those boys I used to play with as a kid still around the locality? Mother wrote me and told me about poor Simon's death, but what about Yanto and Nat? What happened to them?'

'Well, Miss,' Barney stuttered, 'the last I heard, Nat was in a naval prison for beating up an officer. As for Master Gates, he came home a war hero and has been enjoying the fruits of his fame ever since.' Barney sniggered. 'Selwyn Hopkins told me he's just bought a motorbike. Imagine that, at his age. Dunno they're born nowadays.'

Julie laughed. 'Would you say he was still adventurous then?'

'They say he would beat up the devil himself for a shilling,' replied Barney. 'Why do you ask, Miss?'

'Well, I am going to need someone to help me ride over the Severn Bore at Stonebench.'

Barney stared at her aghast. 'You are going to what, Miss?' he stammered.

'I am going to ride over the Bore at Stonebench,' she repeated. 'I have always wanted to do it ever since the first time you took me to see it when I was young.'

The car slowed only slightly as Julie drove through a deserted Berkeley square. She opened the throttle again as she reached the quarter mile straight of Castle Walk.

She took a quick look at the castle, standing huge behind the emerald green foreground of Castle Meadow. 'I see the castle is still standing,' she quipped. Barney who had been deep in thought, spoke as the car thundered past the Berkeley Hunt kennels. 'But just how do you intend to ride the Bore?' he asked.

'I've got a beautiful two-seater kayak canoe in the States,' she replied. 'It's coming over with the rest of my stuff, deep sea. But, as I said, it's a two seater so I shall ask Yanto to come with me.' Two minutes later the Armstrong entered the tiny village of Ham. Barney smiled as Julie negotiated the drive gates leading to the family home. He was trying to imagine Yanto's face when she asked him.

Nine

FRIDAY NIGHT OUT

The motorcycle thundered into life with Bert Midgeley's first kick. Yanto, full of excited anticipation, had raced around to Bert's garage as soon as work finished on Friday. He had found Bert giving the machine a final wipe over with an oily rag. A feeling of total joy swept over him as he inspected the beautiful red and silver machine. Even the aluminium box which served as the sidecar gleamed in the late afternoon sun. 'Listen to the tick-over, Bert,' he whispered. 'What a beauty.'

'Yep, makes me wish I was thirty years younger,' quipped the old man.

As they spoke, Tiny and Joe Jacklin, two brothers who had worked in Yanto's gang on the *Marit*, cycled past on their way home. 'If I ever catch our Jane on the back of that thing I'll give you both barrels,' bawled Tiny over his shoulder.

'One way to get some good blood in the family,' Yanto shouted back with a grin, and gave them the well-known two-fingered salute.

Yanto had paid over his hard-earned money and the log book was in the pocket of his overalls. At last he had his own wheels. He straddled the bike and blipped the throttle. 'Mind how you go now,' said Bert with feeling, 'she's a bit different to those military bikes.'

'I will, Bert, and thanks again.' The late afternoon sun flashed again on red and chrome as he roared away. Bert Midgeley watched him disappear over the hill towards Wanswell and wished for the millionth time that Simon was still with him.

Yanto was in heaven. Savouring the surge of power each time he twisted the throttle. He took to it like a natural. The memories came flooding back. The despatch work in France before Dunkirk. There was no danger now, he could enjoy it to the full. No danger of ambush or sudden death, no creeping around on filtered headlights. This was ultimate freedom. He turned left in the village of Wanswell and blasted the bike over a slight pitch, on into the twisty overgrown lanes that led to the village of Purton. The alternating sunlight and shade caused by the overhanging trees started his eyes twitching. As he raced around one sharp corner he almost ran into the back of a slow-moving lorry. The sight of the familiar two-wheeled hopper which the lorry was towing, plus the overpowering stench emitted by it, made him realise he was about to overtake Terry Gafferty's toilet bucket collection cart.

As the next straight stretch of lane came into view, Yanto took a deep breath, held it, and with a quick twist of the throttle raced past the obnoxious but very necessary vehicle. As he passed, Terry Gafferty turned his thin pock-marked face to his mate, Solly Newport. 'Look at that, mate, the Prince of Purton is mobile. No woman in the bloody county will be safe now.'

Yanto parked the bike in the small alley which separated his mother's cottage from the Post Office and stood back to admire the machine again. Mary Gates came out of the house wiping her hands on her apron and looked at her son's purchase.

'Well, I hope you are happy now,' she said with a grin. 'Fancy a quick trip down the road?' he grinned back. His mother's look was sufficient.

'Come on in,' she commanded, 'your tea is ready.' He obediently followed her into the back kitchen, and gave a delighted whoop when he saw a big pot of homemade faggots and mushy peas simmering on the polished black range.

As he ate, he became aware of his mother watching him. He looked up into her wide blue eyes which were scrutinising him intently over the mug of tea which she was holding with both hands. He sensed that something was bothering her. 'What's up, Ma?' he asked and carried on eating.

She hesitated for a moment, then said, 'I met Sid Watkins in Berkeley today and he asked me if I would like to go to the

Licensed Victuallers' Dinner at the Princes Hotel with him tonight. I said I would let him know this afternoon,' she concluded, a little too quickly. 'He apologised for the short notice. I think he was a bit scared to ask. What do you think, son?' She looked at him intently.

'Well, do you want to go?' he answered, with a smile.

'It would make a nice change,' she replied guardedly. Yanto knew this was a big decision for his mother. Mary Gates had never been out in the company of a man since the death of his father. He decided to make light of it. 'Then go,' he rose from the table with a grin, 'it will do you good. Sid Watkins is a good bloke, who knows, we might even get a better deal with the fish.'

They both laughed. Mary was obviously relieved. 'Well, if you think it will be all right, I will go,' she beamed.

'You're still a good-looking woman, Ma,' Yanto teased, 'you should get more out of life. Anyway, Bill and I are going to test the bike tonight.'

'I suppose that means more wenching and drinking, does it?' she said with mock sternness.

'You know me better than that, Ma,' he laughed.

She smacked him playfully on the bottom with the tea towel. 'You had better get yourself into the washhouse and clean yourself up,' she said, 'I am going round to the Post Office and let Sid Watkins know,' She slipped off her apron and tripped out of the back door like an eighteen-year-old. 'Get me a packet of Woodbines while you're round there, Ma,' he bawled from the washhouse.

Billy Tolboys pulled up the collar of his ancient leather overcoat and hunched down even deeper into the motorcycle sidecar. The rectangular piece of Perspex which acted as a windscreen, provided little if any protection from the cold wind which was currently hitting him at sixty miles an hour. Even so, he was feeling very happy and full of anticipation.

Yanto had picked him up from his home ten minutes before, and they were now racing down the A38 towards Bristol on their first outing on the bike. 'Where are we goin' first?' he yelled over the wind noise. Yanto looked down at him momentarily, his blue eyes watering from the wind.

'I thought we might try The Barge at Thornbury,' he shouted, 'what do you think?' Billy didn't bother to answer, he just raised his thumb in agreement and snuggled even deeper into his coat. What the hell did it matter where they were going, mused Billy, this was living.

To his generation it had been war, ration books, belt-tightening and general hardship. Now, suddenly, it seemed all had changed, reasonably frequent work at the docks, money in their pockets, a great mate to share it with, and their own transport. Man, this was heaven.

Before starting out, Yanto suggested taking the A38 towards Bristol and then turning off to the right towards the river when they felt like it. It would, he said, give them a chance to see how the bike performed on a bit of decent road. The wind velocity gave evidence that the bike was performing very well. As they reached the bottom of the long straight pitch over Milbury Heath, Yanto turned right towards the small town of Thornbury. Thornbury was fast becoming a dormitory town for nearby Bristol, but there were a couple of decent pubs there. They parked the bike in the small yard at the rear of The Barge public house. Neither of them were familiar with The Barge. It had been renovated just before the war and now regarded as quite modern for the area.

The public bar was a large L-shaped room, one half of the L obviously having been a separate snug before the modernisation. It had also robbed the pub of its cosiness as modernisation invariably does. The old open fireplace had been boarded in and a single gas fire now burned in the hearth.

Billy looked around at the considerable number of pictures on the walls portraying various old sailing ships. 'Don't go much on this place,' he grumbled. 'It will do for starters,' Yanto replied, and ordered two pints of half and half cider from the young pleasant-faced landlord. 'Cold wind getting up,' commented the landlord, as he placed the mugs of amber liquid on the bar. 'Yeah, we noticed,' replied Billy, his eyes still watering.

It was still only 8.30 and, apart from themselves and a man and woman sitting in the far corner, the bar was empty. 'Well, I hope we are going to find a bit more life than this,' grunted Billy, as they sat down at a table near the gas fire.

'Stop moaning,' snapped Yanto, 'it's early yet. We can always finish up at The Boar if things don't improve.'

As he spoke, the bar door flew open and a noisy party of four burst in. Two men in their early twenties and two girls about the same age.

It was obvious they had already had plenty to drink. Both girls were pretty, but one, a blonde, was extremely so. Yanto and Billy heard the blonde tell the landlord that it was her birthday as she ordered the drinks.

Billy turned to his friend. 'Things are looking up already,' he murmured with an evil leer. Yanto did not answer. He was staring intently at the blonde.

The more he looked at her, the more he knew he had seen her before. 'What's up, mate?' Billy leaned forward, 'd'you know her?' Then it clicked.

'Yeah. If I'm not mistaken, I pulled a pissed-up matelot off that blonde piece on V.E. night. Remember that bit of bother I had in The Red Hart in Berkeley? The sailor went through the window.'

'Christ,' muttered Billy, 'I remember the talk about that.' His face suddenly lit up. 'You're in then, mate. She owes you.'

The two of them continued to stare at the group. One of the boys in the group was in the process of telling the landlord a joke. This was obviously their local. After the punchline had been delivered and the ensuing laughter had died away, the blonde swayed away from the bar and looked in their direction for the first time. As their eyes met, Yanto sensed a spark of recognition and gave her a broad smile to help her recollect. It worked. She remembered him.

The three other members of her party looked around in surprise as the blonde gave a squeal of delight and walked

59

unsteadily across to Yanto.

Billy's eyes popped out as she kissed Yanto on the cheek and flopped into a chair beside him. 'My hero.' She laughed and looked at Billy. 'He saved me from a fate worse than death, and it was all over so quick I never did get the chance to thank him properly.'

'Well you got the chance now,' grinned Billy, 'What ya drinkin?'

'Call your friends over,' Yanto interrupted, let's have a party.' The blonde did as she was bid. The other girl came over immediately. 'This is my friend Janet,' said the blonde. Billy offered a fourth chair next to him, which the girl accepted. As the two boys walked over, the blonde introduced them as Vic and Benny Travers. After introductory nods between the four men, Billy went to the bar to get a round in.

The blonde, who had introduced herself as Sheila Stevens, then, much to Yanto's embarrassment, began to relate to the other three the incident at The Red Hart on V.E. night. Vic and Benny were suitably impressed by the fate of the sailor. As Billy returned with the drinks, the conversation returned to the antics performed in Berkeley on V.E. night. 'That was some sort of night,' said Sheila, 'they actually turned the marketplace into a dance hall.' This was true. All family rivalries were forgotten. Everybody danced with anybody and as almost every other building was a public house, there was plenty of material spilling out to keep the action going.

During the festivities a hastily built bonfire was set alight in the middle of the market place, and an equally hastily assembled replica of the Japanese Emperor was burnt to a cinder on top of it. It was not until the next morning that the local council realised they had to repair a large hole in the middle of the square.

After several more rounds, things began to warm up in The Barge public bar. The lovely happy hour was approaching. The time when the body begins to warm from the drink and the mind mellows. Tongues loosen and caution takes second place to bravado. The two girls were now paying much more attention to their new-found friends than to their original escorts. At one point, when Janet had kissed Billy's ear, the elder of the two brothers, Vic, had looked as though he was about to protest. One of Billy's evil looks, however, plus the recollection of the sailor's fate on V.E. night, caused him to relax again. Even so, both Yanto and Billy found difficulty in hiding their pleasure when, shortly after, the brothers took their leave. Sheila's remark of 'see you around,' made it painfully obvious they intended to stay.

The public bar had filled considerably and the general clatter of laughter and bustle all added to the good feeling of anticipation which was beginning to invade Yanto. His senses told him he was on to a good thing and his senses were rarely wrong.

He leaned back with a sigh of contentment and, over his fifth pint of cider, observed Billy whispering in Janet's ear. The girl giggled and kissed Billy's ear again. 'He's not doing so bad either,' Yanto mused to himself. As he sipped his cider, Yanto's attention was drawn to a group standing a few feet from their table. A small, bearded old man, obviously a local character, was in hilarious conversation with three young men. As Yanto watched, the old man inclined his head to the right and began jabbing his right index finger into his right ear. As he did so, a fine trickle of sawdust appeared to fall from his ear to the floor. Yanto laughed when he realised the old joker had palmed the sawdust and was allowing it to trickle in such a way as to give the impression that it was trickling from his ear. The old man's next remark explained the charade. 'My old man always reckoned I was a blockhead,' he explained, and brayed with laughter at his own joke.

Yanto laughed again, as did Sheila, who had also been watching the old man's antics. 'We've got one or two like him in our local,' he said to her with a grin.

'What made you come all the way out here just for a drink anyway?' enquired Sheila. 'How did you get out here, pushbike?' While Billy was at the bar ordering another round Yanto told the girls about the motorbike and explained that it was their first outing on the machine. Sheila sat bolt upright. 'You mean to say we have been sitting here for an hour with a motorbike and sidecar parked outside?' She squealed in mock amazement.

'So what,' snorted Billy, who returned with a tray of drinks in time to catch the remark, 'we're enjoying ourselves, ain't we?'

'Well for Pete's sake, let's go somewhere,' Sheila countered.

'Where?'

'I dunno.' Sheila puckered her brow with concentration, then looked up with a grin. 'I know, let's go over to The Windy Ridge, at Shepperdine. They do lovely Severn salmon sandwiches there. It won't take long around the lanes.' She stopped and looked at the other three who were scrutinising her in amused silence. Sheila's full lips pouted slightly. 'Anyway,' she said, 'it is my birthday.' Yanto winked at Billy, who grabbed his mug and said, 'OK, drink up, anything for a quiet life.'

As they left The Barge, Yanto experienced that old feeling in his loins. He had decided what to give Sheila for her birthday.

Billy enjoyed the short trip from The Barge to The Windy Ridge. He had squeezed himself back into the side-car with his long legs stretched flat along the floor of the rectangular alloy box. Janet had little option but to sit on his lap with her legs stretched over his. That's when his enjoyment began. With a mischievous grin on his face, he gyrated his lean anatomy under Janet's neat little posterior in perfect time with the bucking machine. She didn't object.

Yanto looked to neither right nor left as he struggled to keep the bike in the centre of the narrow lane.

He was aware of two things. The rough elder-laden hedgerows rushing past, six feet each side of his face, and Sheila clinging to his back like a koala clinging to its mother.

Suddenly they were there. The narrow lane ended abruptly in the yard of The Windy Ridge public house. Yanto brought the overloaded bike to a skidding halt just short of the sharply rising earthbank, the other side of which lay the muddy banks

62

of the river. Squeaky Sutton, landlord of The Windy Ridge for the past thirty years, looked up as the noisy party clattered down the four steps into his cosy cellar bar. His large round face split into a welcoming grin at the sight of them. 'Evening all,' he squeaked.

The ridiculously high-pitched voice seemed even more ridiculous coming from such a big man and Sheila almost burst out laughing, but caught Yanto's stern glance and managed to stifle it. 'How ya doin' then, Squeak?' Yanto enquired, 'long time no see.'

'Could be better. You know what my regular trade is like, always had to rely on the trippers out here in the sticks, and who wants to come out here during a winter like we've just had.'

'Yeah, reckon so,' agreed Yanto. 'Still, looks like we're going to get a good summer.'

'Can't come too soon for me,' squeaked the landlord. 'What can I get you?'

While Yanto ordered the drinks, Billy and the girls went over to the big open fireplace. The girls sat down on a large pew-style bench in the alcove and laughed at Billy, who was standing with his back to the blazing logs doing his knee-bending policeman act. 'Now this is what a pub should be like,' he said to them with a grin.

Squeaky re-appeared behind the bar with a large enamel jug of cider, and poured out two pints of the golden liquid for Yanto's inspection. 'Looks as good as ever,' smiled Yanto. 'But, isn't it time you got some pumps in here, Squeak?'

'Don't hold with 'em,' he said. 'That's the way I've always done it, and until they carry me out here, that's the way it stays.'

'Suits me, mate,' Yanto laughed. 'By the way, how are the salmon running up here?'

'Not as thick as they used to be,' snorted Squeaky, 'not many big uns either.'

Squeaky whistled in amazement when Yanto told him about his recent monster catch. 'Ant sin one like that in years,' he breathed, 'talk is, the bloody Danes are catching too many of 'em as babees.'

'We're dying of bloody thirst over 'ere,' Billy's voice growled from the fireplace. Yanto grinned at Squeaky, picked up the tray with the two pints and two whisky and oranges, and walked slightly unsteadily over to the fire.

'Thought you'd never stop gassing,' growled Billy and downed a third of his pint in one swallow.

'What's the matter with his voice?' asked Sheila, as Yanto sat down, 'that can't be normal surely?'

'Yeah, I was wondering about that,' interrupted Billy, 'sounds like he ain't got no balls.' He held his hand to his mouth in mock apology as both girls gave him a straight look.

'Well,' Yanto began hastily, 'I was told he got pinned down for a week in no-man's land during the Battle of the Somme. Every time he tried to move he got a burst of machine gun fire. Yelling for help for a week must be enough to knacker anybody's vocal cords. Anyway, that's what I was told.'

A delicious tray of fresh Severn salmon sandwiches had come and gone, as had several more rounds of drinks, and Yanto was getting restless. He became aware of the disapproving looks his noisy party were receiving from some of the older locals who had drifted in over the last hour. The two girls had reached the stage where they were hanging round the boys' necks and roaring with laughter at virtually every word they uttered. Billy was the type that, had he noticed, would have returned the disapproving looks with the two-fingered salute and carried on. Yanto, on the other hand, had always been acutely aware and sensitive about what other people thought of him. With this in mind, plus the fact that the evening's finale was yet to come, he decided it was time to leave.

He caught Billy's eye with a wink and jerked his head towards the door.

Billy's wide mouth stretched into a grin as he winked back. Yanto realised that Billy's instant agreement to leave had nothing to do with embarrassment.

'Time for some fresh air, girls,' Billy spoke and rose from

the table at the same time. Yanto did the same. Sheila looked up at Yanto, 'Your word is my command, o master,' she said in mock seriousness, then giggled and downed the remains of her drink in one go.

Yanto did his best to make a dignified exit, but with the drink he had put away, and Sheila hanging on his arm, it was very difficult. After loud 'good nights' and thanks to Squeaky, the four of them finally staggered out into the cool air of late evening.

Standing together in the backyard of The Windy Ridge, all four of them momentarily experienced that eerie silence that always prevailed on the banks of the River Severn at high water during the hours of darkness. It was as though the wind and tide had decided to have a good rest having expended all its fury achieving the high water mark.

Yanto curled his arm around Sheila's waist and guided her towards the river bank. 'Let's have a look at the river and get some air,' he murmured in her ear. She said nothing, but allowed him to assist her up the steeply rising earthbank. From the top of the bank Yanto noticed Billy and Janet wandering off in the opposite direction. A slight smile curled the edges of his wide mouth as he watched them disappear behind a large veteran hay wagon parked on the far side of the pub yard.

Sheila giggled quietly as they ran down the other side of the bank onto the shore. She rested her head on his shoulder as his arm again curled around her slim waist. 'Lovely, ain't it,' he murmured, 'This river is like a drug to me. Can't keep away from it.' She looked up at his handsome profile silhouetted against the dark sky. There was certainly something different about this one, she thought dreamily, and dropped her head on his shoulder again. The only sound now was their feet rustling through the shore grass, coarse and hard from countless tides of salt water. Even now, the extremities of the grass, where it dipped to meet the mudline, were slowly and silently being invaded by the dark water as the tide reached its zenith.

The old blackthorn tree, twisted and stunted by its choice of birthplace, made a convenient leaning post. Sheila's head tilted back against the rough bark to receive his first kiss. Slowly and sensually he traced the outline of her lips with the tip of his tongue. As the kiss lingered, she was made aware of his hardness as he pressed himself against her. Her excitement mounted as his hands explored the outside of her thighs.

So far, so good, Yanto thought to himself.

Sheila became aware of the hem of her dress slowly rising. Yanto was using his fingers to gather the fine silky material. He carried on bunching the material in his fist, expecting to be stopped any second, until he had the hem of the dress in each hand. Then with a groan, he buried his face in her neck and began stroking her thighs. Encouraged by her lack of resistance, he very slowly began to inch the waistband of her panties down. At this, Sheila showed her first sign of resistance. A gentle two-handed push on his shoulders caused him to sway back on his heels. It was a very gentle push, which Yanto did not believe was a serious attempt to stop him, so as he swayed back against her, he tugged them down another inch. She pushed him again and he did the same again. This continued until Sheila's pants were halfway down her thighs. As his eager hands began to explore her nakedness she suddenly clamped her arms around him like a drowning man. At that point Yanto knew he was there.

As he prepared to take full advantage of the situation he suddenly recalled a horrible memory. He had never enjoyed the thought of making love in a standing position since the embarrassment he had suffered on the last occasion, about a year before. The incident had taken place around the back of the Berkeley cinema, with a very busty and willing Land Army girl. When they had left the cinema, they found it had been raining so Yanto decided the standing position would be favourite.

Unfortunately, as he reached the critical moment when the knees start to tremble, his war wounded leg had collapsed under him, causing a premature withdrawal and an immediate loss of ardour as his bare bottom came into contact with the muddy, wet surface of the cinema bike park. He had never forgotten the outraged eloquence of the frustrated lady as she had hitched up

66

her pants and departed towards the town.

With this ghastly thought in mind, he gently suggested to Sheila that they walk over to a nice patch of grass at the base of the earthbank. She nodded in agreement and with Yanto's assisting arm around her waist, tottered towards the grassy path with a series of short restricted steps. The restriction was caused by her knickers, which were still just above her knees.

As Yanto hurriedly lay his coat out on the grass Sheila turned towards him with a start. 'I hope you've got some things. Have you?'

'Things,' he echoed, looking up with a sinking feeling in his heart.

'You know, those things. My sister had a baby a year ago and her boyfriend wouldn't marry her. My dad would murder me if it happened to me.'

'You don't have to worry about that,' he gushed desperately, very conscious of the fact that he didn't have any 'things'. 'I promise I'll be careful.' But it was no good. She made it very plain: no things, no joy.

'Oh, Christ,' he moaned under his breath. Then he remembered Billy always carried a packet of three. Yanto recalled him boasting in the pub that 'be prepared' had been his motto ever since leaving the boy scouts. 'He'll probably cuss like hell,' Yanto thought to himself, 'but when the Devil drives ...'

'You sit here quiet and watch the river, my love,' he muttered, as he wrapped the edged of his coat around her knees. 'I'll be back before you can say Jack Robinson.' With that he went off down the bank as though all the hounds of hell were after him.

As he reached the top of the earthbank where it overlooked The Windy Ridge car park, he stopped for a breather. He could see the old hay wagon by the light of the yard lamp, but there was no sign of Billy and Janet. 'Silly cow,' he breathed, as he ran down the bank into the yard, 'she'll probably go cold on me while I'm buggering about over here.'

He stood by one of the huge wooden-spoked wheels of the

hay wagon and looked around. 'Ooze that?' Billy's voice was a mixture of apprehension and indignation and it came from under the hay wagon.

Yanto crouched down and peered under the wagon. Two golden shafts of light from the yard lamp crossed their bodies and he could see that they were lying on a mixture of old sacks and loose hay. All he could make out were two white faces and Billy's white behind.

'It's me, Bill,' Yanto whispered urgently. 'I need a johnny fast, got one?'

'Christ, mate, of all the bloody times,' Billy's angry voice left the rest unsaid. 'My jacket, hanging on the wagon. They're in the side pocket. Now bugger off, will yah.' Yanto found the coat and grabbed the little rectangular packet. Before he took off, he couldn't resist another quick peep under the wagon. All he could see now was Billy's bare behind doing an impression of a fiddler's elbow.

By the time he got back to Sheila his chest was heaving. 'Must cut down on the bloody fags,' he told himself. Nothing was said as he sat down beside her. Hoping desperately that she had not changed her mind, he leaned over and kissed her on the mouth. As she responded, he increased the pressure of his lips on hers until she realised what he was trying to do, and slowly allowed herself to be pushed back into a lying position.

Gently, but still breathlessly, only now with excitement, he removed her flimsy pants which were still around her knees. Then, with the minimum of movement, he removed his own encumbrances and fitted the necessary protection. As he moved upon her, the mutual warmth as their thighs made contact caused them to groan in ecstasy. Then there was just their sounds, mingled with the swish of the coarse grass as it moved in unison with the dark water.

'See yah around,' Billy bawled over his shoulder and waved as the bike took off towards the main Bristol road. The fast disappearing figures of the two girls waved back then disappeared as the bike took a left hand bend.

The ride back from The Windy Ridge pub had been quiet and subdued compared to the ride out. But there was nothing strange about that. As with most young men who had succeeded in sowing casual wild oats, it was a case of get away as fast as you can before they start getting ideas. They had promised to see the girls, same time, same place, next week, but both knew that was very unlikely.

Billy, who was now contentedly stretched out in the sidecar with his eyes closed, was suddenly thrown hard against the right hand side of the aluminium box.

Yanto had hardly bothered to reduce speed as he had turned sharp left by Stone school into the narrow lane which would take them back to Berkeley. His cider-sodden mind was causing him to treat his beloved motorcycle in a way he would never have dreamed of a few hours before.

'Watch it, for Christ sake,' Billy bawled into the wind, 'can't you see I've had a hard night.'

Yanto raised his head and laughed. 'We ain't finished yet, mate,' he yelled back, 'we're having a nightcap at The Salvation in Ham.'

'It's nearly twelve o'-bloody-clock,' Billy slurred back from a now almost horizontal position, 'ain't you never had enough? Anyway, they'll be closed.'

'We'll see.'

After another couple of hair-raising bends, they entered the tiny village of Ham, where there was not a light to be seen. Yanto brought the machine to a screeching halt outside The Salvation Inn.

'See I told you,' grunted Billy, pointing at the pub's unlit portals, 'they're closed.'

'Bullshit,' snapped Yanto, 'it's Friday night, mate. Joe Asnett never shuts at weekends till the last bugger drops. They'll be in the back room. Even the local cops won't go in there, short of a murder.'

Billy resignedly followed his friend up the gently rising slope of the car park situated on the left hand side of the building. The old pub looked slightly sinister standing dark against the night sky and Bill shivered as he followed Yanto through the open five-barred gateway into the back garden of the 'Sally', as it was called locally.

To Billy's relief, the large back area of the Sally was partly illuminated by a shaft of golden gaslight showing through the half-open back door.

The floor of the back area was partly grass and partly well-trodden cinders. A high hedge separated the garden from the adjoining apple orchard, and a massive horse chestnut tree completely umbrellaed the whole area, giving it an aura of serenity even in the dark. The old round bench which circled the circumference of the horse chestnut's trunk was solid oak, but its slats were polished and worn by generations of local backsides.

On hot summer evenings this was one of the most popular watering holes for miles around. Joe always made sure there were a couple of swings rigged up to the spread branches for the local children to enjoy. Thus, with the kids occupied, the local mums and dads could enjoy the local brew in the shade of the old tree and listen to the singer. In those lovely days, still unspoilt by materialism and television, there was always a singer. Usually it was a red-faced, moustached elder, who spent his working days milking and dung spreading, but secretly dreamed of the Albert Hall. Probably, in his youth, some tone deaf colleague had told him he possessed a good voice, ever since when, he would arise at every opportunity, usually by reluctant request, and then, po-faced with hand on heart, would bellow 'Come into the garden Maud', watched by a captive audience and a proud, watery-eyed wife.

The two boys walked through the now dark and deserted stage, and pushed the half-open heavy plank door.

Joe Asnett looked up as they walked unsteadily into the small flagstone-floored back room. A stranger could have been excused had he mistaken Joe for a gentleman of Middle Eastern origin. His heavily lined mahogany-coloured face was unsmiling as he looked at them. His long bushy eyebrows, mingling with his coarse black hairline, made him appear to have no forehead at all.

The fierce face spoke. 'Whaddya want?'

'A drink, mine host, if it's not too much trouble.' Yanto's honeyed words were accompanied by a silly grin. The fierce face was still unsmiling as it spoke again.

'You come in 'ere half pissed once a month, usually around midnight, and expect me to jump around for you, now you're bringing your mates as well.' Two of the three remaining customers in the room cackled delight. This unexpected bit of colour materialising just before they were due to fall down came as a bonus.

There was a pregnant pause. Yanto was a bit unsure how to take him as he stood there swaying, and Billy's befuddled mind was getting angrier by the second.

Suddenly Joe's face split into a grin. 'That had you worried, didn't it?' he growled. 'You've made Knocker a rich man, so how about starting on me, regular like?'

Yanto smiled and relaxed. 'I knew you were all heart really, Joe. Pint of mild, please.' Billy also decided to have a beer. 'I've had enough of that bloody scrump for one night,' he growled.

Joe handed the foaming mugs over the bar, and they both collapsed into the little wooden dining chairs set each side of the dying open fire.

They had a conversation of sorts with the two inebriates who had laughed at Joe's opening remarks to them. They were a couple of travelling hedgers and ditchers who were currently working at Baker's Farm down by the river. Both wore the standard dress. Rough tweed jackets and corduroy trousers, complete with wide leather belts and string tied about the knees to stop the mice running up their trouser legs. And their boots! Those huge hobnailed boots could have kicked a hole in Berkeley Castle.

It was the other solitary customer in the room who now held the boys' attention. It suddenly occurred to them that he had not moved a muscle since they came in. He stood bolt upright facing the bar, a half pint of rough cider on the bar in front of him.

The more the boys looked at him the more they realised the man was totally oblivious of his surroundings. Both hands clutched the edge of the plank bar as though his life depended on it, the knuckles showing white against his work-weathered hands.

Joe noticed their interest. 'That's Runner Rowles,' he grinned nodding towards the man, 'a living example, if you call it that, of what a lifetime of too much cider and not enough grub can do to a man!' Joe's discussion of the man as though he were not there, embarrassed Yanto, and Joe noticed. 'Oh, don't worry about him, he can't hear a word we're saying, in a world of his own he is.'

'Why'd they call him Runner?' Billy asked.

'He used to be a very useful runner in his younger days,' Joe explained, 'used to run for the Gloucester Harriers so they say. Only running he does now is when he leaves here with a load on,' said Joe.

'Don't look as though he could do much running to me,' Billy butted in.

'Well he lives in that little cottage at the bottom of the steep pitch just past the green,' Joe continued with a grin, 'as he staggers down the hill his legs have to go faster and faster to stop him falling on his face.'

'What happens then?' said Yanto, fascinated.

'Well, he's usually doing thirty mile an hour by the time he hits the blackberry hedge at the bottom of the pitch, never even gets a scratch as a rule. Sad really.'

Runner still stood motionless, eyes staring straight ahead, the blue veins in his bulbous red nose standing out like lines on a map. 'How come you let him have so much scrump?' Yanto's voice was almost accusing.

'Well, if I didn't some bugger else would,' Joe said defensively. Yanto's words must have cut Joe a little. 'Better get him on his way, I s'pose,' he grunted, as he ducked under the bar flap.

Runner jumped violently as Joe slapped him on his shoulder,

but moved passively as the landlord helped him to the door. 'Mind how you go, mate,' Joe called after him 'make sure you miss the signpost at the bottom of the hill.'

Joe laughed resignedly as he slammed the door. 'Will he be all right?' enquired Yanto, 'don't look too good to me.'

'Course he will,' Joe snapped, 'bin doin it for twenty year. His long-suffering marvellous missus will wash him off and put him to bed. Yes,' said Joe, as he poured runner's unfinished cider into a bottle ready for him the next night, 'he's blessed with a good woman. The quickest way to get a smack in the chops around here, is to bad-mouth Runner in front of Cissy Rowles.'

Joe poured himself a half of beer and pulled a chair up to the fire with the two boys. The two hedgers-and-ditchers were flat out and snoring in the corner pew.

'S'pose you've heard Nat's coming home.' he said, as he settled down.

'Yeah,' said Yanto, without enthusiasm.

'You two won't have it all your own way with the girls when he gets home.'

'You reckon, eh?' growled Billy. Yanto just gazed into the fire.

'Yes, he was a wild one, though I say it myself,' muttered Joe. 'I hope he's quietened down.'

They sipped their beer moodily. The night's events were beginning to catch up on them.

Joe suddenly sat up. 'Hey, that might interest you,' he said. 'I had Barney Summerville in tonight, you know, he works at the big house. It seems young Julie's back from America, you remember the Colonel's daughter?'

The news slowly penetrated Yanto's brain, then registered. He stared at Joe. 'Yes,' Joe said, 'he said she looks like one of them bloody film stars.'

Yanto didn't hear him. His mind was back to those warm childhood days before the war. His first feelings of love had been for that gloriously liberated and beautiful tomboy. He found himself aching to see her.

'Come on, Bill. Time for bed I reckon,' he found himself saying. He had suddenly lost interest in the proceedings.

'Bout bloody time,' said Billy, and heaved himself out of the chair with difficulty. They bade goodnight to Joe and left him struggling with the two inebriates. As they mounted the motorcycle, Yanto stood upright on the footrests and looked over the hedge across the road towards the big house. All was in darkness. 'Roll on,' he thought, and booted viciously at the kickstart.

Ten

THE MEETING

Yanto's head throbbed abominably as he cycled slowly to work the following morning, but at least it was Saturday, he told himself thankfully.

He had decided not to make a habit of using the motorcycle for work. He didn't want to appear flash in front of his workmates. Anyway, his pushbike would keep him fit and conserve the precious petrol for more exciting excursions.

The sight of his motorcycle first thing that morning had made it necessary for his mother to speak sharply to him about his language. As he quickly washed off Friday night's mud, he made a mental note not to take it out on the machine next time he got drunk.

He began to think about Julie Murchison again as he negotiated the narrow viaduct which linked the docks to Station Road. Below him, dockland was beginning to stir in its entirety, like some vast creature emerging from hibernation.

'I wonder what she looks like now,' he mused. He smiled as he thought about the previous night. According to Barney Summerville's report, she was like a film star. 'I'll bet she is to,' he told himself, as he tried to picture her as she was when he last saw her.

They were due to finish unloading the *Marit* by about eleven o'clock and that would be it until Monday morning. By the time he reached the low bridge on the wharves, he had decided to try and see Julie that afternoon.

After carefully avoiding the mooring ropes of several foreign steamers moored along the dock side, he reached the berth of the *Marit* and ditched the bike.

The Norwegian coaster was high in the water, almost

stripped of her cargo of Finnish deal.

Billy Tolboys was sitting on a crane bogie with his head buried in his hands. He looked up slowly at Yanto's greeting. At first sight of Billy's face, Yanto's headache felt better. Billy looked terrible. His face was yellow, and his eyes were as red as rubies. His mouth sagged open and uttered a pitiful croak as Yanto sat down beside him.

'Christ, mate, you look like death. Whaddya come in for?' quipped Yanto with an unsympathetic grin.

'Bloody scrump,' he croaked. 'Spewed me ring up all night, then I went and rode me bike into that mooring rope over there,' he indicated further up the dock. 'Went ass over 'ead. Never again.'

'Not till the next time anyway,' came the laughing reply. 'Come on, mate,' Yanto urged as he stood up, 'we had better get aboard. We can get away early this morning with a bit of effort.'

Work commenced. The crane jib dipped and raised over the deep hold of the *Marit*, each time raising out a neat sling of timber like some massive lucky dip.

The grey clouds that had prevailed that morning began to break up, promising a fine afternoon.

It was 11.30 as Yanto watched the last sling of timber disappeared through the hatch opening high above his head and swing out of sight towards the wharf.

He turned to Billy, whose long-empty stomach had ceased to heave an hour before and who now looked almost human after three hours of hard work. 'That's it then, mate. See you on the Co-op corner half past ten Sunday morning, OK?'

'Oh ah,' replied Billy, with a grimace. 'I forgot all about that bloody picnic. Hope I feel better by then.'

They discussed the coming Sunday excursion as they climbed out of the empty hold and trotted down the ship's gangway onto the wharf.

After another short chat they joined the exodus of dockers leaving the ship. Shouldering their empty bags they jumped on their bikes and after a cheerful 'Watch out for mooring ropes' from Yanto, they cycled off in opposite directions.

Yanto's mind was busy as he meandered slowly through the leafy lanes towards Purton. How could he arrange an accidental meeting with Julie that afternoon? that was the question. His fierce pride demanded that she must assume their meeting had been coincidental. But how?

He suddenly had an idea. If he popped into The Blue Boar for a quick one that lunchtime, he would probably find Selwyn Hopkins in there. Saturday lunchtime was the only time Selwyn visited the pub, owing to the fact that he kept a fifteen-gallon cask of cider in his garden shed.

Although retired, Selwyn Hopkins was a regular beaver where gardening was concerned. As well as keeping his own beloved large patch looking like the Garden of Eden, he still found time to tend Colonel Murchison's land at weekends.

'Let's see,' he pondered to himself. 'If Selwyn intends to go to the Colonel's this afternoon, I could say I had to go that way myself and offer him a lift on the motorbike. Another thought struck him which would add credence to his story. The day before, his mother had asked him to charge the wireless accumulator because the reception was beginning to fade.

The accumulator was very heavy and had to be charged about once a month. This was one of the unwelcome chores, but it would come in handy this time because the wireless agent had his business in the village of Stone which was a couple of miles beyond Ham where Julie lived.

'Yet, that was it,' he told himself, 'If Julie is there I am bound to see her when I drop Selwyn off.' He made a mental note not to be too enthusiastic in front of Selwyn. It wouldn't do to upset Molly.

The problem solved, he smiled and congratulated himself on his devious ingenuity. He began to whistle, and taking his hands off the handlebars he negotiated the last half mile home without touching them again. As he dumped his cycle in the alley his spirits were raised yet again by the glorious aroma of fried onions wafting through the back kitchen window.

The recent spell of warm weather was holding and Julie Murchison was feeling good in spite of the fact that she had spent the last hour in her mother's sick room. Joanna Murchison, always a frail woman, was currently suffering a bout of unseasonal influenza. However, Julie was gratified to see the remarkable change in her mother's general health since she had arrived home. She knew it had been hard for her mother when her father had shipped her off to the United States to escape the war. Colonel Joshua Murchison was a hard, unyielding man and Joanna had drawn great comfort from her beautiful high-spirited daughter. At first Joanna would not hear of it, but had changed her mind after her husband's graphic account of what poison gas could do to people.

She had promised Julie that she would be well enough to get up the following day and they would take a trip in the pony and trap to visit friends in the area whom Julie had not seen for years.

Joanna had insisted on keeping the pony and trap when her husband had bought the Armstrong. She was born of noble stock and loved the old genteel way of life, and the people of the village loved her. During the dark early days of the war, the local people had felt a strange sense of security just to see her pass by. Sitting bold upright in the trap, she would nod at everyone she passed with her proud unsmiling face. Her long dark tailored suits, with ridiculously feathered matching hats pinned to her silvery hair, gave her the respect of all and an air of authority few would dream of challenging. The villagers often joked that if she met a German tank on the road to Berkeley, she would order it off the road and pass on as if nothing had happened. It was that inborn sense of duty that motivated people like Joanna. They would automatically take the helm. Whether it was running the Woman's Institute or assembling and distributing gas masks, it was all the same to them.

Julie ambled happily down the long immaculate front lawn, bordered on each side by miniature fruit trees. Where the lawn narrowed as it skirted the side of the elegant house, it was traversed by a high lattice fence complete with ornate archway. The latticework was interwoven by a rambling rose. So beautiful and so English, thought Julie, causing her spirits to soar.

Luxuriating in the warm mid-morning sun on her shoulders, she walked under the lattice archway and on to the bottom end of the garden. Here the ground was laid to vegetables on one side with a small orchard off to the left. Under a pear tree in the far corner of the orchard was a picturesque timber-built shed. It had that rustic look which only many years of weathering can attain.

Julie smiled, remembering the times she and her friends had hidden in the old shed during hilarious games of hide and seek and sardines.

'Strange how much bigger it seemed then,' she mused, as she stepped through the door. The smell, still familiar after her years away, hit her immediately. The mixture of oil, rusty tools, creosote, and vegetable seeds mingled into a unique scent. Impossible to duplicate or forget.

An old faded deckchair hung from a six-inch nail which had probably been hammered into the shed wall twenty years before. She unhooked the chair, dusted it off, and carried it back to the front lawn.

The last trace of cloud had disappeared from the sky. Julie decided to top up her Californian suntan until Kitty Summerville called lunch, after which she would take a casual stroll to another of her favourite haunts as a child; the old summerhouse on the river bank.

She lay back in the musty-smelling chair, at peace with the world, and allowed the late April sun to envelope her.

Fortified by a beautiful lunch of belly pork and fried onions, Yanto wandered contentedly in the general direction of the Blue Boar. He stopped in the middle of the swing bridge over the canal and watched a couple of local boys fishing from the bank. He returned their wave and gazed down the sun-dappled ribbon of bright water as it meandered its way towards Sharpness docks a couple of miles distant.

It was a beautiful scene. From the left bank of the canal, the green fields of Gloucestershire swept up in the gentle rise for half a mile, there to be terminated by a line of stately elms. A farmer working a pair of shire horses, and probably praying that the weather would hold, moved into his line of vision giving a touch of life to a scene that might have been painted in oils.

On the right hand bank, there was first the well-used tow path. Beyond that lay a few hundred yards of rough, occasionally wooded farmland. There were small pig sties dotted here and there, as many villagers liked to keep a single pig to supplement the still-meagre meat ration. This strip of land was terminated by the estuary. From his spot on the bridge, Yanto could gaze down the seemingly endless reaches of the Severn's mouth. The tide had ebbed, and vast stretches and humps of sand shimmered away into a yellow infinity. Sand which shifted constantly with the tides, making the river virtually un-navigable above Sharpness and necessitating the construction of the canal to Gloucester.

As a youth, Yanto had felt hard done by living 'out in the sticks', as he called it. Now, as he grew older and more mature, especially after his hectic and sometimes horrifying war experiences, he realised how lucky he was to be born and live in such a place.

As he strolled on towards the pub he was surprised at the number of people that were about. Everyone was feeling good in the fine weather. After the war years and the terrible winter they had all endured they had every right to be. There was a feeling of confidence in the air. Some staple foods had come off rations with the promise of more to follow, all adding up to a gradual end to austerity.

Yanto's spirits became even more buoyant as he walked through the always open five-barred gateway into the yard-cum-lawn frontage of The Blue Boar. The familiar figure of Selwyn Hopkins sat on the bench under the horse chestnut tree, gazing out over the estuary. His personal earthenware pint pot was on the ramshackle table in front of him, almost empty.

'Penny for 'em, Selwyn.' The weather-beaten old man squinted up at the handsome young giant who stood grinning down on him.

''Ello, young 'un,' he grunted, 'I was just watchin' 'em lavenettin' on the river there.' He pointed out into the estuary..

Yanto could see several small figures out on the sands. They were local lavenet fishermen, a familiar sight in this part of the country. The tide was now ebbing fast. The ideal time to pursue the sport which many considered to be the purest form of hunting.

The lave net was a simple but very effective contraption for catching salmon. It consisted of connecting poles constructed in the shape of the letter Y, the tail of the Y being the handle. A loose net was fixed between the prongs of the Y and thus, with the open prongs held firmly in the bed of the river, the fisherman would wait quietly for the fish to run into his net.

As soon as the salmon had passed between the prongs and into the net, he would scoop the net up triumphantly to inspect the size of the catch.

It sounds simple, but is not. When the river is nearing low ebb, vast stretches of sand are laid bare, but channels of grey-brown water of varying widths and depths continue to rush out between the sand formations until it meets the next tide coming in, twelve hours later. It is down these channels that the salmon run, making for the sea whilst trying to avoid becoming stranded.

It is also in these channels that the lave fishermen will stand. The man must rely on his instincts to tell him which is the best spot. Full-length waders are essential as it is generally accepted that the best depth to work is knee to waist deep. Leaning hard on his net to counteract the force of the current, he will scrutinise the oncoming water intensely. He is searching for the salmon's loom. This is the mark in the water caused by the fish's dorsal fin. It is essential that he spots the oncoming fish while it is still far away from him. Indeed, even in the fast choppy water the practised eye can spot his prey a hundred yards away.

This is where the pure hunting comes in. Having spotted his prey in a channel which could be fifty yards wide or more, the fisherman must literally read the fish's mind.

Which run would the fish take? Almost blind in the shallow muddy water, it is swimming by instinct, following the deepest sand channels. The prongs of the lave net are probably three to four feet apart, and side- stepping in fast waist deep water is a slow business.; he will only get one chance. If he fails to judge the correct line of the fish's swim, it can pass either side of him; sometimes a frustrating arm's length away.

'They had any luck d'you know?'' Yanto returned his gaze to the top of Selwyn's bald pate, weathered almost black by his long outdoor life.

'Ant heard no shouting. They usually shout to one another when they ketch summat.'

Yanto picked up the old man's mug and walked into the cool bar. The warm weather was certainly bringing people out. Knocker and Renee were both busy serving at the bar. After a brief wait and an exchange of pleasantries with Renee, Yanto carried the two brimming mugs back out into the sun and joined Selwyn on the bench.

No words were exchanged as he placed Selwyn's refill in front of him. Buying each other drinks in this village was so natural and taken for granted that words of thanks were rarely uttered. But woe betide the tight-fisted villager who tried to take advantage.

Yanto took a long swig of cider, then closed his eyes and leaned back against the tree trunk with a sigh of contentment.

No-one spoke for five minutes as they both gloried in the sun and the light fresh breeze. Yanto finally broke the silence. 'I suppose you'll be off to Colonel Murchison's this afternoon with this weather and all?' he said, with tongue in cheek.

'I thought –' Selwyn's reply was interrupted by Renee Nelmes' shrill voice as she yelled out of the bar room window at two boys who were playing on the roof of the concrete pillbox built in the far corner of the pub's front lawn. Built at the start of hostilities, facing the estuary, it was now used by playing children, courting couples, and the odd customer who, thanks to Knocker's cider, had been taken short and decided not to risk trying to get home in time.

Grim-faced, Renee slammed the window, and Selwyn continued, 'I thought about it – might, might not,'

'I'm going over to Stone later on to change our mother's accumulator. Give you a lift in the side-car if you like.' Yanto waited for a reply to his offer with bated breath.

Selwyn's eyes lit up with pleasure. 'I ant bin on a motorbike since the Great War. I'll take you up on that. Can you bring me back too?'

'I 'spect so,' came a cautious reply. Yanto realised he might well have to make a special journey to pick up the old man if Julie happened to be out.

'That'll be lovely,' grinned the old man as he drained his mug and rose to leave. 'You can pick me up about half past two.'

At that moment Yanto notices Herbie Connors cycle into the yard with his bag of empties. He glared at Yanto with dislike as he stomped through the front porch of the pub. Yanto gave him a beautiful smile in return.

'Better get off,' grunted Selwyn, 'our Molly will 'ave me dinner on.' As he turned to leave, they became aware of a lot of shouting from the river. 'Sounds like they caught summat,' said the old man, and cocked his head. As they stood looking and listening, the two boys who Renee had chased off the pillbox earlier, came running back towards the pub from the riverbank.

'What's up, Jackie?' Yanto shouted as the first boy jumped the fence into the pub yard. The boy approached him wide eyed and breathless.

'One of the fishermen just caught a whale or summat. It's a 'ell of a size, t'ent aff big.'

'Silly little bugger,' Yanto laughed. 'You don't get whales in the Severn. Not often anyway. Where is it?'

'Other side of the breakwater,' gasped the boy, 't'ent aff big.'

Selwyn decided his dinner was more important, reminded

Yanto to pick him up at half past two, and wandered off. Curiosity got the better of Yanto however, and having vaulted the fence, he made his way over the hundred and fifty yards of reclaimed field that separated the pub from the riverbank.

'I bet it's a porpoise,' he told himself, as he walked hands in pockets, trying to avoid the now hard ruts caused by the grazing cows during the recent floods. He remembered an occasion about two months before. He had been walking on the riverbank observing a high tide. The water had reached its mark and was lapping the grass that he stood on. It had been a very cold but bright morning, without a breath of wind. The mile of shining water between him and the Forest of Dean had been devoid of a single ripple. As he had watched the silent peaceful seascape, he had been amazed to see a large black dorsal fin lazily break the surface of the water. It couldn't have been more than fifty yards from the bank.

After a few seconds a second fin appeared. Both dorsals must have been a good twelve inches clear of the water. At first he had thought he must be dreaming. They didn't get sharks in the Severn, did they? He had been born and bred on the river, but had never seen anything like it before.

After circling and playing together for probably a minute, the fins had lazily disappeared and Yanto had gone home a mystified man.

Josh Cornock had provided the answer the following morning. Josh was an authority on the Severn from the Bristol Channel to Gloucester.

'They were porpoise, my boy,' he had boomed good-naturedly. 'It's not unusual for the big equinox tides to bring 'em in. Doubt whether they would go up any further than Sharpness though,' he had explained. 'They'd probably get stranded on the ebb tide.'

'Yes, and I bet that's precisely what's happened here,' Yanto told himself, as he reached the riverbank.

The breakwater jutted straight out into the estuary in front of him. A finger of grey granite boulders defiantly standing there in the mud and sand, surrounded permanently by a large lake during low water, much to the delight of the local children in the summer. It was one of man's more successful attempts at curbing the forces of nature. Indeed, had it not been constructed when it was, Peter Scott's Wildfowl Trust, situated further up river at Slimbridge, would probably have lost much of its new grounds to erosion.

Yanto spotted the fishermen immediately. He saw several lave nets lying in an untidy heap on the sand where the fishermen had obviously dumped them in their haste to inspect their colleague's find. Four of them were now standing in the mud trough between the sand and the bank, about fifty yards upstream of the breakwater. A six inch deep channel of water still flowed over their wader-clad feet as they stood in a rough circle looking down at something in the mud.

From where Yanto stood it looked like just another heap of mud. He was not wearing wellingtons, just his working boots, but he decided he must have a look. The four men looked up as he came scrambling down the steep bank. 'What you got there then, boys?' he shouted as he tightrope-walked over a strip of rock strata showing just above the mud trough.

'Dunno, big bastard whatever tis, never sin one before.' The speaker was Lofty Waters, all five feet of him.

Yanto jumped on to a large flat rock, still trying to keep his boots dry, and looked down at the huge mud-covered object. His eyes opened wide with amazement. Lofty was right, it was big. 'Must be nine foot long,' he gasped. One glance destroyed his initial prediction. It was definitely not a porpoise.

'I thought it was a heap of mud and weed,' Lofty said. 'I went to climb over it and the bloody thing twitched, nearly shit meself.'

'Chuck a couple of buckets of water over him, we might be able to recognise what it is,' Yanto suggested. Whatever it was, was well and truly stranded. It had obviously taken the wrong channel and become wedged on a rising shelf of rock strata which traversed the trough about fifty yards before it reached the lake surrounding the breakwater.

'Ten minutes earlier and he would have made it over them

85

rocks into the pool,' concluded Lofty.

One of the group appeared with a battered bucket and commenced throwing water over the mud-covered beast.

The mud, caused by the fish's dying struggles, began to wash away to reveal the bulk of its body.

'Not a native of these waters, that's for sure,' growled another member of the group.

'Look at that mouth, reminds me of the missus.'

'Dead as a tick now,' said another.

'Let's roll the bugger over,' Yanto suggested. Three of them heaved the bulk over on to the high rocks and after a few more buckets of water, they stood back to inspect it further.

Long tendril-like whiskers sprouted each side of the large mouth. What appeared to be a continuous row of sea shells ran down each silvery flank, almost reaching the great crescent tail.

'I remember seeing pictures of a fish like that at school, but I'm damned if I can remember what it was,' said Yanto thoughtfully.

'Well if it eats half as well as a salmon, I shall be 'appy,' grinned Lofty, subtly reminding the others that it was he who had found the fish. The sound of heavy boots sliding down the crumbling bank made them all glance up.

'Here comes happy guts,' someone groaned, recognising the tall figure of Herbie Connors. He had obviously heard about the strange fish from the two boys at the pub, and anything concerning the river was Herbie's concern.

'Afternoon, Mr Connors,' somebody grunted.

'What have we got here?' Herbie demanded, ignoring the greeting. 'I hope all your licences are up to date.' He splashed over the shallow channel and looked down at the monster.

'Any idea what it is, Mr Connors?' ventured Lofty.

'I haven't been a river man all these years for nothing.' The statement was accompanied by a contemptuous downward glance at Lofty. The man's arrogance caused Yanto's nostrils to flare with annoyance. 'However, I will concede that I have never seen one as far upstream as this before.'

'What the hell is it then?' demanded Yanto impatiently.

'For your information, sir, the fish is a sturgeon.'

'Can't be,' gasped Lofty,' they never come out of the Baltic. A sturgeon's a Russian fish.' Yanto closed his eyes and waited for the inevitable. Herbie was incensed.

'Are you contradicting my professional knowledge, you ignorant little reptile?' he yelled. 'I tell you it's a bloody sturgeon.'

'Well, it's my bloody sturgeon,' said Lofty, surprised at his own courage.

'If you touch that fish I'll have you up the steps before you can say Jack Robinson,' hissed Herbie, going blue in the face.

'Whaddya mean?' argued Lofty, 'I found 'im and I gotta licence.'

'Makes no difference in this case, Lofty,' interrupted Yanto, quietly trying to defuse the situation, 'a sturgeon is a royal fish and all of 'em caught in this country must be offered to the King; that's the law.'

Herbie turned his attention to Yanto. 'Who asked you?' he said sourly, 'keep your nose out of it. I'm dealing with this!'

Yanto's fuse ignited. 'Bollocks,' he shouted straight into Herbie's face. 'Who d'you think you are bloody talking to? You come down here and treat everybody like shit.' Yanto was beginning to enjoy himself. 'You're only a poxy water bailiff. Anybody would think *you* were the King.'

Herbie stepped back from the outraged young giant. 'I'm not going to argue with you,' he spluttered, visibly shaken. 'I am going to arrange a van to transport that fish to Berkeley so get it up on the bank.' As he turned to leave he looked again at Lofty. 'If you think you are going to get any caviar out of this fish, forget it. If His Majesty declines the offer, it will come in handy for some civic dinner, I expect.' With a final glare at Yanto, he scrambled back up the bank.

'Bastard,' growled Lofty, 'they'll find him face down in the river one of these days, the way he's goin' on.'

Yanto grinned. 'Well, I'm off home to change,' he chirped, 'got an important date this afternoon.'

He left the four fishermen struggling up the bank with their slippery burden.

Julie smiled with delight. She was enjoying her walk down the quiet country lane towards the riverbank. As she approached the old mill, where the lane was bordered by the mill stream, she noticed a cyclist approaching her. Young Dan Tennant, a farm labourer from Baker's Farm, was on his way home for lunch. Dan had never seen anything like her outside of Berkeley picture house.

She looked like a dream to Dan. A beautiful willowy blonde, sun-tanned and blue-eyed. 'Where had she got a tan like that after the winter they had just endured?' A flared cream pleated skirt that complemented those long perfect brown legs, and a powder blue blouse that matched her eyes a treat. And those breasts. Dan ogled her innocently and unashamedly as he approached her, and continued to gawk over his shoulder after passing. That is, until his bike left the road.

The ensuing crash caused Julie to turn. Dan lay on his back in the grass with his bike alongside him, wheels still spinning.

Another foot and he would have been in the brook. As she started back to check if he was hurt, Dan scrambled back on his bike and cycled off with a final red-faced look over his shoulder.

She smiled again. She was enjoying the effect she was obviously having on the local population. She had stood out in the crowd even amongst the beautiful beach children of San Francisco. But here in rural Gloucestershire, with the war only two years over, well!

She paused by the old flour mill, another landmark of her childhood. As a child, the mill had frightened her. A great grey Victorian workhouse-looking place, with men hanging out of third-storey doorways, pulling up sacks of cereal on pulleys.

One day she had plucked up enough courage to look through the doorway, and had almost choked on the clouds of swirling dust. It looked so different to her now. Smaller, certainly. It never ceased to amaze her how much smaller everything seemed to her eyes. The building, although still basically ugly, looked nicer with the late April sun glinting on the old stonework.

The water scene on each side of the mill could not have been more in contrast. The Little Avon River, upstream of the mill, was a poet's dream. A ribbon of fresh clear water meandering through beautiful unspoilt countryside, providing sport for the local anglers along its willow lined banks. Generations of Berkeley children, including Julie herself, had learned to swim in the brook, as it was called locally. The swimming hole, situated in the castle meadow, was backdropped by the magnificent walls of the castle.

This picturesque beauty however was terminated by the walls and sluice gates of the old mill. On the other side of the mill, in contrast, was a deep high-banked muddy trough meandering the last half mile into the Severn estuary. Had the mill not been built, acting as it was, a barrier across the tidal tributary, the idyllic scene on the other side would have been vastly different. The sparkling fresh water and grassy banks being sullied twice daily by the flotsam and jetsam of the Severn.

Taking care to keep to the well-trodden dirt path between the growing vegetables, she crossed the last field on to the riverbank. Part of the bank here was in the shape of a sea wall, with a miniature promenade running along the top, probably the reason why the locals regarded this particular spot as their own private seaside. Julie stood on the sea wall and moved her head from side to side allowing the fresh wind from the estuary to blow through her hair. She loved this spot. The memories of her pre-war childhood came flooding back. How could she find this scene so enchanting after her years on the golden beaches of California? It mystified her. She gazed across the mile of grey water. The trees of the Dean on the distant bank were taking on a blue haze in the glorious afternoon sun. The blue grey mud banks glittered where wet from the tide, but lay dry and cracked like acres of crazy paving above the high water mark. What was the appeal?

Maybe it was the wild untamed-ness of the river, its banks

populated by real people, proud and self-sufficient, who cared for their neighbours as well as their own. These Severnsiders: a breed apart; that mixture of ancient races mingled over the centuries to form a perfection of self-sufficiency and social harmony. What she did know was that she never wanted to go away again.

Feeling completely happy, she made her way towards the summer house set on high ground a little further down the bank.

'Yippee, go on, son, give 'er the gun.'

Selwyn Hopkins was enjoying himself. Gripping the sides of the sidecar, he urged Yanto to increase the already rapid pace. Yanto grinned and twisted the throttle again. The combination roared along Castle Walk, echoing into the empty courtyard of the Berkeley hunt kennels as it careered up the last hill into the tiny village.

His heart began to thump with apprehension as he brought the bike to a halt outside the drive gates to the big house. Selwyn jumped out of the sidecar like a five year old. 'Ant enjoyed meself so much fer years,' he chirped, a wide grin cracking his brown leathery features. 'Pick me up about half past five, eh?'

Yanto looked at him. 'Yeah, I suppose so,' he said. Selwyn began to walk up the short drive.

'Do you mind if I have a look over the garden,' Yanto called after him, unable to think of a better excuse.

'I didn't know you was interested in gardens.' The old man's surprised reply was tinged with pleasure.

'Well I reckon I shall have to start some time,' Yanto grinned, as he trotted up alongside him.

They walked together through the trellis arch into the back garden. As Selwyn rummaged around the shed for his tools, Barney Summerville came out of the garage wiping his hand on an oily rag. He spotted them and walked over. 'I wondered how long it would be before you young buggers came sniffing around,' he said, with a belly laugh, and looked at Yanto.

'What d'you mean?' asked Yanto, trying to look puzzled.

90

'Don't tell me you haven't heard Miss Julie is back from America.'

'First I've heard of it,' came the seemingly uninterested reply, 'anyway, I'm going steady with Molly, ain't that right, Selwyn?'

'Thought I raised a wench with a bit o' sense,' sniffed the old man as he trundled down the garden path with his wheelbarrow full of tools.

'My missus is making some tea, Selwyn,' Barney called after him, 'you want some?'

'Aah.' Barney took it for granted Yanto would have a cup and made a signal to his wife through the kitchen window.

While they were alone Yanto decided to pump Barney. 'So Julie is back, you say?' Barney nodded. 'Pushed off up to London already, has she?' Yanto said enquiringly. 'Must be finding it pretty dull around here after the States.'

'No,' countered Barney, 'she seems as happy as a pig in poop. She told me she is looking forward to seeing you again.'

Yanto found it hard to conceal his pleasure. 'I don't suppose she even remembers me,' he grinned, going slightly pink.

'Not so,' laughed Barney. 'When I picked her up from the station, she'd asked me about you and Nat before we got into Berkeley. She insisted on driving back herself too, what do you think about that?' Drove that bloody great car back like a good 'un.'

The fact that she had mentioned Nat defused Yanto's excitement somewhat, but the more he heard about her, the more he ached to see her.

Barney pushed his battered trilby to the back of his head. 'She also told me she is going to ask you to help her in a little project,' he said, grinning mischievously. He wouldn't be drawn by Yanto's urgent appeal. 'You'll find out,' he laughed, and left it at that as Kitty, his wife, arrived with the tea.

She was a small, plump, pleasant-faced woman, full of bounce and good intentions, but she could never stop talking. After pouring the tea and talking to Yanto for five minutes about nothing in particular, she turned to her husband.

'I hope that girl doesn't catch cold,' she said. Yanto's ears pricked up.

'Whaddya mean?' growled Barney, 'it's as 'ot as 'ell,' and pushed the rim of his trilby back over his eyes to emphasise the point.

'Well,' Kitty said, 'all those years in that heat, then she walks off to see the summer house and wouldn't take a cardigan. There's always a chill wind blowing off that river.'

'Would it make you feel any better if I took the cardigan down to her?' said Yanto. He decided to throw caution to the wind before Selwyn came over for his tea. 'I've got my motorbike outside and I've got the afternoon to pop over to Stone.'

'Oh, would you?' gushed Kitty. 'I would feel much happier, I don't want her ill as well as her poor mother.' She trotted off and returned two minutes later with a pure white cashmere cardigan.

'You'll find her somewhere near the summer house,' she said, as he rose to leave. Barney gave him a knowing wink.

'We shall be coming to watch this project of yours and Julie's, mind,' he called after Yanto.

When Kitty said 'Oh, she won't really do that,' in an exasperated voice, it only added to Yanto's mystification.

Arthur Jaffe was not a benevolent man at the best of times. Now he was becoming nasty.

Arthur was the ticket clerk at Portsmouth railway station and the heat had been getting to him before the man arrived. 'Get a move on, will you?' he snapped, 'I haven't got all day.'

The man on the other side of the glass was obviously the worse for drink and having difficulty finding his money. Arthur's agitation increased as the woman next in line in the small queue began to fidget. 'Do you mind getting out of the way while I serve the lady?' he stormed. 'What a time of the day to be drunk.'

Suddenly, the man's arm shot through the tunnel shaped aperture in the glass screen of the cash desk like a striking cobra. The hand grabbed Arthur's shirt front and tie in a vice-like grip, and yanked him forward, almost banging his head on the glass. For the first time Arthur had a good look at the man's face. It was a dark, swarthy face, almost Asian in colour, and very handsome. But it was the eyes which caused Arthur's bowels to move slightly. They were cruel, dark, pupil-less eyes, like looking down a bottomless pit.

'Just give me a one-way ticket to Gloucester before I break your fat neck!' Arthur did just that, and the man walked out on to the platform without waiting for his change.

'Wouldn't want to meet him on a dark night,' breathed Arthur, trying to make light of the incident. The slightly shocked woman agreed with him.

Nat Asnett boarded the two fifteen for Gloucester, threw his suitcase onto the rack and slumped down in the corner seat. He was on his way home at last.

Keeping the noisy engine as muted as possible, Yanto negotiated the dirt path until it terminated suddenly at the base of the sea wall. His heart thumping with anticipation, he climbed to the top and gazed around. How would she greet him, he wondered? Then chided himself for getting so excited about one woman, after all the women he had known. Just another wench, he told himself angrily, but deep down he knew different. There was no sign of the girl on the shore. He gazed downstream. The conical roof of the summer house showed above the high hedge about fifty yards down the bank, so forcing himself to act casually, he began to stroll towards it. He skirted the hedgerow and silently approached the unique little building from the rear. His heart lurched as he saw her for the first time for nine years, now in her new role as a woman. Unaware of his presence, she was sitting on the soft springy turf, leaning back against the ancient wall of the summer house and gazing dreamily across the blue haze of the estuary. He just stood and looked at her. The afternoon sun highlighted her blonde hair which hung around her shoulders in reckless abandon, giving her a wild untamed loveliness which took his breath away. His instincts told him she was still the same mad tomboy he had known before the war. He also decided at that moment, to his own amazement, that somehow, some time, he would have her as his wife.

Having made this decision after a minute's observation, not only amazed him, it also caused him to relax completely. Yanto Gates was not given to quick decisions or mad impulses, but the girl in reality matched his dreams of her so perfectly that he had to take it as a sign.

She jumped visibly at his wolf-whistle. She turned to see a very large handsome man holding out a cardigan and grinning like a Cheshire cat.

She squealed with delight as she recognised him instantly. Her beauty made him gasp anew as she moved towards him smiling.

He stood there like an idiot as she clasped him by the arms and kissed him on the cheek.

God, the smell of her. Her fresh expensive perfume, another victim of the recent austere years in England, invaded his senses, making him fight the temptation to grab her and kiss those delicious lips to a pulp. She thanked him as he gallantly placed the cardigan around her shoulders, and explained his reason for being there.

'There is so much to talk about,' said Julie excitedly. 'Let's sit and talk.' They sat down against the summer house wall and talked of each other's activities over the last nine years. Yanto felt he could have sat there for ever. He began to feel his old confidence returning. 'Do you realise,' he said with a grin, 'that this is not a very appropriate place for us to be sitting.'

She looked quizzical. 'Why not?' she asked.

'Well, I know we all call this place the summer house, and it's only used to keep salmon nets and baskets in nowadays, but it is really a gazebo, where the local gentry used to meet their ladies of ill repute in the old days.'

She giggled. 'Well, this is 1947, and it's all different now, isn't it?' she said with seeming innocence.

'Yeah,' he replied, feeling a sudden strong affinity with the

94

gentry of yesteryear.

There was a lull in the conversation as both rested their heads against the smooth warm wall of the old summer house and allowed the afternoon sun to bathe their faces. A gull screeched overhead breaking the dreamy silence, and Julie's eyes flicked open. She gazed again at the peaceful scene in front of her until her eyes rested on an old Severn punt lying high and dry on the foreshore. It lay there on the dry cracked mud below the high water mark, waiting for the next tide to wet its bottom. The sight of the small craft sparked her memory.

'Yanto,' she said. He opened his eyes and looked at her.

'Yeah,' he grunted.

'That little boat over there has reminded me, I need your help in fulfilling a little ambition of mine.' She looked at him with the confidence of a beautiful woman who was used to getting her own way.

'Yeah,' he said again, only this time it was tinged with wariness. He had an idea she was about to explain Barney Summerville's mystery.

'I want to ride over the next big Bore at Stonebench.'

'Oh is that all?' he replied, and relaxed again. 'I'll have a word with Jimmy Myers, he's a skipper on the Sharpness barges. Meets the Bore regular, he does. Can't guarantee we'll meet it at Stonebench though.'

'No, you don't understand,' she said irritably, 'I want you to come with me in my two-seater kayak.' He sat bolt upright.

'You what?'

'I want you to help me ride over the next big Bore in my two-seater kayak,' she replied defiantly.

'Are you sure that Yankee sun hasn't turned your head?' There was a hint of anger in his voice. 'That Bore nearly killed me recently, and that was in the estuary at Purton. It's a damn sight more dangerous at Stonebench. The river's only a hundred yards wide there.'

'You aren't afraid, are you?' she grinned mischievously, 'and you a war hero too.'

Yanto felt annoyed and a little hurt. 'I don't mind putting my neck on the line when I have to, or when there's a percentage in it, but anybody who fools with the Severn in these parts, just for the hell of it, is an idiot.' Now it was Julie's turn to feel hurt.

'Well, if you won't come with me I shall ask Nat when he comes home. I gather that won't be long.' Then to twist the knife, she added, 'He was in the Navy, after all.'

He groaned, She had him. It had now become a direct challenge to his manhood. Where Yanto was concerned that was paramount. 'I didn't say I wouldn't help you. I just said it was stupid. Just make sure you tell your parents that it's your idea. I don't want your old man gunning for me when you get drowned or brained by a tree trunk doing ten knots.'

She smiled as she leaned over then kissed him on the cheek. 'I knew I could count on you,' she cooed. She went on excitedly to explain how her canoe would be arriving in a week or two and she would then telephone the harbourmaster at Sharpness to find out when the next big Bore was due. She insisted that it would have to be a high predicted major tide. This last remark strangely made him brighten up, although he said nothing.

He knew the spectacular Bores only occurred during the equinox periods, February, March, April, and August, September, October. During these periods, the great tides sweeping in from the Atlantic would first feel the initial restriction of the Bristol Channel. As the mass of the water raced upstream, the restriction increased as it reached the ever-narrowing upper reaches. This strangulation of the water continued as the river relentlessly narrowed and the riverbed rose. Finally, this great natural funnel gave the maelstrom no alternative but to rear up into that great familiar wave. And thus, it would roar through the upper reaches of the Severn, twisting and turning through the green fields of Gloucestershire. Crowds of people would line the banks through the little villages, never tiring at the sight of their own local natural phenomenon, until the great waves finally smashed themselves to extinction against the weirs of Gloucester.

Yanto lay back and reflected with satisfaction that they were now at the end of April, and there would be no big tides worth talking about until August at the earliest.

By then, anything could happen. At least it gave him time to try and talk some sense into her. But deep down he had the feeling that sooner or later, he would have to face the big wave with her.

Then she jumped up. 'Come on,' she chirped, 'give me a lift home on the famous motorbike. I must see how Mummy is.'

She chatted into his ear all the way back to the big house, but he stayed silent. He was imagining himself sitting in a tiny kayak in the middle of the Severn looking up at a wall of water, anything from six to nine feet high, depending on conditions, bearing down on him at twelve miles an hour and making more noise than a fast approaching train. 'I must be bloody mad,' he groaned to himself.

He dropped Julie off at the house, then continued on to Stone to charge the accumulator. Selwyn would be ready by the time he returned.

Eleven

THE PICNIC

The brilliant spell of weather was still holding good the following morning. It was Sunday, and Yanto had enjoyed the casual breakfast with his mother, something he rarely had time for during the week. Their chat during breakfast had revealed to him that his mother had enjoyed the previous Friday evening out with Sid Watkins and would probably see him again. Yanto did not like Sundays as a rule. In these rural parts it was usually a case of potter in the garden, or off to church or chapel. This would be followed by a massive Sunday lunch, and then sleep all afternoon. No good for a man like Yanto, who loved the thrust and challenge of life. But today there was the picnic, and who could tell what would happen once the four of them got in amongst the pine coverts of Ham Park.

He felt good as he negotiated the narrow lanes between Purton and Sharpness. His legs, which straddled the powerful motorcycle, were clad in his best grey slacks and his tartan shirt was open to the waist.

He began thinking about Julie Murchison. He had to admit he could hardly wait to see her again. And then there was Molly. Sweet Molly, who he was about to take out for the day and seduce if he got the chance. He grinned to himself. 'Oh, Gatesy, you are a bastard.'

He opened the throttle as he turned left into Station Road. The burble of the exhaust turned to a bellow as he raced down the long gentle slope towards Newtown.

His black curly hair was blown flat across his skull and his ice blue eyes began to water with the force of the wind He was enjoying himself. To his right he could see the panorama of the docks spread out below him. Several foreign ships had arrived

99

within the last twenty-four hours. The *Marit* had sailed and the big Russian timber boat now occupied her mooring. He could also see another large steamer, flying the Swedish flag, further up the dock.

The powerful bike between his thighs, the beautiful morning, and the prospect of a full week's work ahead all made Yanto want to burst with joy. It was sure great to be alive. He braked hard to halt outside the Co-op in Newtown, just as Billy and Mary turned the corner. Mary was carrying what was obviously a large bag of food while Billy nursed a stone jar of cider and a blanket.

'Thought we would let the girls have the tea,' he laughed as he held the jar aloft.

'I'm glad you brought a blanket,' Yanto said with a grin, 'there's no seats in the side-car.' Mary eyed the side-car with trepidation. It was just a rectangular alloy box. Mary climbed into the side-car laughing, and trying to cover her knees from Billy's leering gaze as she sat down. A thought suddenly struck Mary. 'Where's your girlfriend?' she demanded.

'Oh, she's always late, she'll be still cutting sandwiches, so I decided to pick you two up first.'

Billy jumped on to the pillion seat behind Yanto. He handed the precious jar to Mary. 'Hold that tight between your legs,' he said with a laugh. Yanto kicked the bike into life, did a quick turn and, exhaust roaring and rear tyre screeching, departed towards Purton. It took ten minutes to reach Honey Cottage, with Yanto trying his best to scare the pants off Mary. Every turn he threw the combination around was followed by screams and giggles from Mary and wild rebel yells from Billy. 'Hold on to that bloody cider,' Billy yelled. Yanto twisted around on his seat and looked at Billy. 'What was that you were saying yesterday morning when you looked like death warmed up?' he yelled, 'never a bloody 'gain you said. Tommy Handley couldn't best that for a joke.'

On arrival at Honey Cottage, Yanto introduced the two girls. They knew one another vaguely. 'Where's Selwyn?' Yanto asked.

'Where do you think?' Molly answered with resignation. 'Out in the garden somewhere.'

Leaving the happily chatting girls to pack the food, the two boys wandered out into the garden. Selwyn Hopkins' garden was a sight to behold. 'The Garden of Eden must have been something like this,' Billy remarked in awe.

The beautiful half-acre contained every species of vegetable, fruit, herb, and flower that could possibly be grown in England. A small orchard dominated the lower reach of the garden. All varieties of plum, apple, and pear trees grew in unison. The garden was terminated by an immaculate row of sloe trees. Everything was fruitful. The numerous fruit beds were criss-crossed by a network of carefully trimmed and edged grass paths. 'See that, Bill,' Yanto remarked, 'he can get to any part of his garden without stepping on dirt once.'

The two of them stood silent for a while, gazing at the pleasant scene. 'Well, the old bugger ain't out here,' Yanto said suddenly. He walked back around the side of the cottage to the open kitchen window, where the two girls were putting the packed food into a basket.

'No sign of your dad,' he said.

Molly stuck her head out through the kitchen window, and looked around. 'I gave him a jam sandwich just before you arrived. If it's on the tank he must be in the lav, he never takes food in there with him.'

Yanto went around to the back of the cottage where the 'lean-to' lavatory was situated, its door almost inaccessible because of a loganberry bush. Yanto smiled. 'Look at that,' he mused to himself, 'you could have a crap and eat fresh loganberries at the same time.' Standing by the lavatory wall was a large steel tank full of rainwater. It had started out as a ship's boiler but Selwyn had acquired it some years before to ensure a plentiful supply of soft water for his garden. There was a six-inch wide rim around the top of the tank, and sure enough, lying on the rim was a half-eaten jam sandwich. Yanto grinned and pointed it out to Billy as he came around to join him. 'I've found him,' he said quietly, 'and you must admit, he is very hygienic.'

Billy giggled and pointed to a three-foot-square door at the base of the outside wall of the 'lean-to'. 'What's that door for?' he enquired.

'That's the bucket door. Pull out the full 'uns, empty 'em, and replace. All mod cons here, mind.'

'Oh so that's Terry Gafferty's department is it?' laughed Billy. He was referring to the well-known local character whose unenviable job as council dustman included emptying the local toilet buckets, as there was no running water in the area. The local joke was that Terry had no problem getting a drink. When he walked into a crowded bar he always found he had at least half the bar to himself.

'Terry never gets his hands on these buckets, mate,' Yanto laughed. 'Selwyn sees to his own buckets, buries it in his own garden. Nothing gets wasted here.'

Yanto went on to tell Billy about his experience the last time he had used Selwyn's lavatory. 'A couple of months ago it was, on a Sunday afternoon. Must have had some bad cider on the lunchtime. Anyway, I got took short. Just managed to get into Selwyn's crapper in time. I was sat there minding my own business, when all of a sudden that side door opened and sunlight comes flooding in under my ass.' Billy started to double up with laughter.

'Anyway, Selwyn starts pulling out the bucket from under me. I had to yell out for him to hang on a minute.'

Billy was still laughing when the lavatory door creaked open and Selwyn pushed aside the loganberry bush and stepped out.

'What d'you two young buggers want?' he grinned, as he fastened the buckle of his wide leather belt.

'We're taking Molly and her mate for a picnic, Selwyn,' Yanto replied. Selwyn's nut-brown, weathered face split into another grin. 'I thought I raised a wench with a bit of sense, ain't she sin through you yet? Where you takin 'em?'

'Ham Park.'

'Be nice up there today,' Selwyn said as he scanned the cloudless sky, 'but watch out for them bloody stags. They can be nasty when them fawns are getting born.'

He retrieved his jam sandwich from the rim of the tank. 'Have a nice time, and behave yourselves,' he concluded, and walked off in the direction of the garden.

'Christ, ent it bloody 'ot!' Billy Tolboys breathed the words as he took his arm from around Mary's waist and expertly swung the heavy stone jar onto his shoulder and took a deep swig. Five minutes before, the roar of their motorcycle exhaust had broken the Sunday afternoon slumber of the village of Ham. Old Harry James had straightened up from his gardening as they passed, and called to his wife, standing in the window. 'Listen to that, Amy, that Jerry plane that crashed in the park didn't make as much bloody row as 'im.'

They rode over Ham Green and parked the bike on the grass verge by a five-barred gate. After climbing the gate, they shared out the picnic load and began sweating their way up the five hundred yards of steeply rising ground towards the Park wall. That was when Billy paused to take liquid refreshment.

Yanto, who was twenty yards ahead with Molly, turned on hearing the unmistakable sound of cork leaving bottle. 'Steady on, mate,' he shouted, 'that's got to last all day, and there's only a gallon in that jar.'

The game park at Ham consisted of three hundred and twenty-three acres of prime Gloucestershire hunting country.

Being completely enclosed by a wall, ten feet high in places, gave it an air of complete timelessness. In fact, once inside the Park, one had the definite impression of having stepped back into the past.

'Coo, ain't it high,' Mary squeaked, as the party reached the towering wall by the crossing style.

'Yeah,' replied Billy, 'the Great Wall of China must be something like this.'

The stile-cum-ladder was a beautiful piece of woodwork. It had been assisting people over the wall longer than anyone could remember. Built of oak, with steps on either side and a neat little turnstile on the top, it was a typical piece of old world craftsmanship. The girls declined their gentlemanly offer to allow them over first, realising that once at the top, the boys would have a beautiful view of their unmentionables.

'Spoilsport,' Yanto grunted and climbed over.

On the other side of the wall they all experienced a different atmosphere. In the shade of the huge pines it was relatively dark and cool. On their left was the old gatehouse guarding the main entrance to the Park from the road. Many was the carriage and pair that had galloped through that archway. 'Bit spooky 'en it,' Mary whispered as they prepared to climb the short steep bank in front of them. Once at the top of the rise, they found themselves on a flat plateau, of which most of the park area consisted.

Dotted here and there were the various sized pine coverts. These woods gave cover to the herds of wild deer which for centuries had provided sport for the kings and nobility, guests of the Berkeley family at the nearby castle. The deer were now safe apart from the occasional culling their role having now been taken in modern times by the unfortunate fox.

The walking was now easy on the flat springy turf. 'Let's have a blow,' Billy suggested, 'it's getting hotter by the minute. Christ knows what it's going to be like in July if this weather keeps up.'

'What a lovely view,' breathed Mary, as they all stretched out on the grass. The panorama of the estuary was spread out below them like a landscape masterpiece. The river was at high water, and with the green tree-clad Severn grounds sweeping down to the high water mark, it was a sight to behold.

'Best county in the country,' said Billy in a matter-of-fact way.

What they did not know was that in ten years' time, that beautiful picture was to be blighted by Britain's first commercial nuclear power station.

'Just think,' Yanto remarked, 'only a month ago that whole area you can see there was under water. In fact the whole of the Berkeley vale.'

'Yeah,' Billy interrupted, 'the great flood, they called it.

They reckon that half of Gloucester City was under water.'

'Looks like it's going to be a year of extremes,' Yanto grunted.

After a brief rest they walked on across the plateau. Billy suggested they look for a shady spot for the picnic in the covert they were approaching.

'Good idea,' Yanto replied, 'then we can dump all this stuff and have a mooch around.'

As they entered the covert they found it cool and gloomy after the brilliant sun outside. Even their footsteps were silent on the thick carpet of pine needles built up over countless years.

'It's spookier than ever in here,' Mary whispered.

'It's even worse if you see the headless horseman,' Billy replied, with a mischievous grin.

'The what?' shrilled Mary, stopping dead in her tracks.

'The headless horseman,' continued Billy, keeping his face away from her to hide the grin. 'A few years ago one of the old boys from Ham was doing a bit of rabbit poaching up here and a headless horseman went riding by as cool as you please. All glowing and white 'e was. By the time the old boy got home, his hair had gone snow-white. That's what I was told anyway.'

'For Christ's sake, Bill, don't be so bloody daft,' said Yanto angrily. He had noticed Mary's shocked face. 'He's having you on, Mary. Don't take any notice of him.'

'You sod!' shouted Mary, with obvious relief, and threw a large pine cone at Billy, narrowly missing his head.

Shortly afterwards they found the ideal spot. A small glade ablaze with sunbeams. They placed the baskets in a convenient hollow by a large pine and covered them with the blanket. The cider jar was placed in the cool shade. 'Come on then, you lot,' shouted Yanto, 'Let's have a wander and get ourselves an appetite.'

As they wandered happily through the sun-dappled splendour of the woods, Yanto turned suddenly to the girls. 'Would you like to see the fairy princess's castle?' he said with a grin.

'You're kidding,' Mary laughed.

'Come on, you'll see.' They wandered on aimlessly kicking

105

at the pine cones.

'What's that?' Molly remarked suddenly. She was pointing at a recess scraped in the soft earth and pine needles. Scattered around the lip of the hole were several clumps of brown fur.

'Looks like something has been killed there, doesn't it,' she exclaimed. Then she noticed the boys grinning. 'What is it?' she said again suspiciously.

'Well, put it like this,' replied Billy guardedly, 'it means they didn't eat all the deer during the war.'

'What do you mean,' insisted Molly.

'It's a rutting hole,' explained Yanto.

'A what?' interrupted Molly naively.

Yanto tried to be serious as he explained it to the girls, which wasn't easy with Billy's skinny six-foot frame shaking with mirth alongside him. 'Well, when a stag mates with a hind, he first scrapes a hole in the ground. Then he gets her head and shoulders down the hole, leaving her rear end sticking up in the air so he can sort of get at her easier like.'

Both the girls had started to turn pink. 'But what's all that hair?' Molly insisted again, 'There's enough venison around that hole to make a good stew.'

The boys burst out laughing at her remark, then Yanto controlled himself and went on. 'Well, during the action the stag tends to get a bit excited, and starts ripping chunks out of her neck!' Billy looked at the girls' perplexed faces. 'I bet you ent half glad you're not a couple of female deer,' he laughed.

As they broke out of the covert on to the open parkland the bright sun made them squint. 'There you are, Mary, the fairy castle.' Yanto was pointing across the valley to the next hill, on top of which stood a tall ancient tower with turreted ramparts.

'Ooh, I see what you mean,' Mary shrilled excitedly. 'It looks like something out of a story book.'

'Yeah, it was built same time as the castle. From the top of the tower you can see the castle ramparts. They used to signal to each other when there was trouble about.'

'Can we get to the top,' Mary enquired eagerly.

'You can, there's a spiral staircase inside, I gather, but the

106

gamekeeper lives there now and I don't particularly want to meet him.'

'What about a cool off,' Billy suggested.

'Where?' the two girls replied in unison. Billy pointed down into the valley. At the base of the slope immediately below was a small lake. A miniature thorn-clad island dominated its centre, standing out darkly against the surrounding bright water.

'We spent some time in there when we were kids, didn't we, Yant?' Billy shouted, 'fancy a trip down memory lane?'

'Why not?'

The two of them galloped off down the steep grass bank. With squeals of joy the girls hitched up their skirts and charged after them. Five minutes later they stood on the grassy bank, looking down at the brown water.

There was a wooden sluice gate situated in the bank close to where they stood. 'What's that?' came the inevitable female enquiry.

'The pond is fed by an underground stream,' Yanto explained. 'The estate just tops it up when necessary.'

'I wonder if those mirror carp are still here, Yant?' Billy asked with shining eyes. 'Remember, we used to stick 'em with spears. Two buggers used to fill a bucket.' Yanto cast a cautious look towards the gamekeeper's tower, but it appeared to be deserted.

'Well, there's one way to find out. You fancy a paddle?' Yanto looked at the two girls as he spoke.

'How deep is it?' they asked.

'About three foot.'

'We'll get our skirts wet.'

'Hang 'em out to dry when we have the grub,' said Billy, with his usual grin. The girls looked at each other, then agreed.

'Right,' said Yanto, 'then this is what we'll do.'

Ten minutes later they all met together again on the bank. At Yanto's suggestion they had each gone off and found themselves a long thin stick apiece. Billy used his penknife to fashion a needle-sharp point on each of the sticks. While he was thus engaged, Yanto began to explain his plan of action to the

107

girls.

The lake was roughly circular in shape. The island in the middle was also more or less round, thus the distance from the bank to the nearest point of the island was about the same all the way around. It resembled a moat, about thirty yards wide.

Yanto looked at Mary. 'You and Bill go in, spread yourselves out and wade around the island in that direction,' he indicated to the left. 'Me and Moll will do the same in that direction.' He pointed to the right. 'Make as much of a splash as you can and the fish will run in front of you, if there is any fish left in here that is. So your fish will be dashing towards us and our fish will be dashing towards you. By the time the four of us meet up we should have all the fish in the pool between us.' 'And that's when they start to panic,' Billy interrupted, 'then they start flapping around on the surface and we start sticking 'em; dead easy.'

The girls listened in fascination then began to tuck their skirts into their knicker legs. 'They don't bite, do they?' Mary asked as they gingerly entered the water.

'Course not,' came the snorted reply.

The girls squealed as their feet sank into six inches of mud, but they persevered after encouragement from the boys and found the bottom much firmer as they waded out a few more feet. Then they found that their skirts were getting wet. By the time they reached a point halfway to the island the water had reached their hips, so they gave it up as a bad job and began to enjoy themselves.

'Right, let's spread out a bit and get back to back,' said Yanto with a grin, 'you ready, Bill?' The two boys stood back to back, the girls did the same. With a final 'Tally-ho!', they began wading forward, thrashing the water in front of them with their sticks.

By the time they were half way around, Yanto noticed slight disturbances on the surface of the water ahead of them. He began to get excited. 'They're still here, Bill,' he shouted.

Billy and Mary were out of sight behind the island. 'Yeah,' Billy's reply drifted over. The disturbances became more and more apparent as they continued. 'It's like walking in slow motion, isn't it?' laughed Molly alongside him. They saw Billy and Mary appear from behind the island still thrashing the water as they moved towards them.

'Keep bashing the water, Moll,' urged Yanto.

As the gap between the four of them narrowed, fin marks began cutting the surface of the shining water, this way and that. Yanto cast an excited glance towards the tower. It still appeared deserted. Their excitement was such that he doubted if they could stop now even if the gamekeeper did appear. Suddenly, as Billy and Mary got within twenty yards of them, the water erupted. The girls screamed and cowered away as a large, panic-stricken fish surfaced and flapped around in confusion.

'There must be bloody 'undreds of 'em,' yelled Billy, as he lunged his spear at one flapping monster.

Yanto wasn't listening. He was getting a bead on a fish literally trying to run across the surface of the water to his left. Coolly, he thrust the point of his spear into the centre of the foaming maelstrom, and felt the resistance as it struck home.

With a whoop of triumph he lifted his spear into the air with the skewered mirror carp struggling on the shaft. The sun glinted on the silver scales as it struggled in vain. 'Must be five pounds at least,' Billy yelled, as he desperately tried to keep the shoal penned between the four of them. Things had now degenerated into bloodlust. The girls had got over their initial shock, and shrieked with excitement as they thrust at everything that moved.

Another large fish came flapping across the gap. In its blind haste to escape, it came straight towards Molly. 'Stick the bugger,' yelled Billy. In a mad impulsive movement, which Molly later insisted was self-defence, she jabbed desperately at the oncoming fish. Through sheer good luck, or bad luck, depending on whether you were Molly or the fish, the spear struck home. As she lifted her stick in the air she stared in dumb amazement at the big carp jerking in its death throes. 'I didn't mean to do that,' she yelped. Yanto thought she was going to cry. 'Selwyn will be pleased that you did,' he quipped. Suddenly the fish were gone. The only disturbance on the water now was of their own making. 'Sod it,' shouted Billy, 'I ain't got one.' The madness had probably lasted no more than thirty seconds, but they were all breathless from their efforts.

Yanto cast another apprehensive look towards the tower. 'Better get back into the woods, I reckon. If old Jess Purvis is home he must have heard that row.'

'Yeah,' Bill agreed, 'Jess would shag us if he caught us in here with his fish.'

Molly turned on him angrily. She was still upset from her reluctant kill. 'I wish you would show us a little more respect,' she snapped, 'your language is dreadful.' They made their way back to the bank with Billy following, a little more subdued than usual.

The picnic food was excellent. The episode in the lake, plus the walking, had put an edge to their appetites. For the last hour they had done justice to Molly's superb cooking. There was cold faggot with apple chutney, home-made of course. Superb apple pie with sultanas and cloves, interspersed with crusty bread sandwiches of every description. It was a feast, swilled down in the boys' case at least with pints of good cider.

Not for the first time, Yanto realised what an excellent cook Molly was. 'I wonder how Julie stacks up in the grub stakes', he mused to himself.

After filling his cracked white china mug for the third time, Yanto lay back against the mossy bank and gloried in his contentment. He ran his hand up and down Molly's spine as she sat beside him sipping her tea. 'Have a drop of scrump,' he said quietly, and offered her the jar. To his surprise, Molly threw away the dregs of tea in her beaker and held it out for him to fill with the frothing liquor. She took a couple of man-sized swigs, screwed her face up slightly then leaned back beside him.

'This is the life, ain't it, Moll,' he murmured and began to stroke her back again.

'It's lovely,' she breathed. 'I didn't know I could have such a good time so close to home. It's like being on holiday.'

110

'It's the company, Moll,' he whispered mischievously, 'with the right bloke life is a holiday.'

'I know,' she replied and looked at him without smiling. There was no mistaking that look. His chemistry began to work overtime.

Billy and Mary were fooling and rolling about in the sunbeams on the edge of the clearing. The sun and cider were also having their effects on them.

Yanto silently caught Billy's eye and flicked his own eyes to the right. Billy got the message. 'Come on, gal,' he shouted, laughing as he stood up, 'let's see if I can find a deer to show you.'

Yanto and Molly followed them with their eyes until they were lost from view among the trees. Then they looked at one another for a second and kissed passionately. As they kissed Yanto slid his hand under her still damp skirt, and very gently massaged the soft mound of her femininity. She began to moan aloud with uncontrolled excitement. As he took his hand away and began to unbuckle his belt, Molly suddenly sat up.

'What's up, Moll?' he asked breathlessly.

'Oh Yanto,' she moaned softly, 'if we do this every time we see one another, you are bound to get me into trouble, and that would kill our Dad.'

'It won't kill your Dad at all,' he said as he fished in his pocket, 'because I have no intention of getting you into trouble.' He had learned his lesson regarding being prepared from the previous Friday night. He pulled out the little packet of contraceptives and showed them to her.

'What's that?'

He explained the function to her and she relaxed a little. 'This is 1947, Moll, not the dark ages,' he urged. 'Go on, put it on for me.'

She looked at him quizzically. 'How?' she asked. Yanto took her hand, and with his help she began to undo his fly buttons. She gazed in dumb fascination as his erect manhood sprang into view. He ripped open one of the little silver foil packets and handed her the lubricated ring of rubber.

Again with his help, she reverently rolled the condom down the shaft of his erect member. They looked at each other again. It was obvious that she was now completely under his spell. He took her gently by the waist and pulled her on top of him. Even in her naivety she realised what was required of her. She pulled up her skirt, opened her legs, and straddled him. As he kissed her again he slowly felt for the gusset of her panties, pulled them to one side and entered her expertly.

There followed a mad five minutes when they were oblivious to everything, even the possibility of the other two returning. Molly had secretly enjoyed her initiation to sex on the night of Yanto's near-drowning, but then she had had to curtail her natural emotions for fear of waking her father. But this was something else.

She was lost in her own delirium and clawed him unmercifully as she rode the mad race. He gasped with the effect of keeping with her. He felt he was going to climax early and desperately tried to think of other things to take his mind off it in order to last until she was ready.

The sweat was pouring from him when the ultimate moment arrived. They peaked together and rolled onto their sides exhausted. 'Christ, Moll, what happened?' he gasped in awe and rubbed his scored shoulders. Her pretty perspiring face split into a sheepish grin, then became serious again on reflection of being taken over by her baser instincts so completely.

'I don't know,' she muttered, 'I don't know what came over me. That's what you do to me, see.'

He looked at her perturbed face. 'Well, please don't worry about it, love, that's how it should be. I've said it before and I'll say it again, you're some sort of woman.' He lit a cigarette and lay back. He beckoned her to do the same. With a big sigh she lay her head in the crook of his arm and closed her eyes.

Nat Asnett trudged along the deserted castle walk, lost in his own thoughts. Twenty minutes earlier he had alighted from the Gloucester train at Berkeley station. He had spent a couple of minutes chatting to a slightly wary Tom Cotter, the station

112

master, before starting the two-mile walk home to Ham.

Tom had reason to be wary. He had only ever had one bit of trouble with him personally, but he remembered it well. He had caught Nat, then fourteen years old, putting a sleeper across the rails, just to see what would happen to the train.

There had been an aura of menace about the boy even at that age, and Tom had often pondered his real reason for not reporting the incident to the police. Was it benevolence, or fear of reprisal?

As he walked on, Nat pondered on his future. He still smarted from his treatment at the military prison, but realised that he must try to control his violent nature if he was to amount to anything.

He was suddenly shaken from his thoughts by a car which slid silently to a halt beside him. It was a large green Armstrong Siddeley. But it was the driver that made him halt abruptly. It was a girl, and she was indeed beautiful. 'Want a lift?' she said and smiled. There was something vaguely familiar about her. He got in. Julie Murchison pulled expertly away.

Yanto watched the smoke from his cigarette drift lazily up the shaft of the sunbeam which bathed Molly and himself in light through a gap in the greenery above.

He felt at complete peace. His body had now completely relaxed after his frantic efforts with Molly a few minutes before. This, combined with the aftereffects of good food and strong cider, gave him a feeling of total well-being seldom experienced in this life.

His languid mind began comparing this moment to the noise and confusion of Arnhem, the battle that had ended his war. It seemed like only yesterday that he had presented himself at Manchester's Ringway Airport for training with the newly formed Parachute Regiment. He was a raw young bull, itching for more action and glamour in his life. He wanted to cover himself with glory, and what better way than getting accepted by this new elite. The talk was that those good enough to pass the special high standards required by the regiment would receive wings and special regalia, which was sure to appeal to the ladies.

After two weeks he had begun to wonder if he had done the right thing. Hard was not the word. But his confidence had grown as he watched some of his comrades fail the requirements and return to their units. He was still here and he would succeed. Then, after a couple more weeks, that strange phenomenon appeared, just as it appeared after his first two weeks of basic training with the Royal Army Service Corps. It was as though the British Forces were able to instil a form of masochism into their people. The harder it became, the more he and his remaining comrades enjoyed it. Whether it was the competitive spirit, the determination to beat the next man or platoon, or just being super-fit, he didn't know. Anyway, having experienced these things made him able to appreciate times like the present.

A thistledown floated into the bright phallus of the sunbeam and hovered over his face. He watched it, his eyelids growing heavier. 'Looks like a 'chute', he thought dreamily.

'Up eight hundred, four men jumping.' The little Royal Air Force instructor's barked command rang through the still morning air, sending a chill through the four men standing to attention by the cage. It was the first suitable wind-free morning since they had reached first jump status, and this was it. Yanto, the last of the four as they marched into the cage, was desperately trying to control his fear. He kept repeating to himself what his mother had drummed into him as a child. 'Remember, son, you are as good as anyone you will ever meet.'

The instructor smiled as he went to each man in turn and pulled out two full arm lengths of cord from their parachutes before attaching it to the static line. After making each man check that his own line was securely attached, he moved them to the far end of the cage and sat them down on the wooden bench.

A sudden jerk brought Yanto out of his stupor. The winch man was running out the cable, allowing the barrage balloon to rise.

Already they were fifty feet about the ground, and rising. The steel bars of the cage were enclosed by tarpaulin sheets to protect them from the elements, except for one side, which was open with just a simple lift bar to move before exit. Yanto took a quick look between the bars and felt his bowels sag. He resolved not to look at the ground again until he felt his 'chute open. He had taken some comfort from the fact that he had been the last man to board the cage, so at least he could watch Yorky and the others exit, before his turn came. But would he? He looked around.

As they filed aboard, the instructor had moved each man as far as possible up the cage before sitting them down. Yanto realised to his horror he was now the nearest man to the exit bar. The instructor's next words confirmed it. 'Last man in, first man out, lads.' The tough, wiry little man said the words in a cheerful manner, still with a big smile on his face. He was a warm-hearted man, who realised the trauma experienced by the men on their first jump.

Parachuting was still in its infancy, and not without accidents. The new regiment was the Army's first experiment in sending men into battle by this novel method. But the Germans had paratroopers so the British had no alternative. The Royal Air Force were the only experts; hence the little RAF instructor.

As the balloon reached the eight hundred foot marker, he began chatting light-heartedly while at the same time watching the flagman on the ground. The blue flag was showing, which indicated they were still manoeuvring the balloon into position. He carried on his light-hearted banter to the rigidly tense men. Yanto wasn't listening. He was remembering some of the talk during training. Some men insisted that it was not possible to make your first jump without voiding your bowels.

He had laughed at the time, but the way his stomach was behaving now, he began to fear they had not been jesting. 'Please God,' he prayed, 'don't let me shit myself, I would rather die.' The flag showed yellow.

'Stand up, lads,' the instructor smiled, 'first man step forward.' Yanto stood up by the bar looking rigidly into space. The instructor spoke quietly in his ear, reminding him of a few basics, and unobtrusively removed the bar at the same time. Yanto was aware of the wind in his face as the instructor glanced down at the flag man again. 'For God's sake, let's go,' he groaned to himself. He thought he was going to faint. Suddenly a hand slapped his shoulder.

'Go!'

Yanto stepped into space. He fell with eyes clenched shut. He was aware of the wind roaring in his ears and tearing at his clothes. The tug when it came was much gentler that he had imagined it would be.

He decided to open his eyes, and immediately knew how God must have felt when he first observed his new creation. The early morning sun made even the dark distant mass of Manchester look beautiful.

As he slowly revolved he observed all points of the compass with eyes wide in wonder. Woods, fields, brooks, materialised through the morning mist to be dappled into perfection by an early, creamy sunlight. No great master could have done this scene justice. He looked up at that big beautiful canopy of silk billowing above him, the brilliant white contrasting with the blue of the sky. He was bursting with joy. He had done it. Any horrors waiting for him in the future were compensated for by this moment in time. How could a human being experience such total contrast of feelings in a matter of seconds? From deadly trauma to exotic delirium.

He noticed three other parachutes away above him, and couldn't resist yelling and screaming his ecstasy towards them. To cap it all, there would be no need to change his underpants.

Suddenly the ground was racing up to meet him. 'Christ, should he be coming in that fast?' His mind raced over the landing instructions. Legs together, knees bent, mustn't cap this beautiful experience with broken ankles.

He hit the ground hard, but felt no pain.

Following instructions to the letter, he rolled his body, but banged his helmeted head hard against the firm turf of the airfield. He lay there, slightly dazed, but happy. Then he saw the fire. A fire! What fool would build a fire in the dropping zone? To his horror he realised his hand was lying in the embers.

He desperately tried to drag his hand away, but it wouldn't budge. His hand started to burn. He screamed. Then, with a desperate effort threw himself bodily away. There was another scream as Molly was thrown away from his frantic struggles.

'What the hell!' He came to, and knocked the burning cigarette end from between his fingers. He felt foolish as he looked at Molly, who was on all fours amongst the pine needles looking at him in open-mouthed amazement. 'Sorry, love,' he mumbled, 'I've been bloody dreaming.'

Yanto drained the last dregs of cider from the stone jar and watched Molly clear up the remains of the picnic. It had been great fun, much more than he had anticipated.

He watched as Molly flapped the blanket free of crumbs and folded it neatly. She was certainly a terrific girl, he told himself ruefully.

His common sense told him that this was the girl for him, but that sophisticated vision of Julie Murchison kept blurring the scene. 'Where do you think the other two have got to?' she said, and looked around, 'no sign of them.'

Yanto grinned to himself. 'We'll wander back,' he said as he picked up the blanket and baskets, 'expect we'll meet 'em coming back.'

After checking that the two mirror carp were well packed in newspaper, he curled his arm around Molly's waist and they began to stroll back up the track. As they chatted and laughed about the events of the day they almost fell over Billy who was stretched out in the undergrowth snoozing with a contended grin on his face. 'Where's Mary?' Molly demanded. 'She wandered off to find some pine cones,' Billy replied, and stretched his tall skinny frame. 'She said she varnished 'em or summat.'

Billy took one of the baskets from Molly, and the three of them wandered on through the wood. Suddenly they heard Mary calling for Billy in a shrill excited voice.

'Wo's up?' Billy yelled back.

'Come and see, quick,' Mary shrieked. They broke into a trot and found Mary standing in the middle of a thicket. She was holding something. All Molly's motherly instincts erupted when she saw what it was.

Mary was holding a tiny fawn. It couldn't have been more than a few days old.

'Isn't she beautiful,' gushed Molly, 'let me hold her, please?'

'It's a boy,' grunted Billy, after careful observation.

Molly ignored him, and cuddled the beautiful creature. The baby deer nestled in her arms and looked at them with enormous brown unconcerned eyes. The only sign of fear was a nervous tremble in the long spindly legs.

'I saw that bush move as I passed,' Mary jabbered excitedly, 'I was scared for a sec, but I moved the bush and there it was.'

Yanto looked around. 'Its mum and dad can't be far away,' he said. 'Stags are normally nervous, but they get dead vicious when they think their young are threatened.'

Almost as he spoke they heard a crashing in the bushes at the top of the ridge above them. The head and antlers of the magnificent full-grown male appeared on the skyline not fifty yards away. It was a dirty grey-white in colour.

'Christ, it's one of them white buggers,' yelped Billy.

'Put the fawn down and move back,' Yanto commanded. Molly hurriedly put the animal back in the bush, but the damage was done.

With a shake of its magnificent antlers the stag charged down the slope towards them. 'You three run for it,' yelled Yanto. Billy hesitated. 'You look after the girls,' Yanto yelled again. With that the three of them made off as best they could. Yanto had an idea. The stag had stopped momentarily, its spread antlers had tangled in the thick brambles. Yanto shouted

118

at the beast to attract its attention away from the fleeing threesome, while at the same time squeezing himself into a tight batch of young saplings. He prayed that this idea would work. It was either that or tackle the beast with his bare hands. He knew that in this berserk state those horns could open him up like a ripe melon.

The enraged animal freed its antlers from the brambles and with a springing bound, crashed into Yanto's protective cage of saplings. He shrank back fearfully as the horns scythed back and forth among the fragile trees, only a foot or so from his vulnerable body. He couldn't believe that this normally timid creature could be capable of such aggression. As the stag bored it again, Yanto took his chance. Gripping the edge of the blanket he moved as close to the fearsome head as he dared. Then coolly and carefully he tossed the rough cloth over the lowered horns. As the surprised beast lifted its head, the rest of the blanket dropped over its snout and eyes, effectively blinding it. His plan had worked. The stag stood back again, snorting and shaking its head, but the rough material was well tangled in the antlers and stayed put. Yanto broke out of his protective screen and ran as he had never run before. As he raced up the narrow track he took a quick look over his shoulder. The stag was thrusting this way and that, but was still blinded by the blanket. As he reached the edge of the wood, he found the others waiting for him fearfully.

Billy had armed himself with a stout stick. 'Oh, thank God you're safe,' gasped Molly.

As they ran on together across the flat open plateau, Yanto explained breathlessly what he had done. They were congratulating him when Mary screamed and pointed to the rear. They looked back and saw the stag bound out of the wood.

'Christ, he got rid of the blanket,' yelped Billy.

They were now running alongside the wall, but still a long way from the crossing stile. They looked back again. The stag was now at full gallop on the springy turf. 'We'll never get to the stile,' gasped Billy and prepared to turn and face the animal.

'We can get through that hound flap,' screamed Molly, and

pointed ahead. At intervals, all around the park wall, wooden flaps are built into the base of the wall to allow the Berkeley Hunt hounds access into the park during the fox hunting season. During a hunt the wooden flaps were always raised.

The flap which they were rapidly approaching was closed. 'It'll be locked,' groaned Yanto, 'we'll have to tackle the bastard between us, Bill.'

'Try it, for Christ sake,' yelled Billy. Molly pushed desperately against the eighteen-inch high wooden flap. It swung up and open. The drumming of hooves was loud in their ears as Molly wriggled through on her stomach. An almost demented Mary followed her. As Yanto went through, Billy turned and hurled his stick at the oncoming stag, which hesitated slightly.

As Billy reached the other side, there was a sickening crash as antler met wall.

'Christ, that was close,' Yanto gasped, as all four lay on the grass gulping air.

'Yeah,' grinned Billy, 'but what do I say to our Mam, that was her blanket.' They all laughed their relief.

The motorcycle started with the first kick. They sat there for a while feeling drained and empty. 'What time is it?' Billy asked.

'Quarter to six.'

'Stupid bloody licensing laws,' spat Billy, 'I could do with a drink. Joe Asnett's place is just a hundred yards up the road, and don't open 'til seven.'

They moved off. As they passed the silent Salvation Inn, Yanto glanced to the left at the Murchison house. No sign of Julie, but someone was walking up the drive towards the house. Yanto stiffened. He would know that profile anywhere. It was Nat Asnett.

Twelve

THE CONFRONTATION

Yanto was deep in thought as he walked over the canal bridge that evening. What the hell was Nat Asnett doing walking up Julie's drive? He felt a pang of jealousy. Nat could only have arrived home that same day and already he seemed to be queering Yanto's pitch. He pushed it out of his mind as he approached The Blue Boar.

Molly and Mary both had things to do that evening, so Yanto had arranged to meet Billy in The Boar to round off a good weekend. A good weekend it had certainly been. He had enjoyed the picnic much more than he had thought possible. Yes, he and Molly certainly seemed to hit it off well. He felt good.

He had put on his best button-down shirt and striped tie, which together with the tailored worsted slacks had annihilated his clothing coupons. A drop of precious Old Spice aftershave had added the final touch, and now he wanted a drink.

The bar room was warm and inviting as always, and just enough people to be comfortable were enjoying the cosy environment. He spotted Billy lounging against the far corner of the bar talking to Sooty Hill the joker. Billy brayed with laughter at something Sooty had said as Yanto joined them. 'Tell Yant that 'un, Sooty,' Billy commanded between hoots of laughter.

Sooty turned to Yanto, who was already grinning with anticipation. 'Well,' said Sooty, with his usual poker face, 'There was this squadron of French Foreign Legionnaires, see?' Yanto had already begun to laugh at Sooty's serious face. ''Ang on a minute,' Sooty snorted, 'I ant bloody told you yet.' Yanto regained his composure and Sooty continued.

121

'Well, they had been besieged by these hostile Arabs in their desert fort for months, see, and they was bloody starving.' Yanto couldn't help it, he began to hoot with laughter. Sooty was famous for his jokes and it was said he could make a cat laugh just by looking at it. Sooty waited with patient resignation as the two boys regained control. Yanto had to suck in his cheeks as Sooty went on. 'Well, they had eaten all their K rations, see, then they started on the camels and the mules, then the cats and dogs, until finally there was nothing edible left in the fort. Anyway, one morning the Commandant called them all together on the parade ground. "Well gentlemen," he said, "we are faced with a very grave situation. I've got some bad news for you, but I've also got good news."

"Tell us the bad news first, sir," they all chorused.

"Very well,' said the Commandant, 'I am afraid all the food is gone and we are now reduced to eating camel dung." Great groans and gnashing of teeth emanated from the ranks.

"Quick, sir," shouted a trooper, "what's the good news?"

"Well," said the Commandant, "we've got three hundred and fifty tons of it."

Yanto had just taken a swig of cider, and instantly sprayed a dozen regulars as the uncontrollable spasm of laughter erupted. He and Billy were literally on their knees with mirth as Sooty looked on impassively. 'Somebody take the prat away,' groaned Yanto, holding his aching stomach. Unconcerned, Sooty ambled away to join another group.

The next hour passed amiably, by which time the two of them began to feel the effects of the day. The gallon of cider at the picnic plus the four pints of the last hour was giving them that lovely sleepy lethargic feeling.

It was just after ten o'clock, and Yanto began to think of his bed. 'With a bit of luck we should get picked for the Russian ship tomorrow, Bill.'

'Yeah,' Billy yawned back, 'should keep us going for a week at least.' At that moment the babble of voices in the bar ceased, and a hush descended. Yanto saw Billy's mouth drop. Yanto turned and saw Julie Murchison and Nat Asnett enter the bar.

Julie spotted him and walked towards him, smiling. She looked stunning in a beautifully cut peach coloured suit and matching shoes. The navy blouse contrasted perfectly. She looked the epitome of elegance and good taste, with the confidence of a woman who knows she is beautiful. 'Hello again,' she bubbled, 'guess what? I was driving home from Berkeley today and I stopped to give a chap a lift, and look who it was.' She turned and looked towards Nat, who was standing in the doorway talking to one of the locals he knew.

'Isn't it great, all together again, just like when we were kids.' Yanto grunted some inaudible remark and was introducing her to a goggle-eyed Billy as Nat joined them.

Yanto grudgingly admitted to himself that Nat was a fine-looking fellow. The tastefully cut dark blue suit, obviously bought abroad, complemented his dark good looks, giving him a Cary Grant image in the austere setting.

Billy must have been reading his thoughts. 'Christ,' he breathed, 'you two look as though you come straight from Hollywood.' Julie smiled at him but Nat ignored him completely as he stuck his hand out to Yanto. 'Hiya, Gatesy,' he said softly. He still had that same cruel grin which tended to twist the right side of his mouth.

'Hello Nat,' Yanto replied straight faced, 'home at last, eh? How did they treat you?'

'Nothing I couldn't take,' he replied, with the same arrogant grin. Julie stood there looking at one then the other. She sensed a strained atmosphere between them as they exchanged small talk.

Knocker came over to serve them with a slightly worried look on his face. 'What ho, Nat, nice to see you home,' he lied. 'What can I get you and the young lady?'

'Hiya, Knock,' Nat replied, 'nice to see you too. I'll have a double scotch with water,' he turned to Julie, 'what's your poison, my love?' Yanto felt his gut tighten at the term of affection.

'Could you possibly prepare me a John Collins, Mr Nelmes,'

she said with a smile. 'I acquired quite a taste for them in the States.'

'I couldn't,' Knocker grunted, 'don't get much call for 'em around here, but I expect the missus can.' With an irritated raise of the eyebrows, he called to Renee who was observing the group from the other end of the bar, and made the request. Renee shot a disapproving glance at Knocker and began preparing her drink. Nat turned his attention to Yanto and Billy.

'What about you two?' They both ordered cider, which Knocker was drawing as Renee came over and placed the colourful concoction in front of Julie.

'Christ,' said Billy, 'you supposed to drink or eat it?' and gave his usual raucous laugh.

'That is a civilised drink, you peasant,' growled Nat. Billy looked annoyed and was about to say something when Knocker came back with their two pints of cider, looking like tea cups in his massive fists.

'That will be five and ten pence please,' he boomed, sensing the discord among them. Nat pulled out a wad of notes large enough to choke a horse, gave Knocker a pound note, and told him to keep the change. Billy's eyes stared at the wad in disbelief. It must have represented at least three weeks' wages for the average man in the village. Yanto felt a surge of cold anger course through him at this blatant piece of exhibitionism.

'I didn't know they paid that well in the nick,' he heard himself say loudly.

Several people in the bar looked around and Knocker moved closer to the bar flap. Now it was Nat's turn to be annoyed. 'Watch your lip, Gatesy,' he said in a quiet voice, which held more menace than a shout. 'You of all people should know there is always an angle for a bit of profit, like salmon poaching for instance.'

Yanto, flushing with rage, moved towards him. With a loud thud the bar flap flew up and Knocker, with a speed contrary to his barn door dimensions, stood between them.

'I want to go home now, Nathan.' Julie used Nat's real name in a voice shrill with alarm, as several customers in the vicinity moved to the far end of the bar in one fluid movement.

'I think the lady wants to go home,' said Knocker quietly, 'and I think that is an excellent idea, don't you?' He looked at them both in turn. Nat picked up his scotch and tossed it back in one easy movement. He was thinking about his earlier resolve to keep out of trouble, especially with all these witnesses.

Yanto was also having second thoughts about getting into a fight over such a silly incident, and realised it was caused as much by jealousy as anything else. Plus the fact that Nat would be no pushover.

'Well?' said Knocker, eyeing them both again.

'I'll let it go this time, Gatesy,' Nat said quietly, 'but one of these days I shall have to give you what I should have given you when we were kids.'

'Any time you're ready,' Yanto growled, his anger beginning to rise again.

Nat grinned as he turned. 'Evening all,' he said, and walked out into the night.

Julie looked at Yanto. 'Really,' she snapped haughtily, and stalked out. Seconds later they heard the Armstrong start and move away with a screech of tyres.

Knocker mopped his brow. 'I ain't bloody having that every time you two buggers get together, mind,' he said, and went back through the bar flap. The two boys picked up their pints and moved over to a couple of chairs by the fire, just vacated by an elderly couple.

'Christ, Yant,' Billy whispered, 'I can see trouble coming with that bastard.'

'Yeah, as sure as God made little apples.' They both took a deep swig.

Yanto's mind was in a turmoil when he reached home that night. An hour before, he had begun to feel sleepy. Now, the last thing he needed was sleep. The incident with Nat had honed his mind to a razor edge.

He remembered his mother telling him about Sid Watkins' request for another salmon. He grinned to himself. It hadn't taken Sid long to dispose of the monster. Then, of

125

course, there was Bert Midgeley. He still owed Bert a fish over the bike deal. He looked at his watch. It was 11.30. The evening tide had been a modest eighteen-footer and had ebbed to low water an hour ago.

There was a bank of salmon traps over at Clapton which he hadn't visited for ages. These traps were known as putchers, a small basket with a large weave designed specifically for salmon, as opposed to the kipes at Purton, huge baskets with a five foot diameter mouth and small weave, designed to catch anything. Clapton was also an isolated spot where the traps were usually left for a couple of days before being checked. His mind made up, he pushed his bike out of the shed. It started with his first kick, and keeping the machine as quiet as possible until clear of the village, he set off for Berkeley.

Two hours later, a tired but elated Yanto had climbed into bed and nestled into his mother's clean Sunday night linen. His luck had held. That night had been mild with a blustery wind. As always, he had revelled in the wild isolation of the estuary shoreline. Standing by the old timber ponds at Clapton, another of his childhood swimming holes, he had felt his tension being blown away by the eternal winds of the Severn.

There had been some moon which would illuminate the scene suddenly, then be gone as though switched off by the scudding cloud. This had made it easy for him to reach the traps as there were no banks here as such, just flats of mud and rock. To his absolute delight the first trap had held what must have been a seven-pound salmon, plus a couple of mullet which he had ignored. To cap it off, the last but one trap contained a ten-pounder.

Later, as he rode home in the cool night air, a vision of old Bert's delighted face as he presented him with the larger fish invaded his mind's eye, and filled him with contentment.

'Belt up now and listen for your names.' The agent for the shipping line was standing on an upturned milk crate outside the pool hut which was situated close to the entrance to the wharves. Forty to fifty lean tough dockers, who were milling

126

around the hut chatting and laughing, came to an expectant hush at his command. 'These are the men who will work on the ...' The agent hesitated as he tried to read out the name of the Russian ship from the bill of lading in his hand. He gave up. 'On that bloody Russian rust bucket over there.' He waved his hand towards the ship's superstructure which could be seen towering over the dock offices. Some raucous laughter followed the ribald remark. There was another hush. Yanto, who was standing alongside Billy, kept his fingers crossed.

This was important. The gangs had already been selected to work on the other three small coasters which had arrived over the past weekend. Out of the fifty-odd men left, only about thirty would be required to unload the Russian ship, big as she was. The rest faced a week on pool money, no good to man nor beast. 'Turl-Browning-Goulding-Watkins.' The familiar local names droned from the agent's lips and Yanto began to feel apprehensive.

'Gates.' Yanto relaxed, then became concerned for Billy. The married men did, after all, tend to get more consideration.

The list ended with no mention of Billy Tolboys. 'Oh, bollocks,' groaned Billy.

'No sweat, mate,' Yanto tried to console him. 'There's a ship in the basin waiting to come in. You'll probably be picked for her midweek.'

'I s'pose,' Billy spoke with resignation. 'Our Mam bin dropping hints about wallpapering the front room. Looks like she'll get her wish.'

They arranged to meet at The Blue Boar the following Wednesday night, then Billy jumped on his bike to ride home. 'Don't forget, mind, Yant, any fags or booze going on that ship ...' He left the rest unsaid. Yanto nodded, picked up his bait bag, and joined the other lucky ones.

As he walked towards the towering ship he mused over his good fortune. During his first week as a raw stevedore, Cliff Barrett the dock foreman had come aboard the ship he was working on and said something insulting and disrespectful to him. He couldn't remember now what it was, but it had made him blazing mad. Yanto, who would do anything for anybody who asked him nicely, also had a very short fuse when it came to insults, especially in front of witnesses.

He had grabbed hold of Cliff and had him halfway over the ship's side and would have dumped him into the dock had he not been restrained by a couple of his workmates.

He had expected the sack at the time, but strangely enough, he had had more than his share of work from that day on.

'Must be a moral there somewhere,' he mused, as he ran up the gangplank.

By the middle of May, the already warm weather was beginning to turn into an exceptionally hot summer. Nat Asnett, who had been taking it very easy since his homecoming, decided it was time to start work. Between leaving school and going off to war with the Navy, he had worked on the Sharpness tugs for British Waterways.

In this tight community, he had been guaranteed his job back, and was due to start on the coming Monday. So this being his last free Wednesday for a while, he had decided to give himself a treat. One of his old associates he had chatted to in the bar a couple of nights previously, had mentioned how much he enjoyed his regular visits to the Turkish baths in Gloucester. This had interested Nat. His ship had been in Japan just after the surrender and he had enjoyed a couple of visits to the bath houses in Yokohama. A part of the treatment there had included an exhilarating massage carried out by a young girl, who, by standing on his inert naked body and by using her body weight as a substitute for arm muscle, had given him an unforgettable massage with her bare feet. He didn't for one minute expect that sort of treatment in Gloucester, but that was how he would spend this afternoon.

It was while in Japan that he had beaten the Petty Officer half to death in a drunken rage. They had sent him home to do two years in a military prison and his dark oily skin had suffered while inside. He was still suffering from blackheads and other rash problems which jolted his vanity every time he looked in the mirror. A good Turkish bath, his friend had told him, would open his pores and flush out all the impurities. So, with this in mind, he borrowed his father's van and drove towards Gloucester looking forward to a relaxing afternoon in the steam.

The same day, Julie Murchison was sun-bathing on the front lawn when the L.M.S. Railways van drew up outside the big house. Her beloved two-seater kayak had arrived from America at last. Barney gave in to her pleas, and agreed to transport the canoe down to the Little Avon river on the roof-rack of the Armstrong after lunch. The thought of drifting along in the sunbeams, under the willow of the brook with only the frogs and water-rats to keep her company, filled her with glee.

Barney Summerville gave a grunt as he lifted the lightweight canoe off the car's roof-rack. Keeping it raised above his head, he staggered to the edge of the grassy bank and dropped the craft on to the surface of the clear water.

He cursed under his breath as the flat bottom caused the water to cascade over his brown boots.

Two minutes before, he had driven over the humpback bridge by the Berkeley Hunt kennels, then turned immediately left into Mill Lane, alongside the brook, where there was a convenient little spot by the bridge, ideal for launching a small craft.

'You really are a darling, Barney,' Julie laughed, as she lowered herself into the rear of the two individual cockpits and pulled the waterproof liner around her waist. He handed her the double bladed paddle as she said, 'I shall go down as far as Brown's Mill, so could you possibly pick me up here about five-thirty?' Barney nodded resignedly as he gave the canoe a push with his foot, and watched it drift out into midstream.

The underside of the road bridge was of flat construction with about three feet of clearance above normal water level. He watched as Julie lay back in the canoe and moved under the bridge by pushing against the flat underside with her hands.

Being quite a wide road bridge, she had a fair distance to travel in this fashion. With the underside of the bridge only inches above her face, it was as well she was not troubled with claustrophobia. As she disappeared from view, Barney turned and walked back to the car. 'Should 'ave bin a boy,' he grinned as he slammed the door.

'Ahhaa!' Nat's anguished cry rang through the Turkish suite, temporarily disturbing the therapeutic calm. As it was his first visit, the attendant had suggested that he get a good sweat on in the steam room first, then move on to one of the dry heat rooms to continue sweating in comfort on one of the beds provided. He had stepped into the steam room to be met by a blast of hissing scalding fog which caused him to breathe in sharply, thereby promptly burning his nose.

'Breathe through yer mouth.' The gruff voice came through the steam. Nat could vaguely see a figure sitting on the stone slab on the left-hand side of the room. In spite of the steam, he could see that the stone bench, which was a fixture, continued all around the steam room. So, as the other person already occupied part of the left-hand bench, he quite naturally went over to the right-hand bench and promptly sat down. That was when his cry had rent the calm. The bench he had chosen to sit on was part of the inlet system which housed the vents from which the hot steam was emitted. It was blistering hot and definitely not for sitting on. It has also long been a great source of amusement to the more belligerent regulars as they watched the uninitiated stumble in and sit down. Such a regular was Fred Coe.

Nat had gone about three feet in the air. Then Fred's voice came through the steam again, this time accompanied by a cackle of laughter. 'You ent supposed to sit over there, gets too hot and burns your ass.'

'Thanks a bloody bundle for telling me.' Nat barked in annoyance, and moved out into the more bearable climate of the dry heat rooms.

After half an hour on the bed in the dry heat he was really

enjoying himself and was perspiring profusely. He watched the globules of sweat as they oozed from his pores then ran in countless little rivers down his brown skin. He became aware of the excessive beating of his heart, and remembered the attendant's advice not to overdo it on his first visit.

The cold plunge was in the adjoining massage room, and on surprisingly weak legs he made his way there and gratefully dived into the plunge. The ice-cold water made him gasp, but after swimming a couple of lengths of the plunge, he got out feeling an exhilaration beyond belief. Now he could understand why the Finns came running out of their saunas and rolled themselves in the snow. Earlier, he had been amazed by the amount of sludge being discharged by his pores, so before going back to the hot-rooms, he went to the wash hand basin and scrubbed his face with a will, and imagined all his blackheads disappearing down the drain along with the waste water.

'Hello, it's Nat Asnett, isn't it?' Nat awoke from a slumber and sat up. As he did so, the large puddle of perspiration which had accumulated around his body on the rubber sheet of the bed slopped on to the floor.

There was a tall muscular man of about his own age standing naked before him, grinning from ear to ear. 'Don't you remember me?' the craggy features grinned again. Nat remembered.

'Terry Littlejohn,' he grunted and stuck his hand out.

Nat had first started running around with Terry and Terry's twin brother Joe in his mid-teens, and it was then that his many brushes with the law began. He had felt an affinity with the brothers because they were a couple of hard nuts, but he had also found they had definite criminal tendencies.

'I didn't know you were home,' said Terry, as he sat down on the adjacent bed. 'Last I heard you were in detention quarters in Portsmouth.'

Nat flushed, 'I was,' he replied and explained to Terry the reason for his incarceration. 'How's your dad?' He had always

131

liked Reg Littlejohn, who was a widely respected river pilot. He and his wife Rita had been model parents to the twins and had never understood why their sons were basically bad.

'He's OK!' Terry replied, 'he's retiring next year, fit as a fiddle, but still as soft as shit.'

'He's a good old boy,' Nat growled, 'I'm surprised he's still fit having to worry about you two buggers all the time.'

Terry laughed again. 'Well, you have to make a quid somehow and there ain't much money in firewood.' The brothers had a wood business, buying old trees from the various farmers, cutting them into logs and selling them around the locality. Everyone knew it was a front for less savoury operations.

'Talking about work,' said Terry, 'when are you going to start doin' summat?' Nat told him he was due to start back on the tugs on the following Monday. Terry sat up and showed great interest. 'Back on the tugs, eh?' he said quietly, tugging on his moustache, 'we might be able to make a bob or two between us there, mate, what with the old man on the pilot boat as well.' Nat asked what he meant, but Terry wouldn't be drawn, he just tapped the side of his nose and winked.

They continued chatting for a while, in which time Nat got the definite impression that the six months in jail, which Terry told him he had recently endured for receiving stolen property, had taught him nothing at all.

Fred Coe padded by as they talked, with his huge beer belly hanging and flapping in front of him like a charwoman shaking the door mat. He winked at Nat as he passed. 'How's your ass?' he quipped, and disappeared into the small dry heat room, laughing his head off.

'Did you see that guts?' Terry grunted in disgust. 'The state some of these old boys let their bodies get into, old Fred there ain't seen his dick for ten years.' Nat laughed, and told Terry about his burnt posterior episode.

'Yeah, old Fred's a real card, but I'll get him for you tonight.' Terry replied with a grin. 'I always pop into the Prince of Wales for a few bevies when I leave here, so does Fred. He thinks he can play spoof, but I usually come out of the pub legless with as much money as I went in with. He'll never learn.

By the way, you like a drink, fancy coming with me?'

'No thanks, mate,' came the reply. 'I'm on the other side of the bar tonight. Promised the old man. Got to do something to earn my keep.'

Terry shrugged and stood up, 'Please yourself, I need some more steam,' and walked over to the steam room. He tugged open the warped door and was immediately engulfed by the steam from the cauldron within. Before entering, he turned to Nat, 'Don't forget,' he said, tapping his nose, 'I shall be in touch.'

Shortly afterwards Nat decided he had had enough heat for one day. He swam around in the cold plunge for five minutes to close his pores, then towelled himself vigorously before jumping on the scales in the rest room.

He was surprised, there was not an ounce of fat on him, but he had shed five pounds.

Once outside in the fresh air he felt marvellous and made a mental note to attend the Turkish baths regularly. As he made his way back to the van, the thought did occur to him that it might be prudent to stay clear of the likes of Terry Littlejohn. But there again, Nat Asnett had never been accused of being a prudent man.

Thirteen

OLD JESUS

Julie Murchison was in her element. With the odd deft flick of the paddle, she had drifted through the grounds of the Berkeley Hunt kennels and splashed water at the two hound dog puppies which had followed her progress from the bank with noisy curiosity. On her left now was the castle meadow. No willows grew on this section of the bank, and she lay back in the canoe, hands behind her head, and drank in the view of the huge open area of green, with its magnificent backcloth of castle. That Norman masterpiece with its huge terraces and corkscrew chimneys, lying there so naturally as to have been placed there by the hand of God.

With two swift strokes of the paddle she shot under a picturesque little bridge used mainly by cattle, and was then in the part of the river generally regarded by the children of the area as their own private swimming hole. A series of wild shrieks and splashes told her that at least two kids were playing truant that day.

The river widened at this point. One part of the bank was shored up with wooden pilings. This was the small children's area, very shallow with a hard bottom, ideal for the non-swimmers. This part was terminated by the 'cow's drink'. Here the bank was cut away to form a ramp which allowed the cows to drink. The cowpats were numerous, but mattered not at all. These were country kids, the pats just added a naturalness to it all.

On the far side of the cow's drink was the famous gully. This was where the older children loved to show off their swimming prowess.

Julie remembered the gully very well indeed. It was etched

135

into her memory as one of the most exciting days of her childhood. Regardless of how well a child could swim, they had not arrived, as far as their contemporaries were concerned, until they had swum the gully. Ceremoniously escorted by two older boys, the would-be swimmer, wide-eyed with apprehension, would swim across that deep, thirty-five foot psychological barrier, then, delirious with delight, would run all the way home to tell their mum the world-shattering news. Julie remembered the day well. Such is the wonderful world of a child.

She smiled at the two young boys on the bank as she paddled through the gully. They smiled back sheepishly. Their exuberance now replaced by feelings of guilt, brought on no doubt by the appearance of this adult who made them think of another adult, namely their teacher.

Beyond the swimming hole the river ran through a small wood. The two boys silently watched the canoe until it disappeared amongst the trees. Then, with a couple of wild whoops, somersaulted back into the gully.

Jason Bartholomew Selby scrutinised the trimmed-down goose feather float intently as it bobbed on the sun- dappled water.

His piercing blue eyes blazed with excitement as the float suddenly quivered, then vanished beneath the surface. A quick strike with the homemade rod immediately told him he had not hooked the quarry he was seeking. A grunt of disgust escaped his lips as he landed a six-ounce flounder.

With an expert flick, he disgorged the hook from the lucky flat fish and threw it back. His intended victim was a pike, which he knew patrolled a territory from the old flour mill down to the mill race at Brown's mill, a distance of about a mile and a half. Having first spotted it some years before in a shallow sidewater, he had conservatively estimated its weight at between twelve and fourteen pounds. Over the years he had hooked it twice, both occasions resulting in a furious fight with Jason the loser each time. It had now become a very personal duel which Jason intended to win eventually. He fixed another live minnow to his hook and cast again. He was aware of the sun on the back of his neck and felt happy because of it. The fine weather was a great tonic after the grim winter. When you lived in a timber and galvanised shack in the middle of a wood the weather was of paramount importance.

Old Jesus, as he was universally known in his own and neighbouring counties, had known a strange and contrasting life, knowing both ecstasy and tragedy.

As he gazed at the float, the inevitable thoughts began drifting through his mind for the millionth time.

His birth, in 1879, had been to one of the most wealthy and influential landowning families in the county. He had been blessed with a brilliant mind and the tenacity to take full advantage of it. At the age of eleven his father sent him to Gloucester's prestigious King's School, where his academic supremacy regularly caused ripples of comment from the learned masters of an establishment where a high degree of excellence was the norm.

He emerged from King's a mature and totally confident eighteen-year-old, with full honours. Going on to Oxford had been a mere formality, and he had loved every minute of his time there. The easy-going way of life had been a total contrast to the strict discipline he had always known at home. Now there was no holding him.

He had always loved the water, and won his Oxford blue for rowing. Academically he also forged ahead, taking honours in science, while still finding time to take outside courses in advanced agriculture. After university, his father had allowed him to put his knowledge to the test by placing him in sole charge of his farming and forestry empire. Jason had worked hard and had been rewarded by seeing the estate grow with even more wealth and influence. The world was now his oyster, a world of grace and privilege unknown at this time anywhere else in the world, and jealously guarded by the British nobility.

He had never been a man for the ladies. Work and self-betterment had always taken predominance with him, even when the yells and taunts of 'Swot!' had echoed around his ears at college. But that chaste period of his life had ended for him early in the year 1914, when he had met Joanna Farraway.

He had accepted an invitation to the Berkeley Hunt Ball, which was to be held at the castle. During the riotous evening of merriment, he had met Joanna. It was love at first sight for Jason, and after a few weeks his love was reciprocated by this beautiful woman. She was twenty-five and the only daughter of Elton Farraway, the wealthy Bristol shipping magnate. Life hit a dizzy peak for Jason at that time, and he thought it would last forever.

On the August Bank Holiday of that year the Great War began and, as with millions of people around the world, the good times ceased for Jason.

Always a God-fearing Christian man, he resisted the local fervour to join up, realising he could never bring himself to kill another human being. Then, after almost a year of war, with most of the eligible men already at the front, he received that terrible letter.

It contained a single white feather, the symbol of cowardice. Although the letter was anonymous, the familiar scent lingering on the envelope told him it was from Joanna.

His world fell apart that morning. Without a word to anyone, he enlisted the same day, and after several weeks of hell called basic training, found himself in France as a member of the newly formed machine gun corps. His education and social background meant an automatic commission. So Second Lieutenant Selby began presiding over his part of the greatest slaughter the world had ever known.

He was a brave and honourable man and as officer in charge of his machine gun platoon, unlike some officers of the day, made the well-being of his men his main concern, and they loved him for it. As the machine gun corps, they had the dubious advantage of being issued with bicycles. This was to enable them to quickly transport themselves and the heavy machine gun to any part of the front that was being hard-pressed. It also meant that they saw more than their fair share of action.

The months rolled away. Months of filth and agony, seeing

his small bunch of charges being killed and maimed one by one, writing to their next of kin and knowing what devastation that slip of paper would cause at the end of its journey. To help keep his sanity, Jason began writing poetry during the quieter periods. Some reflected the horrors of war that surrounded him.

But more often, they concerned the animals and birds of his beloved home country. Others were sad, because his astute mind realised that the lovely unrushed way of life at home before the war could never be quite the same again. Even people's attitudes to each other would be changed by this gargantuan conflict. His mind began to suffer.

Things finally became too much for him during the terrible fighting on the Somme. A shell landed on his section and wiped it out to a man. Jason miraculously escaped with a minor flesh wound. As his head cleared he saw the German infantry charging his position over open ground, not five hundred yards away. For the first time he would have to man the gun himself.

Up until then, as officer in charge, he would issue range instructions and general orders to his non-commissioned officers and men. But now his men were dead. The moment he had always dreaded had arrived. He would have to do the killing himself.

With dread in his heart, he pulled the two dead bodies of his men away from the gun, which had been blown off its tripod. The grey-clad German troops were now less than three hundred yards away, firing as they ran. He heaved the heavy Vickers back into position and like a man in a dream, commenced firing. He watched those thirty mothers' sons fall away like corn before the scythe. They were gone, and he had been their executioner.

Unaware of where he was, he continued firing even after the attack had broken up. The water-cooled machine gun finally became red-hot and jammed. When they found him he was still sitting behind the gun, horror filled eyes staring straight ahead, trigger still depressed by hands that gripped the traversing handles with such force that his knuckles glowed white. It was a complete breakdown, from which he would never fully recover.

After a period in the military hospital he seemed normal enough. Words of congratulations and promises of a medal for his heroic stand came from his commanding officer, but fell on deaf ears. It was simply the end of the road for Jason. As far as he was concerned, the war was over.

He refused to return to the front. For weeks he ignored the threats and persuasions of his superiors. His only reply was 'Shoot me if you wish.' Had he been a private soldier that is exactly what they would have done, but he was an officer with a hitherto exemplary record.

After taking into account his previous good record and also the state of his mind, they finally sent him home with that heartless tag, L.M.F. (lack of moral fibre) attached to him. The tag meant disgrace. He returned home to a different world from which he had left seemingly a century ago. His mother had died whilst he had been away and he met a stony silence from his father, who like many of his kind, carried the banner for King and Country but had never had to fire a shot in anger in their lives.

Joanna, who had sent the white feather under duress from her family, wanted to see Jason but was forbidden by her father ever to see him again. In such a family at that time, to go against her father's wishes was unthinkable. Six months later she married a military man who was acceptable to the family. He was the son of a Cornish tin mine owner. Second Lieutenant Joshua Murchison.

The oppressive, miserable atmosphere, plus the news of Joanna's marriage, was the last straw for Jason. One fine morning he packed a few essentials in his military webbing packs and took to the road. For a month he walked the back roads and byways of Gloucestershire and the surrounding counties, thinking about nothing at all. He had taken what cash he had with him and when that began to run out, he forced himself to approach local farmers for casual work. The farmers, although sceptical at first, found him to be a hard worker with an enormous knowledge of agriculture. Because of the war there was a critical shortage of manpower and word soon got around the farming communities regarding Jason's abilities. Work was assured when and where it suited him.

It was a fine spring and after a few weeks Jason began to feel the therapeutic benefits of his new life. His ramblings gave him the opportunity to study and appreciate the abundant wildlife which he loved; which in turn prompted him to continue writing his poetry.

He began using the public libraries on his travels and read avidly on subjects which always intrigued him. He had long held strong convictions on deep subjects like reincarnation, time, and the meaning of life. He developed theories on these subjects which, had he expressed them to the locals, would probably have got him committed to an institution for the mentally insane.

All in all, Jason Bartholomew Selby had found his niche in life, and was re-finding his happiness.

After two years of this life, he decided to make some sort of base in which to carry on his writing and studying between his travels. A kindly farmer for whom he had worked on numerous occasions allowed him to convert a disused cowshed on the edge of a small wood near Brown's Mill. It was isolated enough to suit him, and the town of Berkeley was close enough for provisions.

He accumulated a few permanent essentials: bed, oil stove, oil lanterns and such like, which although primitive, now seemed like the lap of luxury to Jason.

From that day forth, that was his life. Going on his walkabouts when the mood and the weather suited him. Studying and reading until he was on a par with probably any professor in the land. His gifts were many.

Eminent people had been known to look Old Jesus up for services ranging from curing their warts, to water divining during droughts. Yes, Old Jesus was quite a famous character. But at this moment in time he was concentrating on just one thing; catching that elusive pike.

Thoughts were also clouding Julie Murchison's mind as she

drifted through the beech wood.

With her hand idly dragging in the water, she wondered about her father. Why was he such an unfeeling man? He had hardly bothered to speak to her since her return home. He was more or less the same with her mother. He had been offhand for as long as she could remember, but her mother had confided in her that, in recent months, he had become downright rude to everyone. In his position as local magistrate and manager of the prestigious Berkeley estate, it was becoming very noticeable and tongues were beginning to wag. Julie suspected that the worry of it was partly responsible for her mother's periodic bouts of ill-health.

Then there were the boys. She knew there was an intense rivalry between them, and that they were both very fond of her. She liked Nat, but could sense the undertones of violence and insecurity just beneath the surface.

With Yanto it was different. Although she had never encouraged him in any way, she felt easy with him and enjoyed his company. He had an enormous sexual presence and a confidence in himself which indicated a bright future when he eventually settled down. Yes, she wanted to see more of Yanto, but did not wish to cause trouble by seeming to favour one of them.

She cleared her mind of such thoughts, and with a sigh, lay back in the canoe and watched the sun flicker through the branches above her.

She heard a plop in the water near the right-hand bank. She glanced over and saw the circle of ripples where the water rat had dived. A flash of colours in the water suddenly caught her eye. She froze in alarm and realised why the water rat had dived. The snake glided serenely from under the partly submerged bush, with myriad colours reflecting from its twenty-four inches of length as it zigzagged through the shimmering water.

Julie had had a terror of snakes since that day with Aunt Polly in America. Aunt Polly had taken the young Julie on a camping holiday to Lake Tahoe in the neighbouring state of

Nevada. While travelling through the desert they had stopped for a picnic lunch among some rocks which gave a semblance of shade. Julie had wanted to explore among the rocks, so Aunt Polly had toddled along behind, eating ice cream off a large dinner plate as she walked.

Suddenly, as she had paused to look into a small cave, a terrible whirring rattle rang through the still air as the rattlesnake, which she had almost stood on, brought its evil head back, ready to strike.

The petrified girl stood there gazing in horror at the deadly reptile in front of her.

Aunt Polly had saved her life that day. With a reflex action which would have surprised an athlete, she hurled the plate of ice cream at the snake. The rattler's strike was thwarted as the plate smashed against the rock, throwing fragments of china around its flat head. Aunt Polly grabbed the still-frozen girl and pulled her away. Julie had suffered nightmares for weeks after, and had abominated snakes ever since.

Stiff with apprehension, she watched the snake swim diagonally across the river on a course that would take it within six feet of the canoe. It swam with its head jutting out clear of the water, emphasising the silent menace. As it came closer she could clearly see the V on the back of its head and the dark tell-tale zigzag down its back. It was a big adder. She suddenly had horrible visions of it climbing up the paddle which lay in the water.

In a panicky moment she whipped the blade out of the water. The ensuing splash caused the snake to notice the canoe for the first time, and to her absolute horror she saw it turn directly towards her. The terrified girl knew instinctively that it was going to attack her.

She lay rigid in the canoe and prayed the thing would pass her by, then almost fainted as she heard it brushing against the side of the craft. There was a moment's silence and she began to think her prayer had been answered. But no: like a vision of evil, the snake's head plus six inches of its length appeared above the freeboard of the canoe.

143

The demonic head looked at the frozen girl with its little black forked tongue flicking in and out, not two feet from her face. Suddenly something snapped inside Julie. It was not a conscious thing. It was as if her nervous system had leapt into life independent of her mind. She screamed like a banshee and whipped the blade of the paddle around in an arc towards the abomination.

Such was the frenzy of her movement that the flimsy craft immediately capsized.

She was now in the grip of sheer panic. Finding herself submerged beneath the boat would not normally have alarmed her. Many times when canoeing in America she had deliberately turned the craft over, then by using the paddle as a lever had expertly flicked herself upright again, in what was termed an Eskimo roll.

But now it was different. She had lost her paddle as she lunged at the snake, and the more she thrashed around under the canoe the more she became tangled in the wet liner around her waist. Her legs were also jammed well forward in the slim craft, making it very difficult for her to extricate herself. On top of this, her tortured mind expected to feel the stinging bite of the adder any second.

Julie was in fear for her life.

The combined effects of the warm sun and the reflections on the water around his float was having a hypnotic effect on Old Jesus. It was warm. It had to be warm for him to discard his shin-length old mac, which he had done half an hour before.

His raggedy twelve-inch grey beard bobbed up and down his chest as he slowly nodded off. Visions of a young Joanna, smiling and standing precariously in a punt drifted through his languid mind. They were at Henley Regatta on that fateful August Bank Holiday in 1914, their last truly happy time together. She screamed excitedly as the punt threatened to capsize. Then she screamed again, but it wasn't Joanna screaming.

Another scream pierced his befuddled mind and he was

144

suddenly awake and fully alert.

It had come from the river, not fifty yards from where he sat.

It was not the excited screams of the children in the swimming hole that he had heard earlier. It was a scream of terror, the like of which still haunted him from the war.

The last scream had stopped abruptly. Now all he could hear was a violent splashing in the water.

He leapt to his feet in a fashion which made nonsense of his sixty-eight years. In his plimsoll-clad feet he dashed along the wooded bank, showing a surprising turn of speed as he dodged between the saplings and clumps of brush. He saw the canoe, or rather the bottom of it, through a gap in the trees and by the way it was bobbing and gyrating in the water, there was obviously somebody underneath it. His astute mind calculated the fact that at least half a minute must have elapsed since the screaming had stopped, so whoever was under the canoe must be in real trouble by now.

Without breaking his stride, he half jumped, half plunged into the river from the low bank, and with a couple of wild strokes reached the upturned craft. He was a tall man and was gratified to find he could just touch the bottom at this point, which would give him more leverage to right the canoe.

By dipping himself under the craft he felt for and found the still struggling occupant.

He dug his feet into the muddy bottom and with one hard sustained heave, succeeded in righting the canoe. The half-conscious girl began to retch and cough as, with great difficulty, the old man manhandled her and the swamped canoe towards the bank. Once in the shallower water he grasped the limp girl around the waist and freed her from the clinging wet liner. Then, after words of encouragement from him, she limply kicked her legs free from the cockpit and clung grimly to his neck, still gasping.

Jason found he was too exhausted to push the girl out of the water and onto the bank, so while still chest-deep in the water, he began tapping her cheek and talking to her. As he did so he gently removed the long shards of golden hair that matted her face. For the first time he realised how beautiful she was. A strange sensation swept over him as he looked at her.

He had never seen her before, he was sure of that. But there was something so familiar, so close about her, and although it was ridiculous in their present situation, it just seemed so right to be holding her like this. He felt mystified. Suddenly she became fully coherent and began looking around wildly.

'Where's the snake?' she gasped, clinging to him desperately, almost pulling him under the water.

'What snake?' he demanded.

Between sharp intakes of breath, she told him about the big adder and the subsequent capsizing. He looked around. 'Well, it's gone now, my dear,' he said reassuringly. 'They are usually more afraid of us than we are of them. Look, you hold on to this,' he indicated to a tree root sticking out of the bank, 'then I can get out and pull you out as well. We can't stay here all day,' he laughed, trying to quieten the still frightened girl.

As she did as instructed, the old man used the exposed tree roots as a ladder and hauled himself out.

He then reached down, grabbed her hand and, after some slipping and sliding, managed to haul her out on to the grass. Jason then sat her down on a tree stump and gently pushed her head between her knees a few times until she indicated that she was fully recovered.

It was then that she really looked at her rescuer for the first time. 'I know you,' she said, remembering the times during her childhood when the boys used to catcall after the familiar tramp as he had passed them by. He would always turn and smile, then wave back at them good-naturedly. 'You're Old Jesus, aren't you?' she said, then immediately regretted it. 'Oh, I am sorry,' she gushed, 'but that's the only name I knew you by. Please forgive me.'

His watery blue eyes twinkled and his leather brown face split into a grin. 'Nothing to forgive, my child,' he said, 'to be associated, if only by name, to our Lord, can only be a compliment.

As she smiled back he noticed she began to shiver. He

146

became concerned that she may be experiencing some delayed shock. 'Come along,' he commanded, 'my place is just along by the edge of the wood. You can dry off there and I think a nice cup of tea will do you the world of good. Come along,' he said again, and extended his hand. To her own surprise, she accepted his hand and followed him through the wood like an obedient child. She felt easy in his presence and liked him immediately, and not only because he had probably just saved her life. There was an aura of good about the man that calmed her.

She tried not to look too surprised as they approached the converted cowshed. It wasn't much bigger than their garage at home. Then she felt sad that such a person should live like this. It was as if the old man had read her thoughts. 'I know it doesn't look much,' he said to her smiling again, 'but I've been very happy here.'

She followed him into the shack after treading carefully so as not to step on the profusion of flowers which lay thick and colourful right up to the front door. It was then she received her second surprise, and for the totally opposite reason. The interior of the shack was lovely.

Over the years Jason had converted his dwelling into an ideal according to his way of life. The upright timber and galvanised walls were now clad with tongue and groove matchboard, which was varnished and polished until they shone. The partitioned bedroom section had walls hung with hessian, so expertly and lovingly fitted as to have graced the drawing room of a stately home. The original concrete floor was sealed with roofing felt, but covered almost wall to wall by a magnificent Indian carpet which, Jason explained, had been given to him by a grateful farmer's wife after he had given up many evenings to successfully tutor her son through his eleven plus.

Then there were the books. Julie had never seen so many books. One complete wall was shelved from floor to ceiling and packed with volumes. A large, ancient writing desk stood in the recess to one side of the wall of books, with a highly polished ornate brass oil lamp standing on top of it reflecting the sunlight like burnished gold.

She stood there looking around in fascination, until Jason hustled her towards the blacked and polished wood-burning stove situated in the kitchen alcove. The stove was alight even in this warm weather. The old man kept it going continually in order to make tea and warm up his food. It helped to conserve the previous fuel oil, and there was, after all, plenty of wood around here.

As she warmed herself, Jason re-appeared with a towel and a woman's housecoat. Although old-fashioned, the housecoat was washed and pressed.

She was surprised to see a female garment in such a male-orientated environment, but said nothing.

He indicated to the bedroom section. 'Dry yourself and slip that on while I make some tea,' he instructed, and again she obeyed him instantly. She pulled the hessian curtain across the doorway and shed her soaked clothes. After towelling dry, she slipped on the old housecoat and smiled at herself in the full-length free-standing mirror. Although old-fashioned, she realised it must have been very expensive in its day. The inserts of silk brocade and real Maltese lace were hand-sewn, and must have belonged originally to a lady of substance.

As she turned to go back into the living quarters, she noticed something hanging on the wall over the head of the bed. It was a picture frame containing a poem. The frame was crude and obviously homemade, but the poem was written in beautiful broad pen script. It was simply entitled 'Joanna', and as Julie read it she felt strangely moved.

Country lass with golden hair
Down-soft skin, complexion fair
Take my love, this heart of mine,
Be my maid, my Columbine.

Flowers bow as you pass by,
Jealous is the butterfly,
Your golden smile that lights my day

Is warming, as the month of May.

It tears my heart to know the truth,
You are the memory of my youth.
Of Halcyon days that oft-times pass,
And take you with them, country lass.

Jason was pouring the boiling water into his billy can-cum-teapot as she returned to the living quarters. He turned and smiled at her. Then, as he looked at her standing there in the old housecoat, his smile slowly turned to a look of sheer perplexity. She noticed the change in his expression and asked him if anything was wrong.

'No, no, my dear,' he said hurriedly, as he placed the teapot on the stove to brew. 'It's just that for a second I thought I had shot back in time about thirty-odd years.'

'How was that?' she asked, looking slightly mystified.

'Well, you do look remarkably like someone who was very dear to me in the past.'

'Was it the lady who owned this?' she said with a mischievous smile, and plucked at the lapel of the old housecoat. She suddenly realised she was being rather forward and apologised.

'Not at all, my dear,' he replied with a sheepish grin, 'as a matter of fact it was. Must have been rather obvious, I suppose. Anyway,' he continued, dismissing the subject with a wave of his hand, 'come and sit down and have some tea. I mustn't bore you with an old man's memories.'

She declined the biscuits he offered her, but gratefully accepted the mug of hot sweet tea. They began talking, and as they did so, Julie found him more and more fascinating, and wondered how he could have become a tramp and virtual recluse.

'I noticed that lovely poem above your bed while I was changing,' she said. 'Did you write it yourself?'

'Yes,' he replied, 'I have always loved poetry. I find writing it relaxes me and helps protect me from the harsh realities of life.'

'My mother's name is Joanna,' she remarked casually.

'Lovely name,' he said with a smile, and took a sip of tea. 'Talking of names, I don't know your name, do I? I can't say I remember seeing you before. Do you live around her?'

'Well, I have been living in the United States since just before the war, and I've only just returned. My name is Julie Murchison and I live at Parklands, the big house opposite The Salvation Inn at Ham.'

She went on to say how her parents would want to thank him personally for what he had done for her, but he wasn't listening.

The sudden knowledge that he had just saved his lost love's child, penetrated his brain and exploded. Of course, what a fool, now he knew why she had seemed so familiar to him. He found himself thanking God that he had been in a position to save her. The thought of the devastation that the loss of such a girl as this would have had on the woman he still loved from afar filled him with dread.

She had stopped talking and was looking at him with concern. 'Are you sure you are all right, Mr Selby? You've gone rather pale.'

He pulled his thoughts together, patted her hand, and smiled. 'Of course, my child. Probably too much sun on the riverbank today.'

Julie looked towards her clothes which were still steaming around the old stove. 'Maybe I should go,' she said, 'and give you a chance to rest.'

'Nonsense,' he gushed. 'I get very little chance to talk to anyone, especially since Mr Venables died last year. He was the farmer who allowed me to set up home here. A real Christian gentleman. Would you believe, when he died he left this shack and the plot of land to me in his will, God rest his soul.'

A tear appeared in the old man's eye. 'Anyway,' he said, as he brushed the tears away with a little embarrassment, 'you must stay. Have some more tea, your clothes will soon be dry.' She did so, and they continued to talk. Then suddenly Julie shivered violently.

The old man took her hand and asked her what was wrong. She looked at him with fear in her eyes.

'I have just realised, Mr Selby,' she said, 'if it wasn't for you then, like your friend the farmer, I would probably be dead now, in a perpetual darkness.' She shivered again. 'I've always been terrified at the thought of dying.'

He held her hand tightly and looked at her with a serious face. 'Now listen to what I am about to say to you and remember it,' he said. She looked into his eyes and listened. 'Never, never be afraid of death,' he said quietly. 'In your case it is probably a long time away anyway, but never be afraid of it. When you do eventually die, there will be no blackness. You will simply enter a state of bliss and serenity, compared to which life on this planet is nothing but penal servitude. Unfortunately, this will not last. The next thing you know, you will be back at your mother's breast again. Back to penal servitude.'

'You're talking about reincarnation,' she said in an awed voice. 'Do you really believe in all that?'

'Implicitly,' he replied, 'like the flowers in the field and the leaves on the trees, we are condemned to return, time after time after time.'

The total conviction in his voice excited Julie and her fascination for the old man increased in leaps and bounds, and she knew she was talking to no ordinary man.

She pumped him for more information. 'Do we return to our original country each time?' she demanded. He looked at her steadily again.

'Logic and my own theorising indicates that we return to the country of our last incarnation, provided we died in that country. Although, it could be in the past or in the future, because time is not as it may appear, but that is an even deeper subject. Suffice to say, we shall probably return to our own countries. I know it instinctively, but I have not as yet proved the link to my own satisfaction. But I shall.'

'You should be out there lecturing to the people,' she said, with the same note of awe in her voice, 'not just sat here enlightening me.'

'Why, my child, to be chided and rebuked and called a crank by the "when you're dead, you're dead" brigade? These people have a total lack of imagination, and are incapable of profound thought.'

'Well, there are plenty of sensible people out there as well,' she said, with a hint of annoyance, 'intelligent people who would appreciate your views.'

'You are probably right, my dear,' Jason agreed resignedly, 'but I fear I've been away from people too long to change now. But anyone who wants to is welcome to read my manuscripts.' He waved his hands towards the reams of handwritten documents stacked on the wall shelves along with the books.

'Would you mind if I called periodically and read some of your work?' Julie asked.

Jason's eyes shone with delight. 'Nothing would please me more,' he said, and she could see that he meant it. She looked at the old cuckoo clock on the wall above his desk, and was surprised to see it was now 5.30.

'Goodness, I must rush,' she said, as she grabbed her clothes which were now quite dry. 'I asked my father's man to pick me up by the bridge at 5.30. He'll be jumping up and down by now.'

Jason was standing by the front door when she came out. 'You will call on me again, won't you?' There was a hint of pleading in his voice.

'I certainly shall,' she replied, and stood looking at him a little awkwardly. 'I don't know how to thank you for what you have done for me. I dread to think what would have happened if you hadn't been there.'

'The fact that I was there is reward enough for me,' he said with a smile.

She stood on tiptoe and kissed him on the cheek. 'See you soon,' she said, and ran off towards the bank. She suddenly stopped fifty yards from him and turned. 'Could you beach my canoe for me, Mr Selby? I'll send Barney to pick it up tomorrow.' He nodded and smiled. She waved and ran on.

He watched her until she disappeared around the edge of the wood. 'So that's Joanna's daughter,' he said to himself. 'She would have been mine but for that filthy war.' He experienced feelings of regret and a little bitterness for the first time in many years. He had deliberately avoided meeting Joanna all these years, and he didn't really know why. Was it shame or feelings of inadequacy? He didn't know. All he knew was that he had been unable to face her, which was crazy when he considered the fact that it was her white feather that had started it all in the first place.

On one occasion during the Second World War, he had been standing by the sandbag pillbox on the castle walk, waiting for the rag and bone man. He had had a couple of successful days rabbiting and the skins were worth three pence each to the rag and bone merchant. He saw the merchant coming down High Street hill out of Berkeley with his horse and cart. So intently was he watching him approach and with the clip-clop of the approaching hooves he failed to hear the clip-clop of another set of hooves coming in the opposite direction from Ham.

Joanna pulled up in her pony and trap at the same time as the rag and bone man. She had called him from across the road. When he saw her so close for the first time since going to war, he had panicked and run back across the castle meadow, watched by a sad-faced Joanna and an irate rag and bone man. It was only when he had reached the shack that he realised he still had the bag full of rabbit skins, plus two freshly killed rabbits – one down each trouser leg.

Now, especially after talking to Julie, he began to realise how foolish he had been and made a resolution to speak to Joanna the next time he saw her.

Later that evening, Julie waited for her father to go out before going upstairs for her usual pre-bedtime chat with her mother.

Joanna had magnificent golden hair which, although now streaked with silver, was still a sight to behold. The hair was long, to well below her shoulders, and despite chides and pleas from her daughter, Joanna insisted on wearing it as a huge bun during the day. Julie sat her mother down at the dressing table and began releasing her hair from the restrictive bun. As she brushed it out she began telling her about the events of the afternoon in great detail. At first Joanna was shocked to hear about her daughter's brush with death, but Julie went on to tell her about the strange man who had helped her and then taken her home for tea and dried her out. She left nothing out. She chatted on about Jason's beautiful shack, his books and how impressed she had been just talking to him. Then there was the poem over his bed, and the old housecoat.

'He made me promise to call on him again,' she said finally, 'and I shall.' Joanna had been strangely quiet afterwards, and Julie had put it down to tiredness. Shortly afterwards she had kissed her mother goodnight and retired to her own room.

Had she looked in a minute later, she would have seen her mother, shoulders shaking and quietly weeping.

Fourteen

BACK TO WORK

Nat Asnett was feeling good. His transition back to life on the tugs was progressing smoothly. On the Monday morning, he had joined his old tug, the *Resolution*, which he found had been converted from steam to diesel engines in his absence.

The great throbbing diesels were cleaner, easier to work on, and more efficient, but he found they lacked the charisma and the excitement of the old steam engines which he remembered with affection. Sam Torrence was the skipper now, and Nat liked him from the start. He was a short, stocky man of forty-eight, with a mane of red hair that warned of a terrible temper, and gave a ring of truth to the stories Nat had heard about him not suffering fools gladly. Sam seemed to take to Nat also.

They were both ex-Royal Navy, with Sam doing his bit as a stoker with the Grand Fleet during the First War, and had seen action at the Battle of Jutland. 'I was in when they were needing 'em, not feeding 'em,' he said to Nat with a laugh, during their first conversation.

The work was more or less the same as Nat remembered. Picking up the silt barges was a never- ending chore, because it was only the constant work of the dredgers that kept Sharpness viable as an inland port. Then there were the regular trips up the canal to Gloucester Docks, with cereal and timber barges which Nat remembered as the most boring part of the job.

It was on the Wednesday of his second week that the *Resolution* went out into the estuary for her first trip downriver since Nat had joined her.

A larger than average steamer bound for Sharpness had been told to lighten her load at Avonmouth before proceeding. To navigate the narrow deep water corridor, which snaked between the sandbanks that abounded further upstream, was difficult enough at the best of times, but an overloaded ship could make it downright hazardous.

The ship's deck cargo had been offloaded into lighters, and the *Resolution* had been ordered to Avonmouth to bring them on up to Sharpness. This was the tug work that Nat liked best.

The normal working crew of the *Resolution*, when engaged on canal and dock duties, was three. Sam, Nat, and Sam's only son, Terry, who was seventeen years old and a promising light-middleweight with the Berkeley Boxing Club. He was also the apple of Sam's eye. When on river duty, a fourth member was called for, so prior to their departure, Otis Summers, or Hairpin as he was known in dockland, came aboard. Hairpin was a tall, skinny, gangling man of fifty, and had been with the waterways for years. Nat remembered him from his old tug days.

After waiting for high water in the lock, the great dock gates were opened and they moved out into the racing grey waters of the river. As they cleared the dock entrance, it began to drizzle. It was the first rain for some weeks and Nat found it refreshing. He was never at his best in the heat. The drizzle increased to a steady downpour, so he climbed up into the wheelhouse and joined Sam, who was at the wheel with a roll-up hanging from one corner of his mouth.

As the gently throbbing diesels increased to a low constant roar, Sam grunted and pointed to his right. 'There you are, son,' he said, 'a monument to what happens if you try to get into Sharpness without one hundred per cent concentration.' The big ocean-going steamer lay there, deserted and dead. Even with the grey tide sucking and swirling around her, it was obvious she would never be ocean-going again.

The *S.S. Stancliffe* had run aground off the north pier two months before, on April the second, with three thousand tons of logs on board. She had made the fatal mistake of overshooting the narrow entrance to the docks, and when that happened there was no way back against the force of the Severn tide. She was now stuck fast in the shifting sands, with each tide digging her

156

deeper and deeper into her grave.

'She ain't the first ship to come to grief in the estuary, and she won't be the last,' said Sam philosophically.

'Yeah,' Nat grunted, 'I heard about her running aground, but that's the first time I've seen her. I hear there was a fair bit of looting going on when she first bought it, wasn't there?'

'Looting,' laughed Sam, 'I'll say there was looting. The crew deserted her almost immediately, and the locals were going out to her in anything that floated. Anything that wasn't welded to her got nicked.' He paused, grinning at the memory. 'The compass, all the fittings went,' Sam said, 'even the bloody chart table walked. Christ knows how they got the table out, it was built in when they built the ship. They must have cut the bugger in half. Anyway, nobody around here will be cold next winter, everybody local has got at least one of them logs hidden in the back yard.'

'Well, we are all rogues given half a chance,' grunted Nat.

'Some more than others,' growled Sam. 'Them bloody Littlejohn brothers got the lion's share. I saw 'em out there with old Reg Littlejohn's boat meself. Bad lot, them two buggers.'

Nat grinned to himself as he remembered Terry Littlejohn's crafty nose-tapping at the Turkish baths, and wondered when he would hear from them.

As the *Resolution* pulled out into mid-stream, the rain stopped and the sun came out again, transforming the grey scene into a colourful sun dappled seascape.

A huge bow wave developed as Sam turned on the power, and the *Resolution* dug her nose into the incoming tide.

Yanto stood in the cake shop in Berkeley Square and breathed the delicious aroma of fresh-baked bread and cakes, which wafted through from the bakehouse at the back.

He decided there and then that no other smell in the world could compare with this. It was Monday morning, the sun was shining and he was between ships, so he had decided to take a trip into Berkeley to pick up his watch from Merryfields Watch Repair, where it had been for some time. His mother had asked him to pick up a bag of doughnuts while he was in town, and he was doing just that.

'Gangway, please.' The deep voice came from the back of the shop. Yanto and the two ladies in front of him at the counter looked up and saw the familiar boiler-suited figures of Terry Gafferty and his mate Solly Newport coming through with their usual burden from the back.

All three squeezed tightly against the counter to allow maximum freeway for the two men and the four buckets of raw excrement which they had just collected from the shop's outside privy. The delicious aroma in the shop changed dramatically for a few seconds, but apart from a quick pinch of the nose by the two ladies, no further notice was taken. Such a sight would probably have caused a health and hygiene man of later generations to faint, but with no running water in the town and no back entrances to many of the premises in the square, such sights were commonplace. But not for much longer.

In the near future, a well-known MP named Nye Bevan, would condescend to cross the water from his Welsh constituency to officiate at the opening of the town's first waterworks. Thus, by pressing a switch, bringing Berkeley into the twentieth century.

Yanto collected his doughnuts and wandered out into the sunlit market place. He spotted Old Jesus sitting on the town hall seat looking surprisingly smart. He was wearing a quaintly old-fashioned, but obviously once expensive, tweed country suit. His usually unruly mop of hair was slicked down with brilliantine and shone in the morning sun.

The old man smiled as Yanto sat down beside him. 'Going to a wedding, old mate?' Yanto grinned and pointed to the large daffodil pinned to the old man's lapel.

'No,' he replied, 'You are looking at a new me,' and left it at that.

Yanto leaned back in the ancient seat and allowed the morning sun to bathe his face. He wondered what had come over the old tramp.

'You know a bit about fishing, don't you?' Jason said

suddenly.

'A bit.'

Jason went on to tell him about his unsuccessful battles with the big pike. 'Hooked the devil twice,' the old man continued, 'what am I doing wrong?'

'What hook you using?' Yanto spoke without opening his eyes.

'Number eight.'

'That's what you are doing wrong,' said Yanto, eyes still closed, 'you need a Jardine snap.'

'Never heard of it,' Jason replied.

'That's why you have never caught a pike,' Yanto said as he turned and looked at the old man. 'A Jardine snap is like a miniature grappling iron, with three hooks. Put a live two to three-inch roach on. Best way is to jam just one of your hooks under the roach's bottom jaw, then when you pull your line in it looks as though the fish is swimming, to a pike it would anyway. Once he gets that lot down him he'll never get off,' Yanto said in conclusion.

'Sounds expensive to me,' the old man grunted.

'Well, tie three number eights back to back and it's the same thing roughly. Use rabbit snare wire to tie 'em together. You got plenty of that, ain't you?' the last sentence was accompanied by a wide grin.

'Thanks a lot, young 'un,' the old man said enthusiastically. 'I shall certainly try that next time.'

With that he strolled back to his motorcycle, put the doughnuts in the pannier, and went into Merryfields.

Julie Murchison felt both thrilled and proud as she stood in Berkeley High Street, looking up at the newly painted shop front with its brand new sign which said 'New Dawn'.

This was her first morning as a dress shop proprietress. True to her word, Joanna Murchison, who long ago had promised her daughter a shop of her own, had purchased the lease of Shoreland's ladies' outfitters. Jesse Shoreland, who seemingly had run her dress shop for centuries on the corner of the High

Street and market place, had recently decided to throw in the towel. Being an old friend of Joanna, she had given her first refusal on the lease, which Joanna had accepted immediately. Julie had been over the moon, and threw herself into the task of supervising the decorating and renovation of the ancient premises.

Julie realised that after the drab, deprived war years, women of all ages could hardly wait to kill off austerity and experience the thrill of new clothes again, in spite of the clothing coupons.

She had painted the frontage as brightly as the authorities would allow, and Amy Trout, who had worked for Jesse Shoreland for years, had agreed to stay on under the new boss and help her become established.

Julie knew she was going to be happy with the new shop. It was only eleven o'clock on the morning of her first day and already she had sold two cardigans, a skirt, and two hats.

She was now in the process of selling Tom Hook, the butcher whose shop was just up the High Street, a new dress for his wife's birthday the following day. Using a bit of thoughtful diplomacy, Julie tied a little greetings card to the neatly packed purchase before giving it to the smiling butcher. 'There you are, Mr Hook,' she chirped, 'now all you have to do is write a nice sentiment on it.'

'My word,' grinned the delighted man, 'that will really please my old lady. That's what I call service. I shall see if I can find you a nice little piece of steak!'

She walked to the door with Tom and waved as he walked back to his shop. As she turned in the doorway she noticed a red and silver motorcycle parked outside Merryfields, the watch repairer on the opposite side of the square. She recognised it at once as Yanto's. The sight of the machine made her buoyant spirits rise even more and she wanted to see him.

As she watched he came sauntering out of Merryfields strapping on his wristwatch. He looked up and grinned with delight at her call.

He strolled over the square towards her, looking as handsome as ever in a pair of light beige slacks and one of the newly introduced American T-shirts, which was white and emphasised his deep suntan. 'Crikey,' she giggled, and pretended to swoon as he approached her.

'What's up?' he said, still grinning.

'Well, you look so manly,' she replied. 'Got one of the new T-shirts, I see.'

'Got to keep up with the fashions,' he said. 'I heard about the dress shop. What's it like to be a budding tycoon?'

'So far, so good,' she said with that beautiful melting smile that always enchanted him. 'Why not come in and buy Molly a new dress, she is your girlfriend, isn't she?' The last sentence was almost an accusation and Yanto noticed.

'Oh we knock about a bit, nothing serious though,' he replied nonchalantly. Then in the same breath said, 'fancy a quick one in the B.C. to celebrate your first day in big business?' She hesitated then looked into the shop. There were no customers in and Amy had just returned from the back of the shop after her mid-morning tea break.

She looked back at him and smiled again. 'Why not,' she said with a mock look of grim abandon, 'it is something to celebrate and I wanted to speak to you anyway.'

'Shan't be long, Amy,' she called over her shoulder and the old lady raised her hand in acknowledgement.

'I usually go in the back bar meself,' Yanto grunted, as they negotiated the revolving front doors of the Berkeley Chase Hotel, 'but I suppose you will want to go in the saloon.'

'Of course,' she snapped haughtily, 'I'm not Molly, you know.'

'Molly don't drink,' Yanto replied with a spark of barely concealed annoyance, as they entered the saloon bar. He was surprised by her bitchy remark, but decided to make light of it as he ordered a pint of best bitter for himself and a gin and orange for Julie.

The bar was busy with people in for the weekly auction sale of second-hand furniture and bric-a-brac, which was held in the Berkeley Chase car park, but they found a small table in the corner and sat down. As they relaxed with the drinks, Julie asked him why he was not at work. 'I'm between ships,' he explained, 'so I've got a couple of days on the pool.'

They sat back, not speaking for a while, enjoying the cosy atmosphere of the bar. A great sunbeam blazed through the bar room window, alive with twists of blue tobacco smoke appearing like animated tattoos. The babble of country voices blended into that acceptable decibel reading, where you could talk normally to the person next to you without lowering your voice, yet without fear of being overheard.

'You said in the shop that you wanted to speak to me about something,' Yanto ventured. Julie jerked out of her comfortable malaise.

'Oh yes,' she chirped, 'well, as you said at the shop, this drink we are having now is a little celebration, but I would like to celebrate the opening of the shop properly. I was wondering if we could go out to dinner Saturday evening and celebrate in style. It will be my treat, of course!' Yanto was taken aback, but showed no sign as his self-confidence rose even higher. Already he was becoming aware of the envious faces of the wealthy farmers in the bar as they shot self-conscious glances at his companion. Even so, he was determined to play it in his usual cool manner.

He looked at her with a steady gaze. His wide set ice-blue eyes drinking in that lovely oval face with the pouty lips. 'I would be delighted to take you out to dinner,' he began, 'but I can't pretend to have made a habit of it. In fact, I have never done it before.'

'Then it's time you did,' she smiled mischievously.

'OK, it's a date,' he replied with a shrug, then held up his index finger with a stern expression on his face. 'You realise you'll have to ride in a sidecar, and as for it being your treat, forget it. I've never allowed a woman in my company to pay yet, and I don't intend to start now.'

It sounded like male arrogance, but she realised it was not in this case, and she respected him for it. 'OK,' she said smiling again, 'I accept the second part, but as it's a celebration, I shall ask Daddy if I can borrow the Armstrong, OK?'

'OK,' he agreed, then asked where she fancied going.

'I thought we could eat here. Is that all right with you?' For a second Yanto regretted his insistence on paying the bill. Of course the Berkeley Chase was all right by him, but it was one of the most expensive places to eat in the county.

Then it was agreed. He had to swallow his pride when she insisted on picking him up in the car, but what the hell.

Suddenly she stood up.

'I must fly,' she beamed, 'I suddenly had a vision of Mrs Trout being inundated with desperate customers. See you Saturday at eight. Thanks for the drink,' then she smiled and was gone.

He gave a great sigh, shrugged his shoulders and went back to the bar, to be greeted by a knowing wink from Sid Watkins. He engaged Sid in urgent conversation for five minutes before a deal was struck concerning the coming Saturday night's dinner bill, and Sid's next salmon.

Fifteen

THE COLONEL

Colonel Joshua Murchison was a very worried man. His secret life had always cost him a lot of money and considerable worry, but now things were really coming to a head. He knew he had never been easy to live with, but the strained, worried looks he had been getting from his wife and daughter of late were beginning to get to him. He was also aware that a lot of gossip was circulating regarding his public work, or the lack of it.

His mania for gambling seemed to be getting worse as he grew older. As a serving officer, his weakness had caused him many problems. The late-night card schools had drawn him like a magnet, which, had he been a proficient card player, would have been understandable; but he wasn't.

Even so, the more he lost, the more he sought out the big game. On many occasions he found himself unable to meet his mess bills and only his wife's generosity had saved him from being shamed in front of his fellow officers.

It was worries of this nature, plus the hope that a new environment might help him escape his compulsive gambling urges, that decided him to resign his commission at the end of hostilities. In spite of his brilliant war record, he had left the army under a cloud. He had kept the dark secret of the Irish incident well, but he knew the army had always had suspicions.

Shortly after his return home, he had landed the prestigious job of estate manager to the noble Berkeley family. His military record had helped, but he suspected that being married to one of the wealthiest and most influential women in the county had had more to do with it. Even so, within a year he had met all the right people and was generally regarded as a pillar of society. Yet, during that time he had still been unable to control the dark

165

side of his nature. A gambling crony had introduced him to Nick Sarrazin, a wealthy Anglo-Indian, who ran a very plush illegal gambling house on the outskirts of Bristol. It had a sophisticated air and was frequented by his type of people, and at the first he had won considerable amounts of money. Then, inevitably, the euphoric winning streak had evaporated and he began to lose heavily.

At first Sarrazin had readily allowed him credit. But when the debt had reached into the third thousand, the clamps came on. Then there was Danielle. She was a croupier at Sarrazin's tables, a beautiful olive-skinned Eurasian girl, half his age. He had fallen for her, hook line, and sinker. She had taken an obvious interest in the tall, handsome military man, when Sarrazin had first introduced them and his vanity would not allow him to ignore it. During his initial winning streak, he had rashly set her up in a fashionable apartment in Henleaze and was visiting her twice a week.

Now the crunch had come. He was broke. Sarrazin was threatening to expose his debt and infidelity to his wife and his employers. He was becoming desperate. One afternoon, as he sat moodily in the estate office, he came to a decision. He would have to take up the Irish option.

Not for the first time, his mind ran back to that day in 1941. He had been just a major then. Having been a regular soldier since 1915, he should have been a colonel, but slow promotion had been another result of his peacetime gambling fiascos. He was commanding a rifle company in Ireland at the time, carrying out routine patrols on the border with the Republic. It was a cushy posting after Dunkirk, and they were making the most of it before being posted to North Africa.

On the day in question he had taken a scout car to visit the main force of his men, who were patrolling the border near Newry. On his arrival he was informed that his second-in-command, Second Lieutenant Gorse, had taken two scout cars with five men and gone on ahead.

Having satisfied himself that all was well with the main force, he carried on alone to find Second Lieutenant Gorse.

166

When he arrived half an hour later, he found them brewing up and gratefully accepted a mug of hot tea, which he enjoyed while listening to his second-in-command's day and he had decided to go along with them for a while before returning to HQ.

As the patrol had reached the top of a steep track, two men in civilian clothes were spotted crossing a field about five hundred yards away. The patrol suddenly appearing over the top of the ridge seemed to catch the two men unawares, and they immediately began running towards the edge of a large wood about two hundred yards away. At this point they were about a mile inside British territory, and from the direction that the two men had been walking, plus the fact that there was no official crossing point in the immediate area, it seemed a safe bet that they had crossed from the South illegally.

'Stop them, Lieutenant,' the major snapped. The two men ignored the loudhailer commanding them to stop, and ran on desperately towards the safety of the trees. Both men were carrying what appeared to be a large suitcase, which impaired their progress considerably.

Warning shots were then fired which caused gouts of soft earth to fly up in front of the fleeing men. Suddenly, one of the men, or boy as it turned out, did a very stupid thing which had amazed the major at the time. He produced a handgun and commenced firing at the patrol as he ran. Firing at an army patrol while on open ground had the inevitable fatal consequences. The Brens on the scout cars opened fire simultaneously, cutting them down only yards from cover.

'Silly little bugger,' his anguished sergeant had yelled, as they looked down at the boy, his face now mute in death. 'He ain't got no business firing real guns. Should be home playing cowboys.'

'This is Ireland, Sergeant,' the major said softly. 'He panicked, so let's see what's in the suitcases that is worth dying for.'

Fearing booby traps, the two cases were opened very gingerly. Finally, when revealed, the contents of the two cases

167

had every man present rooted to the spot in amazement. Both cases were crammed with British banknotes. Wads of snowy white, brand new five-pound notes were crammed into every available inch of space within the large cases. One of the soldiers, a bank teller in civilian life, was ordered to make a quick inspection of the money. After five minutes the corporal looked up at the Major.

'Must be somewhere between nine hundred thousand and a million quid here, sir,' said the incredulous man.

Major Murchison's mind was racing. He had heard the reports regarding German efforts to undermine sterling by flooding the UK with high-quality counterfeit bank notes.

Official sources reported that the enemy were using every possible method to funnel the money into Britain.

In the South of Ireland at this time there were many who sympathised with the Nazi cause, and as always, many who were hostile to Britain. The Major recalled the numerous reports and rumours of U-boats being spotted off the coast. There were also suspicions that U-boats were being refuelled secretly by certain elements in the South. If this was the case, what better opportunity could be presented to the enemy for funnelling the illicit currency into Britain?

This money had to be counterfeit. He needed time to think.

He called over his second-in-command, who came smartly to attention. 'In view of the circumstances,' he said quietly, 'I shall take this money straight back to HQ. You take the bodies and meet up with the rest of the company, then report to me on your return to HQ.'

His mind had coolly considered the situation as he drove back alone. The money would be burned as soon as it was confirmed counterfeit, that much was certain.

The reports had stated that only an expert could detect the notes as forgeries. So many thoughts were rushing through his head. Even if Germany was defeated, and that seemed unlikely at the moment, would he survive the war? Even forgeries of this quality would be very handy after the war if he did survive. How much in the pound would the right people pay for such perfect forgeries? Greed finally got the upper hand. He made his decision.

'God damn it,' he grated, 'this is war! Why the hell shouldn't I get something out of it? The armament people are making a fortune without even risking their necks.'

He was driving along the west shore of Strangford Lough, and approaching a place called Killyleagh. At this point the road ran through a small wood.

After looking around and seeing no sign of life, he drove off the road and into the trees. He opened both cases. The money felt so real. The crackling of the notes sounded like music to his ears. What had the corporal said, nine hundred thousand to a million? Working quickly, he took an equal amount from each case, in total approximately one hundred thousand, and stuffed the money into a large webbing backpack. There was a gas cape lying in the scout car. He took the cape along with a trenching shovel which was stowed in a rack on the side of the car, and walked deeper into the wood.

Half an hour later, with the webbing pack securely wrapped in the waterproof cape and buried in a spot known only to him, he coolly drove back to base camp. The money was duly found to be counterfeit and destroyed.

The official enquiry into the incident had finished on a sour note however. The Corporal had duly repeated that, in his opinion, and given the time that he had had to check, the cases had contained between nine hundred thousand and a million pounds sterling. In fact, only eight hundred and fifty thousand or so had been burned. As the major had taken the money back alone, he was also questioned.

The presiding officer had started out by commending him on the action, then started to delve in to the question of the possible discrepancy. He pointed out that in the odd cases where couriers had been caught red-handed they had been carrying one million pounds and that amount appeared to be the norm.

Major Murchison had remained coolly impassive and maintained that if there had been a shortfall, the couriers must have helped themselves. Then, with a suitable hurt expression on his face, said that apart from the details already known to the investigating officer, he could help him no further.

Nothing else was said in public, but the major knew that this being the army, which was well aware of his gambling weaknesses, much more would be said behind closed doors.

He had then put the incident firmly behind him and felt comforted by the knowledge that come what may, it was nice to know the money was there.

After that, it was as though he had led a charmed life. He led his men through the North African campaign without a scratch. Promotion to Lieutenant Colonel came after he distinguished himself at Tobruk. Then, after Alamein, it was on to Italy. They experienced terrible fighting in this new theatre, until one joyous day he received the news that he and his command were being shipped back to England. On their return home, however, it soon became apparent that they were being prepared for the biggest show of all; the invasion of Europe.

But first there was the heaven of home leave.

After that blissful interlude he had kissed Joanna goodbye, quite convinced that he would never see her again. Yet Lady Luck still courted him. When he and his men landed on Sword Beach on that first eventful day, he remained alive and unscathed in a sea of death and destruction. Many of his best men died during those first days in France, including his friend and second-in-command, Lieutenant Gorse, who had been told of his promotion to Major only days before his death. This had saddened him greatly. He and Jimmy Gorse had gone a long way together and Murchison began to yearn for an end to the fighting. But it was far from over. They slogged their way through France, over the Rhine and into Germany. He thought of the money on only the odd occasion; staying alive was his predominant thought at this stage.

Recognition came again in the form of a full colonelcy, and then, during the lulls in the fighting, he would sit back and luxuriate in the thoughts that he had earned his nest egg; albeit an illegal one. Finally it had all ended, and here he was in this impossible predicament. In all this time he had never really expected to recover the money. It had just been a dream, something to keep him going.

Money, however, was the only thing that could save him now, so the dream would have to be implemented. But how?

The Army, he knew, was like an elephant. It never forgot. If he went dashing off to Ireland now, him being a man of stature and substance, it would be noticed. A trip to Ireland so soon after the end of the hostilities could possibly rekindle Army suspicions about him, regarding the shortfall in the recovered money. The risk was unacceptable. It would have to be a clandestine operation. He suddenly had an idea.

Terry Littlejohn was feeling evil and moody as he drove the battered ex-military Bedford QL through the Breadstone Lanes. It was a remote place and it took all his concentration to keep the truck and its trailer full of logs from wandering into one of the deep ditches which flanked both sides of the narrow strip of asphalt. He was on his usual weekly run, delivering logs to the more isolated hamlets around Berkeley. Normally his twin brother Joe would be with him to help hump the big wicker baskets of logs into the cottages, but today Joe had cried off, claiming to have the flu.

'I bet the big, fat, lazy bastard jumped straight into the hammock as soon as I disappeared,' Terry thought savagely. Terry had acquired an ex-navy hammock a couple of weeks before and had rigged it up between two plum trees outside the family home. His obese bother had taken quite a shine to it.

His thoughts were interrupted by lights flashing in his rear view mirror. A large green car was tight up behind him and as he squinted at it the car's lights flashed again. 'You've got no bloody chance, mate,' growled Terry as he waved two fingers out of the truck's open window. The car then began to blow its horn while still flashing its lights. Terry began to get really angry, then a thought suddenly flashed through his mind. It could be a police car and the road fund licence disc that should have been on the windscreen was conspicuous by its absence.

'Don't look like a cop car,' he muttered to himself. 'It ain't a

Wolseley, but you never know nowadays. Better pull in.'

There was a small layby coming up. These laybys were placed at intervals to allow traffic to pass and Terry reluctantly pulled in. The car passed, then to Terry's surprise and not a little consternation, pulled quickly in front of him and stopped with its wheel almost in the ditch.

Terry could now see the make of the car from the chrome badges on the boot lid. It was an Armstrong Siddeley. 'I know that car,' Terry muttered to himself, 'it's that toffee-nosed manager of the estate.' Several times Terry had attempted to buy trees from the Berkeley Estate, until Colonel Murchison had made it very plain that he wanted nothing to do with him.

The car door swung open and the tall, elegant figure of the Colonel emerged. The lean, tough-looking face was unsmiling as he approached the truck.

'Took your time pulling over, didn't you?' he snapped.

'Well there was no layby, was there,' Terry replied, feeling a little uneasy. 'Anyway, why should I?'

'Don't give me any lip, laddie.' The tone was that of a man used to giving orders and being obeyed. 'Anyway, Mr Littlejohn,' the Colonel continued, his tone softening somewhat, 'I have been checking your movements for some time and I would like a word with you, now! Would you mind stepping to the car?'

Terry was perplexed. What on earth could a man of this calibre want with him? His curiosity got the better of him. 'Yeah, OK,' he grunted warily, and jumped out of the truck. The car door closed with a solid clunk and he breathed in the pleasant aroma of grained leather.

'Right,' said the Colonel softly, as he settled himself. 'As I said, I have been making enquiries about you.'

'Why?' interrupted Terry indignantly, then fell silent after a steely glance from the Colonel.

'And it soon became obvious to me that you are basically a crook.' Terry was about to interrupt again, but decided against it. 'But,' the deep, cultured voice went on, 'it also became clear that you could be loyal and be relied on to keep your mouth shut, especially when you were well-paid.'

Terry was becoming interested. The Colonel looked at him again. 'I understand you have access to an ocean-going boat and that you are quite adept at handling it.'

'Our dad got a deep-sea fishing boat, had it for years.'

'Can you navigate?'

'Yeah, Dad taught me when I was a kid. He wanted me to train as a pilot with him.'

The questions were now becoming sharp and businesslike. 'Does he ever arrange organised fishing trips or anything of that nature?'

'No,' said Terry, 'but he used to take a few mates fishing occasionally off Swansea and places like that, but that was a long time before the war.'

A good half minute passed before the Colonel spoke again. 'Well,' he said, 'I have a proposition for you. I want you to take me sea fishing off the east coast of Ireland. Can you do it?'

'No sweat, if you make it worth my while,' Terry said, with a new confidence creeping in. 'But why all the third degree just to go sea fishing?'

The Colonel smiled for the first time. 'Because I want to keep it quiet for personal reasons. It will only be a couple of days, but while we are there I shall want to slip ashore for a few hours to see someone. So make sure you take a tender or a dinghy.'

Terry asked him why they couldn't pull into a local village for the night, but the Colonel said that meant harbour dues and officialdom and he wanted none of that. They would have to sleep on the boat.

'So all I want from you,' the Colonel continued, 'is a safe passage there and back, and your word that not a word will be spoken about the trip once we are back, especially about my going ashore.'

'And what's in it for me?' countered Terry.

'All the trees from the estate as they become available in future, and two hundred pounds for the trip.'

Terry almost fainted. The average weekly wage for a man

173

was about eight pounds a week. Two hundred pounds was a fortune. Murchison noted the shocked face. 'Yes, it is a lot of money, and it will be paid in cash within a week of our return. But let me down, or breathe a word, and I'll break you, financially and physically.'

Terry looked at the grim, handsome face and knew that the Colonel meant every word. He stuck his hand out. 'Sir, you have got a deal.'

The Colonel shook his hand. 'Arrange things for the first week of July. I shall be taking a week's leave then, and I shall contact you shortly as to my exact destination.'

'By the way, sir,' Terry said suddenly, 'you do realise I shall need one other man aboard to look after the engines, cook food and the like. Safety demands it.'

Murchison thought for a second. 'I appreciate that,' he said, 'I will leave that to you. You will have to pay him what you think out of the two hundred, and remember, all he must know is that I am chartering the boat for fishing. You understand?'

Terry nodded. 'Do you have anybody in mind?' the Colonel asked.

Terry grinned. 'I know just the man.'

Sixteen

THE DINNER DATE

At 8.30 on the Saturday evening following the meeting between Colonel Murchison and Terry Littlejohn, Yanto and Julie entered the Berkeley Chase Hotel via the front entrance revolving doors.

The son of Mary Gates felt good. He was wearing his best pre-war dark suit for the first time since returning from the recent unpleasantness. It was gratifying to find that it still fitted him a treat. His white shirt, freshly washed and pressed by his fussing mother, was complemented by a dark blue, red and silver, diagonally striped cricket club tie. The white pyramid-shaped handkerchief which jutted from his breast pocket stood out against the royal blue suit material like a snow-clad Mount Fuji.

But the main reason for his feeling of well-being and confidence was the quick four pints of Dutch courage obtained from a sympathetic and understanding Knocker Nelmes half an hour before Julie honked outside his door.

Mary Gates had wanted to invite Julie in for a sherry. She had bought the bottle specially after her son had told her about the arrangements. But after suitable threats of death and mutilation from her son, she contented herself with a little wave from the front door to the occupant of the big car purring outside. Then, with a nervous wringing of hands, she watched the tail lights disappear down the lane.

Sid Watkins, after prior instructions from Mary Gates, was in the foyer to greet them. Even Sid, used to the coming and going of the blue-blooded country elite, was staggered at the sight of Julie Murchison. 'Jesus Christ,' he muttered under his breath; 'what a doll.'

175

Had she not looked so stunning one could almost have accused her of ostentation at this still austere time. Her obviously new clothes had hidden labels that screamed 'Made in the U.S.A.'

Julie's cornflower blue pencil dress, which ended six inches above her ankles, was classic and unfussy. Such a body needed no trimmings. Walking would obviously have been a problem had not it been for the daring eighteen-inch slit, front centre of the hem. Her blonde hair was stacked in seemingly abandoned fashion on top of her head, emphasising her perfect neck and fine jaw. This, together with the matching blue high-heeled court shoes, gave an overall impression of almost Greek Goddess proportions. She wore no jewellery. To have done so would have been superfluous. Sid ceremoniously removed her short white stole and showed them to an alcove table for two in the elegant oak-panelled dining room.

Half the tables in the room were already occupied by the local well-to-do, and every eye in the place was on them. Yanto smiled around and thanked God for the four pints of cider in him. Without it he would have felt decidedly uncomfortable.

Sid waved away the waiter as he approached, having decided to look after them personally as a favour to Mary Gates.

He handed them a large menu apiece. 'Can I order you an aperitif, folks?' Yanto was sure he detected a quick wink in Sid's eye as he looked first at him and then Julie.

'I'll have a dry white port, please,' Julie smiled at him.

'And sir?' Sid looked at Yanto, tongue in cheek.

'A pint of best please, mine host,' said Yanto, who was already beginning to relax and enjoy himself. Sid snapped his fingers at one of the waiters standing by the elegant sideboard festooned with silver tureens. The waiter scurried off with the drinks order then Sid continued. 'And starters, sir, madam?'

They both studied the menu. It might have been Greek for all Yanto knew. 'What do you recommend, Sid?' It was almost a plea.

'Well we do have a particularly fine local duck pate, sir.'

'Suits me,' said Yanto thankfully.

Sid looked at Julie 'I did rather fall in love with seafood at Fisherman's Wharf when I lived in San Francisco,' she said enthusiastically, 'could you oblige?'

'I expect we can rustle something up,' Sid smiled. 'I have got just about everything, bar lobster, is that all right?' Julie nodded. 'Now, what about main course? I do have some excellent local salmon.' Again Yanto noticed the slight smirk on Sid's face.

'Oh, I'm not a fishy person,' snorted Julie.

'That goes for me too, Sid,' Yanto joined in, 'red meat, that's me.'

'Well,' said Sid leaning a little closer, 'I wouldn't mention this to everybody, but they culled a few deer in the Park this week. I managed to get just one.'

'Ooh, venison,' Julie squirmed with delight, 'I haven't had venison since I was a child.' Yanto had never tasted it at all. So it was agreed; a haunch of venison with a bottle of good pre-war burgundy to swill it down.

Sid walked away with a quiet 'Enjoy your meal' and a wink. Then the drinks arrived. A pianist in black tie and tails, who had arrived earlier, ceased shuffling his sheet music and began to play 'Summertime' quietly in the corner alcove. Immediately everyone in the room seemed to relax, and the previously whispered conversations raised a few decibels.

Yanto took a deep swig at his pint and leaned back with a sigh of contentment. 'This is OK, ain't it, sweetheart? I think I could get used to this high life.'

Julie smiled and sipped her port. 'Tell me, Yanto,' she said in her sexy whisper, 'your name has always fascinated me. It's not local, is it? How did you come to get a name like that?'

Yanto was a little surprised at the question. 'It's an old Welsh name,' he explained. 'Dad was a Welsh miner. When the local pit closed he moved to the Forest of Dean and went opencast mining. He met Ma, who was a Coleford girl, married her, and when I was born he called me Yanto after his dad, simple as that.'

'Fascinating,' she said, and sipped some more port.

The young, efficient waiter arrived with the impeccably presented starters. Julie's seafood platter had the lot. Prawns, crab, mussels, squid, scallops – right down to a couple of rollmop herrings. There they lay in regimented patterns. Even the bed of lettuce leaves seemed to lie in perfect symmetry. The pink sauce and lemon wedges completed the colourful display.

Julie took a forkful and closed her eyes with bliss. 'San Fran all over again,' she breathed.

Yanto's pate was to gourmet standard, but Yanto was no gourmet. 'Nice,' he grunted after the first toast soldier, 'but hot buttered toast in front of the fire with bloater paste is better.'

'Philistine,' Julie said with a grin.

The wine waiter appeared with the burgundy, poured a small amount into Yanto's glass, then looked at him expectantly.

It was fortunate that he had seen this rigmarole several times at the pictures during dinner scenes, otherwise he would probably have asked the waiter what he was playing at and to get the glass topped up. Instead, he ceremoniously picked up the glass and with the stem between thumb and forefinger, twirled it expertly in front of the burning candle to inspect the colour. Then, after poking his nose into the glass, he took a sip. It was lovely. Thus having satisfied himself that he had appeased convention, nodded to the waiter. Had it tasted like neat vinegar he would still, no doubt, have nodded at the waiter. Suitably impressed, the waiter topped up the glasses. He ordered another pint for himself and a gin and tonic for Julie and relaxed again.

The pianist began to play 'Stardust'. He gazed at her exquisite face across the burning candle. He was beginning to mellow. 'You are absolutely beautiful, you know that, don't you?' he said uncharacteristically.

'It's always nice to be told,' she whispered seductively.

She suddenly changed the subject with a toss of her head. 'What are you doing on the thirtieth of August?' she said matter-of-factly.

'God knows, why?' came the inevitable reply.

'I rang the District Engineer at the Severn Catchment Board in Gloucester to enquire when the biggest Bore tide was due this year.' Yanto groaned inwardly. He had hoped her encounter with the snake in the brook had caused her to think twice about her crazy ambition.

'And?' he said resignedly.

'He told me the highest tide for the remainder of the year was predicted on August thirtieth. It's a thirty-three foot tide. The wave will reach Stonebench at around twenty past nine a.m.' She paused. 'It's a Saturday morning, are you still game?'

'It means having a morning off work,' he said hopelessly. 'Look, are you sure you want to do this? Do you realise what a thirty-three-foot tide means? With a high predicted tide and the right conditions ...' He left the rest unsaid.

'Listen,' she replied grimly, 'with the war over, the world is going to get smaller, with people flying all over the world.' She was getting excited. 'What we have here is a river that is unique, well almost anyway. Over the next few years all sorts of people will be coming over. Americans and Australians with their surfboards, just to ride our wave. I want to be first, that's all.' There it was, that pout again. He smiled in defeat. 'What are you grinning at?' she demanded.

'I was just thinking,' he said, still smiling. 'I read an interesting article recently. On the twentieth of January, 1607, a high tide was predicted for the Severn. On that occasion all conditions were perfect. The result was two thousand people drowned in the Severn estuary alone.' He paused for effect. 'And you want to meet that lot coming up a channel a hundred yards wide?' Yanto shook his head.

'You're scared,' she said.

'You're damn right I'm scared,' he replied, and left it at that.

She was about to speak again then bit her tongue as the main course arrived. Sid was doing the honours personally. He arrived at their table bearing the large domed silver dish and wearing a smile from ear to ear. The young waiter trailed behind with two smaller dishes containing the vegetables. People on the neighbouring tables began craning their necks to

179

see what the dishes contained. They must have begun to think they had a couple of VIPs in their midst. Sid placed the dish in the centre of the table and raised the domed lid with the seeming reverence of a master actor. The exotic haunch of dark venison must have weighed best part of three pounds. The deliciously scented steam, which rose and spread as the lid was raised, made the saliva glands work overtime. They, and half the occupants of the dining room watched as Sid carved.

'None of this razor blade carving, mind, Sid,' chortled Yanto, as he took another long pull at his pint, 'cut thick.'

Sid did just that. Slice after tender slice fell away from the knife as he carved expertly. As he did so, Julie took the opportunity to powder her nose. Sid placed the oversized portions of sliced succulence on the heated plates then removed the lids from the vegetable dishes. 'Mostly home grown,' he said to his friend. The small new potatoes gleamed white, showing up the green sprigs of parsley scattered over them in careless abandon. Fresh baby carrots added their colour to the occasion. Broccoli spears, sage and onion stuffing, chipolatas, peas, and the essential gravy boat now lay before them. It was a meal fit for a king.

'What a feast,' groaned Yanto.

'You're at the B.C. now,' Sid said with a grin, 'and if that lot ain't through you in twenty-four hours, you're a dead 'un.'

He nodded to the young waiter and they began to withdraw. Yanto caught his arm 'You've done us proud, Sid,' he said earnestly, 'I shan't forget it.'

'For Mary Gates's son, anything,' Sid replied and withdrew.

Julie returned, obviously enjoying the envious glances of the ladies in the room, and a few lustful glances from the men for good measure.

With a little squeal of delight she began selecting vegetables from the dishes and placing them carefully on what limited space was left on her plate. Yanto did the same. Then there was silence between them as they tucked into that most glorious meal. The pianist began to play 'That Ole Devil Called Love'.

An hour later they were beat. Neither of them could face

dessert and they were both flopped out in easy chairs in the lounge. The drinks waiter was still in evidence however, scurrying between the saloon bar and the cosy chintzy little lounge. Yanto began to notice the odd slur in Julie's excited chatter. She had virtually finished off the bottle of burgundy herself, as Yanto was no wine drinker, and the gin and tonics were by now too numerous to count. The world was taking on a very rosy hue for both of them.

'Oh, Yanto, thank you for a wonderful evening,' she said with a tipsy giggle. From his slumped down position in the chair he just raised his hand and grinned.

With the other diners now conspicuous by their absence, Julie looked at her watch, 'Goodness, do you realise it is eleven-thirty already?'

Another silly grin from him. 'Shall we go?' she said and giggled again. As they both rose rather unsteadily, Sid appeared as if by magic with Julie's stole. The pianist, who must have been a glutton for punishment, began to play 'As Time Goes By'.

Sid saw them to the revolving doors, then Yanto took his hand before departing. 'Many thanks, old mate,' he said, 'I shall be seeing you within the week.' Sid understood, and they left.

As they walked to the car Julie turned to him. 'You didn't pay the man.' She giggled.

'We have an understanding,' he said.

The marketplace was dark and almost deserted as they walked back to the car. A solitary policeman watched them pass from his position by the café. As they walked under the streetlamp by the Town Hall she cuddled up to him affectionately. He couldn't help it. He decided to take the bull by the horns and kiss her properly for the first time. He stopped, pulled her into him almost roughly, and crushed those lovely pouty lips in a long, lingering, scented kiss. He was surprised by her eager response.

Nat Asnett had had a lousy night. He had become bored at his father's pub when his two mates, with whom he normally

181

shared a few jokes and games of spoof, had decided to go to the boxing show at Gloucester Baths. The bar had been quiet at The Salvation Inn, so he had decided to leave his father to it and walk into Berkeley for a drink. Berkeley had more than her fair share of pubs, and Nat had managed to visit most of them in the course of the evening. He was now the worse for drink and in a foul mood at the thought of having to walk back to Ham.

As he walked unsteadily out of the George in the market place, he saw two people obviously kissing under the Town Hall lamp. It took his befuddled mind a few seconds to recognise them in all that finery, but as he did so, a great black mixture of self-pity, frustration, rage and hate, coursed through his entire being.

He was about to snarl a challenge and beat his arch rival to a pulp in front of the girl, when he spotted the policeman in front of the café. As he stood there trying to decide what to do, the couple disentangled and walked on. 'You stinking bastard pig, Gates.' The grated obscenities poured from Nat's lips and his fury was terrible to behold. He suddenly calmed down. 'That's it, boy,' he said quietly, 'the next time I see you, I'll cripple you.'

Julie drove the big car to Wanswell and turned right towards the village of Brookend. The pretty coloured lights on the walnut dashboard were having a hypnotic effect on Yanto's languid mind as he absent-mindedly stroked the back of Julie's neck. It was a novel event for him to be taken home by a girl, but he had to admit, it had been a wonderful evening and he was looking forward to that goodnight kiss.

He suddenly went rigid with shock. Was he dreaming? No, he wasn't, Julie had her hand on his thigh. She giggled and moved her hand provocatively nearer to the danger area. He could not believe what was happening. All the girls he had taken out. All the struggling and cajolery to get what he wanted, many times without success, and now here was this exotic girl of his dreams taking the initiative. He had had no intention of trying his hand with her tonight. Up until now she had seemed so remote and untouchable.

Such noble thoughts now went out of the window in a flash. He took her hand and guided it the rest of the way. She gasped softly as her hand came into contact with his bulging loins, then began to undo his fly buttons one handed while driving with the other.

'For God's sake, Julie, pull in there.' They were approaching an open five-barred gateway into a field on the right-hand side of the narrow lane. 'Drive in there,' he groaned. She removed her hand and drove through the open gateway and on into the field a short distance until the car was screened from the road by the hedge.

A kind of madness gripped them. He couldn't wait for the car to stop. As soon as it did he took hold of her and kissed her long and passionately, while exploring her firm hard breasts.

Her tongue forced its way between his lips tantalisingly. 'My God,' he thought deliriously, 'what the hell had she been up to in the States?' He had never known a girl as sensuous as this.

He began to undress her slowly and deliberately. He was more excited now than he had ever been in his life before, but he was determined not to rush it. This was going to be something to remember.

He undid the long line of small cloth covered buttons at the back of her evening dress, right down to the small of her back. Then she meekly held her arms out to allow him to tug the top half of the dress forward and away from her. The smell of her and the sight of those beautifully filled flimsy brassiere cups, filled him with wonder and longing.

It was too much. When was she going to come to her senses and push him away? He breathlessly undid the back buckle of the bra and allowed it to fall away. Her breasts, showing snowy-white in the subdued fluorescence of the car's dashboard lights, rose and fell with her excited breathing before his fascinated eyes. She groaned uncontrollably as he fell upon them with his mouth, and sucked those raspberry-like nipples with the fervour of a hungry babe.

She went for his belt and fly buttons like a tigress. He raised himself off the leather seat and allowed his suit trousers to fall down. She tore his pants down and took hold of his painfully erect member and began to do delicious things with it. It was impossible to take things slowly with such a woman. He eased her up and manipulated the lower half of her dress over her hips until it fell in an untidy heap around her ankles. Then, feverishly, his hand slid around that wonderland of flesh between stocking top and panties, and explored her femininity in a rhapsody of glorious lust.

It was as well they were in a field. The sounds she began to make would almost have woken the dead. He could stand it no longer. He kicked open the two front doors of the Armstrong and laid her flat on the large bench seat. Then, with his feet sticking out of the passenger door, he thrust into her. He was not the slightest bit surprised to find she was not a virgin. With a groaning shriek she threw those long wondrous legs around his waist and held him like a vice.

For the first time with a local girl, the thought of taking precautions had not even crossed his mind, and no way did he intend to withdraw prematurely. Not that he could have anyway, not with Julie's legs wrapped round him like a demented boa constrictor. Not that it mattered. Julie was already arching and shrieking like a banshee. It crossed his mind, even at this stage, that if the local policeman should happen by, he would probably think a murder was being committed over the hedge.

It was over as quickly as it began. They lay together sweating and panting for five minutes before he began the difficult disentanglement. They dressed and drove the last mile back to Yanto's home in a complete and embarrassing silence. Even when he kissed her coyly on the cheek and said 'good night', she made no sound.

As he watched the tail lights disappear he began to wonder if he had dreamed the whole episode. 'Julie,' he murmured to himself, 'you are beautiful, charming, sophisticated and exciting, but you have got to be a nympho.'

As he went in the door he found his mother waiting

anxiously. 'Did you have a nice time? Did Sidney look after you?'

'We had a wonderful evening, Mam,' he replied, 'and Sid was magnificent.'

He started up the steep narrow staircase. Halfway up the stairs he stopped. 'Mam,' he shouted.

'Yes, son,' she replied, poking her head up the stairwell.

'It ain't my birthday today is it?'

'Course not, you twerp. What are you on about?'

'I just wondered,' he said wearily, and went to bed.

Seventeen

THE BIG FIGHT

On the following Monday lunchtime, Nat Asnett sat moodily eating a basin of faggots and peas in the bar of the Sharpness Hotel. The *Resolution* was tied up in the dock by the lock entrance, waiting for the tide. Even the thought of another trip down river failed to bring him out of his black mood.

Ted, the landlord, looked over to where Nat was sitting alone, and shook his head. Nat had only been in three-quarters of an hour and already he had sunk five pints of cider. 'Christ, he's in some sort of mood,' he said quietly to one of the old regulars at the bar. 'Somebody had better start runnin'', that's for sure.'

That same lunchtime, Yanto sat on the sun-warmed planks of one of the dock basin piers, chin in hand and deep in thought.

He still found it difficult to believe what had happened that previous Saturday night. The memory of Julie's raw lust persisted in his memory, reducing him almost to a state of shock. It was the total unexpectedness of it all that he couldn't get over. There he had been, in his naivety, looking forward to that goodnight kiss, then wham bam, thank you ma'am.

The tall, gangly figure of Billy Tolboys moved into his line of vision, trailing his elver net in the muddy waters of the basin.

Having nothing better to do during the lunch hour Yanto had accompanied Billy to the dock basin, where he hoped to catch a feed of elvers for his parents. 'Bit different to last time, Yant,' Billy called over, 'cock all about now. Can't understand it, the bloody gates are open.'

Yanto began to get bored. 'Come on, Bill, you're wasting your time. Let's get back to the ship.'

187

'S'pose you're right,' Billy said dejectedly, and picked up the bucket with a dozen or so baby eels writhing inside, and threw them back into the basin with a snort of disgust.

They walked back along the edge of the lock talking about nothing in particular.

Somebody shouted Yanto's name. They looked up and saw Nat Asnett walking a little unsteadily over the lock gate catwalk twenty yards in front of them. Nat looked like hell.

'Wo's that nasty prat want?' Billy snorted.

'Dunno,' Yanto replied, with a sinking feeling in the pit of his stomach. He had seen that look on Nat's face many times over the years, and he knew it meant trouble with a capital T.

Nat stopped in front of Yanto, a picture of complete menace. 'I want you, you bastard,' he spat.

'Watch your mouth, Nat,' Yanto growled back. 'You're pissed. What the hell have I done?'

'I *saw you* Saturday night,' he rasped, with his fists clenching and unclenching. 'I saw you farting and flaunting with the Murchison dame.'

'So what?' Yanto fired back at him.

'Because she's my meat, that's what,' Nat almost yelled, 'so I'm goin' to do you, right now.'

'Your meat, bollocks,' Yanto spat back. 'That's why she invited me out and not you, is it?' Nat moved towards him with fists raised and murder in his eyes.

Billy jumped between them. 'Don't be a prat,' Billy yelped in Nat's face. 'If you fight on dock property it's the sack for both of you, that's for sure.'

Nat thumped Billy in his skinny chest and sent him staggering back. Billy righted himself and with a snarl, went for Nat. Now it was Yanto's turn to get between them. He clamped his hands on Billy's shoulders and stopped him dead in his tracks.

'OK, mate,' he smiled into Billy's mad eyes, 'thanks anyway, but forget it. This is my fight.'

He pushed Billy away then turned on Nat. 'Right, you evil bastard,' he said quietly, 'let's get to it then.'

Sam Torrence and his son Terry sat back from the table having just demolished a large plateful of shepherd's pie, chips, and peas in the lockside café.

Terry had spent the lunch break telling his father about the problems his boxing club was currently experiencing. The Berkeley Boys Boxing Club, like most sporting clubs, was having a hard time getting going again after the war years. The finances just weren't there.

Suddenly there was a commotion outside the café by the lockside. Sam peered out of his window. What he saw made him throw back his chair and dash out of the door. He saw the two young giants circling each other preparing to fight, and by the looks on their faces they meant business. He could also see that one of the contestants was his crew member who should be accompanying him down river within the next ten minutes.

'Nathan,' he yelled, with that note of authority that only Sam could muster.

Nat hesitated, then stood back as Sam jumped between them. Several other dockers now came running over to see what all the fuss was about. 'What do you think you are playin' at, eh?' Sam stood there looking up at Nat with his hands on his hips, doing his impression of a brick outhouse.

'I am going to cripple that bastard, that's what,' Nat breathed, and began to move around Sam.

'Not on my time you ain't' Sam snorted. 'Fight on this dock, Nat, and I shall have to let you go, I mean it.' Then he turned to Yanto. 'And I shall see to it that Cliff Barrett hears about it, Yanto,' he said 'you know what that means too.'

'It's his idea, Sam,' Yanto shrugged, 'but you know me, I don't run from no man!'

'OK, Gatesy,' Nat said quietly, 'I'll be waiting for you outside the docks at five o'clock, OK?'

'OK by me,' Yanto replied grimly.

One of the onlooking dockers rubbed his hands with glee. 'This will be the fight of the century,' he chortled.

Sam looked at the docker with a thoughtful expression on

his face, then had a brilliant idea.

'Boys,' he said, looking at the two of them with a grin, 'come back in the café with me. I'll buy you both a cup of tea, then I want to put a proposal to you.'

Two minutes later they were around the café table drinking tea. Sam paid for the teas. He also remembered to pay for his lunch. For a minute or two the anxious café owner had thought he had a runner on his hands.

Sam sat at the table with Yanto, Nat, and his son Terry. Billy and the three excited dockers stood looking on. 'What's the point,' Sam began, 'of you two boys knocking each other's brains out for nothing. It will mean that either me or Cliff Barrett, or maybe both of us, will be a man short and what will it achieve?'

'It will achieve satisfaction for me,' Nat broke in.

Sam raised his hand. 'My way you will both get satisfaction, raise some money for a good cause, and make a bob or two for yourselves.'

'Go on,' somebody said. 'Well, as you know, my boy here,' he nodded at Terry, 'boxes for the club over at Berkeley. Like all clubs at the moment they are having a hard time. So suppose I arrange a grudge fight in the ring, with prize fight rules.'

There followed a fascinated silence, then Sam continued. 'Both of you boys are famous for miles around, I know that, and a lot of people would pay a lot of money to see you two fight to the finish.'

Terry jumped up with a gleam in his eye. 'Dad, you're a genius, a bloody genius,' he yelped.

Sam looked at him and he sat down.

'I reckon we could get at least five hundred blokes to watch a fight like that. We can work out the financial details later. But I reckon five bob a head would be about right.' He paused and wrinkled his brow as he did some mental arithmetic. 'That's a hundred and twenty-five quid.'

'Christ, that's real money,' one of the dockers breathed, 'I'll be there, you can count on that.'

'How you gonna get 'em all in the club?' Terry chipped in.

'I'll get the club to fix a ring in a nice quiet field somewhere handy,' Sam replied, grinning, 'what with this weather and all they'll come flocking. Well,' he said in conclusion, 'what do you both think of my idea?'

Nat looked at Yanto. 'As long as I get the chance to bust him up,' he grinned evilly.

'Suits me,' Yanto replied.

Sam was still way ahead of them. 'Competition gloves and prize fight rules, I reckon,' he said, lost in thought. 'A knock down signals the end of a round, OK?' There was a general agreement.

'Great,' said Sam as he stood up, 'leave the organising to me. Christ,' he grinned, 'once the word gets around who knows how many we'll get there, 'specially if this weather holds.' He slapped Nat on the back and looked at Yanto. 'In the meantime,' he said, 'you two shake hands, that's an order.' They did so reluctantly.

'Right,' Sam looked at Nat, 'get yourself aboard that tug. We got work to do.'

With one last withering look at Yanto, Nat left. Yanto and Billy went back to the Swedish ship they were working on and the three dockers ran to spread the word.

Later that evening Nat was helping his father in the bar at The Salvation Inn.

'D'you reckon you can take him, son?' his father asked, 'he's a big, tough bugger mind, and there's goin' to be a fair bit o' money changin' hands over this, so I gather.'

'Put yer shirt on me, Dad,' Nat replied, as the bar door opened. Terry Littlejohn sauntered in looking as flamboyant as ever.

'Evening Joe, Nat.' He caught Nat's eye with a wink and nodded towards the far end of the bar where it was quiet. Nat pulled him a pint and joined him.

Joe Asnett cast a disapproving eye towards the two of them huddled together across the counter, then carried on chatting to a regular.

Terry told Nat about Colonel Murchison's proposed fishing

191

trip in every detail, except of course, the two hundred pound fee.

'Just take four days off, the first week in July,' Terry said earnestly, 'we are going on the morning tide, Sunday the sixth. We shall be back for work on the Friday, and,' he said with another wink, 'there's twenty quid cash in it for you.'

Nat looked into his half pint of beer. 'Come on, mate, don't let me down,' Terry breathed urgently. 'It's either you or our Joe, and I don't particularly want to take that twat with me.'

'What's the catch?' Nat said suddenly.

'That's the beauty of it,' Terry replied, 'there ain't one. Just a straightforward fishing trip. I think the old bugger is up to something because he wants to slip ashore for a couple of hours, quiet like, but that's nothing to do with us. All we have to do is take him, bring him back, and keep our mouths shut. What do you say?'

Nat looked at him. Something told him Terry was dealing straight for once. 'Count me in,' he said.

The word was out with a vengeance. From just a handful of knowledgeable sources, the word had travelled the length and breadth of the Berkeley Vale within a couple of days.

Both boys were six foot plus. Both were hard tough natural fighters, who know what a roughhouse was all about. They were also well-known and well-liked characters in their own right and had been bitter rivals all their lives. The talk locally was about nothing else.

The public's imagination was stirred, and if Jack Dempsey and Gene Tunney had been billed to fight that night, the excitement could not have been greater. Knocker Nelmes was in his element. He took complete control of Yanto immediately and was to endure many cussings from Renee for absenteeism over the next couple of weeks. He rigged up a makeshift gym in his large attic at the Boar and made out a strict training schedule for his protégé. The heavy bag which he hung from the rafters was an ex-army kitbag, well stuffed with God knows what. His old free-standing punchball also came out of mothballs to tantalise the sweating, panting Yanto. It's very easy to miss a fast moving punchball.

The Berkeley Boys Boxing Club had gone for it in a big way and agreed to erect the ring and supply the necessary equipment. But a word of caution was uttered. There was the question of the police.

By the already considerable excitement being created, it was obvious that a lot of people could be expected and prize fighting was, after all, illegal.

The committee members agreed to put their heads together and figure out the best way to tackle this hitherto unconsidered aspect. Sam Torrence came to the Boar on the Wednesday evening to announce that the fight was fixed for the following Saturday week, all being well, to start at six p.m. sharp.

Then the work really began in earnest. 'I've got five quid on you, mind,' Knocker announced solemnly as he hurled the medicine ball into Yanto's screaming solar plexus.

'I wish to Christ Sam hadn't been in that bloody café,' Yanto groaned, 'would all be over now, one way or t'other.'

'Crap!' Knocker grunted, as he heaved the ball at Yanto again. 'You are going to make a tidy penny out of this, I can feel it in my water.'

When Billy Tolboys heard that Terry Torrence was visiting the rival camp at The Salvation Inn to act as sparring partner to Nat, he turned up at The Blue Boar to offer his services. But this act of benevolence lasted just one evening. Yanto found it impossible to hit anyone unless his blood was up or he had first been hurt by someone he disliked. Anyway, Billy was no fighter, and the sight of his familiar face trying to look menacing made Yanto burst out laughing every time he came at him.

'You're about as much use as a one-legged bloke in an ass kickin' contest,' Knocker bawled unkindly.

So after that Yanto contented himself by smashing his gloved fists into the large padded mitt held by the staunch Knocker, and imagined it was Nat's face.

Then there was the roadwork. This part was becoming

decidedly embarrassing to Yanto. He deliberately avoided the local pubs on his runs, as it invariably caused something akin to mass hysteria within the precincts of the watering holes. Even so, the sight of the two of them sweating their separate ways around the local lanes brought thumbs up and cheers from the locals as they tended their gardens and allotments.

Yes, the road work was the hardest part. After a day's work on the docks, then an hour with Knocker in the gym, that evening run was almost the last straw. But Knocker insisted.

'Run on the river bank,' he said, 'grass running won't jar you too much; if it gets too hard, walk awhile, then run again, OK?'

'OK, O-bloody-K,' Yanto said through gritted teeth, as he ran along the bank of the Berkeley Pill on the following Saturday evening. He wore his old army PE shorts and a pair of heavy boots. Not a pretty sight, but, 'when those heavy boots come off on fight night and you get into a pair of lightweight boxing boots,' Knocker had proclaimed solemnly, 'your feet will move faster than shit off a shovel.'

It was a lovely balmy evening. He had laid off the cigarettes temporarily and was beginning to glory in his new-found fitness. Not since the completion of his army training had he felt so good. He was also gratified to find that his war-wounded leg was bothering him less and less.

As he ran along the lip of that narrow winding muddy slit, the Berkeley Pill, he saw a couple of figures about a hundred yards ahead of him. They were both heaving on a rope, the end of which was obviously attached to something submerged in the muddy water.

As he drew closer he recognised Herb Meadows, who farmed most of the land around here. The other fellow was Herb's cowman, who Yanto knew only as Tom. Herb was in his seventies, but probably worked harder and longer hours than most men half his age.

As Yanto stopped for a grateful breather, Herb stopped pulling on the rope and straightened his back. 'Give us a pull, young 'un,' he cackled, 'It'll help build them muscles up for the fight.' Yanto was beginning to wonder if there was anyone who hadn't heard about the coming confrontation.

'What you got on the end of that rope?' Yanto asked, mystified.

'The missus fancied some eels and elvers for supper,' Herb replied, rubbing his back.

'Elvers,' Yanto gasped, 'never saw an elver you had to get out with a rope yet, where's your net?'

'Net, my ass.' Herb almost spat the words out, 'when the missus wants elvers, she wants elvers, not promises. Those daft prats could sieve from here to Gloucester and maybe not catch a single bugger. Wot I got 'ere is a guarantee. Come on, give us a pull.'

The mystified Yanto took hold of the rope and the three of them pulled together.

The revolting apparition that broke through the glutinous water and came sliding up the Pill bank filled Yanto with amazement and disgust. It had once been a sheep, but after being in the Pill for a few days it now bore scant resemblance to its former being.

The great bloated body, with its legs stuck out straight and still, looked huge in comparison to the tiny head. The head, with the rope knotted around the neck, came up first. The black sockets where the eyes had once been stared at Yanto as it reached the top of the mudslide like something out of a Dracula movie.

'Heave it over onto the grass, Tom' Herb grunted. Yanto stood there panting and wide eyed, scrutinising the loathsome spectacle.

Suddenly the rear end of the sheep twitched and seemed to come alive. He leaped back with a cry of alarm as a three-pound eel sloughed and writhed its way out of the dead sheep's anus.

'Grab 'im, Tom,' the old farmer cried excitedly. Tom whacked the eel across its tail with his thumb stick, which seemed to have a paralysing effect on it, then picked up the twisting silvery length of agonised fury and rammed it into a small sack.

As he did so another large eel emerged the same way.

'OK, Tom,' Herb shouted excitedly, 'open 'er up.' Tom whipped out his jack-knife, flicked it open, and bisected the bloated monstrosity with the dexterity of a master surgeon.

The great repulsive belly fell apart with the hiss of escaping gas and a cascade of giblets and foul water. The stench was enough to fell a strong man. There, amongst the blue-grey and vermilion innards, writhed at least a dozen prize eels. As they watched, masses of tiny elvers began to materialise from every liquid crevice. Herb and Tom first grabbed the eels then began scooping up the elvers with old tin mugs and sloshing them into a bucket until all visible life within the carcass had disappeared.

Yanto watched this scene of excited barbarism with fascinated eyes.

'Fancy some mutton-fed supper, young 'un?' cackled Herb, 'plenty 'ere.'

With his stomach heaving, Yanto ran on. Later he decided he had had enough for one day and ran directly home.

'I done me washing today,' Yanto's mother said shortly after his return home. 'Why not have a nice hot bath, there's plenty of hot water in the copper.'

'Good idea, Ma,' he grunted and went out into the back yard where the large zinc bath hung on a nail on the wash-house wall.

After manhandling the bath into the back kitchen, he began ferrying buckets of hot water from the great copper bowl in the wash-house into the back kitchen. The dying embers of the fire still flickered in the firehole beneath the old boiler.

Two other small tin baths lay on the wash-house floor containing the family whites, which his mother had left to soak. The water in the baths was an impossible blue, brought about by the little bags of Reckitts Blue which were considered essential by women who wanted perfect whites. And they all did. Most women of the time would rather have died than have their billowing washing seen as anything but pristine.

He was about to strip off for his bath when his mother

knocked on the kitchen door.

'You decent?' she whispered.

'Yeah.'

Mary stuck her head around the door. 'You've got a visitor, it's Molly.'

'Oh, tell her to come in,' Yanto said, with surprise in his voice.

'I did,' his mother whispered again, 'but she won't, she just wants to see you. By the look of her she's been crying,' Mary went on almost accusingly. 'You haven't been up to anything with that girl, have you?'

'Bloody hell, Ma,' he snorted, and went through to the front door. Molly stood by the front gate, tall, elegant and pretty, still in the two-piece navy suit she wore to her work at the dock office. She looked upset and had obviously been crying.

'Hello Moll, what's up?' he asked.

'You may well ask,' she replied in a small quavering voice. 'Someone at work today delighted in telling me all about your association with that new girl from Ham. I don't expect to be taken out for expensive meals, but I do like a little consideration. I will not be a laughing stock for you or any man. How dare you compromise me in this fashion?'

He was lost for words.

'Anyway,' she continued, 'I just called to say I don't want to see you any more, and I hope Nat knocks your block off.'

With that she turned on her heel and walked towards Honey Cottage with as much dignity as she could muster. He watched her go, open-mouthed.

It shook him badly, and it was a very thoughtful Yanto who later lay soaking in the suds.

Old Jesus sat on the makeshift bench outside his shack, humming happily in the sun. He was fashioning the 'do-it-yourself' Jardine snap. He grunted as he heaved on the snare wire with two hands to tension the three hooks together.

He had decided that when circumstances made it impossible to stay on the brook bank, he would leave a bank line in place,

197

with a tin of metal washers attached to the line.

Being only a few yards from the bank he should be able to hear the rattle caused by the frantic pulls of a large fish.

'And then, my beauty,' he muttered to himself, 'with twenty-four hours' coverage, I am bound to get you sooner or later.'

A flash of colour suddenly caught the corner of his eye. He looked up and saw the portly figure of Mrs Venables appear around the edge of the wood. She was the widow of his old friend the farmer who had left him his shack and the surrounding plot in his will. He had not seen her for some weeks, which was strange, as the farmhouse was only one small field away from his own abode.

He put down the tackle and walked towards her with a smile. Her rosy face tried to smile in return, but he could see she was deeply troubled. 'Hello, my dear,' he said, and held her hands at arms' length, 'and where have you been lately?'

'Oh, Jason,' she whispered, 'I just had to get out of the house for a while. I can't sleep and I have been worried to death.'

She began to sob quietly.

'Come on,' he said briskly, as he guided her towards the shack, 'I can see this is something that needs talking about.'

They walked back to the shack in silence.

Not until she was sitting in an easy chair and the kettle put on the stove, did he speak again. 'Now tell me all about it, Tilly.'

'Well, it's our Arthur, you see, Jason,' she said, dabbing her eyes. 'They told me yesterday that he is going to die. They can't do anything else for him.' She began to cry again with great shuddering sobs.

'Oh my God,' he gasped in horror. 'I knew he was ill, but not to that degree.'

Arthur Venables was forty years old. A big strong happy man. A simple man, who, not having been bestowed with looks or charm, was happy just to work his great heart out on the farm and live with his mam forever. He had always loved Jason, and

198

as a teenager had spent hours with this mysterious man who had suddenly taken up residence in one of his father's cowsheds.

Jason had taught the lad a great deal. Another reason why old Jack Venables had shown his appreciation by willing Jason his home. 'Why on earth didn't you let me know before?' Jason said.

'Well, you were so good to us when Jack died I didn't want to trouble you with all this,' she replied hopelessly. Jason stood up thoughtfully and began to make the tea.

'Does Arthur know?' he asked.

'Yes,' Tilly replied, dabbing her eyes again, 'he insisted, you know how strong-willed he is.'

'Yes, I do know,' Jason replied still lost in thought. He handed Tilly the mug of tea and sat down beside her. 'Where exactly is the growth?' Jason enquired. 'In his stomach,' she whispered, 'we thought he was cured after the operation, but it was not to be. What am I going to do, Jason?' she quailed. 'First Jack, now my lovely boy.'

'There, there,' he said and patted her hand, 'I shall just have to do something about it myself, won't I?'

She looked at him with open-eyed amazement. 'What can you do, Jason?' she almost sobbed; 'the doctors have given up.' He noticed the desperate gleam of hope in her eyes.

'Now, Tilly,' he cautioned, 'please don't get your hopes up too much, please. Our doctors are marvellous and if they give up, things must be bad. But,' he continued, 'as you know by now, my methods and ideas are unconventional, to say the least, but I got rid of your warts, didn't I, and they're growths of a sort.'

Tilly remembered. Years before, she had been plagued with warts on her hands. They would stick to her woollen mittens, causing sore darts of pain every time she put them on, and in winter they bled profusely as she helped her husband with the milking and other farm chores. She remembered them as pure misery, and a visit to the doctor resulted in something to dab on them which did no good at all.

She knew that people came from far and near to have Jason

charm their warts away, so one day, in spite of her husband's jibes, she had asked Jason if he could rid her of them.

'How many warts have you got there?' he had asked, seemingly uninterested. She had counted seven. He had looked at them fleetingly. 'Just forget 'em,' he had said, and walked away.

She had felt angry and rejected at the time. 'He's not interested because I didn't offer him any money,' she remembered thinking at the time.

'I remember it so well,' she said perking up visibly as she sipped her tea.

'The funny thing is, I did forget them completely. For the life of me I still can't imagine how I put those mittens on without remembering. But I did. It was just as if you had erased the very thought of them from my mind. Anyway,' she said, giggling at the memory, 'when I did think about it a couple of weeks later, there was no trace of them.'

'Well, a wart is a growth. Not like the devil growing in Arthur's stomach, but I can try.' He rose and put his empty mug in the washing up bowl. 'When you have finished your tea,' he said, 'I will have a chat with young master Arthur.'

When Tilly Venables ushered him into Arthur's sick room later, all the smells of medication and illness hit him and brought back harsh obnoxious memories of the war.

'Hello, Uncle Jason.' The excited childish phrase coming from this grown man brought a lump to Jason's throat. Arthur leaned over from the pillows that were propping him up in bed, and with a stroke, knocked a pile of farming magazines off the bedside chair. 'Thanks for coming over,' he beamed, 'take a seat.' Jason took his hand. The great strong work-calloused hand that he remembered had already gone soft and limp.

'Hello, my boy,' he said, and looked into Arthur's trusting eyes. The round jovial face was already sunken cheeked, with that pallor that said more than words.

'I am sorry to hear about your trouble,' he said softly.

'Yeah,' Arthur replied, as he smacked his hand over his stomach; 'it looks as if the bastard is going to do for me this time.'

'Please don't talk like that, son,' his mother implored.

Jason turned to her. 'Give me ten minutes alone with him, please, Tilly. I would love a cup of tea.'

'Of course,' she whispered, and withdrew. Then Jason turned to Arthur with a gleam in his eye. 'Right, young man,' he said, 'you and me together are going to lick this bastard. Are you game?' Arthur was full of questions, but he was game.

He pulled up the chair and leaned close to an attentive Arthur. 'Do you remember,' he said quietly, 'a few years ago when you and me had that great mountain of dung to shift?'

'Wot, when we was dung-spreading?' Arthur chortled. 'Christ, that was some sort of dung 'eap, wudd'n it?'

'Well, Arthur,' Jason began earnestly, 'I want you to imagine that the growth in your stomach is that bloody great dung heap. OK?'

Arthur looked perplexed. 'Yeah,' he said, 'what then?'

'I know you are very strong-willed and stubborn, and I want you to do exactly as I say. Then it's up to you. I can't do it for you. Do you promise?'

Arthur nodded. 'Just tell me what to do,' he said.

'You see, my boy,' Jason went on, 'I believe that the most powerful force in the universe is the human brain. Harness that power and anything is possible!' Arthur nodded again. 'Right,' Jason snapped, 'from now on, during every waking minute of your day, I want you to imagine you and I are digging away, shifting that dung heap in your stomach.

'Close your eyes. Can't you see us, sweating and cussing, the stink is awful and the sweat is pouring off us, can't you see us, Arthur?'

Arthur, who already had his eyes closed, nodded his head, 'I'm sweating already,' he said.

'There we are,' Jason whispered to him, 'digging that filthy dung heap out of your stomach, shovelful after shovelful, day after day. Do it, Arthur. Live it. Then, when that dung heap is gone, so the growth will be gone. Faith can move mountains, my boy. Once you have totally convinced yourself, the rest is all downhill.'

As Jason watched, a fine film of perspiration appeared on Arthur's brow.

'Go to it, son,' Jason urged as he stood up. 'Trust me.'

Arthur, still laid back against the pillows, held his hand out to him. 'I trust you, Uncle,' he whispered. 'I can do it. Just you wait and see. You have given me something to fight with.'

Jason wiped a tear from his face. 'I'm going now, son,' he said, 'but I shall call in a week's time and I shall expect to find a lot of that dung hill shifted and you feeling a bit better.'

He closed the door quietly, leaving Arthur to fight for his life. He shared a cup of tea with the anxious Tilly and tried to explain to her what he had done.

'Don't go into his room unless it is absolutely necessary, Tilly,' he urged. 'He's fighting now. We can only help him by leaving him alone.'

'Bless you, Jason,' she said tearfully, 'I will pray for you both.'

He left her and went back to his Jardine snap.

That last week of work, then training on top, seemed to creep by for Yanto. Then suddenly it was Saturday, Fight day; and he had done all the training he intended to do.

Under orders from Knocker, he had forgone his usual Saturday lunchtime bevvy at The Boar, and it was a very tense Yanto who sat watching his mother ironing that afternoon.

It seemed everything was arranged.

The boxing club had erected the ring that morning on the far side of the Castle meadow, not far from the swimming hole, but well away from the road. In fact it was completely screened from civilisation by the great brooding profile of the castle. The word had travelled far and wide and a good crowd was expected. But just how many was anybody's guess.

Thankfully the weather was still holding perfect. The boxing club boys would be at every possible entry point to the venue, to collect five shillings from anybody who wished to witness the spectacle.

Sam Torrence had suggested the castle meadow as a venue for several reasons. First, it was well out of the way. Also, it was quite common to see large groups of people walking over the meadow at this time of year. Gangs of kids were always making for the swimming-hole. Parents also, to witness their offspring's prowess in the water. Also the meadow lay between the two camps, so only Yanto's supporters would have to travel through the normally quiet Berkeley Square. It wouldn't do to rub the authorities' noses in the fact that something was up.

This was important, because there was still the worry of the police. Sam said there was little likelihood of anyone reporting it, or making an official complaint, but with so many people knowing about the fight, even though the word had been passed to keep it as quiet as possible, it seemed unlikely that the police would not get to hear about it.

'We shall have to take a chance on that one,' Sam had said. 'If the police stop it and the boys are fined, then the gate money will have to be used to pay the fines. If on the other hand, everything goes all right, I reckon half of the gate money should go to the boxing club and the other half to the two boys. Say, sixty per cent to the winner and forty per cent to the loser.' Both camps had agreed.

A motorised regular from The Boar had been called up to transport Yanto and his seconds, that was Knocker and Billy, to the venue. He would be picking them up at five thirty. 'Plenty of time, that,' Knocker had said briskly, 'I don't want my boy hanging around getting cold or nervous.'

Yanto lay back in the easy chair and watched his mother put the heavy flat iron, which had cooled as she worked, back into the rack which was attached to the front of the open fire grill. Using a cloth to protect her hand, she took the second iron which had been heating up as she used its twin, and inspected it. She deposited a small droplet of saliva on to her index finger and dabbed it on the hot base of the iron. It hissed angrily. Then satisfied it was hot enough, she carried on with her task. By the time this iron cooled, its twin would be ready. Like all women's chores at this time, ironing was a laborious and time-consuming business, but still conducted with great pride.

'Penny for 'em, son,' she said without looking up.

'Oh, I shall just be glad when it's over and done with,' he grunted. 'I shall have a skinful tonight, either way.'

'You should have more sense, all of you,' she snorted. 'Like a bunch of schoolboys. Just wait till I see that Nathan Nelmes.'

'It ain't Knocker's fault, Ma,' he protested, 'I'm lucky to have a bloke like him to help me.'

'Well, just remember,' she said, as she changed irons again, 'if he hurts you tonight, just go down and stay down. You don't have to prove anything to the cider-sodden twerps around here.'

'OK, Ma, anything you say,' he lied.

This time Mary didn't bother to spit on her finger to test the iron. She spat directly on the iron. The little globule skated off the hot iron with a hiss and disappeared into the corner of the room.

He lapsed into a moody silence again. Visions of Molly and Julie began to invade his mind. He had only seen Julie once since that night. He had taken her to Berkeley Pictures on the Wednesday evening to see *Gone With the Wind*. He had tried hard, but things had been cool and miserable between them. It was as though any possibility of a lifetime of love and happiness they may have had together, had been burned away in that mad ten minutes of lust and passion in her father's car.

But it was Molly who was predominant in his thoughts now. His respect for her had increased in leaps and bounds since she had bawled him out.

He smiled to himself as he recalled her face as she reprimanded him. The finely chiselled jaw sticking out defiantly and the pretty little elfin face puckered up with proud indignation. He was like most men, and most women come to that: he hadn't appreciated what he had until it was gone. The more he thought about her, the more he realised what an idiot he had been.

He needed a good woman. He was twenty-eight years old after all, and he suspected that it was only a matter of time before his mother decided to marry Sid Watkins. Yes, he decided there and then. He would have to eat humble pie for the first time in his life and ask Molly to forgive him.

The car arrived promptly at five thirty. All kit was being supplied by the boxing club, so Yanto sauntered out to the car empty-handed and seemingly unconcerned. He was, in fact, as uptight as a bow string.

The three faces in the car grinned with excited anticipation as he came out. 'You're gonna kill 'im, Yant,' and other such words tumbled from Billy's lips, falling on Yanto's deaf ears as the car pulled away.

As it did so, the curtains of the front room fell back into place as the worried face of Mary Gates withdrew.

Another worried face watched from the window as the car passed Honey Cottage. Molly Hopkins had been watching the cavalcade of excited supporters pass the cottage for the last half hour, and as the car passed, Yanto was looking at the cottage. She was sure he had seen her at the window. She felt miserable and dejected. She didn't really hope that Nat would knock his block off.

As the little Austin dropped into bottom gear and chugged its way up Station Hill, they began to pass the tail end of the predominantly Gates supporters. The modes of transport were many and varied. Brisk walking pedestrians were being overtaken, but only just, by the numerous bicycles. One or two of the bicycles had sidecars attached to them containing some lucky docker or other, who would yell and wave at the passing car as his panting, red-faced mate laboured at the pedals.

Horses and traps trotted sedately between the large hay wagons. These wagons, the flagships of the Gloucestershire farming hierarchy, moved cumbersomely along, their great iron-shod wheels rumbling on the road surface and a magnificent Shire between each set of shafts, snorting and tossing its great maned head at the shouting throng.

'Christ, what have we started here?' Knocker groaned, 'we shall never get away with it.'

As they passed Wilf Tillett's hay wagon, alive with half a dozen of his cider jar-armed labourers, Knocker wound down the tiny window and jammed his massive head through it. 'Spread yourselves out, for Christ sake, Wilf,' he bawled, 'or we'll have the bloody cavalry down on us before we throw the first punch!' Wilf, who was sitting on the driving board like the King of Siam, raised his hand. So did all the singing occupants.

Knocker looked apprehensively out of the window as the little car shot through Berkeley Square and on up the High Street. There was not a blue uniform to be seen. The large number of people making their way through the market place were quiet and subdued, as though praying that the strong arm of the law would not intervene at the last second to spoil their sporting evening.

The car pulled up with a jerk by the old wartime sandbag pillbox which guarded the entrance to the castle meadow. The entrance consisted of a five-barred gateway with a neat little stepover stile alongside it, which indicated that it was also a public footpath.

As Yanto and his seconds hopped over the stile, the driver drove on up the castle walk to find a less conspicuous place to park.

It had been arranged that the larger forms of transportation, horses and carts and the like, should be moved on elsewhere for the duration of the fight. Many farm boys had volunteered when two shillings a head had been suggested. To leave horses and carts herding about in one place would have been asking for trouble.

As they commenced the half-mile or so walk across the meadow to where the ring had been erected, Knocker kept up a constant flow of instructions to the tense Yanto, while Billy did his best to keep well-wishers and back-slappers away. Yanto was beginning to realise how the Christians must have felt when they entered the Roman arenas.

As they reached the ring, Yanto was shocked and worried by the sheer number of people milling about. The ring itself looked slightly ridiculous standing out in this beautiful setting.

Knocker guided his bemused protégé towards the changing area which consisted of nothing more than a couple of canvas windbreaks fitted together. He glanced across as he entered and caught a wicked look from Nat, who was about to enter his quarters with Sam and Terry Torrence.

The butterflies really began to work as Knocker started kitting him out. But he had to admit that Knocker knew his business.

When those great heavy boots were wrenched from his feet and the boxing boots laced up in place of them, he felt like a trotting pony.

They were to fight stripped to the waist. 'None of that amateur stuff tonight,' Knocker grinned, as he taped Yanto's hands. Then he stood back admiring Yanto's rippling lean torso. 'My God, son,' he said seriously, 'to look at you, you could be fighting for a world title.'

Patch Parsons came breezing into their changing area as Knocker laced on the competition gloves. 'All set, gents?' he asked.

Patch was the original founder member of the Berkeley Boys Boxing Club and had been a serious contender at featherweight in his youth. That was until an accident with a blowtorch at John Harker's shipyard had taken away his eye and his hopes in one fell swoop. Now, in his fifties, this dark tough little fellow spent all his spare time trying to train local boys for the glory that had cruelly eluded him. Patch had been the obvious choice for referee. 'Christ! Knock, what a spectacle out there,' he breathed, as he watched Knocker massage Yanto's legs. 'They be coming from all directions. Must be five hundred buggers out there already.'

'Any sign of the boys in blue?' Knocker asked anxiously without looking up.

'Nope,' Patch replied, 'the local inspector's a mate of mine and a real boxing nut, but it's in the lap of the gods I reckon. Oh, by the way,' he said, 'I got old Doc Saunderson at ringside, you know, he retired last year. I got him to bring his bag just in case.

'Tell that to the other side,' Knocker growled, 'my boy won't be needin' 'im.'

Patch sniffed, adjusted the ever-present eye patch and looked out between the canvas sheets. 'Looks like they're ready, Knock,' he said excitedly. 'You OK, son?' he said, looking at Yanto.

The very self-conscious Yanto was amazed again by the number of people as he made his way to the ring. A great hush descended on the multitude and latecomers could be seen running towards them from all directions as they sensed that the show was about to commence. The boxing club boys were also running to intercept them with their buckets full of two bobs, half crowns, and tanners.

The two camps had great difficulty getting through the excited throng. Then one inebriated enthusiast, who had brought along his hunting horn, gave the two boys a tuneless blast as they climbed between the ropes.

The Boxing Club had taken the fight very seriously. Flat boxes of resin were present in both corners, for the contestants to rub the soles of their boots in to avoid slipping on the canvas.

Bottles of water and snow-white towels were there. It was all very professional.

Patch called them together in the centre of the ring. 'Well, boys,' he said softly, 'I know this is a grudge fight, but I want Queensbury rules observed. No butting, kicking, or gouging. Prize-fight rules will apply. A knockdown will indicate the end of a round, OK?' He paused, then continued. 'When a man is knocked down he will have one minute to return to the centre of the ring and show that he is still able to defend himself.' Patch paused again. 'I know it's a bit unorthodox, there ain't bin a prize-fight around here since 1882, but do you both understand?' They both nodded.

'Right,' said Patch earnestly, 'I want a good clean fight and may the best man win. Now shake hands and come out fighting.'

They touched gloves, then, with a last dark look of withering hate from Nat, they returned to their corners.

The sharp clang of the bell rang through the warm electricity-charged air.

Molly Hopkins slammed the flat iron down with a frustrated snort, 'Blast the man,' she grated to herself, 'why should I care if he does get hurt.'

Selwyn had gone to the fight along with everybody else it seemed. It was like a ghost village outside. Molly had decided to do a bit of ironing to take her mind off things. But it was no good.

'God damn it all,' she almost shouted, then stalked outside to the shed. Selwyn had left his wheelbarrow just inside the shed door, effectively blocking in Molly's bike. With a show of erupting rage she booted the barrow on its side, snatched her bike, and cycled off in the direction of Berkeley.

Nat came out of his corner with a half-smile of evil anticipation on his face.

Yanto had decided to play a defensive waiting game initially, hoping that Nat would tire. Knocker watched pensively as Nat let loose the first punch of the fight, a tremendous right-handed roundhouse. A great yelling cheer erupted from the Asnett supporters but died quickly as Yanto easily blocked it with his left arm, then immediately stung Nat's nose with a stinging jab from the same arm. Nat then calmed as they circled each other warily, each looking for that opening.

Nat's style was orthodox, but Yanto favoured the 'peek-a-boo' style: both arms held high in front of his face and a crouching stance. Nat came in again, aggressively, but this time more controlled, and caught Yanto high on the head with a left jab, then connected with a right cross. It was a good punch, it caught Yanto on the jaw, causing stars to flash momentarily as the other side of his jawbone clicked ominously.

All thoughts of caution then left Yanto's mind as he went in two-handed. For the next couple of minutes the brutal slugging match transformed the crowd into a mad frenzy.

Even the quick swigs from the cider jars ceased for fear of missing the knockout punch. The two combatants were hurting each other badly now and the crowd bayed for blood.

In the midst of the mad melee, a sucker punch caught Yanto on the point of the jaw and he went down. Patch ordered a grinning Nat to his corner as Knocker and Billy sprang through the ropes and helped the dazed Yanto to his corner. Billy flapped the towel madly in Yanto's confused face as Knocker mopped it with a wet flannel and spoke urgent instructions in his ear.

'For Christ sake, box 'im,' Knocker implored, 'don't lose your temper.' Yanto's head cleared and a grim resolution coursed through him. They came to scratch for the second. Nat came in again, impatient to hurt him and finish it, only to be met by a shuddering short left jab in the face.

Nat's nose began to run bloody and he was becoming more angry by the second. He thudded punch after punch into Yanto's body, but they had no effect.

Yanto had always been impervious to body blows; you could have fired a cannonball into his stomach without effect. He was happy to let Nat tire himself that way, knowing that he was only really vulnerable to the head.

Yanto, always the thinker, was beginning to realise that it was just the opposite with Nat. He had smashed full-blooded blows into Nat's face and jaw, there was plenty of blood flowing but they didn't seem to slow him. But the odd blow to Nat's body seemed to affect him badly. He suddenly realised he had cracked it. He must concentrate on Nat's body.

Sam Torrence was also scrutinising the fight closely from Nat's corner and suddenly realised where his man was going wrong. A minute later, more from a push than anything else, Yanto tripped over his own feet and fell over. As Nat returned to his corner Sam whispered urgently in his ear. Nat grinned and nodded. At the start of the third, following Sam's instructions, Nat went straight for Yanto with over-the-top swinging blows. Yanto anticipated well, ducked, and landed a full-blooded right-handed blow to the centre of Nat's solar plexus, following it up with a hard swinging left to his ribs.

Nat's grunt could be heard yards from the ring as he fell to his knees, then doubled up with the top of his head against the canvas. Now it was Yanto's turn to stroll back to his stool as Sam and Terry dashed in and half carried Nat back to his corner. The dockers and all of Yanto's supporters went mad. Many were now half-inebriated as they danced and yelled with delight.

Both boys were now very tired. In the fourth it began to get really hard. Both had trained religiously, but that only meant so much. They had already absorbed more punishment than any referee would have allowed in a legitimate fight. Yanto had a bad cut across the bridge of his nose and Nat's mouth and nose streamed blood.

But this was a fight to the finish and it was far from over. As Nat rushed in for another attack, Yanto caught him full on the nose with a hard, beautifully timed straight right. He felt Nat's nose break under the hammer blow. Nat also knew his nose had gone. The dreadful pain, plus the knowledge that his arch enemy had probably just ruined his good looks for life, sent Nat totally berserk. He bounced back from the ropes then went for Yanto in a way that drew a sudden awed silence from the hitherto delirious crowd. Yanto backpedalled, desperately trying to ride out the murderous attack, but Nat overwhelmed his defence and landed a vicious right and left high to his head. Had the blows landed on his chin the fight would have been over there and then. Even so, such was the force of the blows that he fell back headlong against the ropes.

The hastily constructed ring was not up to a contest such as this. The ropes fell away and Yanto fell with them, finishing up on his back in the grass. As he staggered back to his feet the demented Nat leapt from the ring. Yanto covered up desperately as more blows rained upon him from every angle.

The ringside crowd moved back like a retreating wave as Patch grabbed Nat from behind and tried to pull him away, while shouting for them to get back in the ring.

With a snarl Nat turned away from Yanto and swung a tremendous roundhouse at Patch's head. Luckily the little man saw it coming and ducked in the nick of time. He then withdrew rapidly. All bedlam was now breaking out in the crowd. Nat's attack on the referee had given Yanto the vital seconds he needed. As Nat turned his attention back at him he was ready. Yanto's gloved fist started at ground level and finished deep in the pit of Nat's stomach. It contained just about all his remaining strength. The wind that whistled out through Nat's teeth would have blown out an oil lamp from twenty paces. He bent double. Then, in that split second, as Nat's head and neck jutted out like a crowing rooster, Yanto's left arced round like a sledgehammer, and connected on Nat's jaw with a sickening thud. He sprawled full length on the grass, out cold. Yanto knew without a shadow of a doubt that he would never make scratch for the next round, and sank thankfully on to the grass himself. Somebody threw a bucket of water over him and then strong arms picked him up.

Molly, who had arrived in time to witness the last terrible five minutes, watched them carry him shoulder high back to the changing area. 'Yes, my love,' she murmured, 'you are certainly some sort of man.' She gave a big sigh, then turned on her heel and made her way back across the meadow; all her anger dispelled.

'Steady on,' growled old Doc Saunderson, 'how do you expect me to fix his nose with you pratting about.' An excited Knocker, who had been hugging and kissing Yanto, stepped back with a sheepish smile. Then he stuck his great crew cut head out between the canvas sheets.

'Back to my place, boys,' he bawled, 'we shall be along in a minute.' A great cheer rang out as they began trekking back to the road. Most of them had done very well with the bookies. Nat had become firm favourite once word of Yanto's war-wounded leg had circulated. But most people who knew him stayed firmly with him and were now very happy that they had.

Five minutes later a tired but warmly contented Yanto made his way back with Knocker, Billy, and the Doc. He felt a little self-conscious of the strip of plaster running down the full length of his nose. As they walked, Doc had explained he had been unable to do anything about Nat's nose, it had been too badly broken, so he had told Sam to take him straight to the hospital. 'I expect they will have to take him to Gloucester.'

'Serves 'im right,' Billy spat, 'that will stop him farting in church.'

Wilf Tillett's hay wagon was waiting for them. It was a quarter full of sweet-smelling hay, and with a moan of ecstasy, Yanto lay back in it and closed his eyes.

For the second time that day, the cavalcade passed through Berkeley market place. There was still no sign of the police. 'Gawd bless 'em,' Knocker growled under his breath, 'they must have turned Nelson's eye on us.'

Police-public relations were probably at an all-time high at this time. Most of the big bobbies were veterans of one or the other of the great wars, and had seen their share of death and misery. They knew when to be lenient. Many local boys, who probably in later generations would have been landed with a record for life for pinching apples or riding their bikes with no lights, escaped with a clip around the ear and a cussing from those tough, kind-hearted coppers. They were probably the best there was ever to be.

'Ere, 'ave a snort of this,' chortled Knocker happily, as the cart passed through Brookend.

He handed his hip flask full of fine malt whisky to the laid back Yanto, who took a long pull at it and lay back again. He was so thankful that it was all over and his reputation was still intact.

His nose hurt like hell, but Doc Saunderson had done a good job and it was a small price to pay for that rosy glow of satisfaction that was coursing through him.

'Gonna be some sort of night at the Boar tonight, eh, Knock?' he said happily.

'You can bet your balls on that, chum!' Billy interrupted, as he helped himself to Knocker's whisky. 'Here's to you champ,' he laughed and took a swig.

When the column finally reached the Boar it was 8.30, and then things really began to jump. Word had got back to the village early by way of the motorised regulars who had taken them to the venue, and already the pub was half full of excited villagers eager to spend their winnings. 'Open the lounge up,' Renee,' Knocker ordered, 'it's gonna be a busy night.'

A couple of sober locals were called up for bar duty as the real drinking began. The stragglers were still arriving and Knocker had to arrange extra benches and upturned barrels on the lawn.

'Thank Christ it's a warm night,' Knocker murmured to himself. A pianist was summoned to re-activate the ancient piano and it wasn't long before the renderings of 'Annie Laurie' and 'We're Going to Hang Out the Washing on the Siegfried Line' drifted out over the estuary accompanied by dozens of appreciative voices.

As the evening wore on, the cider began to take its inevitable toll. Some had staggered home, while others lay in dreamless sleep on the lawn.

Yanto and Billy were laughing and holding each other up in the bar when they were cornered by Sooty Hill.

'Did you hear the one about the two real old farmers from around here?'

'No, but I reckon we're about to,' laughed Billy.

'This is a true story, mind,' Sooty said with a straight face, and the two boys began to laugh.

'Well,' said Sooty, 'these two real old farmers was in the bar together, see. This bar I think t'wus, come to think of it. Anyway,' he continued, 'this old farmer said to t'other, "Hey," he said, "your boy took my daughter out las' night."

"Oh aah," said t'other.

"And that ent all," said the first. "E never got 'er 'ome til gone two."

"Oh aah," said t'other.

"And that ent all," said the first again. "'E broke my daughter's virginity."

"Oh aah," said t'other, "he always was an awkward bugger. 'E broke my tractor las' week.".'

The boys fell down, hysterical. Yanto thought his nose was splitting again. 'Piss off, Soot, for Christ sake,' he groaned.

A few more were staggering home now. Even Sammy

Pockets managed to mount his bike and rode away in a figure-of-eight fashion.

It was then that Windy Willoughby, one of the local bargees, sank his tenth pint of cider of the night. Windy had a unique abdomen and could fart louder than anybody in the county. Some said if the wind was in the right direction it was quite audible even when his barge was in mid-river. The two pounds Windy had won on Yanto had almost gone, and his round chubby face glowed with ecstasy as he braced himself for the act for which he was notorious. He watched Renee disappear into the back room and decided the time was right.

All attention suddenly focussed on Windy as the thunderous fart echoed through the bar. Unfortunately, Renee returned just in time to catch the blast.

Renee fixed a steely gaze on the perpetrator. 'Get out, you dirty sod,' she screamed. As she did so, she saw his jovial face change from ecstasy to sheer horror. It was obvious what had happened. 'Oh no, Nathan,' she screeched, hitting top C, 'he's shit hisself in my bar! Get out, you dirty old bugger!'

As the bar flap thudded open and the massive head appeared, Windy did the rapid stiff-legged strut, long associated with a surfeit of cider in these parts, out of the door. Knocker watched him disappear into the pillbox on the lawn and slammed the bar door.

'Nathan,' Renee shrilled, 'for God's sake leave the door open.'

At that moment young Jackie, one of the local boys who had been allowed to stay out late, burst into the bar panting and wide-eyed.

'Mr Nelmes,' he shrilled over the row, 'Sammy Pockets is in the cut again.'

'Oh, bloody 'ell, not again,' Knocker groaned. 'Quick, you two,' he ordered, 'my grappling hook and rope. It's on the wall in the yard. If 'is mac gets saturated he could go down like a stone.'

Yanto and Billy dashed from the bar as fast as their condition would allow. They found the grappler and ran the few hundred yards to the canal towpath. Sammy hadn't even made it on to the towpath this time. He had obviously made some sort of effort to negotiate the ninety-degree turn on to the path, but the fact that he was now floating happily only twenty feet from the swing bridge indicated that it had been somewhat half-hearted.

He made a funny sight floating there. His old long mac had risen up and now lay around him on the surface with big bumps of trapped air sticking up. His bald head shining in the half-light, along with the red nose and yellow scarf, made a beautiful centrepiece.

'You look like a bloody great water lily,' laughed Billy as he threw him the rope.

Sammy was totally incoherent and the two boys almost went in themselves as they manhandled his dead weight on to the bank.

As Yanto half carried him the two hundred yards to his cottage, Billy grappled for his bike.

Ten minutes later, with Sammy and his bike safely deposited, they took the short cut along the river bank back to The Blue Boar. It was relatively quiet in the pub now, with just a handful of First Division boozers left. Sam Torrence was standing at the bar talking to Knocker. Sam turned to Yanto as he came to the bar. 'Congratulations, son, he said, and stuck his hand out, 'it was a great fight and you won fair and square.'

'Got Knocker's training to thank for that,' Yanto chipped in.

'Anyway,' Sam continued, as he threw down the remains of his pint. 'I just popped in to let you know you got fifty quid comin' to yah.'

'Fifty quid.' Yanto gasped.

'Yep,' said Sam, 'we took a hunner'd and sixty quid. Eighty quid to the club, fifty for you, and thirty for Nat.' He looked at Yanto, grinning like an idiot. Yanto was doing some mental arithmetic.

'Christ, that's six hundred and forty people!'

'Yep,' Sam said again as he made for the door,' 'worth it, wuddn't it. Good night all.'

'Talkin' of money,' said Knocker, 'I ant counted the takin's yet, but it's got to be my best night ever, even better than V.E. night.'

'All's well that ends well, champ,' Billy slurred as he threw his arm around Yanto's shoulders.

Knocker pushed two large malts across the bar. 'Special night cap for yah,' he grunted. As the two boys picked up the glasses the flame from the gas lamp filtered through the golden nectar within.

Eighteen

IRELAND

It was eight o'clock in the morning, and the oppressive Sunday morning silence hung over Sharpness docks like a sunlit cloak. Not a ripple disturbed the surface of the bright water, causing the mirrored reflections of the grain warehouses to appear as solid as their originals.

The *Rita* lay motionless at her moorings between the high and low bridges, with the morning sun lighting up the coats of yacht varnish lovingly applied to her hull over the years.

She was a clinker-built West Country fishing boat, forty-five feet long and eighteen feet in the beam. A good deep sea boat born in a Devon dockyard at the turn of the century, when working boats were built to last forever. Reg Littlejohn had acquired her in 1930 and had been lovingly restoring and adapting her to his own requirements ever since. The former working hack now boasted all the mod cons. Three comfortable bunks, four at a push, were set forward in the bow. The modern efficient galley, accessible by means of a slide-topped hatch forward of the wide roomy stern well, would have put many of the local houses to shame. Her upper works, glistening in dark brown and white paint, plus the matching colours of the seat padding and cushions, indicated that Rita Littlejohn had had a hand in the renovation.

Reg had also adapted the steering system to his own requirements. The boat could be steered by the polished wheel in the wheelhouse, the chains plainly visible running along the scuppers. But she could also be steered by the long tiller bar situated on the raised poop deck at the stern, which was six feet long. Too long, one might have thought. But the *Rita* was a heavy boat and the extended tiller gave greater leverage to steer the vessel.

'After all,' Reg had said many times as he lay back steering in the sun, 'I bought the boat for pleasure, not hard work.'

It was already very warm, indicating a scorcher to come, and Terry Littlejohn worked up a sweat as he stowed away stores and fishing gear. He had spent freely getting in high-quality food and drink for the trip. He now had a great deal of respect for the Colonel and was determined to impress him. Any doubts Terry had harboured regarding his receiving the astonishingly high fee of two hundred pounds had been dispelled a week before, when the Colonel had waylaid him again. Much to Terry's delight Murchison had given him fifty pounds in advance. He had also given him their destination. It seemed he wanted to fish in Strangford Lough in County Down, on the east coast. So Terry had plotted a course accordingly.

The *Rita* was still rigged for sail, but Terry had never used her that way. His father had acquired the big Perkins marine diesel engine from somewhere during the war, which pushed the boat along at a steady ten knots, twelve flat out, and Terry was quite content with that.

Feeling the boat rock slightly, he looked out of the galley porthole and saw Nat yawning and stretching himself in the stern well. He carried an overnight bag and looked fit and well; apart from his nose, which still looked a mess.

As Terry showed him where to stow his kit, the Colonel's car slid to a halt on the quayside. Barney Summerville jumped out and opened the door for the Colonel, who looked elegantly casual in rough tweed trousers and an expensive windcheater.

The Colonel reservedly returned Terry's chirpy 'Good morning.' As he did so, Nat leaned over the rail and took the fishing paraphernalia plus the two travel bags from the red-faced Barney and dumped them on the warm planking of the stern well. After introducing the Colonel to Nat, it became obvious to Terry that Murchison intended to remain as remote from them as possible, but he shrugged as he thought of the money and continued preparing the *Rita* for departure.

As Nat busied himself checking the engine, Murchison

turned to Terry. 'When do you estimate we shall be returning? I need to inform my man when to pick me up.'

'All being well,' Terry replied cautiously, 'we shall be back here on the late afternoon tide next Thursday.' Murchison instructed Barney to pick him up at that time and after a smart salute, Barney departed.

Half an hour later, with the lockage fee paid and the Colonel below, the *Rita* moved out into the estuary. Terry was at the wheel as the turning tide gripped them and pushed them effortlessly downriver. He gazed thoughtfully through the wheelhouse window as his father's departing words drifted through his mind. 'Bring that boat back in once piece or don't bother to come back at all.'

As the *Rita* passed Berkeley House Farm, the Colonel emerged from below and joined Terry in the wheelhouse. 'We'll run to Barry on this tide,' Terry explained, 'that should take us about five hours comfortable.' The Colonel nodded. 'We'll hang over there for the next high water,' Terry continued, 'then shoot down to Milford Haven. If I keep her on a steady ten knots that should take about twelve hours.'

'What about fuel?' the Colonel asked.

'I'll fill up at Milford,' Terry replied quickly. He still felt nervous in this man's presence. 'I brought extra fuel cans, so we can run from Milford to Strangford Lough and back to Milford without refuelling again.'

'What's your estimated time of arrival at Strangford Lough?' There was almost a hint of a smile on the Colonel's face as he asked the question.

Terry wrinkled his brow as he calculated. 'Depending on conditions, around Tuesday midday.'

The Colonel was lost in thought for a while. 'Right,' he said briskly, 'immediately on arrival I would like to enter the Lough and endeavour to catch some sea trout until dusk on Tuesday. 'Then, I want you to anchor off the village called Killyleagh and wait while I use the dinghy to nip ashore for an hour or two.' He jerked his thumb towards the stern, where the little wooden dinghy danced along behind them at the end of the tow rope.

'You're the boss,' Terry grinned.

'Good lad,' smiled the Colonel uncharacteristically, as he slipped on a pair of sunglasses. He was beginning to relax and enjoy himself. Everything was going smoothly and in a few short days his troubles should be over. Then, with surprising agility for a man of his age, he swung himself out of the wheelhouse, jumped down into the stern well, and began sunning himself.

A week or so after his first visit, Old Jesus called at the Venables farm again, to see how Arthur was getting along. Tilly Venables fussed him inside and insisted that he join her in a cup of tea before going up to Arthur's room.

Tilly seemed to be of mixed feelings. 'Oh, Jason,' she murmured, as he sipped his tea, 'he's wearing himself out. He lies there day and night sweating buckets and working his poor shoulders. Even when he's asleep I'm sure he's still working in his mind.'

He leaned over and patted her hand. 'That's good, Tilly,' he said soothingly. 'He knows it's his only chance and he is taking it. I am praying that that stubborn determination of his will prevail.'

Tilly suddenly brightened up as a thought struck her. She looked at him smiling. 'I was very pleased yesterday,' she said, 'I was cooking myself a bit of lamb stew for dinner and it smelt lovely. Anyway, Arthur suddenly started hammering on the floor upstairs. When I went up he asked me if he could have some. Said he was starving, poor lamb.'

'Go on,' Jason said hurriedly.

'Well, I took him some up and he got it down 'im like a good 'un. Didn't bring it up neither. That's the first food he's been able to keep down for ages.'

Jason jumped up excitedly. 'That's marvellous news, Tilly,' he jabbered. 'Don't you realise what a hopeful sign that is? I am sure he is going to make it.'

Then, after quickly draining the remains of his tea, they went

222

up to Arthur's room.

Jason slipped in quietly. The room was in semi-darkness, but he could hear his friend breathing, heavy and regular.

As his eyes grew accustomed to the gloom, he could see Arthur's shoulders moving rhythmically under the covers. He appeared to be almost trance-like in his concentration and was completely unaware of Jason's presence.

Jason decided it was best not to disturb him, and joined Tilly who was hovering outside the bedroom door. Together they went back to the kitchen.

'Well, what do you think of him?' she asked, wringing her hands together.

'I am very pleased,' he replied earnestly, 'but we mustn't get our hopes up too much. Having said that, I feel very confident.'

'Well, I shall just keep praying,' Tilly said resignedly. 'The doctor's coming on his routine visit tomorrow. I wonder what he will make of him?'

'I'll call again in a week or so,' Jason said, as he rose to leave. 'Maybe I shall be able to have a talk to Arthur then.'

'Where d'you think you're going?' Tilly asked, as he made for the door.

'Home.'

'Oh no, you don't,' Tilly said firmly, 'I am going to cook you a nice bit o' dinner. That's the least I can do.'

Jason sat down again.

Colonel Murchison idly watched the smudge of Lundy Island appear and then slowly disappear off the port bow as the *Rita* trudged her way up the St George's Channel. She had refuelled at Dale, Milford Haven, and was now on the last leg of the outward journey.

The Players cigarette hung forgotten from his lips as his mind analysed past events and future solutions. He mulled over his meeting with Nick Sarrazin, which had taken place the evening before he had given the fifty pounds advance to Terry Littlejohn.

Sarrazin had numerous connections with the big city

underworld and although the Colonel was in debt to him to the tune of three thousand pounds, Sarrazin knew he was an officer and gentleman, and respected him for it. With this in mind, after the Colonel had put the proposition to him, and graphically described the high quality of the counterfeit money, he had made subtle enquiries. Sarrazin had finally offered to exchange, or to use his own words, launder the money for five thousand pounds, legit.

'Five per cent?' The wily Colonel had pretended to be outraged and said he would go to London and do the job direct. Sarrazin had then made his final offer. Five thousand pounds, up front in cash, provided the counterfeit money came up to expectations, plus he would return the Colonel's IOUs for the three thousand pound debt. A total of eight thousand.

The Colonel still showed a pretext of disappointment, when in fact he was delighted. The deal was struck.

He flicked away the half-smoked cigarette and leaned out over the bow rail. As he watched the *Rita*'s cumbersome bow cut through the now clear water, he made a resolution. Once this trip was over and he was out of the financial mire, he would cease his gambling and generally make amends to his wife and daughter for his past misdemeanours.

His thoughts were interrupted as Nat came forward stripped to the waist and carrying a huge mug of tea. 'With the skipper's compliments, sir,' he said with a grin. The Colonel smiled back as he accepted the tea, then went back to his thoughts.

'Is there anything I should know about this lough?' Terry asked the Colonel as the *Rita* slowly made her way up the narrowing water channel towards the entrance to Strangford Lough. The land they were passing to starboard was the tip of the Ards Peninsula, which isolated the lough from the Irish Sea. It was eleven o'clock on the Tuesday and it had been a perfect, uneventful trip, with the sun blazing down on a ripple-free sea all the way.

The Colonel mopped his face with a large handkerchief before replying.

'I was stationed around here for a while during the war.' He replied. 'The lough is about twenty miles long if I recall, and about five miles wide at the widest point.'

'What about the depth?' Terry asked him without taking his eyes away from the ever narrowing channel. 'Any shallow sandbars and the like?'

'No problem for a boat of this size,' came the curt reply. 'There's a small ferry service across the bar entrance between Strangford and Portaferry. We shall be able to see it soon. About a quarter of a mile wide there.'

Terry nodded as he concentrated. 'Once we are through the bar, make for the west shore.' The Colonel smiled as he spoke and patted his stomach. 'I'm starving, and would like some grub before having a go at those trout.'

'This'll do, Nat, sling the 'ook over.' Terry's voice rang through the still morning air. The Colonel had indicated the spot and was now standing in the bow thoughtfully scrutinising the peaceful pastures lying half a mile away from the motionless *Rita*. The cluster of buildings that represented the village of Killyleagh was quite visible lying under the shimmering heat haze. It was a beautiful morning and a beautiful spot. One to gladden the heart of anyone. Especially a fisherman.

The mirror bright surface of the lough sparkled and shimmered in the morning sun, with little islands dotted here and there. On the shore, misty green grazing and agricultural land seemed to sweep right to the water's edge. The memories of that day in 1941 invaded the Colonel's mind, and again he went over the well-memorised markers which would indicate the spot where he had buried the hundred thousand pounds.

He knew he would recognise the spot when he saw it, even at dusk. But was the money still in good condition. Would the webbing pack and gas cape have protected it over those six years in the soil of Ireland? Sarrazin would use any excuse to cut the price.

Finally, the glorious aroma of bacon, eggs, and coffee cut through his nagging doubts, and with a sigh he went through to the galley.

'Hey! You got a cracker there, Colonel.' Nat leaned over the rail excitedly as the line screamed out of the reel. Two respectable sea trout, one four pounds, the other six, lay twitching in a basket in the stern well. The Colonel, now fully relaxed again, fought and guided this latest catch expertly. The sweat began to pour from his brow and into his eyes. Terry mopped the Colonel's brow good-naturedly as Nat grabbed the long-handled net. As the Colonel finally manipulated his quarry to the *Rita*'s side, Nat scooped up the specimen trout with a whoop.

'If that ain't eight pounds then my dick's a bloater,' Terry said in admiration.

'Toast and bloater paste for tea?' Nat said with a grin. But when weighed it was indeed eight and a quarter pounds. The Colonel could not remember when he had enjoyed himself so much, but as the light finally began to fade, the main reason for his being there began to cloud his mind.

With the big trout safely in the basket, he turned to Terry and asked him to prepare the dinghy for his trip ashore. 'I'm going down to change,' he said curtly, and handed the rod to Nat. 'Here, you keep up the good work,' he said, as he went below.

With less than half an hour of daylight left, the Colonel beached the little rowing boat on the lough shore and began making his way across the fields towards the Killyleagh Road. The road ran adjacent to the lough shore and the Colonel had judged his landing point accordingly. The wood where the money was buried was less than a mile from Killyleagh and Murchison had been able to see the wood quite clearly with his field glasses from the *Rita*.

He made his way through a herd of grazing cows, and after climbing the five-barred gate, found himself on the road. Turning to his right he could just see the first cottages of Killyleagh village. To anyone who saw him he was a well-to-do hiker. Plus-four trousers were in evidence along with heavy

Fenn boots. The tweed hacking jacket, with collar and tie, gave off an air of respectability that few would dare to challenge.

He wore the flat cap of the country elite and carried a large hiker's backpack which appeared to be well packed with something. In fact, it was well packed with old newspapers and anything else he had been able to find, which would eventually finish up occupying the hole which currently concealed the counterfeit money bag. On his return to the boat he wanted Terry and Nat to see him as he was when he left them. No point in raising their curiosity any more than was necessary.

The twilight turned to deep gloom as the road entered the wood and he became concerned lest he found difficulty in locating the markers.

He increased his already brisk pace. The road was just as he remembered it, and quite deserted, which suited him fine.

He came to a bend in the road which he remembered encountering immediately after leaving the burial spot in the scout car. If his memory served him well, there should be a pull-in off the road immediately around the bend on the right. And there it was. Just as if he had buried the money yesterday. He took a final look around before walking unhurriedly into the pull-in. Then on, into the wood itself.

He thought of the traumatic things that had happened to him since he was last in this spot, as he searched for the tree with the corkscrew trunk.

It was now almost dark and he gave an audible sigh of relief as he located the tree. He glanced to his right. There was the other marker; a tree with a split trunk, looking like a letter Y.

He took a straight line between the two trees and counted out ten paces from the base of the corkscrew tree. Originally he had counted twenty paces between the two trees and planted the money half way between them. Simple but effective.

He took a sharp hand trowel from his backpack and began to dig. Thick grass had grown over the spot, so first he removed the turf from an area of approximately six square feet and placed it to one side. The soil beneath felt dry and loamy. Obviously well drained, which made him feel more confident that the money would still be in mint condition.

He dug quickly through the soft soil, pausing every half a dozen trowelfuls to listen. But apart from the soft rustle of the leaves, all was still.

As he reached a depth of about two feet, he stiffened with excitement as the trowel encountered something soft and pliable. After a few more feverish digs, he scooped the loose earth out with his hands. There was the bag, still wrapped in the gas cape and as dry as a bone. 'Thank God,' he groaned under his breath as he dragged the burden out of the hole and brushed off the loose dirt.

Working quickly, he unwrapped the gas cape and stuffed it back in the hole, along with the newspapers and other rubbish from his hiker's pack. He then filled in the hole with the loose dirt and replaced the turf. The Colonel was a meticulous man.

Then, with the webbing pack containing the counterfeit money stowed out of sight in the hiker's bag, he made his way out of the now pitch dark wood towards the road.

PC Daniel O'Rourke cursed as the front lamp on his bicycle went out for the third time. He pulled the lamp from its bracket and gave it a good thump, but this time it refused to light. 'Blast it,' he growled, as he jumped back on his bike and cycled on up the dark deserted road.

He was on his way back to Killyleagh police station after his nocturnal patrol of the surrounding rural backwater. It grew even darker as the road entered the small wood, but his eyes were now becoming accustomed to the night.

He stiffened suddenly and his heart began to pound as he saw a dark figure emerge from the wood fifty yards ahead of him.

He had been told to watch for poachers and it looked as though he had inadvertently surprised this one red-handed, what with his bicycle lamp not working.

He allowed the bicycle to silently free-wheel to within a few yards of the unsuspecting man's back before challenging him. 'And what have we here?' he said loudly. He was unable to control the nervous tremor in his voice. The Colonel jumped violently and turned to face the big youthful policeman. Murchison's heart sank, but his mind was racing. If he was found with the counterfeit money on him, all was lost and his life would be in ruins.

He cursed his luck under his breath. Then he cursed himself for his negligence. What a fool. The trip over, the recovery: everything had gone like clockwork. He should have realised something was bound to go wrong.

The policeman lay his bike gently on the ground, watching him like a hawk as he did so, then stood facing the Colonel.

'Just you stay quiet,' he warned, 'while I see what you've got tucked away in there.' He reached cautiously for the backpack which hung loosely over the Colonel's left shoulder. He used his left arm, which, for a second, left him wide open. The spectre of his wife's shamed face as she visited him in jail flashed before the Colonel's eyes. It was now or never.

The vicious right hook landed perfectly on the constable's unprotected jaw. Murchison felt the jaw break as the blow landed.

He also felt his own hand break at the same time. The sickening, jarring pain shot up his arm, making him gasp out loud in agony.

PC O'Rourke dropped without a sound and lay still.

Using his good left hand, the Colonel pulled the inert constable and his bicycle off the road and onto the grass verge. It was bad enough having to hit the policeman, so he certainly couldn't take the chance of him being struck by a passing vehicle. He was in enough trouble already.

He undid one of the buttons on the front of his hacking jacket and painfully managed to insert his useless hand inside. It acted as a crude sling and gave him some respite from the pain. Then shouldering the heavy money bag as best he could, he made off through the trees towards the lough shore and the boat. He couldn't even imagine how he was going to get the dinghy back to the *Rita*.

Nat was leaning over the bow rail enjoying the warm night air and smoking a cigarette. He suddenly became totally alert like a startled animal.

He could hear something splashing the water. It sounded about forty or fifty yards from the boat, towards the shore. It must be the Colonel he told himself, as he grabbed the spotlight. But why make all that noise with the oars?

He switched on the powerful light and swept the area from which the splashing seemed to come. What he saw made him gasp. The Colonel was kneeling on the floor of the little wooden dinghy, facing forward. He was using the one oar like a paddle, gripping the oar with his left hand and pushing on the end of it with his right elbow. It looked even more awkward when every other stroke had to be transferred to the starboard side of the dinghy in order to keep it in a straight line.

'Wo's up?' Nat called.

'Put that bloody light out and throw me a rope, for God's sake,' the Colonel shouted harshly. Nat jumped into the sternwell and grabbed a coiled rope. He stuck his head into the galley as he did so where Terry was making two mugs of cocoa.

'Better make that three mugs, mate,' Nat said softly, 'he's back, and it looks like he's hurt.'

'Oh ahh,' Terry said to himself, 'I wondered when the trouble would start. Two hundred quid for a fishing trip, there had to be a catch.'

He came out of the galley as Nat threw the rope. The Colonel managed to wrap his arm around the rope and they pulled him in.

Before they got him over the side the colonel told Terry to get underway for home. 'What? Are you crazy?' Terry yelped. 'We can't see a thing. It's like peering up a crow's ass at midnight out there.'

'We'll manage,' the Colonel snapped. 'Something has come up. It's imperative we leave now,' he continued, 'otherwise I shan't be leaving at all. And that means no fee, of course.'

'Is there somebody after you?' Terry looked him straight in the eye.

230

'There will be if we don't get the hell out of here before dawn.'

'OK, let's go,' Terry said resignedly, 'pull up the hook, Nat.'

The tone in the Colonel's voice had conveyed the urgency of the situation to the two boys and the response was immediate.

Terry disappeared into the wheelhouse to start the diesel, and Nat leapt up into the bows to winch in the anchor. Doing his bit, the Colonel grabbed the rope attached to the dinghy and manoeuvred the little craft around the *Rita*'s side and hurriedly secured the rope to the stern with his good hand.

With a muffled roar the diesel burst into life. Slowly and carefully they made their way across the lough towards the narrow exit bar.

'Tide's going out, at least that's in our favour,' Terry grunted. The Colonel stood beside him in the wheelhouse, anxiously staring ahead. Nat was up in the bow keeping his eyes peeled. The lights of Strangford and Portaferry were plainly visible ahead. 'I'll just make for the black bit in the middle,' Terry said with a chuckle.

As the *Rita* neared the bar she began to pick up speed.

'Bloody 'ell,' there was concern in Terry's voice, 'we've got some sort of current here.'

'Oh yes,' the Colonel came out of his thoughtful trance. 'I do recall some local chap telling me that this tide goes out through the bar at nine knots.' 'Christ,' said Terry, as he doubled his concentration.

Nat had noticed the increasing speed of the *Rita* as she neared the bar, but was unconcerned as his eyes were now fully accustomed to the light. He could see there were no hidden obstacles in their way and the bar showed up clearly between the lights of Strangford and Portaferry.

Nat suddenly became aware of a strange sound. It was an eerie, blood chilling moan. As the *Rita* drew nearer and nearer to the bar the unnerving sound increased. Nat went back and stuck his head in the wheelhouse feeling thankful for the light and the company.

'Here,' he said, 'come and 'ave a listen to this, weirdest

bloody sound I've ever heard.'

'Is it a moaning sound?' the colonel asked, unable to hear anything over the noise of the diesel. 'Yeah,' Nat replied, 'I'm beginning to wonder if there's any truth in them stories about the Irish Banshees.'

'No, that's something else the old locals told me during the war,' the Colonel said quickly. 'It seems the force of the water pushing through the bar as the tide goes out sets up this weird moaning sound. They call it the moaning lough. It's a phenomenon. Nobody knows what causes it.'

'Thank Christ for that,' said Nat, as he returned to his post in the bow.

The Colonel laughed at Nat's back, then stiffened with a little cry as a spasm of pain shot through his damaged hand.

Terry suddenly remembered Nat saying that the Colonel was hurt. 'What's the matter?' he demanded, 'you hurt your arm?'

'No it's my hand,' the Colonel grunted. 'Fell over getting back to the dinghy.'

'I'll get Nat to take a look once we get through the bar,' Terry replied, stiff with concentration, 'he did first aid in the navy.'

Two minutes later the *Rita* shot through the bar like a Bondi surfer.

Thanks to the outgoing tide, the stretch from the lough bar to the open sea was rapid but uneventful. All three of them, the Colonel especially, were visibly relieved to be at sea and on course for the Bristol Channel.

Later, as Nat inspected his hand, Murchison had to force himself not to cry out. Already the hand was all colours of the rainbow.

'Christ! That's a bad break,' Nat breathed, 'I'll bind it the best I can, but you had better get to a doctor fast when you get home. How'ja do it anyway?'

'Fell on it,' came the curt reply. Nat looked at him and said nothing. He had seen enough punch-broken hands to know the Colonel was lying. He voiced his suspicions to Terry later when the Colonel was sleeping.

'Yeah, he had trouble while he was ashore, OK,' Terry agreed, 'but it's nowt to do with us. We just keep our traps shut when we get home. Remember that, Nat, OK?'

'How long have you known me?' Nat's voice was a growl.

'Yeah, a long time,' said Terry hurriedly, 'sorry, mate.' He went to a small locker in the corner of the wheelhouse and took out a bottle of scotch. 'Let's drink to a safe trip home, then you get some kip, OK.' They sipped their scotch in a moody silence, with the subdued wheelhouse light shadowing their faces as they thought their own thoughts.

Then Nat threw down the remains of his drink in one go and looked at his watch. It was 3 a.m. 'It's the pit for me,' he grunted, 'what time d'you want relieving?'

'I'll give you a shout about 6.30,' came the reply. 'G'night, mate.'

It was seven o'clock when Terry woke him by stamping on the floor of the wheelhouse. But to Nat it seemed as though he had been asleep about five minutes. Getting to sleep had been difficult with the Colonel fretting and talking fitfully in his sleep on the next bunk. Nat got up quietly and left the curtains drawn. The colonel seemed to be sleeping peacefully now.

It was a glorious morning, made even more beautiful by being at sea. Nat felt great as he jumped down into the stern well clad only in his underpants, and sloshed some cold water into a bowl. He washed the sleep from his eyes with a will, then rubbed his face vigorously with a rough towel before stretching and looking around. God, it was gorgeous. But it was different. He stood there looking over the stern and scratching his belly. What was different?' Something was missing. 'Christ, the dinghy. 'Hey, Terry,' he yelled, 'the bloody dinghy's gone.'

Terry dashed from the wheelhouse. 'Oh, bollocks,' he groaned. 'My old man'll bloody kill me. Who tied the bastard up?'

'Must have bin the Colonel,' Nat grunted.

As they stood there vainly scrutinising the horizon, the Colonel appeared on deck, looking haggard. 'You didn't do a very good job tying up the tender, Colonel.' There was an accusing note in Terry's voice.

Murchison, who had just emerged from the dark horrors of his dreams into the bright reality of the beautiful morning, was unperturbed. 'I'm sorry, m'boys,' he chortled, as he prepared to wash using his good hand. 'Tying her up one-handed, that's what it was, but don't worry about it; I shall replace it on our return, never fear.'

Terry turned to Nat as the Colonel washed. 'More bad luck,' he said and banged his hand on the bulwark. 'I wonder what else will go wrong before we get home?'

Nineteen

THE RETURN

On that same Thursday morning, Joanna Murchison was off to do something she had secretly wanted to do for the last thirty-three years.

She was going to pay a visit to Jason Selby. The official reason was to thank him personally for saving the life of her daughter. A sound enough reason for a woman of her status to visit a man, she told herself.

As she drove her pony and trap along the sun-dappled castle walk, many thoughts were infiltrating her mind. She was on her way to visit the only man she'd ever truly loved. The smouldering love which she had successfully suppressed all those years had suddenly re-kindled after her daughter's graphic account of the man who had saved her life.

Her husband, although a hard man in many ways and very weak in others, had been basically good to her. But it had been a loveless life for her, and being human, the warm wonderful memories of those days with Jason before the Great War refused to die.

It was a hopeless love for a woman in her position, she knew that, but at least she now had a good reason to visit and talk with her lost love.

She dismounted at the entrance to the castle meadow and pushed open the five-barred gate then, having driven the pony and trap through, made sure the gate was securely fastened. Obeying the country code was an automatic thing to her class. A sudden wave of elated abandon swept over her as she drove the swaying trap along the grass track through the meadow. With the castle looming on her left, and a total absence of the trappings of the time, she was back in the carefree days of her youth. She was calling on her man, a real man, whose generation had all but perished in 'the war to end all wars'. The fact that he now lived in a converted cowshed, instead of the great country house of her last visit, was neither here nor there.

She tied the pony to a sapling near the brook side and walked over the picturesque little bridge. Her nerves began to play on her as she picked her way between the cowpats. How would he react? The last time she had seen him close up, he had run a mile.

She had avoided wearing her normal stern, sober clothes and had dressed casually. She didn't want to frighten him off again. She wore a long green tartan skirt, along with a tasteful but simple blouse and matching cardigan.

The shoes were sensible flat walking shoes, and there was the inevitable walking cane. Most daring of all was the absence of the bun. Her daughter had won the day. The naturally wavy hair, blonde and silver, had been stylishly cut just above the shoulders, which no doubt helped contribute towards her feelings of daring.

With a lightness in her step, she walked around the edge of the wood.

With a grunt, Old Jesus leaned out and pulled in his bank line for checking.

Yes, something had been nibbling at the roach in his absence all right, but it wasn't the pike. 'Just small fry,' he muttered to himself as he attached a fresh roach to the triple hook. He carefully tossed the line back into the favoured spot, then after a quick shake of his tin of washers alarm system, made his way back towards the shack. As he reached the edge of the wood he stopped dead in his tracks. He could see his shack, and there was a woman standing by his ever-open door. It wasn't Tilly. Too slim. As the woman turned and gazed around, his knees turned to jelly.

'God, it's Joanna.' Panic welled up inside him. He was about to run back into the seclusion of the woods: then he chided himself as he remembered his recent resolve.

He looked down at himself and was glad that he had decided to tidy himself up. His hair was combed, his beard was trimmed. He had discarded his old plimsolls in favour of a pair of smart country brogues. Even the well-washed corduroy trousers had a discernible crease in them. Yes, he felt presentable. He also felt decidedly lightheaded. Why had she called after all this time? He remembered Julie's words at the shack. 'My parents will wish to thank you personally.' Yes, it had to be that. He took a deep breath and walked determinedly towards her.

She watched him approach with a little smile on her face. He couldn't find the words to speak. 'Hello, Jason,' she said softly. 'You look marvellous. How have you been?'

He laughed, feeling foolish, and shrugged his shoulders before pointing at the shack. 'As you see me,' he said and laughed again. She turned towards the shack and scrutinised the garden. He felt an overwhelming desire to hold her and kiss her.

'I think you have carved a lovely little piece of England out of these pastures, Jason,' she said, 'but you always were an industrious man.'

She turned and smiled at him again.

'I came home for some tea,' he blurted, 'would you care for some?'

'I would indeed,' she replied, 'thank you.' As they entered the shack Joanna made approving noises as Jason brushed non-existent crumbs from a chair before offering it to her. He busied himself making the tea, unable to think of anything to say.

'You know why I called, I expect,' Joanna said suddenly.

He paused and looked at her. 'Not really,' he replied, 'but I'm very glad that you did.'

'You saved my daughter's life,' she said in a whisper. 'If I live to be a hundred, I could never repay you for that.'

He didn't know what to say at first. Then he did. 'She could have been mine, you know, but for circumstances.' He couldn't believe he had said it. He looked at her and she averted her eyes to the floor.

'Oh, Jason,' she said softly, 'the things we did to appease

convention. I did come here to thank you,' she went on hurriedly, 'but I admit that was not the only reason.' He took the tea to the table, unable to believe what he was hearing. As he sat down he noticed her eyes had grown moist. 'I know I ruined both our lives,' she continued sadly, 'but no one has regretted it more than I.'

Tears welled up in his eyes and he yearned to hold her. 'You can't imagine what it means to me to hear you say that,' he said, and covered her hand with his on the table. 'All the misery and hardship I have endured has been worth it, just to have you here saying these things.' He felt he had to say it all.

'I know it's impossible,' he went on, 'but I want you to know I have loved you all my life and I will love you till the day I die.' She began to sob. 'There, I've said it,' he said, 'and I'm glad I said it. Now, drink your tea, then we'll talk of happier days.' She laughed back at him, and they did talk. About their grand nights together at the glittering balls, and their weekends away at the regattas and races. About a different world of privilege and splendour, when they were young and time mattered not.

For each of them it was the happiest hour they had spent for thirty-three years.

When he finally waved after her as she departed in the pony and trap, he felt drunk with delirious joy.

The great tree had once stood tall and proud on the banks of the Severn's mouth at Beachley. Generations of local children had swung out over the grey water from the improvised rope swings that had hung from its spreaded branches. Over the years the relentless tides had ripped at, and undermined the bank around its roots; until one windy night several weeks before, it had given up the ghost and with one great protesting groan, had fallen into the waiting arms of the river.

Ever since then, it had journeyed back and forth up and down the estuary, going nowhere, like some grotesque *Flying Dutchman*. Sometimes it would lie for hours, high and dry on the sandbank. The next high water would effortlessly pluck it up and push it down the familiar path again. The lesser branches were long gone, and the muddy waters gradually and insidiously soaked and softened the great hard trunk.

Now, on this day, Thursday the tenth of July, it lay waterlogged and almost submerged in mid-river off Berkeley House Farm.

The outgoing tide had met its replacement coming in, and for a while it lay stationary, going neither this way nor that. But as the influx of new water gained predominance, the great log yawed around, then slowly and almost invisibly began to drift up river towards Sharpness.

After waving goodbye to Joanna, Jason returned to his shack and lay back in his easy chair. He was a completely happy man, totally at peace with himself and the world. He could never have her, he knew that, but they had made their peace together, and to know that she still cared for him, and had done all these years, filled him with wonder.

A knock on the open front door jerked him from his rosy thoughts. He turned and saw the plump figure of Tilly Venables framed in the sunlit doorway.

'Come in, my dear,' he said and jumped up. Tilly bustled into the room, smiling and breathless.

'Oh, Jason,' she breathed, 'I had to come over. I'm so excited.'

He sat her down, then sat opposite here and held her hand. 'Tell me,' he said. 'Well, the doctor, 'ee's just left. 'Ee couldn't get over our Arthur. Proper perplexed 'ee was.' She couldn't blurt the words out quick enough. 'There was my boy, sat up in bed eatin' boiled eggs and brown toast, with more colour in 'is face than I've seen in weeks. 'E ent been sick fer a fortnight, neither. Oh, Jason,' she said again, 'the doctor is sendin' 'im back to Gloucester Infirmary fer new tests and X-rays.'

Jason leaned forward and covered his face with his hands. 'Oh, glory be,' he whispered, 'the Lord had recognised me at last.' Tilly began to cry in her hopeful excitement.

'Come on, girl,' he soothed, 'he ain't out of the woods yet, so let's go and give the boy a bit more encouragement.'

The thunderstorm that had been threatening for the last hour, began as the *Rita* passed Bevington on the late afternoon tide.

Terry looked up as the first large spots began to spatter the wheelhouse windows.

'Blast it,' he snorted to Nat. 'Bloody sod's law, never fails. Another hour and we'd be home and dry. It's tricky enough getting into Sharpness without this bloody lot.'

The *Rita* was due into Sharpness at high water, seven o'clock, and the Colonel was standing in the bows fully dressed for disembarking. He was deep in thought. 'Just a few more miles and I've done it,' he told himself, as he unconsciously pulled at the webbing straps securing the hiker's pack to his back. His excitement was tinged with a nagging worry. Was the policeman all right? Yes, he was young and strong. They'll probably blame some local poacher for it anyway. As the first spots of rain began, he cast his worries aside and went below. Then after donning an oilskin and sou'wester, he went back to the bows and revelled in the rain.

As the *Rita* approached Sharpness the storm reached the height of its fury. The wind-driven rain lashed the boat in unremitting sheets as it swept along in the fast deep water.

Thunder echoed and rolled over the dark tree-lined western shore and the lightning rent the black cloudbanks with angry flashes of crimson. The Colonel still clung to the bow bulwark, excited and stimulated by the spectacle of nature's violence all around him. Thunderstorms had always held a fascination for him. The sudden unleashing of the elements, after the initial grumbling threats, held an almost sexual attraction for him.

'Look at the silly bastard,' Terry mouthed the words at Nat as he struggled with the wheel and vainly tried to see out through the rain lashed wheelhouse window. 'Serve 'im right if he gets struck by lightning.

To enter Sharpness docks a vessel does not simply turn right. The four-and-a-half knot tide race would contemptuously flush it past the entrance on to a waiting sandbank, where it would meet the same fate as the *S.S. Stancliffe*. To enter safely it was necessary to overshoot the dock entrance while way out in midstream, then execute a wide loop to approach the dock gates against the tide. Thus, the skipper has control over the situation.

Terry turned on full power as he began to swing the *Rita* round against the fearsome current. As he did so, the Colonel turned from the rail to go below.

At that precise moment in time, almost like keeping a date with destiny, the *Rita* hit the submerged tree trunk. The sickening impact as the heavy boat met the unyielding object shook the *Rita* from stem to stern.

It caught the Colonel totally unawares and in mid-step. With a terrible cry he toppled over the wooden bulwark into the racing grey maelstrom. He came to the surface shocked and wild with panic. Already his heavy clothes and backpack were dragging him down. His horror-filled eyes saw the *Rita* grow more distant by the second as the great hand of the tide sucked him towards the Severn railway bridge and its whirlpools, three quarters of a mile upstream. In wild desperation he grabbed for the straps of the backpack, hoping to dispose of its dragging weight. The fact that it contained one hundred thousand pounds was no longer of any consequence.

But he was sheathed in the oilskin. He gulped in mouthfuls of filthy salt water as he ripped at the buttons of the oilskin. In his panic he used his right hand. The sheer agony from his smashed hand as he dragged at the clinging shroud was too much.

He opened his mouth to scream but no sound came. His burden had relentlessly dragged him below the surface.

As he breathed in the salt water just before he died, he was tempted to laugh at the irony of it all. For a second just his hands appeared above the surface, one bandaged, the other like a claw trying to hang on to life. Then he was gone.

Terry and Nat's horrified eyes watched the Colonel go over, but their nightmare was just beginning. The forward motion of the heavy boat caused the bows to rear up and over the tree trunk. Terry braced himself, closed his eyes and prayed, as for a second, the *Rita* lay balanced across the log.

'Please, God almighty, don't let it take the prop.' God was otherwise engaged that day. With a sickening scraping rumble from beneath their feet, the *Rita* slid forward and over the massive obstacle.

As the stern came down hard on the log, there was a tearing ripping thump, and the engine revolutions increased to a screaming crescendo as the propeller sheared.

'Oh Jesus, we've 'ad it now,' screamed Terry, 'if only we had the dinghy.'

'Don't panic,' Nat shouted, 'I'll drop the hook.'

'She won't hold. We're drifting too fast already,' cried the demented Terry. As Nat scrambled into the bows, Terry looked wildly through the rain and mist. He could see the great steel bastions of the Severn Bridge looming in the distance. He looked towards the dock entrance. Several figures were running around waving wildly from the open gates, but they were powerless to help.

The *Rita*, now free of the log, was drifting faster and faster towards the bridge and disaster.

With a metallic roar, Nat released the anchor. There was a jolt for a second, after which the *Rita* continued her headlong drift. 'She's dragging her anchor,' Terry yelled, and dived into a locker. He emerged with two lifejackets. As Nat returned to the wheelhouse, Terry threw one to him.

'We'll have to swim for it,' he said wildly, 'with no power the boat will get sucked into the bridge piers, and with those whirlpools ...' He left the rest unsaid.

'Look,' Terry jabbered, as he pointed ahead to the right. 'The shore sticks out there like a small headland, see. If we go now and swim like stink, it's only a couple of hundred yards. If we don't it'll be too late, we'll get sucked up to the bridge.'

Nat donned his lifejacket but made no move. 'Come on, mate, for Christ sake,' Terry yelled, with his legs over the side. Nat rubbed his eyes clear of the still sheeting rain. 'You go on, mate,' he shouted, 'I'm going to try and steer her through the bridge piers.'

Never in all his life had Nat told anyone about his secret dread. He could swim, provided he was within his depth, but the thought of deep water under him had always filled him with frozen terror. The nightmares he had endured during his wartime navy services were too harrowing for words.

'You're bloody mad,' Terry screamed over the wind and rain, 'it's your funeral.' With that he jumped. Nat wondered if he had made the right decision as he watched Terry strike for the shore.

Then, as the peril of his situation hit him again, he leapt into action. He dashed into the wheelhouse, only to find the wheel jammed. His heart sank. 'Must have knackered the rudder as well,' he gasped, as he jumped into the stern well. He slipped on the wet planks and fell heavily on his elbow, sending an agonising pain through his arm.

Sick at heart, he clambered up to the raised stern. He ripped the long tiller bar from the rack and jammed it into the rudder socket. He had done some service as a sea boat helmsman in the navy and he hoped it would come in handy now.

The rudder was damaged but as he heaved on the extended tiller like a madman, it seemed to free itself. He realised that even with the rudder free he would have virtually no control over the boat. He was drifting, and with no forward movement through the water, there would be little if any response from the rudder anyway.

But he was a brave man, and a grim resolve gripped him as he watched the great piers of the bridge loom closer.

'It's shit or bust,' he told himself grimly as he bent to the task.

'Come on, mate, I'm getting bloody soaked down 'ere', Yanto yelled from the bottom of the ship's gangplank to Billy, who was still on board. Billy appeared on deck, then pulled up his coat collar against the rain before sprinting down the gangway.

It was 6.45 p.m. on the Thursday evening. They had been unable to finish unloading the Swedish coaster by five o'clock, so the gang had been asked to work on until she was finished. The skipper had wanted to leave at high water and already was making preparations to sail.

'Wo's the rush?' Billy demanded, as the rest of the gang came bouncing down the plank.

'I'm bloody parched, that's what,' Yanto replied as he impatiently tweaked the throttle of the motorbike. 'Let's grab a quick 'un at the Shant before we go.'

'OK by me, pal,' Billy's boyish face split into a wide grin, 'but do us a favour first, will ya?'

'Wo's that?' Yanto asked.

'I forgot to give me pools coupon to Jacko, lunchtime,' Billy explained, 'give us a lift up to the gates, Jacko's on duty tonight.'

'Hop on,' Yanto said resignedly. Yanto had guessed he would be on overtime today, so he had decided to ride the motorbike to work. With a roar they took off up the now deserted dockside. After shaking a few windows in Dock Road, they turned sharp left down past the dry dock and skidded to a halt on the edge of the tidal basin. The main entrance gates were open as they invariably were at high water. So the tidal basin was full, waiting to accommodate any incoming traffic.

'Keep 'er runnin,' Billy chirped, 'shan't be a tick.'

'Wo's all that shoutin' and bawlin' about?' Yanto asked as he glanced towards the main gates. Several of the lock gatemen were shouting and waving out into the river.

'I'll find out,' Billy snapped, and sprinted off in the direction of the gate house.

Yanto sat on his bike and watched curiously as he saw Billy bent talking to Jacko who was pointing out into the river. Two minutes later Billy came haring back. 'Bloody hell, Yant,' he gasped, breathlessly, 'it's Reg Littlejohn's boat. Terry and Nat are on board and they're in trouble. The bloody boat's drifting towards the bridge.'

'Christ, with no power they'll hit the bridge,' Yanto gasped, as he booted the bike into life, 'then they're done for.'

'They're trying to raise the rescue boat,' Billy said, as he jumped on the pillion, 'but there ain't no time.'

Yanto raced the bike into Dock Road then turned left for the shore. After negotiating the flotsam-strewn bank, he took the bike almost to the high-water mark and jumped off. The rain had stopped in spite of the great black cloud that still persisted overhead. In stark contrast, the sky over the west bank glowed with a pearly opalescence. Yanto took in the situation at a glance. The boat was already upriver of them. Less than half a mile from the bridge.

'There's some bugger swimmin', look,' Billy shouted and pointed. The lone swimmer was a hundred yards from the shore being swept along in front of them. 'It's Terry Littlejohn,' Billy yelped.

'So that must be Nat on the boat,' Yanto grunted, as he tore off his coat and threw it over the bike. 'Look after Terry, Bill,' he yelled over his shoulder as he began to run up the bank.

'What ya gonna do?' Billy bawled after him. But Yanto was gone.

Nat was terrified and becoming more so by the minute. He was hypnotised by the spectre of the bridge yawning in front of him. His resolve began to melt away as he saw the grey tide ripping between the towering six-foot diameter piers, causing bow waves to form around their base.

The spans between the piers were a hundred and thirty-four feet wide at this part of the bridge. Not very wide for a heavy boat with no power and virtually no steering capability. The *Rita* began to drift broadside. 'Come round, you cow,' Nat screamed, as he held the tiller hard over, but she would not answer. 'Christ, if I can't keep her straight she is bound to hit,' he wailed out loud. The thought of those khaki deep water whirlpools waiting for him beyond the bridge filled him with dread. He doubled his efforts at the tiller.

He screamed obscenities into the wind as he wrenched the tiller round again. Slowly, slowly, the bow came into line. Then he found that by oversteering violently first one way then the other, he was able to keep her in a semblance of a straight line.

In this fashion, Nat aimed for the centre of the span directly ahead. In doing so he was making a deadly mistake. As the river men knew well, to negotiate the bridge successfully, it was necessary to steer directly at the pier to the left of the span that you intended to go through. This necessity was caused by the strong current coming from Wellhouse Bay on the west shore. This current, ever present in the vicinity of the Severn Bridge, pushed hard towards the east shore. Thus, by steering straight at the pier, the current would push an upriver bound vessel to the right and hence safely through the centre of the span. Nat was not aware of this nautical fact. The *Rita*'s already rapid drift accelerated suddenly. With just a hundred yards to go she was now caught up in the sucking motion of the tide as it roared between the bridge piers. His eyes opened wide with horror as, at the last moment, she began to broadside to port with the stern being drawn like a magnet towards the pier to the right of the span. With all his weight still on the hard over tiller, he closed his eyes and prayed. There was nothing else he could do. It was as though a giant hand had taken hold of the lumbering craft. She almost went through broadside. Almost, but not quite.

The stern struck the pier with a passing blow that echoed and reverberated across the breadth of the estuary.

Even so, he thought he had done it. She was almost through and still in one piece. But it was not to be. The rudder was still hard over, jutting out at right angles to the boat. At the last second, the rudder snagged on the masonry that supported the pier and was whipped violently into line. The long steel tiller bar that Nat desperately clung to was directly connected to the rudder. It flashed around in a vicious arc with the force of a sledgehammer blow.

Nat was aware of his ribs caving in and of flying through the air before he blacked out.

Yanto ran like a lunatic. He had no love for Nat, but neither could he let him drown. Yanto knew that when the boat hit the bridge, as hit it it must without power, then it would either break up or turn turtle.

Either way it meant curtains for Nat.

A small creek snaked inland from the river just ahead of him and he knew one of the locals kept a punt moored there winter and summer. He ran on, trying to keep the *Rita* in view while leaping over the tangled debris on the shore. Several times he slipped and fell on the muddy banks and got up cursing Nat. As he reached the muddy slit of the rhene he could see the *Rita* closing rapidly with the bridge, and Nat wrestling with the tiller like a madman.

The square-nosed punt which bobbed in the flooded rhene, was a quarter full of water from the heavy rain. Yanto grabbed the mooring rope and pulled the craft close in to the slimy bank. The hollow crash that suddenly echoed across the estuary thrust any thought of caution from his mind. He leapt over the three-foot gap into the partly floored craft. It rocked crazily and almost capsized, but he grabbed the gunwales and was able to steady it.

There was no time to bail the water from the punt. The crash had seen to that. He grabbed the oars, and within minutes was rowing hard out of the mouth of the rhene into the tide race.

Immediately, the current caught the little craft and almost ran him into the shore, but by rowing like a man possessed, he gradually made headway out into the river. As he approached the bridge he rowed flat out towards the nearest pier, then the current flushed him through like a canoeist shooting the rapids. The punt shipped more water and once through the bridge he was forced to stop and use the fisherman's maggot tin to bail. He could now see the *Rita* clearly. Mercifully she was still afloat and bobbing drunkenly in midstream. It was only a matter of time before she stranded herself on a sandbank.

But where the hell was Nat? There was no sign of him. The black clouds had scudded away and the strange pearly light illuminated the surface of the water with a bright sheen, which tended to highlight floating objects. Yanto was gaining fast on the lumbering *Rita* when he spotted the dark bundle bobbing off to the left in the water. There was still no sign of life on the boat. 'He must have been chucked overboard,' Yanto told himself, and changed course towards the floating object.

As he approached he gasped with relief. It was Nat and he had had the sense to don a life jacket.

'Nat,' he yelled, 'you OK?' There was no response. Nat just lay there, head back with his eyes closed. Yanto juggled with the oars, then shipped them as he came alongside the motionless man.

He grabbed the collar of Nat's jacket with both hands and manhandled him to the square stern of the punt. To have attempted to haul him over the side would have been courting disaster. With a carefully balanced heave he managed to flop Nat's chest over the stern of the punt. Then, with both hands clamped to the loose cloth of his backside, Yanto heaved again.

A sigh of relief whistled through his teeth as the seemingly lifeless form rolled limply on to the floor of the punt. He made a quick inspection of Nat's condition. The normally dark, handsome features were the colour of putty. Small droplets of bright water clinging to the coarse jet-black hair shone like pearls in the eerie light, giving him an almost serene appearance. Suddenly he gave a little cough and a thin line of bright blood dribbled from the corner of his mouth. Yanto quickly grabbed the oars and rowed hard for the east shore.

During the rescue proceedings the tide had been pushing them relentlessly upstream. After a quick scan around, Yanto realised they were approaching Purton east. He could see the tide rushing over the almost submerged breakwater. As he continued to row hard for the east bank, he calculated that his best course of action was to try and beach the punt this side of the breakwater. Then it was just a short dash to The Blue Boar. Knocker had one of the very few telephones in the village.

Yanto pulled close to the bank trying to find a suitable spot to beach the punt. He was looking for a stretch where the mud was flat. Most of the bank consisted of great mounds of mud which could swallow a man completely. He allowed the punt to drift as he searched. At this distance the banks seemed to flash past, showing again the tremendous speed and power of the Severn tide. Then he saw it. A forty foot gap between two mud banks, it was as likely a spot as he could hope for on this stretch of the bank. He would have to wade through a good thirty yards of mud to reach the grass line. He pulled hard on his right hand oar to bring the nose of the punt in line with the gap.

Then, by using the power of the current as his ally, he rowed like a demon towards it in order to drive the flat-bottomed punt as far up the liquid mud as possible. The punt hit the mud, slithered for six feet, then stuck firm.

Nat was beginning to moan quietly. Yanto leaned over him, told him to lie still, and explained quickly what he intended to do. He wasn't sure if Nat heard him or not. With that he jumped over the side. The glutinous mess immediately rose to his waist. He half waded and half crawled towards the grass line.

As he did so, he was amazed and gratified to see several men run down the bank and through the mud towards him.

Knocker Nelmes and Sooty Hill grabbed his arms and began assisting him up the bank.

Sammy Pockets, Tiny Jacklin, and Tiny's brother waded past in the mud to reach Nat.

'Go easy on him,' Yanto called over his shoulder, 'he's hurt bad.'

Then he almost passed out with exhaustion.

An hour later, Yanto felt much better. Knocker had washed him off and he now sat in Knocker's private quarters, shrouded in a blanket with a double scotch in his hand.

It transpired that Sammy Pockets had spotted the *Rita* in trouble as he got his bike out to go to The Boar for his usual tipple. Consequently, Yanto's rescue of Nat had been observed, albeit from a distance, by the entire clientele of the pub.

The ambulance had arrived quickly from Berkeley. The ambulance crew, suspecting that Nat's smashed ribs had punctured a lung, transported him rapidly to Gloucester Royal Infirmary. Yanto had made a mental note to visit him in a few days. He had respect for Nat, if nothing else.

Billy had arrived at The Blue Boar on Yanto's motorbike. He had no licence, but that was Billy. Billy had also brought the whisky up for his mate. Then, before dashing off to get clean clothes for him, they talked.

It seemed Terry Littlejohn had managed to make it ashore, exhausted, but otherwise unscathed by the ordeal. He had gone immediately to Sharpness Police Station to report the falling overboard of Colonel Murchison. Boats were out at this moment and word had been flashed upriver to keep a look out. But nobody expected him to be found alive. Fatalities in the River Severn had always been, and always would be, a regular occurrence. It was usually several days before she gave up her dead. Sometimes she never did.

Yanto had been shocked to hear about Colonel Murchison and wondered what impression it would have on Julie. If nothing else, it should make her give up her silly idea of riding over the big Bore.

There was a knock on the door. 'Come on in, Bill,' he said. But it was Knocker who stuck his head around the door. 'You fit to receive a visitor?' he grinned.

Yanto pulled the blanket around him. 'Yeah,' he said cautiously.

Molly Hopkins walked in, tall and slim and as pretty as ever. Knocker closed the door quietly.

'Hello, hero,' she said with a smile. 'Can't you ever keep out of the news?'

Yanto smiled with delight at seeing her. 'Seems not,' he replied with a wide grin. 'Sit down,' he pointed to the other chair.

'I can't stop,' she said quickly, 'I just called to see if you were all right. I can see you are.' She stood, unsure of what to say, looking embarrassed.

'Moll,' he said 'I'm sorry I let you down, It wasn't intended. You know me, I just don't think.' He paused and looked at her. 'Would you consider going out with me again?'

She was taken by surprise. 'What about the girl from Ham?' The smile was gone now.

'There's nothing between us now. Never was really, come to think of it,' he replied.

The funny thing was, as he said it, he realised he meant

250

every word. 'I understand her father was killed today,' she said.

'Looks like,' he replied. 'Anyway, what do you say, Moll?'

'I don't think so, Yanto,' she said and looked away. 'I don't think I could trust you again.'

'Oh, Moll,' he whispered, putting on the charm. 'I shall be twenty-nine in a few days. Reckon it's time I started thinkin' about settlin' down.'

She looked at him straight with that old-fashioned look of hers. 'We'll talk about it sometime,' she said, 'now I must go. Dad'll want his supper.' She gave him a little smile and went out.

'Ain't goin' to be as easy as I thought,' he pondered. Five minutes later Billy arrived with his clothes.

'Come on, pal,' he grinned, 'they're all waitin' for you in the bar.'

They found the body of Colonel Joshua Murchison on Rodley Sands, six days later. It was not a pretty sight.

The hiker's pack was still attached to him. It caused a big stir and a lot of questions were asked. Terry Littlejohn was interviewed, and he simply told them about the Colonel's chartering of his boat. He also mentioned the Colonel's nocturnal trip ashore. Then the army became involved, and somehow it was all hushed up. For the army, however, a longstanding question had been answered.

Yanto went to the big funeral at Berkeley church. Both Joanna and Julie looked grim, but composed. Afterwards, before getting into the car with her mother, Julie came across to Yanto.

'Don't forget the thirtieth of next month,' she said grimly.

Yanto looked at her in amazement. 'You can't be serious,' he gasped, 'not after your father?'

'Especially after my father,' she snapped, sticking her chin out. 'I hate that river now, and I'll beat it, with you or without you. You agreed to do it, or are you backing out now?' The dare and devilment flashed in her eyes.

'I'll be there,' he said resignedly.

Twenty

TO CHALLENGE THE BORE

On the Saturday afternoon following the Colonel's funeral,
Yanto took his fight winnings from the top of his wardrobe and
rode his motorcycle into Gloucester.

He parked the machine outside a large jewellers in the
Oxbode, and entered the shop. The first and only other time he
had been in this shop had been with his mother on his twentieth
birthday. The war was imminent and Yanto was joining up.
Mary Gates had insisted on buying him a gold signet ring for
his birthday. She had always planned to buy him one for his
twenty-first, but there was no way of knowing if he would be
around then.

The assistant, a smartly dressed man around his late fifties,
came to the glass topped counter, smiled, and asked if he could
help.

'Yes, I am interested in buying an engagement ring for my
lady. Could I see some please?' There was a confident,
authoritative ring in Yanto's voice.

'Of course, sir. Many congratulations. About how much did
you wish to spend?' Yanto looked thoughtful, but did not
answer. The assistant took a tray of rings from under the glass-
topped counter.

'The rings on this tray range from seven pounds up to twelve
pounds, sir. Do you see anything that you particularly like?'

'Hmmm,' Yanto studied the array of rings slotted into the
blue velvet backcloth. They looked nice and were quite
expensive, but they were mainly small emeralds or sapphires,
dispersed with diamonds that looked more like chippings to
him, He thought of his mother's engagement ring, which she
treasured. It was a solitaire diamond. 'Much more sense to put

253

your money into a real diamond, than a sackful of chippings,' she had once told him.

He left the assistant standing there and began to browse around the various stands and counters. Then he spotted it. It stood out from the rest like the Koh-i-Noor diamond. The ring was in its own ornate little box, which lay open in a well-secured glass cabinet. The light coming through the glass-panelled front door caused it to flash in myriad colours. It was a large solitaire diamond, set in twenty-two carat gold ring. Unfussy and classically beautiful in its simplicity.

'How much is this one?' Yanto asked, still studying the flashing stone.

The assistant hurried from behind the counter. 'Ahh, sir. I do admire your taste. A magnificent stone, but very expensive, I'm afraid.' Yanto looked at him and waited. 'That ring is an investment at forty pounds ten shillings.' Yanto was expecting the worst, but the price knocked him back. The assistant noticed.

'A lot of money, I admit, sir, but, as I said, an investment at the price!' Yanto squeezed the fifty pounds fight money in his pocket. He would need money for the week, plus there was ten pounds which was earmarked for something else before he returned home.

'I'll take it for thirty-five pounds,' Yanto said briskly.

The assistant raised his hands. 'Oh, I'm sorry but, as I said, the ring is an investment at that price.'

Yanto thought for a second. 'All right,' he said, 'I didn't anticipate having to spend so much, but I will go to thirty-seven pounds, and that's my final offer. You don't sell rings of that calibre every day.'

'I really am sorry, sir.' The assistant stood looking sympathetic, with his hands together as if in prayer.

'Ah, well,' Yanto said, as he walked to the door, 'I'm sorry we couldn't do business.'

'Well, wait a second sir,' the assistant said hurriedly. 'The owner is upstairs in his private rooms. I can but ask him, but I fear the answer will be no.'

Yanto prowled around the shop for five minutes before the man returned. 'It must be your lucky day, sir,' the assistant burbled, as he unlocked the glass cabinet and removed the ring.

Yanto felt pleased with himself as he watched the assistant wrap the tiny valuable parcel. He paid the man, then as he reached the door, he turned. 'Please convey my best wishes to the owner,' he said.

'Thank you, sir, I am the owner, I ...' He suddenly realised he had forgotten himself and blushed to the colour of a turkey cock. Yanto smiled and left.

'Crafty old bugger,' he chuckled as he started the bike.

He had one other errand to see to. As he rode out of Gloucester, he turned left into the Southgate Street entrance of the Gloucester Royal Infirmary, and parked the bike.

Then, after purchasing a bag of black grapes from a nearby shop, he entered the hospital and spoke to the lady in reception.

'Could you tell me which ward Mr Nathan Asnett is in, please?'

The receptionist scrutinised her sheet. 'You'll find him in ward F1. He's coming along very well after his operation.' She smiled pleasantly and gave him directions to the ward.

He found Nat propped up in bed looking bored with a bandage-swathed chest showing through his open pyjama top. He looked up in amazement as Yanto walked in.

'Hiya, Nat. How ya feelin'? Bought you some grapes.' Yanto helped himself to a grape then placed the bag in the bedside locker.

Nat looked at him straight and unsmiling. 'They tell me you saved my life?' he said suddenly.

'I was in the right place at the right time,' Yanto answered with a shrug of his shoulders. 'You'd have done the same for me.'

'That's beside the point,' Nat replied, then grimaced with pain as he tried to change his position. 'Anyway, I owe you, and I shan't forget it.'

They talked about various things for a while, then Nat looked at him seriously. 'You realise you was lucky to win that fight,' he said, 'could have gone either way, y'know.'

'That's another reason why I called.' As he spoke Yanto took two five-pound notes from his pocket and placed them in Nat's locker drawer.

'Wo's that for?' Nat demanded.

'I got fifty quid for the fight, you got thirty. Now we got forty apiece. Let's call it a draw, OK?'

'Don't be bloody daft, I ...'

Yanto cut him short. 'I've been intendin' to do it ever since the fight, so no arguments.'

Nat looked at him in puzzled respect. Then he grinned and stuck his hand out. 'You ain't a bad old bastard, are you, Gatesy. Put it there.' They shook hands.

That handshake sealed a friendship that was destined to last the rest of their lives.

Yanto was in high spirits when he got home. He had made his peace with Nat, and that had pleased him. Also, there was that beautiful ring. He had finally come to the decision that Molly was the girl for him and he felt confident that the ring, plus a bit of charm, would do the trick.

He was honour-bound now to accompany Julie on her hair-brained scheme, so he decided to wait until that little episode was out of the way before tackling Molly in earnest, Then he could tell her in all sincerity that he would not be seeing Julie again.

He found his mother in the kitchen preparing tea. Her best dress was in evidence, and one look at her hair told him that she had been to Berkeley for a perm that very afternoon.

'You look good enough to eat, Mam,' he said, as he watched her lay out the three plates of fresh salad. Three plates? His mother's opening remark explained it.

'Sid's here, son,' she said, 'he's come for tea.'

Yanto went through to the cosy little parlour. He found the table laid with his mother's best linen and tea service, looking as though the King himself was coming to tea.

Sid jumped up from the easy chair as he entered, and they

256

shook hands and exchanged greetings. 'You're being honoured, Sid,' Yanto laughed, 'that's the first time I've seen that tea service out of the glass cabinet. Have we won the pools or summat, Ma?' he asked, as Mary came in with a plate of fancy cakes.

'No, we haven't,' she replied quickly, 'but Sid and I would like to talk to you before we have tea.'

Here it comes, he thought. He had been expecting it. Mary sat on the arm of Sid's armchair and looked at him with a slightly worried look.

'Sid and I have decided to get married, son. I hope you will be happy for us.'

Yanto, who had rehearsed many times what he would say when this expected moment arrived, jumped up. He kissed his mother and shook hands with Sid. 'I'm absolutely delighted, Ma,' he chuckled. 'You couldn't have picked a nicer bloke. Now I know you'll be all right.'

'Thank you, Yanto, that was much appreciated,' Sid said seriously.

'Come on, this is an occasion,' Yanto shouted, and clapped his hands, 'let's have a drink.'

His mother smiled broadly as she watched him go through to the kitchen. He reappeared a minute later with a bottle of Black and White whisky and the bottle of sherry his mother had bought for Julie's expected visit.

It was a very enjoyable tea, during which Mary told him they planned to be married at the local registry office in October. 'Just a quiet family do,' she said happily, 'and the autumn is my favourite time of year.'

After the tea things were cleared away they sat drinking and chatting in the easy chairs. It was then Sid broached the subject of accommodation.

'I would like Mary to move into my private quarters at The Chase once we're married,' he said. 'As you know, it's big and modern, but she's worried about you. What do you think, Yanto?'

'I want you to have the cottage anyway, son,' Mary

intervened, 'but you've never been used to seeing to yourself, have you?'

Yanto held up his hands. 'Look, Ma,' he said, 'I am quite capable of looking after myself. Anyway, I do have plans of my own.'

'Oh, and what might they be?' his mother asked curiously. Yanto didn't answer. Instead he went out to the kitchen and returned with his precious little parcel. 'Got something to show you,' he said simply.

His mother craned her neck as he stripped the wrapping from the little box. She almost fainted when she saw the magnificent ring. 'Good grief, Yanto,' Sid gasped, 'it must have cost a fortune.'

'Used me fight money,' he grinned. 'Think she'll like it?'

'Well she is a wealthy girl,' his mother said, still ogling the ring, 'but that has got to be something special, even for her.'

'It's not for Julie Murchison, Ma, for God's sake,' he snorted. 'It's for Molly.'

Mary threw her head back and clapped her hands with joy. 'Oh glory be,' she shrilled. 'Molly's a wonderful girl. I'm just glad you've got the sense to see it. When did she agree to become engaged?'

'She ain't yet, but she will,' he said with a grin. Mary looked puzzled but said nothing. 'Anyway, I shall be quite happy on me own here 'til I get wed. Then I shall buy a place of my own.'

'What's wrong with this place?' Mary asked in a surprised little voice.

'Nothing,' he replied, 'but it's your cottage, and when it's sold the proceeds will go to you. 'Bout time you had a bit of luxury in your life.'

'We'll see about that when the time comes,' Mary replied, as she looked at Sid. 'I've got all the luxury I want in life with the two of you.'

'Let's have another drink,' Sid suggested.

'But I tell you it's regressing, sir.' The junior doctor in the X-ray department of the Gloucester Royal Infirmary could not believe his eyes.

'Can't be,' snorted the consultant, as he came across to inspect the plates. Arthur Venables' original X-ray plates hung on the illuminated panel alongside the new film, taken that day. The consultant rubbed his chin as he scrutinised them.

'Something very strange going on here, John.' The consultant spoke half to himself and half to his colleague. The ominous grey area of the carcinoma showed up clear and unmistakeable on the original plates. Yet on the new film it showed less than a third of its previous size.

'By all rules the man should be dead by now,' the consultant said quietly, 'yet here he is eating normally and putting on weight.'

He continued to inspect the film. 'What did the fellow have to say about it?' he said suddenly.

'He just said his uncle told him how to do it,' the young doctor replied with an incredulous tone to his voice. 'He's a bit incoherent, but from what I gather, it was some sort of mind over matter method.' The consultant took his eyes from the plates and looked at the young doctor.

'Go on,' he said.

'The only other thing I could get out of him,' he continued hurriedly, 'was that he had nearly finished shifting the dung heap.'

The consultant pondered for a while, then spoke. 'I read a paper about this way-out treatment recently, and heard talk about it from time to time, but this is the first time I've ever witnessed it personally. With all the marvellous advances in medicine ...' He left the rest unsaid as he smiled and shook his head. 'I would never have believed it, but I suppose if you have somebody strong-willed enough, anything is possible.'

'Well, he's that right enough, sir,' the young doctor broke in. 'He refused point blank to take his socks off in bed. Even Matron couldn't budge him, and you know Matron ...'

The consultant laughed out loud. 'Well, I would certainly like to meet this uncle of his.'

On the evening of Friday the twenty-ninth of August, Yanto walked moodily through the rain towards The Blue Boar, where he had arranged to meet Billy. He felt like a drink. In fact, he felt like getting drunk.

The rain did nothing to help his already sombre mood. The long hot spell had broken two days before and it had rained hard ever since. He looked over at the drizzling greyness of the river as he entered the pub, and wondered what horrors the morrow held in store for him.

He found Billy in the bar talking to a very happy Terry Littlejohn. 'What's up, Yant?' Terry said chirpily, 'you look as though you lost a quid and found a tanner.'

'I got good reason,' Yanto growled. 'Anyway, what you got to be so cheerful about?'

'Well,' Terry said, as he leaned closer. 'I 'ad nuthin' to be 'appy about this mornin'. The old man wanted to kick me out for all but wreckin' 'is boat and losing the dinghy.'

'So,' Yanto growled again.

'I 'ad a caller this afternoon,' Terry continued happily. 'Mrs Murchison called over in that big chauffeur-driven car of hers. Paid in full for the fishing trip, plus paid me compensation for the loss of the dinghy. Now there's a real lady if you like.'

'Well, you can afford to buy me a pint of scrump then,' Yanto grunted, as he leaned heavily on the bar.

'Come on mate, wo's up?' Billy chipped in.

He told them about Julie Murchison's determination to ride over the Bore at Stonebench next morning, and the fact that he was honour-bound to accompany her.

Billy and Terry were aghast. 'You gotta be bloody mad,' Billy gasped. 'That's the biggest tide of the year tomorra'. I was talking to Herb Meadows in the Sally earlier, and he's driving all his sheep onto high ground tonight. They're expectin' floods an' Christ knows what.'

'Well I promised her, so there's nothing I can do about it,' Yanto snorted angrily.

'Well you won't catch me on that bloody river again in a

hurry, I can tell you,' Terry broke in for good measure.

Yanto was getting bored with the proceedings and threw back the remains of his pint. 'I think I'll have an early night, boys,' he snapped; 'be seeing you.'

'I bloody hope so, mate,' Billy said earnestly, as he watched him go out into the rainy night.

In the grey of early morning, an ominous scenario was developing in the wide emptiness of the Severn Estuary.

A strong westerly wind pushed and agitated the gathering swell, flicking the grey water into white horses as it prepared itself for the violent invasion into the heart of Gloucestershire. Blustery gusts tantalised the wheeling gulls showing shiny white against the dirty grey backcloth of the clouds.

Had one been walking on the broad, flat Waveridge Sands, lying high, dry, and yellow off Sharpness that morning, one could have witnessed the birth of the Severn Bore. A birth so new, yet as old as time.

The tiny froth-capped embryo wave, barely two inches high, rolled evenly and playfully over the hard flat sand, giving no hint of the unlimited power following closely in its wake.

The miniature wave moved over the sand at the pace of a briskly walking man.

But in the low-lying mud troughs that flanked the estuary to east and west, it was a different picture. Already the troughs were subject to the tide's full onslaught. If the fictitious briskly walking man on the sands had been a real man, his life would now have been in deadly danger. As happens on the very odd occasions the requisites to turn a big Bore into a freak Bore were well in evidence.

This was one of the highest predicted tides of the year. There was a strong westerly wind blowing, and the barometer had dropped alarmingly. On top of this already threatening situation, the rain of the last few days had raised the level of the river a good two feet above normal in the ever-narrowing upper reaches.

An old retired riverman stood watching the great onslaught

from the safety of his cottage garden high on the river bank. He turned to his grandson by his side. 'Reckon they be gonna need the sandbags up river today, son,' he grunted. As they continued to watch the fascinating spectacle, the sand flats and humps began to disappear like sand through a giant's fingers.

The tide was gaining momentum now. Relentlessly, the grey surge pushed past Frampton. Then to feel the beginnings of strangulation as it entered the aptly named Horseshoe Bend.

The water mass now began to rise up as if the entire Atlantic Ocean had decided to squeeze itself into the narrowing confines of the Severn's upper reaches.

Great flocks of gulls and other water birds would suddenly rise screeching and flapping into the overcast sky, their breakfast abruptly terminated as the advancing monster engulfed and drowned the hitherto dry sandbanks.

Yanto groaned inwardly as the car horn honked outside his door. Even at this late stage he had hoped that the recent rain, plus the dark dismal morning, would have caused Julie to call it off.

He cursed quietly under his breath as he laced up his plimsolls. Then, after gulping down the remains of his mug of tea, he pulled his favourite fishing blouse over his shoulders.

Made from sailcloth, with three-quarter length sleeves, it was windproof and comfortable, but more important, it was light. This, combined with the plimsolls and the lightweight waterproof trousers, would make things a little easier if he had to swim for his life. This, he realised, was a distinct possibility.

The horn honked again as he went outside. Barney Summerville sat at the wheel grinning wickedly, with a po-faced Julie sat beside him. The flimsy canoe was strapped to the roof-rack of the car and a couple of lifejackets were lying on the back seat.

'Perfect old day for a drowning,' he said without humour as he flopped himself in the back seat.

'Good morning, pessimist,' she said, as she turned to look at him. She was wearing a short yellow oilskin jacket, brown corduroy slacks and turned down Wellington boots. The little yellow sou'wester perched on top of her yellow hair made her look as cute as ever, in spite of her sullen face.

'Which way ya' going?' Yanto asked Barney, as the big car pulled away. 'If we go through Frampton then up the side of the river, we shall overtake the Bore.' He looked at Julie, 'then we can see what we've got to contend with.'

Julie turned to him again. 'No,' she said, 'we are going up the A38. I don't want to see the Bore until we are face to face.'

'Then I got an idea you'll wish you'd stayed in bed,' Yanto grunted. She turned away from him with a snort, and looked sulkily out of the window.

As the car joined the A38 at Berkeley Road, large spots of rain began to slap the windscreen intermittently, and the ominous black clouds seemed to press down on them.

'What am I bloody doin' here,' Yanto groaned to himself.

The office of the Severn Catchment Board in Gloucester's Clarence Street was very busy that morning. They knew they had a big one on their hands, and with these conditions they knew they could expect a very dangerous surge.

As many warnings as possible had been sent out to the more vulnerable pubs and communities scattered along Severnside, advising them to sandbag their properties as much as possible. The terrible memories of the previous winter were still fresh in their minds. Memories of pianos floating in front rooms, and water marks six feet up the walls of public bars, take a bit of forgetting.

Many farmers had made an early start by driving their grazing stock on to high ground, knowing that much of the low-lying ground bordering the river would be swamped and flooded.

The district engineer tapped the barometer again. Then a thought struck him. He called in his secretary. 'That phone call I received from the young lady in Berkeley some weeks back. Do you recall it?'

She puckered her forehead as she thought about it.

'She was enquiring as to the date of the highest predicted tide this year. I'm sure I gave her today's date,' he concluded with a frown. That sparked the secretary's memory.

'Oh yes, I remember,' she chirped, 'she said she wanted to ride over the wave in her boat or something.'

'That's the one,' he replied, 'she didn't leave a phone number, did she?'

'Not with me.'

The district engineer looked troubled as he thought for a moment. 'Well,' he said finally, 'if she is silly enough to try riding on the river today, she'll be very lucky to get out alive.'

The wave broke at Denny Rock, Minsterworth. Now the Bore proper was in evidence. Now it gave warning of its advance with that distant whispering roar, like that of a steam train fast approaching, but still out of sight behind the last bend.

As it roared along Elmore Back, scattered groups of early Bore watchers were forced to retreat from the banks as it smashed and danced its way through the narrows. With the impatient tide pushing and harrying from behind, the three great waves of the advance guard noisily violated the peaceful low water channel meandering through the green fields ahead, oblivious of the misery perpetrated in its wake.

Occasionally, on straight obstacle-free stretches, the breakers would mutate back to a more ominous deep-water surge, breaking here, and spilling there. Until the next bend or obstacle, when with a thunderous roar, it would break again, sending spectacular cascades flying as the waves struck the eroded protrusions of the banks.

It was 9.15 a.m. now, and the Bore was passing Weir Green. In a few more minutes it would arrive at that spectacular curve which caused the wave to rise to its maximum. It was the favourite spot for people to witness the phenomenon. It was called Stonebench.

Yanto sat in the rear cockpit of the kayak, staring at the back of Julie's head and feeling foolish. Twenty minutes before, they

264

had turned off the A38 just prior to it entering the City of Gloucester, and negotiated the narrow lane down to the riverbank. Many times it had been necessary for Barney to sound his horn at the numerous groups of people making their way down to the viewing point. Much excitement was shown by the people already assembled on the river bank as they saw the car arrive and the canoe removed from the roof-rack. This was a thrilling bonus they had not expected.

Willing hands had helped with the difficult launch down the steep slippery bank, and now for better or for worse, here they were. The river was about a hundred yards wide at Stonebench and, with deft strokes of her paddle, Julie had negotiated the canoe to midstream about one hundred yards upstream from the bend.

'You're determined to catch the full force, ain't you?' Yanto snorted.

'If something is worth doing, you might as well do it properly,' she said over her shoulder.

He was very conscious of the large number of people jumping around excitedly on the bank, and felt a distinct affinity with the goldfish in its bowl.

'Hey, you're a lucky sod, mate,' one of the spectators shouted, as he ogled Julie.

'Come and take my place if you like, pal,' he shouted back. The clouds had begun to break up and the sun was doing its best to shine. The wind had also dropped, and a silence descended on the scene, as though everything was holding its breath for the big finale.

Yanto's nerves were like bowstrings as he tried to figure out how best to ride over the beast. 'If it's a big 'un, mind,' he said hoarsely, 'make for the inside curve over there,' he pointed to the right-hand bank. 'The wave won't be so pronounced on the inside bend. And make sure we hit it bow on, or we've had it.'

'We should have kept the wet liners,' she said accusingly, 'we could easily be swamped without them.'

Yanto had earlier insisted they get rid of the wet liners. 'If we go over, I want to be able to get out quick,' he replied.

'Chicken,' she laughed.

'Chicken, my ass,' he grated angrily. 'You know damn all about this river, so do as I say. If you knew the risk you were taking you wouldn't be here at all.'

'This canoe took the biggest waves the Pacific would throw at her in California,' she rasped.

'OK, but sea waves are spread out, and you can get the rhythm going,' he fumed, 'with the Bore you normally get three big waves, almost on top of one another. I've seen 'em swamp big boats before now.' She said nothing.

So they sat and waited in ridiculous silence. 'I can 'ear 'er cumin',' somebody yelled on the bank. Yanto cocked his ear. Yes, there it was, that unmistakable sound around the bend.

'Now do as I say,' he grated, as he grabbed his paddle.

A great 'Ohhh' went up from the crowd as they caught their first glimpse. In fact they saw the spray and cascades of spume leaping over the bank, before it appeared around the bend. Barney Summerville's eyes opened wide with horror as it appeared. It was still out of sight for Yanto and Julie at this stage. 'Yanto,' he yelled, 'get out, for God's sake, it's a monster.'

Then it appeared in all its majesty. It was an awesome sight. The advance wave must have been nine feet high and rising as it heaved around the outside curve of the bend. But such was the sheer volume of water pushing up the channel, that even on the inside curve the wave seemed enormous.

'God help us,' Yanto gasped. 'It's a freaker.' Julie froze with horror. The Bores she witnessed as a child were nothing like this. The wave roared towards them, its great height accentuated even more by the fact that they were sitting at water level.

The spectators suddenly realised to their horror that the wave was flooding over the bank as it careered around the bend. With screams and the grabbing of children they ran from the bank in total panic and disorder.

'Make for the inside bend, for Christ sake,' Yanto yelled, as he desperately dug his paddle into the water which was ridiculously calm, compared to what it was about to become any second now.

Something in the tone of Yanto's voice cut through Julie's paralysis and she too dug frantically with her paddle. But such was their panicky haste that they lost their co-ordination, and suddenly found the craft broadside on to the wave. The wall of water was now less that fifty yards from them.

'Stop paddling,' Yanto screamed. 'Leave it to me.'

By the time the wave hit them Yanto had almost succeeded in getting the canoe bow on. It was as though they were being lifted by a giant hand. Deafened by the noise and shocked by the drenching spray, Yanto was amazed to find that the canoe had actually managed to raise itself to the crest of the first gigantic wave. He also noticed that Julie had lost her paddle. Once over the top, the kayak dived almost perpendicularly down into the trough between the first two waves. But without the wet liners it was almost full of water already.

Somehow, Yanto didn't know how, the partly swamped craft made its cumbersome ascent to the top of the second wave. But now it was wallowing broadside on. As it dropped into the next trough it was totally engulfed by the third wave.

In a terrifying bedlam of tearing, tumbling water Yanto kicked himself free of the swirling, useless craft and came to the surface coughing and thanking God for the life-jacket. He looked around wildly, trying to catch a flash of yellow from Julie's lifejacket.

'Julie,' he yelled again dementedly. God! If she was still amongst the great breakers at the head of the Bore, they could keep her down indefinitely.

He began to swim desperately towards the Bore's crazy head. Then he saw a flash of yellow. There were parts of trees and debris of every nature rushing along with him, and he became aware of the tree branches on the bank flashing past at an unbelievable rate. He saw the blur of yellow again, about twenty yards ahead, and a little towards mid-stream of him. He swam like a lunatic towards it, then almost screamed with despair as the yellow tumbled out of sight again.

A dead sheep tangled up in an uprooted bush appeared

alongside him. With a bellow of rage and disgust he pulled himself around it. Then he saw the flash of yellow yet again, not ten feet away. He prayed as he lunged for it. His prayer was answered. He grabbed her and pulled her face up into the air. He didn't know if she was alive or dead. He just knew he had to get her out fast.

The river twisted to the left just ahead. If he could just get close into the bank and find an eddy out of the main current, he might be able to grab a branch or anything that was handy.

With his left arm clamped around Julie's neck he pulled hard towards the bank. A branch hung almost to the water ahead of him. He was still in the grip of the main current and moving very fast.

He grabbed desperately at the drooping branch, but was unable to hold it. The current tore him away and he screamed terrible oaths at the river as the branch tore most of the skin from the palm of his hand.

He began to smack Julie's death-like face as they swept on. But there was no response.

Again he thanked God for the fact that they were both wearing life-jackets. At least they didn't have to worry about simply keeping afloat. As they came out of the bend he spotted a prominent protrusion in the bank ahead. The narrow sapling-clad peninsula jutted out into the river a good fifteen feet or more.

The current was swirling madly around it, but he knew he would find a quiet current-free patch on the far side.

As the tide swept them out and around the outcrop, he struck madly for the bank. He was right, there was no rush of tide here. He was able to drift in and up to the bank. The earth around the protrusion was badly eroded, and the roots of the small trees stuck out like dead men's fingers.

He managed to get a foot- and hand-hold, then quivering like jelly with effort, he heaved and pushed Julie's dead weight up and on to the low earth jetty. After scrambling out unsteadily himself, he immediately began attempting to revive her.

He lay her face down on the grass with her head lying on her crossed hands. Then, after thumping hard between the shoulder blades a couple of times, he commenced artificial respiration. 'Come on, gal, you can do it. Come on,' he pleaded. He kept pumping on her, but he was beginning to despair. 'Breathe, you silly cow,' he yelled, 'your dad's dead, if you go too, it will kill your mam, so bloody breathe, will ya.'

Suddenly Barney and several other people came running up. They had been scouring the bank for them. 'Oh, Yanto,' Barney groaned as he dropped to his knees beside him, 'is she ...?'

Julie jerked and gave a little cough.

'Come on, my beauty,' Yanto bellowed in delight, and doubled his efforts.

She coughed again and began to moan quietly. Yanto ceased pumping and with Barney's help, got her into a sitting position where after a while she became coherent.

Then, with tears streaming down his face, Barney cradled her head to his shoulder. 'Thank God,' he said, 'and thank you too, Yanto.' Yanto flaked out on his back, totally exhausted.

Ten minutes passed by before they started back towards the nearest bit of road. Once there, they sat thankfully down on the grass verge while Barney ran to get the car. There were towels and a vacuum flask of coffee in the car, so while Barney fussed and dried Julie off as best as he could, Yanto helped himself to the coffee. After all the foul water he had drunk that morning it tasted like the nectar of the gods.

When they were finally on their way home, Yanto looked into Julie's pale expressionless face. 'Well you did it, kid,' he grinned, 'but if you ever get any more bright ideas, leave me out of them, there's a good girl.'

As the Armstrong travelled homewards with its tired but thankful passengers, the Severn Bore entered the city.

Here, at Lower Partings, the river splits into two channels. Some of the surging water mass was siphoned off and went rolling up the east channel to meet its Waterloo at Llanthony Weir. But most roared on unabated down the west channel, towards Maisemore Weir.

A group of people had gathered at this weir to witness the

obliteration of the great wave.

'It looks like hundreds of sheep running towards us, doesn't it?' one excited spectator commented, as they watched the head of the Bore approach. The noise was tremendous and twofold. On one side there was the thundering waterfall as the outgoing water tumbled over the weir. Added to this was the crescendo of noise from the approaching waves. Then, as the advance waves hit the weir, the spectators experienced a strange sensation. After the commotion of the Bore's impact with the weir had subsided, there was a deathly hush.

The great waves were no more, and all sound from the weir had ceased as it now lay drowned beneath the swirling deep water.

The two channels would shortly converge again and the surge of water would continue to Tewkesbury and beyond. But the Bore proper was no more.

The wave had travelled twenty-two miles. Now it was over. All bar the mopping up.

Twenty-one

THE PROPOSAL

Yanto was as stiff as the proverbial board when he came down to breakfast the following morning. But it was Sunday, and after a good dose of bacon, eggs, and his favourite slices of fried potato, he began to feel human again. He listened good-naturedly to his mother's plans for the wedding, then took his mug of tea and the Sunday paper out into the back yard.

As he sat there soaking up the sun, he began to think of Molly. She was a real little 'she-cat' when she was roused. He smiled at the memory of her outraged face when she called at the cottage.

I shall have to do something about her, he told himself, and today is as good a day as any.

Molly Hopkins paused from her task of washing up the breakfast things and gazed out of the kitchen window. She smiled at her father who was sitting on the low wall which separated the small paved courtyard from his magnificent garden. Earlier that morning he had decided to spend the day patting for eels. He had dug up a good cache of earthworms and was now engaged in the tricky task of threading them on a long length of cotton.

He was using what could only be described as an oversized darning needle. The needle was a good six inches long and a three foot length of cotton was attached to the eye at the end of it. First he threaded the needle through the length of the earthworm then slid the still-squirming creature to the end of the length of cotton. Then he did the same with the next worm, and the next; until he had a three-foot length of continuous worm.

271

Then he took what appeared to be a half ball of solid lead with several little hooks embedded in the flat underside. Selwyn had cast the weight himself by pouring molten lead into an empty goose egg- shell. He then hung every six inches or so of the luckless length of worms to the various hooks until he had one mass of worm hanging and wriggling on the underside of the lead weight. All he needed now was a stout beanpole and a long length of hairy baling string, which he would attach to the wire eye on the top of the lead weight, and then he was ready to go patting.

Molly had accompanied her father on the odd eeling expedition when she was younger, and he would simply allow the worm-clad lead weight to lie in the mud at the bottom of the Pill or river, wherever he went, and wait.

The eels, it seemed, would chew on the abundant feast of worms and promptly get their teeth caught up in the cotton within.

Rarely had she seen Selwyn pull in the lead weight without at least two eels attached. Anyway, he always took two buckets with him and they were always full when he returned.

Molly placed a Tizer bottle of rough cider in her father's canvas fishing bag, along with a pack of freshly cut bread and cheese, and took it out to the courtyard.

'My word, it's so hot already,' she exclaimed.

'Ahh, and it'll get 'otter still,' Selwyn replied. 'Well, I be off,' he continued. 'Can't wait to get in among them eels.' He strutted off spritely in the direction of the river.

'Don't fall in, mind,' she shouted after him. He waved without looking back. Molly walked morosely back into the house and continued her chores. It was such a lovely morning. She thought of that other lovely Sunday when the four of them went on the picnic to Ham Park. Then she thought of Yanto.

He hadn't been near her in weeks. She had been so angry with him. But the more she thought about it, the more she realised she had had no right to be. He was an attractive man of the world and it wasn't as if they were married, engaged even. 'I expect he'll finish up with that rich girl from Ham,' she told herself sadly, 'more his style.'

She heard a knock on the front door. 'Who on earth can that be?' she asked herself. The paperboy had called half an hour ago, hadn't he? She dried her hands on her apron as she went down the passage then tugged open the seldom-used front door.

She was amazed to find Yanto standing there. He wore a white T-shirt and a pair of white shorts. The sporting theme was completed by a pair of white daps on his stockingless feet. He also wore a very wide grin.

'Hiya, Moll,' he quipped, 'fancy a swim?'

'What do you want?' she asked sternly, but her heart was fluttering like a moth in a jam jar.

'Like I said, I called to take you swimming,' he grinned again, and tugged on the towel which hung casually around his neck to emphasise the point.

'You've got a nerve ...' she began.

'Please,' he interrupted her, still smiling. 'It's too hot to fight, and we do need to talk.'

Molly was lost and she knew it. He was the epitome of manhood. She felt herself physically melting under the steady gaze of those icy blue eyes.

'I'll get my costume,' she said simply, and went back up the passage. With her mind in a whirl, she walked with him over the swing bridge and down the canal towpath.

They didn't talk but as they walked he took her hand.

'Mornin', folks.' The greeting came from Sammy Pockets, who was sitting on a dining chair in the doorway of his canalside cottage, enjoying the morning sun.

Yanto smiled, and nodded at Sammy sitting there with his trouser braces over his bare shoulders.

A short distance past Sammy's cottage the towpath ran on to a little flat bridge that traversed the overflow channel from the canal to the river. Here, any excessive water in the canal would automatically discharge itself into the adjacent Severn. A couple of local children were already paddling happily in the unofficial children's area. This concrete bottomed, three foot deep area beneath the bridge, was separated from the eighteen foot deep canal by wooden pilings, the rotting tops of which could be seen sticking up a couple of inches above the water. It was reasonably safe for children and had long been claimed as their private beach.

'Shan't be long,' Molly said, as she ran down the slope from the towpath to the river shore. Yanto watched her disappear behind the decaying hull of one of the numerous old barges that were beached along this part of the Purton shoreline. He was wearing his trunks beneath his shorts and stripped off in a matter of seconds.

He stretched himself and looked around. It was a glorious morning and a lovely spot. The canal looked inviting with its water sparkling between the daisy-strewn banks. And there, just a few yards of coarse grassed bank away, lay the silent sunlit emptiness of the estuary. The tide was out and the humps and hollows of yellow sand stretched away to the distant smoky green of the Forest of Dean.

God! he felt great.

A dredging barge lay moored against the canal bank, close by. It lay low in the water, already full of mud and rock which had been dredged from one of the local waterways. He vaulted easily up on to the hot steel deck of the barge, then, after balancing himself precariously on the prow for a few seconds, executed a perfect jack-knife dive into the deep water. Unlike the sea, the water in the canal was never too cold for comfort. Even as a child, when he was invariably the first kid to venture into the swimming hole after the winter, it still seemed just right.

Using a stylish American crawl, he sprinted across the ripple-free forty yard stretch to the opposite bank. Then, with the minimum of effort, he floated leisurely back, glorying in the dual delights of the cool water on his body and the hot sun on his face.

As he clambered over the submerged fence into the children's area, Molly appeared on the bank. She looked lovely. Her bobbed dark hair complemented her beautiful complexion, and the black one-piece costume clung to her tall slender body in the right places, giving her an aura of health and beauty. 'Cor,' he could hardly wait.

He reached the top of the bank in time to see Molly hop up on to the barge.

Then, after slipping on her rubber swimming cap, she performed a perfectly acceptable dive off the bow.

He laid the two towels on the grass then stretched out on his back and waited for her to join him. After swimming around for a while using a graceful backstroke, she scrambled up the bank and flopped down beside him on the other towel. 'That was sheer heaven,' she breathed, as she pulled off the skull-hugging cap and shook her hair free. But she still looked very unsure of herself.

He rolled over on his stomach, and with his chin in his hands, looked at her smiling. She turned and looked at his grinning face with the bright droplets of water clinging to his black hair and shining like diamonds.

'Well, my sweet,' he murmured, 'can we get back together again, do you think?'

'What about Julie what's 'er name?' she said quietly. 'I gather you were with her yesterday. Saved her life even.' She turned away and gazed across to the opposite bank.

'We finished awhile back,' he replied, with a serious face. 'I was honour-bound to go with her yesterday. I didn't want to, but I promised. Just as well I did, as it turned out.' She didn't reply. 'I wanted to get yesterday out of the way so that I could honestly say I wouldn't be seeing her again.'

She continued to gaze silently across the water.

'Please, Moll,' he said urgently. 'I really want us to get together again.' He took a deep breath. 'In fact I want to marry you.'

Her jaw dropped and she looked at him in open-mouthed amazement. Christ, he had actually said it, and he was glad.

'What did you say?' she asked incredulously.

'I want to marry you.' He had said it again.

She dropped her face into her hands. She couldn't believe it. Was this really Yanto Gates proposing to her? Her body began to pulsate with little silent sobs. He sat up quickly and put his arms around her warm wet shoulders.

'Come on, Moll,' he pleaded, 'nuthin' to cry about. Will you marry me, for Christ sake?'

'Oh Yanto, I don't know,' she moaned. 'I've always loved you, you know that, but you can be so insensitive and hurtful. How can I tell if you're really serious?'

'I've got something to show you,' he said, as he jumped up and went over to his clothes. After taking the little box out of the pocket of his shorts he sat down beside her again.

She looked at him with shining eyes as he handed her the box. 'That's a token of my sincerity,' he quipped.

When she clipped open the little box she just stared in disbelief. She could not believe her eyes. The beautiful solitaire flashed and sparkled in the morning sun like red-hot embers. All doubts and animosity left her at that moment. She was Scarlett O'Hara and he was her Rhett Butler.

'Oh, Yanto,' she shuddered, 'it's too much. You shouldn't have.'

'Nothing's too good for you, Moll,' he said with a half-smile. 'What do you say?'

'I would have married you with a copper washer on my finger if necessary,' she sighed, as she rested her head on his shoulder.

'So we're engaged then, OK?' he beamed.

'Anything you say,' she murmured helplessly.

He lay her down on the grass and kissed her passionately. As he did so he couldn't help exploring her breasts with his free hand. She sat up with a start.

'I want to make one thing clear, Yanto, my love,' she said curtly.

'Wo's that?' he said, as he sat up beside her.

She looked at him coolly. 'I will marry you, and come what may, I will love you forever, but there will be no more shenanigans until the day, understood?'

He could see she meant every word. 'OK, my love. Anything you say,' he laughed, 'but look out after!'

A surge of joy swept through Molly's being such as she had never thought possible. Jamming the ring firmly on her finger she looked at him. 'Last one in's a cissy,' she squealed, then jumped up and ran towards the barge.

He leapt up and followed her, but she hit the water a good two seconds before him.

Twenty-two

HAPPY EVER AFTER

It was a short engagement. Yanto married Molly Hopkins on the last Saturday in September.

Molly's mother had been a Berkeley girl, and had married Selwyn at Berkeley Church. It had always been her wish that her daughter would also marry in that magnificent old church.

And so it was to be. Yanto had held a stag party at The Blue Boar on the previous Thursday night. It was pay night so its success was guaranteed. Just about every male in the village had attended to honour its favourite son. Even Nat attended and his behaviour was impeccable.

During the evening Billy had drawn Yanto to one side. 'I'm bloody glad you're getting married, mate,' he had said sheepishly.

'Why?' Yanto had asked.

'Well, I've put Mary in the club.' Yanto had started to laugh. 'She's a great kid, mind,' Billy had gone on hurriedly, 'and I shall do the right thing by her. So I shall be getting married meself, see. But I feel happy about it now, the thought of you randying around every night, with me married, would 'ave driven me round the twist.'

The longest, hottest summer for many a year was still holding, and this Saturday was no exception.

The bells rang out over the old town and the church was decked out with flowers in no mean fashion. The origins of Berkeley Church were dim with the mist of time, but like the town itself it, is steeped in history.

The bullet holes and hatchet marks, still visible in the west door of the nave, bear silent witness to its Royalist stand against Cromwell in the siege of 1645. Also, in the same churchyard, stands the hut where Doctor Edward Jenner injected cow pox into the arm of little Jimmy Phipps of Ham. Thus signalling the arrival of vaccination and the eventual demise of the scourge of smallpox.

The old town also played its part in the early origins of the mighty United States. Twenty-five staunch men and women from Berkeley (known in American history as the Berkeley Hundred) pioneered their way from Bristol to the New World on the good ship *Margaret*. On arriving at what is now Virginia, they immediately conducted a Christian Service to give thanks for their safe deliverance. That ceremony is now officially recognised as the first Service of Thanksgiving ever to be held in the New World.

When one considers the fact that this event occurred one year before the Pilgrim Fathers sailed, one wonders why the *Mayflower* received all the good press.

But that, as they say, is history. Today, on the other hand was a day of merriment and rejoicing.

The church was packed. Relatives from both sides, many not seen for years, were there. Mary Gates looked beautiful, sitting beside her husband to be, having a little weep.

Knocker and Renee Nelmes sat right at the front, with Knocker looking slightly ridiculous in a suit. Everybody was in their seldom-used finery; with the ladies eyeing each other smugly or self-consciously, and the men pulling at stiff collars and sweating profusely in this heavy unfamiliar garb, with a huge rose or some other horticultural specimen sprouting from their lapels. It was going to be a happy day. Yanto and Billy, his best man, sat in the front pew feeling calm and composed after the three swift snorts of brandy in the bar of the Chase earlier.

But Yanto still jumped visibly as the organist suddenly began to belt out the 'Wedding March'. The two boys sprang to their positions in front of the solemn vicar, not daring to look back.

Had they done so, they would have seen a proud, beaming Selwyn leading the beautiful bride up the aisle. Her dress had been made by a crippled seamstress who lived in the village, and who kind-hearted Molly had helped many times over the years. Things like doing a bit of shopping for the old lady, and pushing her around in her wheelchair had never been too much trouble for Molly.

The old seamstress had repaid all these favours to Molly with interest when she made her wedding dress out of the vast amount of material left over from her long career. She refused payment. 'That's my wedding present to you, my dear,' was all she said.

The dress would have graced a royal bride.

As she came alongside him, Yanto stole a quick self-conscious look. She took his breath away. As he looked at her, she lifted the veil from her face and draped it back over the little pearl-studded tiara which was pinned to her hair. She smiled at him, her face radiant with happiness. Her pale, flawless complexion, toned with the white silk and cream brocade, yet highlighted her dark hair and violet eyes, to form an exquisite picture of true beauty.

Yanto continued to stare at her lovely profile even after the vicar had begun his address to the gathering.

He knew he had made the right choice.

Joanna Murchison felt sad and empty as she mounted her trap in the stables behind the Berkeley Chase Hotel.

She and her daughter had taken lunch together, during which Julie had told her that she wanted to return to the United States for a while. She told her mother life over there had more to offer, and she felt that she could advance herself more.

Joanna didn't argue with her. She was weary of considering everybody else to the detriment of her own happiness. All her life, it seemed to her, it had been duty and appearances. She was beginning to feel old and careworn by the responsibility of it all. Everybody had remarked how splendidly she had stood up to her husband's death. Like the true noblewoman she was, they all said.

But Joanna knew the truth of it. The Colonel had been a good man, all things considered. But it had been a loveless marriage, and his death had borne no great devastation for her. 'If only,' she said to herself, as she flicked the long whip over the pony's flanks and drove out towards the High Street.

Joanna had to rein in and wait a while before driving out into the High Street. The Berkeley Hunt was passing through. Her pony tossed his head excitedly as the colourful cavalcade of horses and hounds trooped noisily past them up the High Street and into the Square.

The Huntsman and the Whipper-in raised their riding crops respectfully to her as they trotted past, resplendent in the bright yellow coats, unique to the Berkeley. Joanna acknowledged them with a weak little smile, then trotted off towards High Street Hill.

As she approached the brow of the steep slope, she saw groups of smartly dressed laughing people emerging from Church Lane and Castle Drive, into the High Street.

'Oh, it's a wedding,' Joanna said to the pony, as she halted the trap. As she watched the excited throng make their way towards the Berkeley Chase Hotel, Bert Midgeley's big black Humber, resplendent with white ribbons, moved sedately down Castle Drive towards her. It stopped momentarily at the bottom of the drive before turning right and accelerating up the hill and into the High Street.

Joanna recognised Yanto as he chatted happily to his bride in the back seat. She sat there pondering for a good five minutes after the guests had disappeared.

'I think I've done enough, and waited long enough,' she told herself firmly as she flicked the whip at the pony. It was just two hundred yards from the Castle Drive to the entrance onto the Castle meadow. Joanna pulled into the entrance, then after opening the gate and closing it firmly behind her, she drove slowly across the meadow with her head held high.

Jason Bartholomew Selby was light-headed and happy after being wined and dined at the Venables Farm.

Arthur Venables had received an official clean bill of health, and was back working on the farm. Tilly Venables had kissed him and lavished everything on him to an embarrassing degree.

'You're a wonderful man, Jason,' she had said, 'and anything I own is yours for the asking.'

Jason had settled for a roast beef dinner, a bottle of good wine, and Arthur's big grinning red face. 'Got something to show you, Uncle,' he had beamed, as Tilly had cleared away the dishes.

They had gone out into the barn where Arthur proudly showed him the brand new Ferguson tractor, gleaming away with its shiny grey paint. 'Bought it to celebrate, Uncle,' he had said, 'never thought I'd live to see the day.'

Yes, Jason was a happy man as he returned to his shack and put the kettle on. As he waited for the kettle to boil, he finished off a verse of poetry that he had doodled with a few days ago.

A sound outside made him look up. Through the open doorway he saw Joanna stepping down from her trap. She had driven over the little bridge this time, right up to his shack.

A surge of joy swept over him at the sight of her. He dashed straight out to greet her.

'What a wonderful surprise,' he said with feeling, as he took her hand and guided her into the living room. 'And what wonderful timing. The kettle's just boiling.'

She sat there serene and smiling as he made the tea. He began to broach the subject carefully. 'I was very sorry to hear the news about the Colonel, my dear,' he began, 'I wanted to call at the time but ...'

'Let's not talk about that,' she interrupted. 'That part of my life is over and gone forever.'

An impossible hope began to invade his mind as he poured the tea. 'What's this you have been writing, Jason?' she asked, as she saw the poem, written in his beautiful broad penscript. 'May I read it?'

'Of course,' he replied with a smile, 'just something I jotted down in one of my more sombre moments.'

She started to read the verse. It was entitled 'Autumn Days'.

Beside the river running free,

Through fields that man has left alone,
I wander, just my thoughts and me,
Thinking of my youth that's gone.

The hours, the days, the weeks and months
then ambled by, so slow,
Did seasons pass as quickly then,
As they now seem to go?

Joanna looked at him as she put the paper down.

'It's lovely,' she smiled, 'but you will never grow old, Jason.'

He looked at her with bated breath. Why had she called? he anguished himself. And this was the second time. There must be a chance. He threw caution to the winds.

'Not if I had you beside me,' he quavered.

She continued to smile with that strange look in her eyes.

'Do I have a chance, Joanna?' he said, as he stood before her.

Her eyes spoke volumes. 'I want you to court me all over again, Jason Selby,' she said quietly. The smile was gone now. 'I want us to be back at Henley Regatta, that August Bank Holiday before the Great War began. I want us to forget everything that happened between then and this moment.'

He was unable to take it in at first. Then he dropped his head and began to sob. She stood up and lay her head on his shoulder. The scent of her brought him out of his state of shock, and he immediately entwined her in his arms. 'Oh my lovely, lovely girl,' he whispered, as he buried his face in her neck. 'You will never know how I have dreamed and prayed for this moment.' He stood there rocking her in his arms. He held her and allowed the sheer joy to engulf him as the reality of it all began to sink in.

There was a tinkling in his brain. *A tinkling?* He brought his head up with a start. Yes, there was a tinkling sound, but not from his brain. It was coming from the direction of the brook bank.

'I've got him at last,' he yelled. Joanna looked at him in

stunned amazement.

'I'll explain in a minute, my darling,' he yelped, 'but I must go.' He kissed her on the cheek as he sat her back on the chair. Then he hared off towards the brook like a ten-year-old.

As he arrived at the bank he noticed that the slender sapling, which his bank line was attached to, was flexing visibly and wildly, and the washers in the tin can were rattling noisily. 'There's only one fish in this brook that is capable of doing that,' he panted, as he twined the line around his sleeved arm. He ran a short distance down the bank to take the tremendous pressure of the line, and the fish began to dash downstream as he did so. Then he moved to the edge of the bank and began to play the fish skilfully as it began pulling again. That is, until the soft earth at the lip of the bank collapsed and he fell in.

Such was his excitement that he hardly noticed the water which was up to his chest. He continued to play and tire the fish from this watery position, his eyes bright with excitement and concentration. That was how Joanna found him as she arrived at the bank five minutes later. At first she was flabbergasted, then she began to laugh heartily for the first time in weeks when she realised what was going on.

Slowly the fish began to tire, and Jason was able to begin hauling himself out of the brook one-handed. He grabbed at the small tree growing out of the bank and, with the laughing Joanna assisting him, he managed to climb out on to the grass.

Then, taking great pains not to snag the line on the branches which dropped to water level, he began to pull in his prize. He didn't have the luxury of a net, so as he finally manipulated his quarry into the bank, he gave one hard sustained heave, and succeeded in pulling the fish on to the grass, where it lay flapping and heaving in its agony. It was a magnificent pike. 'Must be seventeen pounds at least,' shouted the elated Jason. Joanna looked at the great green creature in amazement as it squirmed on the grass, with its flat jaws full of razor-sharp teeth opening and closing helplessly. Its struggles began anew as Jason grabbed it firmly with both hands.

After sitting himself down, he hauled it across his lap.

He held it firmly until the struggles subsided again. Now he was able to disgorge the triple hook. He looked at the magnificent specimen and speculated silently as to how long the pike must have lived in the brook to reach such a size.

Then he looked at Joanna's smiling face bending over him. 'It's your lucky day, my beauty,' he soothed, 'you caught me, or rather I caught you, at a very rare moment in my life.'

He carried the great fish to a nearby spot where the bank dipped almost to water level. Gently, he submerged it in the water. It lay there between his hands for a few seconds, then, with a sudden wild flap of its tail and a splashing of water, it was gone.

'We shall meet again, mind,' he called after it. Then he turned and went back to his lifelong love. They sat down together on the grass and put their arms around each other. Nothing was said. The past was dead.

There was only the future.

The small party of revellers stepped smartly back from the edge of the platform as the little tank engine with its two carriages arrived at Berkeley Station. It halted with a metallic screech of brakes, then emitted a blast of escaping steam, not unlike some demented dragon who had suddenly discovered his fire had gone out. Molly kissed her father, then her new mother-in-law, before stepping aboard.

Yanto in turn kissed his mother, then shook hands solemnly with Selwyn, Sid, and Bert Midgeley, in that order, before following her.

'Have a lovely time,' Selwyn quavered, whipping out a bright red handkerchief and dabbing his eyes.

They were both leaning out of the window as the guard waved his flag. Then with that familiar rumpus that had decided generations of kids to become engine drivers, the local donkey began to grind it way towards the Severn Bridge. The little group waved wildly until the train took that slow right-hand bend and they were lost from sight.

With a great sigh of relief the newlyweds then collapsed into

286

their seats opposite each other in the empty compartment.

'Well, Mrs Gates, what d'you reckon then?' he quipped with that smile of his. She just smiled back at him with a look that made any reply superfluous.

As the little train rolled and rattled the short distance to Sharpness station, they talked about their day. It had been a wonderful wedding, and the reception at the Berkeley Chase had been equally wonderful. Sid's staff had seen to that. After that memorable spell of eating and drinking, there had been the long drawn-out farewells from the guests before dashing off to their respective homes to change.

It had been arranged that on their return from honeymoon they would live for a short while with Selwyn at Honey Cottage. Then, once Sid and Mary had married and moved to the Chase, they would move to Mary's cottage. But, Yanto insisted, that would only be for as long as it took him to buy a place of his own. Selwyn had tried to assure Molly that he would be all right on his own, but Yanto knew that Molly would be calling on him every day. So did Selwyn, secretly.

Sid and Mary had driven them to the station in Sid's nearly new Ford Eight. And Bert Midgeley, who had provided his black Humber for the wedding free of charge, had driven Selwyn to see them off.

So now they were off to the land of Yanto's father.

Selwyn's younger brother Jack, who owned a small-holding at Newquay in North Wales, had immediately accepted when Selwyn wrote to him inviting him to the wedding. In fact, he had written back stating that he would like to stay for a week's holiday with Selwyn afterwards. The two brothers had not seen each other for years. He had also suggested that if the newlyweds had not already made plans, they might like to spend their honeymoon at his seaside bachelor abode.

They hadn't made other plans, and when Yanto heard that Jack also owned a boat and a local patch of lobster pots the decision had been easy.

As the train chuffed its way out of Sharpness station, Yanto looked out at the wharves and warehouses of the docks with the colourful steamers and coasters tied up here and there. 'I shall have to get stuck in and consider my future seriously when I get back,' he mused to himself.

The dull rumble of the wheels changed to a hollow metallic clatter as the local train ran on to the Severn Bridge. Yanto looked down at the wide expanse of grey water, with the tide swirling around Wheel Rock.

He was beginning to miss it already.

Then he looked at his bride. She looked a picture in her peach coloured 'going away' costume with the pleated skirt and matching pillbox hat. Her smart court shoes were also matching, and those beautiful long legs were clad in sheer nylon. Once again he began to experience that old feeling. Molly, true to her word, had kept him at bay since his proposal at the swimming hole. He gave her an evil smile. She smiled knowingly back.

'It's a while before we change trains at Lydney Junction, my love,' he whispered, 'and there ain't no corridors on this train.' He looked into her eyes and saw only love.

Shivering with anticipation, he reached for her.

THE END

Root of the Tudor Rose
Mari Griffith

1421: Henry V and his young bride, Catherine de Valois, are blessed with the birth of a son – but their happiness is short-lived. Catherine is widowed and when her father, the French king, also dies, her son inherits the crowns of France and England. Just ten months old, Henry VI needs all his mother's watchful care to protect him from political intrigue.

But Catherine is a foreigner at the English Court. Lonely and vulnerable, she is held in suspicion by those with their own claims to the throne. Only with another outsider, a young Welshman named Owen Tudor, does Catherine find true friendship but their liaison must be kept secret at all costs. Catherine, Queen of England is forbidden to remarry and she is in love with a servant...

Scorpion Sunset
Catrin Collier

1916, Mesopotamia. The Turks order prisoners from the siege of Kut to march the hundreds of miles to Baghdad. The men are weak from starvation after the five-month siege, with many suffering from dysentery, scabies, and malaria. Hundreds of men die on the march, the stragglers killed by Arab tribesmen; those too ill to move are left behind to die.

Soon, though, the tide of war turns, and eventually the British march victorious into Baghdad. Having taken control of Mesopotamia, the British find they do not have the resources to govern it. What will be the country's fate? Meanwhile, the POWs who survived imprisonment re-enter an uncertain world – among them John Mason, his health ruined and future unsure.

His old friend Charles Reid is more optimistic as love blossoms. But nothing is clear-cut anymore ...Harry Downe remains with his Bedouin wife's tribe: how much of his past does he truly remember? His journalist brother Michael seeks answers amidst the ruins of war as, for their friends and comrades, the struggle to survive goes on despite the conflict's end.

For more information about **Ray Pickernell**
and other **Accent Press** titles

please visit

www.accentpress.co.uk